PEACHES FOR
MONSIEUR LE CURÉ

PEACHES FOR MONSIEUR LE CURÉ

Joanne Harris

WINDSOR
PARAGON

First published 2012
by Doubleday
This Large Print edition published 2012
by AudioGO Ltd
by arrangement with
Transworld Publishers

Hardcover   ISBN: 978 1 4713 0300 5
Softcover   ISBN: 978 1 4713 0301 2

British Library Cataloguing in Publication Data available

Printed and bound in Great Britain by
MPG Books Group Limited

To my father, Bob Short,
who would never let good fruit go to waste.

NEW
MOON

NEW
MOON

CHAPTER ONE

☾

Someone once told me that, in France alone, a quarter of a million letters are delivered every year to the dead.

What she didn't tell me is that sometimes the dead write back.

CHAPTER TWO

☾

Tuesday, 10th August

It came on the wind of Ramadan. not that I knew it then, of course. Paris gets windy in August, and the dust makes little dervishes that skate and scour the sidewalks and leave little sparkling flakes of grit on your eyelids and your face, while the sun glares down like a blind white eye and no one feels like eating. Paris is mostly dead right now, except for tourists and people like us who can't afford a holiday; and the river stinks, and there is no shade, and you'd do almost anything to walk barefoot in a field somewhere, or to sit under a tree in a wood.

Roux knows how it is, of course. Roux wasn't made for city life. And when Rosette is bored she makes mischief; and I make chocolates for no one to buy, and Anouk goes to the internet café on the Rue de la Paix to talk with her friends on Facebook, or walks up to Montmartre cemetery and watches the feral cats that slink among the houses of the dead, with the sun coming down like a guillotine between the slices of shadow.

Anouk at fifteen. Where does the time go? Like perfume in a bottle, however tight the seal, evaporating so slyly that, when you open it to look, all you find is a scented smear where once there was enough to spare—

How are you, my little Anouk? What's happening in your strange little world? Are you

4

happy? Restless? Content? How many more of these days will we have before you leave my orbit for good, shooting away like a rogue satellite, vanishing into the stars?

This train of thought is far from new. Fear has been my shadow ever since Anouk was born, but this summer the fear has grown, blooming monstrously in the heat. Perhaps it's because of the mother I lost—and the one I found four years ago. Or maybe it's the memory of Zozie de l'Alba, the taker of hearts, who almost robbed me of everything, and who showed me how fragile our lives can be; how easily the house of cards can fall at the smallest breath of wind.

Fifteen. *Fifteen.* At her age I'd already travelled the world. My mother was dying. The word *home* meant any place we stayed for the night. I'd never made a real friend. And love—well, love was like the torches that burn at the terraces of cafés at night; a source of fleeting warmth; a touch; a face half glimpsed in firelight.

Anouk, I hope, will be different. Already she is beautiful; although she is quite unaware of this. One day she will fall in love. What will happen to us then? Still, I tell myself, there's time. So far, the only boy in her life is her friend Jean-Loup Rimbault, from whom she is usually inseparable, but who this month has had to go into hospital for another operation. Jean-Loup was born with a heart defect; Anouk doesn't speak of it, but I can understand her fear. It's like my own; a shadow that creeps; a certainty that nothing lasts.

She still sometimes talks about Lansquenet. Even though she is happy enough here, Paris seems more like a stopping-place on some as yet

5

untravelled road than a home to which she will always return. Of course, a houseboat is not a house; it lacks the conviction of mortar and stone. And Anouk, with the curious nostalgia that affects the very young, remembers in rosy colours the little *chocolaterie* across from the church, with its striped awning and hand-painted sign. And her eyes are wistful when she speaks of the friends she left behind; of Jeannot Drou and Luc Clairmont, and of streets where no one is afraid to walk at night, and of front doors that are never locked—

I shouldn't be so anxious, I know. My little Anouk is secretive, but unlike so many of her friends, she still likes her mother's company. We're still all right. We still have good times. Just the two of us, tucked up in bed, with Pantoufle a hazy blur at the corner of my eye and the screen of the portable television flickering mystic images against the darkened windows, while Rosette sits out on the deck with Roux, fishing for stars in the silent Seine.

Roux has taken to fatherhood. I really hadn't expected that. But Rosette—eight years old, and the image of him—seems to have drawn something out of Roux that neither Anouk nor I could have known. In fact, there are times when I think that she belongs more to Roux than to anyone; they have a secret language—of honks and hoots and whistles—in which they can confer for hours, and which no one else shares, not even me.

Otherwise, my little Rosette still doesn't talk much to anyone, preferring the sign language she learnt as a child, in which she is very proficient. She likes drawing and mathematics; the Sudoku on the back page of *Le Monde* takes her only minutes

6

to complete, and she can add up great lists of numbers without ever having to write them down. We tried sending her to school once, but that didn't work at all. The schools here are too large and too impersonal to cope with a special case like Rosette. Now, Roux teaches her, and if his curriculum is unusual, with its emphasis on art, bird noises and number games, it seems to make her happy. She has no friends, of course—except for Bam—and sometimes I see her watching the children who pass on their way to school with a look of curious longing. But on the whole, Paris treats us well, for all its anonymity; still, sometimes, on a day like this, like Anouk, like Rosette, I find myself wishing for something more. More than a boat on a river that stinks; more than this cauldron of stale air; more than this forest of towers and spires; or the tiny galley in which I make my chocolates.

More. Oh, that word. That deceptive word. That eater of lives; that malcontent. That straw that broke the camel's back, demanding—what, exactly?

I'm very happy with my life. I'm happy with the man I love. I have two wonderful daughters and a job doing what I was meant to do. It's not much of a living, but it helps pay for the mooring, and Roux takes on building and carpentry work that keeps the four of us afloat. All my friends from Montmartre are here; Alice and Nico; Madame Luzeron; Laurent from the little café; Jean-Louis and Paupaul, the painters. I even have my mother close by, the mother I thought lost for so many years—

What more could I possibly want?

It began in the galley the other day. I was making truffles. In this heat, only truffles are safe; anything else runs the risk of damage, either

7

from refrigeration, or from the heat that gets into everything. Temper the couverture on the slab; heat it gently on the hob; add spices, vanilla and cardamom. Wait for just the right moment, transmuting simple cookery into an act of domestic magic.

What more could I have wanted? Well, maybe a breeze; the tiniest breeze, no more than a kiss in the nape of my neck, where my hair, pinned up in a messy knot, was already stinging with summer sweat—

The tiniest of breezes. What? What possible harm could that do?

And so I called the wind—just a little. A warm and playful little wind that makes cats skittish, and races the clouds.

> *V'là l'bon vent, v'là l'joli vent,*
> *V'là l'bon vent, ma mie m'appelle—*

It really wasn't very much; just that little gust of wind and a glamour, like a smile in the air, bringing with it a distant scent of pollen and spices and gingerbread. All I really wanted was to comb the clouds from the summer sky, to bring the scent of other places to my corner of the world.

> *V'là l'bon vent, v'là l'joli vent—*

And all around the Left Bank the sweet wrappers flew like butterflies, and the playful wind tugged at the skirts of a woman crossing the Pont des Arts, a Muslim woman in the *niqab* face-veil, of which there are so many these days, and I caught a glimpse of colours from underneath the long

8

black veil, and just for a moment I thought I saw a shimmy in the scorching air, and the shadows of the wind-blown trees scribbled crazy abstract designs across the dusty water—

V'là l'bon vent, v'là l'joli vent—

The woman glanced down from the bridge at me. I couldn't see her face; just the eyes, kohl-accented under the *niqab*. For a moment I saw her watching me, and wondered if I knew her somehow. I raised a hand and waved to her. Between us, the Seine, and the rising scent of chocolate from the galley's open window.

Try me. Taste me. For a moment I thought she was going to wave back. The dark eyes dropped. She turned away. And then she was gone across the bridge; a faceless woman dressed in black, into the wind of Ramadan.

CHAPTER THREE

☾

Friday, 13th August

It isn't often you receive a letter from the dead. A letter from Lansquenet-sous-Tannes, a letter *inside* a letter, in fact; delivered to our PO box (houseboats don't get mail, of course) and collected by Roux as he goes every day on his way to fetch the bread.

'It's just a letter,' he told me, and shrugged. 'It

9

doesn't have to mean anything.'

But that wind had been blowing all day and all night, and we have always mistrusted the wind. Today it was gusty and changeable, punctuating the silent Seine with little commas of turbulence. Rosette was skittish, practising jumps along the quayside and playing with Bam by the water. Bam is Rosette's invisible friend—though he isn't always invisible. Well, not to us, anyway. Even customers see him sometimes, on days like this one, watching from the side of a bridge or hanging by his tail from a tree. Of course Rosette sees him *all* the time—but then, Rosette is different.

'It's just a letter,' repeated Roux. 'Why don't you open it and see?'

I was rolling the last of the truffles before packing them into boxes. It's hard enough keeping chocolate at the right temperature as it is, but on a boat, with so little space, it's best to keep to the simplest things. Truffles are very easy to make, and the cocoa powder in which they are rolled keeps the chocolate from blooming. I store them under the counter, along with the trays of rusty old tools— spanners and screwdrivers, nuts and bolts—so lifelike that you'd swear they were real, and not just made from chocolate.

'It's been eight years since we left the place,' I said, rolling a truffle across my palm. 'Who is it from, anyway? I don't recognize the writing.'

Roux opened the envelope. He always does what's simplest. Always in the moment, speculation isn't really something that concerns him.

'It's from Luc Clairmont.'

'Little Luc?' I remembered an awkward teenager; paralysed by his stammer. With a jolt

I realized that Luc must be a man by now. Roux unfolded the paper and read:

Dear Vianne and Anouk,

It's been a long time. I hope this letter gets to you. As you know, when my grandmother died she left everything to me, including the house, what money she had, and an envelope not to be opened before my twenty-first birthday. That was in April, and inside was this. It's addressed to you.

Roux fell silent. I turned and saw him holding out an envelope—plain, white, a little scuffed, marked with the passage of years and the touch of living hands on the dead page. And there was my name in blue-black ink, written in Armande's hand—arthritic, imperious, painstaking—

'Armande,' I said.

My dear old friend. How strange—how sad— to hear from you now. And opening the envelope, breaking a seal grown brittle with time, an envelope you must have licked, as you licked the sugar spoon in your cup of chocolate, gleefully, greedily, like a child. You always saw so much further than I—and you made me see, like it or not. I'm not sure whether I'm ready to see what's in this note from beyond the grave, but you know I'll read it, nevertheless.

Dear Vianne (it says).

I can hear her voice. Dry as cocoa dust, and sweet. *I remember the first telephone to make it into Lansquenet. Whee! What a commotion it made. Everyone wanted to try it out. The Bishop, who had it in his house, was up to his eyes in presents and bribes. Well, if they thought that was a miracle, imagine what they'd think to this. Me, talking to you from the dead. And, in case you're wondering, yes they* do *have*

11

chocolate in Paradise. Tell Monsieur le Curé I said so. See if he's learnt to take a joke.

I stopped there for a moment. Sat down on one of the galley stools.

'All right?' said Roux.

I nodded. Went on. *Eight years. A lot can happen, eh? Little girls begin to grow up. Seasons change. People move on. My own grandson, twenty-one! A good age, I remember that much. And you, Vianne—did you move on? I think you did. You weren't ready to stay. Which doesn't mean you won't, some day—keep a cat indoors and all it wants is to go outside again. Keep it outside, and it cries to get in. People are not so different. You'll find that out, if you ever come back. And why would you, I hear you ask? Well, I don't claim to see the future. Not precisely, anyway. But you did Lansquenet a good turn once, though not everyone saw it that way at the time. Still, times change. We all know that. And one thing's for sure; sooner or later, Lansquenet will need you again. But I can't count on our stubborn curé to tell you when that happens. So do me a final courtesy. Take a trip back to Lansquenet. Bring the children. Roux, if he's there. Put flowers on an old lady's grave. Not from Narcisse's shop, mind, but proper flowers from the fields. Say hello to my grandson. Have a cup of chocolate.*

Oh, and one more thing, Vianne. There used to be a peach tree growing up the side of my house. If you come in summertime, the fruit should be ripe and ready to pick. Give some to the little ones. I'd hate the birds to get them all. And remember: everything returns. The river brings everything back in the end.

With all my love, as always,
Armande

12

I stared at the page for a long time, hearing the echoes of her voice. I'd heard it so many times in dreams, balanced at the edge of sleep with her dry old laughter in my ears and the scent of her—lavender, chocolate, old books—gilding the air with its presence. They say that no one ever dies as long as someone remembers them. Perhaps that's why Armande remains so very clearly in my mind; her berry-black eyes; her impudence; the scarlet petticoats she wore under the black of her mourning. And that's why I couldn't refuse her, even though I wanted to; even though I'd promised myself never to go back to Lansquenet, the place we'd loved best of all, the place where we'd almost managed to stay, but from which the wind had driven us, leaving half of ourselves behind—

And now that wind was blowing again. Blowing from beyond the grave, prettily scented with peaches—

Bring the children.

Well, why not?

Call it a holiday, I thought. A reason to leave the city behind; to give Rosette a place to play; to give Anouk the chance to revisit old friends. And yes, I *do* miss Lansquenet; the dun-coloured houses; the little streets that stagger down towards the Tannes; the narrow ribs of farmland that stretch across the blue hills. And Les Marauds, where Armande lived; the old deserted tanneries; the half-timbered derelict houses leaning like drunks into the path of the Tannes, where the river-gypsies moored their boats and lit their campfires along the river . . .

Take a trip back to Lansquenet. Bring the children.

What harm could it do?

I never promised anything. I never meant to

13

change the wind. But if you could travel back through Time, and find yourself as you used to be, wouldn't you try, just once at least, to give her some kind of warning? Wouldn't you want to make things right? To show her that she's not alone?

CHAPTER FOUR

☾

Saturday, 14th August

Anouk received the news of our trip with vivid, touching enthusiasm. Her schoolfriends are mostly away for August, and with Jean-Loup still in hospital, she spends too much of her time alone and sleeps more than is good for her. She needs to get away for a while—as do we all, I realize. And Paris *is* dreadful in August; a ghost city, crushed in a fist of heat; shuttered shops, streets bare of everything but tourists, with their rucksacks and their baseball caps and the traders who follow like swarms of flies.

I told her we were going south.

'To Lansquenet?' she said at once.

I hadn't expected *that*. Not yet. Perhaps she read my colours. But her face lit up at once, and her eyes—which are as expressive as the sky, with all its variations—losing the squally, ominous look that seems habitual nowadays and shining with excitement, just as they did when we first arrived in Lansquenet, eight years ago. Rosette, who mimics everything Anouk does, was watching closely, awaiting her cue.

'If that's all right,' I said at last.

'Cool,' said Anouk.

'*Coo*,' said Rosette.

A ricochet on the oily Seine signalled Bam's approval.

Only Roux said nothing. In fact, since Armande's letter he has been unusually silent. It is not that he has any particular affection for Paris, which he tolerates for our sake, and because he regards the river, and not the city, as his home. But Lansquenet has not treated him well, and Roux has never forgotten it. He still bears a grudge for the loss of his boat, and for what happened afterwards. He has a few friends there—Joséphine is one of them—but on the whole he sees the place as a den of small-minded bigots who threatened him, burnt his home, even refused to sell him supplies. And as for the *curé*, Francis Reynaud—

In spite of his simplicity, there is something sullen about Roux. Like a wild animal that can be tamed, but never forgets unkindness, he can be both fiercely loyal and fiercely unforgiving. I suspect that in the case of Reynaud he will never change his mind, and as for the village itself, he feels nothing but contempt for the tame little rabbits of Lansquenet, living so quietly by the bank of the Tannes, never daring to look beyond the nearest hill, flinching at every breath of change, at the arrival of every stranger—

'Well?' I said. 'What do you think?'

For a long time Roux stayed silent, looking into the river, his long hair hanging in his face. Then he shrugged.

'Maybe not.'

I was surprised. In all the excitement, I'd

15

forgotten to ask what he felt. I'd assumed that he too would welcome the chance of a change of scenery.

'What do you mean, *maybe not*?'

'The letter was addressed to you, not me.'

'Why didn't you tell me before?'

'I could see you wanted to go.'

'And you'd rather stay here?'

He shrugged again. Sometimes I think his silences are more articulate than speech. There's something—or *someone*—in Lansquenet that Roux doesn't want to revisit, and I knew that no amount of questioning would make him confess to anything.

'It's OK,' he told me at last. 'Do whatever you have to do. Visit the place. Put flowers on Armande's grave. And then come home to me.' He smiled and kissed my fingertips. 'You still taste of chocolate.'

'You won't change your mind?'

He shook his head. 'You won't be there long. And besides, someone has to look after the boat.'

That was true, I told myself: but still, it makes me uneasy to think that Roux prefers to stay behind. I had assumed we would travel by boat; Roux knows all the waterways. His route would have taken us down the Seine and through a maze of canals to the Loire, and from there towards the Canal des Deux Mers, the Garonne, and at last into the Tannes, through locks and lifts, fast water and slow, past fields and castles and industrial estates, watching the water change as we go from broad to narrow and back again, from oily to green, fast-moving to slow, brown to black to yellow to clear.

Each river has its own personality. The Seine is urban; industrious; a highway crammed with barges piled with timber; crates; shipping containers; metal girders; car parts. The Loire is sandy and treacherous, silver in the sunlight but rank below the surface, riddled with snakes and sandbars. The Garonne is bumpy; irregular; generous in certain parts, so shallow in others that a houseboat—even a small one like ours—would have to be hoisted by mechanical lift from one level to the next, taking time, precious time—

But none of that happened. We took the train. A better option in so many ways; besides, to move a houseboat on the Seine is no straightforward task. There is paperwork to fill in; permissions to be granted; the mooring to be secured and countless pieces of administration to be seen to. But somehow it makes me uneasy to come back to Lansquenet like this; suitcase in hand, like a refugee, Anouk at my heels like a stray dog.

Why should I feel this sense of unease? After all, I have nothing to prove. I am no longer the Vianne Rocher who blew into town eight years ago. I have a business now; a home. We are no longer river-rats, moving from village to village in search of mean pickings; itinerant work, digging, planting, harvesting. I am in charge of my destiny. *I* call the wind. It answers to me.

Why then—why this urgency? Is it for Armande? For myself? And why is it that the wind, far from easing as we leave Paris, seems to have grown more persistent as we travel south, its voice acquiring a plaintive note—*hurry, hurry, hurry*?

I keep Armande's letter in the box that I carry with me wherever I go, along with my mother's Tarot cards and the fragments of my other life. It isn't much to show for a life; all those years we

17

spent on the road. The places we lived; the people we met; the recipes I collected; all the friends we made and lost. The drawings Anouk made in school. Some photographs; not many. Passports, postcards, birth certificates, identity cards. All those moments, those memories. Everything we are, compressed into just two or three kilos of paper—the weight of a human heart, in fact—that sometimes seems unbearable.

Hurry. Hurry. That voice again.

Whose is it? My own? Armande's? Or is it the voice of the changing wind, which blows so softly that sometimes I can almost believe it has stopped for good?

Here, along the last stretch of our journey, the roadside is covered with dandelions, most of them now gone to seed, so that the air is filled with bright little particles.

Hurry. Hurry. Reynaud used to say that if you let dandelions go to seed, the next year they get into everything—roadsides, verges, flowerbeds, vineyards, churchyards, gardens, even the cracks in the pavement—so that in a year's time, or maybe two, there are nothing but dandelions left, marching across the countryside; hungry, indestructible—

Francis Reynaud hated weeds. But I always liked the dandelions; their cheery faces, their tasty leaves. Even so, I've never seen quite so many growing here. Rosette likes to pick them and blow the seeds into the air. Next year—

Next year—

How strange, to be thinking of next year. We are not used to planning ahead. We were always like those dandelion seeds; settle for a season, then

18

blow away. Dandelion roots are strong. They need to be, to find sustenance. But the plant only flowers for a season—even assuming someone like Francis Reynaud hasn't already uprooted it—and after it has gone to seed, it has to move on with the wind to survive.

Is that why I find myself drawn so readily back to Lansquenet? Is this a response to some instinct so deep that I am barely conscious of the need to return to the place where once I sowed these stubborn seeds? I wonder what, if anything, has grown there in our absence. I wonder whether our passage has left a mark, however small, on this land. How do folk remember us? With affection? Indifference? Do they remember us at all, or has time erased us from their minds?

CHAPTER FIVE

Sunday, 15th August

Any excuse for a carnival, *père*. At least, so it is in Lansquenet, where folk work hard and anything new—even the opening of a shop—is seen as a break from the daily routine, a reason to stop and celebrate.

Today, it is the Sainte-Marie, the festival of the Virgin. A national holiday, though, of course, most people try to get as far away from the church as they can, spending their time in front of the television, or going to the seaside—it's only two hours' drive to the coast—coming home in the early hours with sunburn on their shoulders and the furtive look of domestic cats that have stayed out all night up to no good.

I know. I have to be tolerant. My role as a priest is changing. The moral compass of Lansquenet is held by others nowadays; by city folk and outsiders, by officials and the politically correct. Times are changing, so they say, and the old traditions and beliefs must now be made to comply with decisions made in Brussels by men (or even worse, by women) in suits who have never been out of the metropolis, except maybe for a summer in Cannes, or ski-ing in the Val d'Isère.

Here in Lansquenet, of course, the poison has taken some time to reach the pulse points of the community. Narcisse still keeps bees as his father and grandfather did, the honey still unpasteurized in defiance of EU restrictions—though nowadays he gives it away, flamboyantly and with a gleam in his eye, *absolutely free*, he says, with the postcards he sells at 10 euros apiece, thereby circumventing the need to conform to the new restrictions, or break with a local tradition that has remained unchanged for centuries.

Narcisse is not the only one to sometimes defy the authorities. There's Joséphine Bonnet—Muscat, as was—who runs the Café des Marauds, and who has always done whatever she could to encourage the despised river-gypsies to stay—and the Englishman and his wife, Marise, who own the vineyard down the road, and who often hire them (off the books) to help bring in the harvest. And Guillaume Duplessis, long since retired from teaching, but who still gives private lessons to any

20

child who asks for them, in spite of new laws calling for checks on anyone working with children.

Of course, there are some who welcome innovation—as long as they are somehow involved. Caro Clairmont and her husband are now zealous disciples of Brussels and Paris, and have recently made it their mission to introduce Health and Safety into our community, checking pavements for evidence of neglect, campaigning against itinerants and undesirables, promoting modern values and generally making much of themselves. Traditionally Lansquenet has no mayor, but if it had one, then Caro would be the obvious choice. As it is, she runs the Neighbourhood Watch, the League of Christian Women, the village Book Club, the Riverside Cleaning Campaign and ParentWatch, a group designed to protect our children against paedophiles.

And the church? Some would say she runs that, too.

If you'd told me ten years ago that I would one day sympathize with rebels and refuseniks, I would probably have laughed in your face. But I myself have changed since then. I have come to value different things. When I was younger, Order reigned; the messy, disorderly lives of my flock were a constant irritation. Now I have come to understand them better—if not always to approve. I have come to feel—not affection, precisely, but something almost approaching it when dealing with their problems. It may not have made me a better man. But I have learnt over the years that it's better to bend a little than be broken. Vianne Rocher taught me that, and although I was never happier to see anyone leave Lansquenet than when she and

21

her daughter moved away, I know what I owe her. I know it well.

Which is why, on the tail of this carnival, with change in the air like the scent of smoke, I can almost imagine Vianne Rocher coming back to Lansquenet. It would be so very like her, you see, to roll into town on the eve of a war. Because a war *is* coming, that is certain, and it smells like a storm about to break.

I wonder, would she sense it, too? And is it wrong of me to hope that this time she would take my side, instead of joining the enemy?

CHAPTER SIX

☾

Sunday, 15th August

I don't often return to places I've left. I find it too uncomfortable to deal with all the things that have changed: cafés closed, paths overgrown, friends moved away, or settled rather too permanently in cemeteries and old folks' homes—

Some places change so completely that I can hardly believe I was there at all. In a way that's for the best: I am spared the routine heartbreak of once-familiar places and times reduced to reflections of themselves in mirrors that we broke when we left. Some change only a little, which is sometimes harder to bear. But I have never returned to a place where nothing seemed to have changed *at all*—

Not until today, at least.

We came on the wind of the carnival. Eight and a half long years ago, on a wind that seemed to promise so much; a mad wind, full of confetti and scented with smoke and pancakes cooked by the side of the road. The pancake stall is still there, and the crowds that line the side of the street, and the flower-decked cart with its motley crew of fairies, wolves and witches. I bought a *galette* from that very stall. I bought one now, to remember. Still as good, just the right side of burnt, and the flavours—butter and salt and rye—help reawaken the memory.

Anouk was standing beside me then, a plastic trumpet in her hand. Now she stood wide-eyed and alert, and Rosette was the one with the trumpet. *Prraaaaaaa!* This time it was red, not yellow, and there was no hint of frost in the air, but the sounds and voices and scents were the same; and the people in their summer clothes—overcoats and berets giving way to white shirts, straw hats; who'd wear black in this heat?—might almost be the same ones, especially the children who bounced along in the wake of the cart, collecting streamers and flowers and sweets—

Prrraaaaaa! went the trumpet. Rosette laughed. Today, she is in her element. Today she can run like a mad thing, swing like a monkey, laugh like a clown, and no one will notice or criticize. Today she is normal—whatever *that* means—and she joined the procession behind the cart, hooting with exuberance.

This must be the fifteenth of August, I thought. I'd almost forgotten what day it was. I don't really follow the Church's festivals, but I could see her, the Mother of Christ, in plaster with a gilded

23

crown, being carried in state by four choirboys under a flowery canopy. The boys were wearing surplices, and slightly resentful expressions. Well, it must have been hot under those robes, and the others were having much more fun. For a moment I almost recognized the face of one of the choirboys—it looked like Jeannot Drou, Anouk's little friend back in the days of La Céleste Praline—though of course it couldn't have been. The boy must be seventeen by now. But the faces *were* familiar. A relative, a cousin, perhaps, maybe even a brother. And that girl on the cart with the fairy wings looked just like Caroline Clairmont. A woman in a blue summer frock could almost have been Joséphine Muscat, and that man with his dog, standing too far away for me to see the face under the hat, might easily have been my old friend Guillaume.

And that figure in the black robe, standing slightly apart from the rest of the crowd in silent disapproval—

Could that be Francis Reynaud?

Prraaaaaaaa! The trumpet was garish and off-key, like the bright red plastic of its manufacture. The black figure seemed almost to wince as Rosette scurried past, with Bam (quite clearly visible today) screaming and scampering in her wake.

But it wasn't Reynaud. I could see that now as the figure turned to look back at the procession. In fact it wasn't a man at all. It was a woman in *niqab*—young, from her figure, and veiled in black even to her fingertips. In this brutal heat she wore gloves, and her eyes, the only part of her that could be seen above the veil, were long and dark

24

and unreadable.

Had I seen her before? I thought not. And yet she was strangely familiar, perhaps because of the colours that swam around her black, immobile shape; the colours of the carnival, the flowers, the streamers, the bunting, the flags.

No one spoke to her. No one stared. In Paris, where folk are so jaded that hardly anything invites comment, people still notice the *niqab*, but here, where gossip is currency, the face-veil attracts no second glance.

Out of tact? Maybe. Out of fear? The crowd parted around her on either side, allowing a space to contain her. She might have been a ghost—standing unseen in the slipstream with the scent of fried food and candyfloss distressing the air around her and the cries of children like fireworks hurled into the hot blue sky.

Prraaaaaaaa! Oh, my. That trumpet again. I looked for Anouk, but she had disappeared, and for a moment my city senses prickled with anxiety—

Then I saw her in the crowd, talking to someone—a boy of her age. Maybe a friend. I do hope so. Anouk finds it hard to make friends. Not that she is antisocial. Quite the opposite, in fact. But others sense her otherness, and tend to give her a wide berth. Except for Jean-Loup Rimbault, of course. Jean-Loup, who has already skirted death so many times in his short life. I sometimes despair of my little Anouk, who has already endured so much loss, choosing as her closest friend someone who may not live to see twenty.

Don't get me wrong. I like Jean-Loup. But my little Anouk is sensitive in ways I understand only too well. She feels responsibility for things that

25

are beyond her control. Perhaps because she's the eldest child; or perhaps it has something to do with what happened in Paris, four years ago, when the wind nearly blew us away for good.

I scanned the crowd for faces again. This time, I recognized Guillaume, eight years older, but just the same, with the dog that was a puppy when Anouk and I left Lansquenet now walking sedately at his heels, and a small group of children following, feeding treats to the little dog and chattering excitedly.

'Guillaume!'

He did not hear me. The music, the laughter, were all too loud. But the man at my side turned abruptly, and I saw his very familiar face; the features small and sharp and neat, the eyes a chilly shade of grey, and I caught a glimpse of his colours as he turned with a look of astonishment—in fact, were it not for those colours I might not have known him without his soutane, but there's no way of hiding who you are under the skin of the mask you wear—

'Mademoiselle Rocher?' he said.

It was Francis Reynaud.

Now forty-five, he has hardly changed. The same narrow, suspicious mouth. Hair slicked severely back to fight its tendency to curl. The same stubborn set of the shoulders, like a man carrying an invisible cross.

He has gained weight since I saw him last. Although he will never really be fat, there is a perceptible roundness in the region of his midsection that points to a less austere regime. This suits him—he is tall enough to need a little extra bulk—and, still more surprising, there are lines

26

around those cool grey eyes that might almost hint at laughter.

He smiled—a shy, uncertain smile that has had too little practice. And with that smile, I understood what Armande meant when she wrote to me that Lansquenet would need my help.

Of course, it was all in his colours. His outward appearance was that of a man firmly, completely in control. Still, I know him better than most, and I could see that beneath his apparent calm Reynaud was deeply agitated. To begin with, his collar was misaligned. A priest's collar fastens at the back— in this case with a small clip. Reynaud's collar had slipped to one side; the clip was clearly visible. To such a meticulous man as Reynaud, this was no trivial detail.

What was it Armande said?

Lansquenet will need you again. But I can't count on our stubborn curé—

Then there were the colours themselves; a turgid confusion of greens and greys, shot through with the scarlet of distress. And the look in his eyes; the careful blankness of a man who does not know how to ask for help. In short, Reynaud looked as if he were standing on the edge of a precipice, and now I knew I could not leave until I knew what was happening.

And remember: everything returns.

Armande's voice was clear in my mind. Eight years dead, and still she sounds as stubborn as she did in life; stubborn and wise and mischievous. There's no point trying to fight the dead; their voices are relentless.

I smiled. I said, 'Monsieur le Curé.'

Then I prepared to ride the wind.

27

CHAPTER SEVEN

Sunday, 15th August

My God. She hasn't changed at all. Long black hair; laughing eyes; bright red skirt and sandals. A half-eaten *galette* in one hand; jingling bracelets on one wrist; her daughter scampering in her wake. For a moment it was almost as if Time had stopped; even the child had scarcely aged.

Of course, it wasn't the same child. I realized that almost at once. For a start, this one has red hair, while the other one was dark. Besides which, looking closer now, I could see that Vianne Rocher *has* changed; there are fine lines around her eyes and she wears a guarded expression, as if eight years have taught her mistrust—or perhaps she's expecting trouble.

I tried a smile, though I am aware that my personal charm is somewhat lacking. I do not have the easy social graces of Père Henri Lemaître, the priest from Toulouse who now serves the neighbouring parishes of Florient, Chancy and Pont-le-Saôul. My manner has been described (by Caro Clairmont, among others) as *dry*. I neither attempt to woo my flock, nor flatter them into submission. Instead I try to be honest, which earns me little gratitude from Caro and her cronies, who much prefer the kind of priest who attends social functions, coos over babies and lets his hair down at church fêtes.

Vianne Rocher raised an eyebrow. Perhaps my smile was a little forced. Given the circumstances, of course, it was to be expected.

'I'm sorry, I didn't—'

It's the soutane. I don't suppose she'd ever seen me without it. I've always thought there was something comforting about the Church's traditional black robe; a visible sign of authority. But nowadays, I simply wear the collar over a plain black shirt. I do not stoop to wear blue jeans, as Père Henri Lemaître so often does, but Caro Clairmont has made it clear that my wearing of the soutane (outside of religious ceremonies) is no longer entirely appropriate in these days of progress and enlightenment. Caro Clairmont has the Bishop's ear, and in the light of recent events I've learnt that it pays to play the game.

I felt Vianne's eyes move over me, curious, but not unkind. I waited for her to say I'd changed. Instead, she smiled—a real smile, this time—and kissed me lightly on the cheek.

'I hope that's not inappropriate,' she said, with a hint of mischief.

'If it were, I doubt you'd care.'

She laughed at that, and her eyes shone. The child at her side gave a gleeful hoot and blew into her plastic trumpet.

'This is my little Rosette,' she said. 'And of course, you'll remember Anouk.'

'Of course.' How could I have missed her? A dark-haired girl of fifteen or so, talking to the Drou boy. Standing out without meaning to in her faded jeans and daffodil shirt, with her dusty feet in their sandals and her hair tied back with a piece of string

29

while the village girls in their festival gear walked past with a contemptuous eye—

'She looks like you.'

She smiled. 'Oh dear.'

'I meant it as a compliment.'

She laughed again at my awkwardness. I never did quite understand what provokes her laughter. Vianne Rocher is one of those people who seem to laugh at everything—as if life were some kind of perpetual joke, and people endlessly charming and good, instead of being mostly stupid and dull, if not downright poisonous.

Cordially: 'What brings you here?'

She shrugged. 'Nothing special. Just catching up.'

'Oh.' She hadn't heard, then. Or maybe she had, and was toying with me. We'd parted on uncertain terms, and it may be that she still bears a grudge. Perhaps I deserve it, after all. She has the right to despise me.

'Where are you staying?'

She gave a shrug. 'I'm not sure if I'm staying at all.' She looked at me, and I felt those eyes again, like fingers on my face. 'You look well.'

'You look the same.'

That concluded the pleasantries. I decided that she knew nothing of my circumstances, and that her arrival—today, of all days—was nothing but coincidence. Very well, I told myself. Perhaps it was better to keep it that way. What could she do, one woman, alone, especially on the eve of a war?

'Is my chocolate shop still there?'

The question I was dreading. 'Of course it's there.' I looked away.

'Really? Who runs it?'

'A foreigner.'

30

She laughed. 'A foreigner from Pont-le-Saôul?' The closeness of our communities has always been a joke to her. All our neighbouring villages are fiercely independent. Once, they were *bastides*, fortress towns in a fretwork of tiny dominions, and even now they tend to be somewhat wary of strangers.

'You'll be wanting to find somewhere to stay,' I said, avoiding the question. 'Agen has some good hotels. Or you could drive to Montauban—'

'We don't have a car. We hired a cab.'

'Oh.'

The carnival was nearing its end. I could see the final *char*, decked with flowers from stem to stern, staggering down the main road like a drunken bishop in full regalia.

'I thought we might stay at Joséphine's,' said Vianne. 'Assuming the café still has rooms.'

I pulled a face. 'I suppose you might.' I knew I was being ungracious. But to have her here at this sensitive time was to subject myself to unnecessary anxiety. And besides, she has always had the knack of arriving at just the wrong moment—

'Excuse me, but is something wrong?'

'Not at all.' I tried to assume a festive air. 'But this is Sainte-Marie's festival, and it's Mass in half an hour—'

'Mass. Well, I'll come with you, then.'

I stared. 'You never go to Mass.'

'I thought I might look in at the shop. Just for old times' sake,' she said.

I could see there was no stopping her. I prepared myself for the inevitable. 'It isn't a chocolate shop any more.'

'I didn't think it would be,' she said. 'What is it

31

now, a bakery?'

'Not exactly,' I said.

'Maybe the owner will show me around.'

I tried to suppress a grimace.

'What?'

'I don't think that's a good idea.'

'Why not?' Her eyes were inquisitive. At her feet, the red-haired child was squatting in the dusty road. The trumpet had become a doll, and she was marching it to and fro, making little sounds to herself. I wondered if she was entirely normal, but then children seldom make much sense to me.

'The people aren't very friendly,' I said.

She laughed at that. 'I think I can cope.'

I threw down my last card. 'They're foreigners.'

'So am I,' said Vianne Rocher. 'I'm sure we'll get on like a house on fire.'

And that was how, on the festival of Sainte-Marie, Vianne Rocher blew back into town, bringing with her her usual gift of mayhem, dreams and chocolate.

CHAPTER EIGHT

☾

Sunday, 15th August

The procession was over. Sainte-Marie in her festival robes was on her way back to her plinth in the church, her crown put away for another year, her wreath already fading. August is hot in Lansquenet, and the wind that blows across from the hills strips the land of moisture. By the time we arrived, the four of us, the shadows were already lengthening, with only the top of Saint-Jérôme's tower still shining in the sunlight. The bells were ringing for Mass, and people were making their way to church; old women in black straw hats (with the occasional ribbon or bunch of cherries to relieve half a lifetime of mourning); old men in berets that gave them the look of schoolboys slouching to class, grey hair slicked hastily back with water from the pump in the square, Sunday shoes capped with yellow dust. No one looked at me as they passed. No one looked familiar.

Reynaud glanced over his shoulder at me as he led the way to church. I thought there was something reluctant in the way he approached; although his movements were as precise as ever, he somehow seemed to be dragging his feet, as if to prolong the journey. Rosette had lost her exuberance, along with the plastic trumpet, discarded somewhere along the way. Anouk was walking ahead of us, iPod earpiece in one ear. I wondered what she was listening to, lost in a private world of sound.

We passed the corner of the church and stepped into the little square, and faced the *chocolaterie*; the very first place Anouk and I had ever really called *home*—

For a moment neither of us spoke. It was simply too much to register: the empty windows, gaping roof, the ladder of soot climbing the wall. The smell of it was still half fresh—a combination of plaster, charred wood and memories gone up in smoke.

'What happened?' I said at last.

Reynaud shrugged. 'There was a fire.'

33

In that moment he almost sounded like Roux in the days that had followed the loss of his boat. The warily uninflected tone, the almost insulting neutrality. I wanted to ask if *he*'d started the fire— not because I believed he had, but just to break his composure.

'Was anybody hurt?' I said.

'No.' Again, that apparent detachment, though behind it his colours howled and spat.

'Who lived there?'

'A woman and her child.'

'Foreigners,' I said.

'Yes.'

His pale eyes held mine almost like a challenge. Of course, I too was a foreigner, at least by his definition. I too was a woman with a child. I wondered whether his choice of words had been intended to convey something else.

'Did you know them?'

'Not at all.'

That, too, was unusual. In a place the size of Lansquenet, the parish priest knows everyone. Either Reynaud was lying, or the woman who had lived in my house had managed the near-impossible.

'Where are they staying now?' I said.

'Les Marauds, I think.'

'You *think*?'

He shrugged. 'There are lots of them now in Les Marauds,' he said. 'Things have changed since you were here.'

I was beginning to think he was right. Things *have* changed in Lansquenet. Behind the half-known faces and the houses and the whitewashed church; the fields; the little streets

34

staggering down towards the river; the old tanneries; the square with its strip of gravel for playing *pétanque*; the school; the bakery—all those landmarks that had seemed to me so comforting when I arrived, with their illusion of timelessness— all now coloured with something else; a shadow of disquiet, perhaps; the strangeness of familiarity.

I saw him glance at the church door. The worshippers had all gone in. 'Better get your robes,' I said. 'You don't want to be late for Mass.'

'I'm not the one saying Mass today.' His tone was still perfectly neutral. 'There's a visiting priest, Père Henri Lemaître, who comes on special occasions.'

That sounded rather odd to me, although, not being a churchgoer, I was reluctant to comment. Reynaud offered no further explanation, but remained, rather stiffly, at my side, as if awaiting judgement.

Rosette had been watching with Anouk. Both seemed unable to keep their eyes from the *chocolaterie*. Anouk had taken off her iPod and was standing by the charred front door, and I knew that she was remembering us soaping and sanding the woodwork; buying the paint and the brushes; trying to wash the paint from our hair.

'It might not be as bad as it looks,' I said to Anouk, and pushed at the door. It was unlocked; it opened. Inside, there was worse: a jumble of chairs piled in the middle of the room, most of them charred and useless. A carpet, rolled up and blackened. The remains of an easel on the floor. A flaking blackboard on the wall.

'It was a school,' I said aloud.

Reynaud said nothing. His mouth was set.

Rosette pulled a face and said in sign language:

35

Are we sleeping here?

I shook my head and smiled at her.

Good. Bam doesn't like it.

'We'll find somewhere else,' I told her.

Where?

'I know just the place,' I said. I looked at Reynaud. 'I don't mean to intrude. But are you in some kind of trouble?'

He smiled. It was a narrow smile, but this time it went all the way to his eyes. 'I think you could probably say that.'

'Did you ever *intend* to go to Mass?'

He shook his head.

'Then come with me.'

Once more he smiled. 'And where are we going, Mademoiselle Rocher?'

'First, to put flowers on an old lady's grave.'

'And after that?'

'You'll see,' I said.

CHAPTER NINE

Sunday, 15th August

I suppose I'll have to explain myself. I thought I might avoid it. But if she is staying in Lansquenet— and everything points to the fact that she is—then she will hear it eventually. Our gossips pull no punches. For some strange reason she seems to believe that she and I can somehow be friends. I may as well tell her the truth before she gets too used to the idea.

This was my thought as I followed her to the cemetery, pausing every few minutes as she and the children stopped to pick a handful of roadside flowers—weeds, for the most part—dandelions; ragwort; daisies; poppies; a stray anemone from the verge; a fistful of rosemary from someone's garden, pushing its shoots through a dry-stone wall.

Of course, Vianne Rocher *likes* weeds. And the children—the young one especially—lent themselves to the game with glee, so that by the time we reached the place, she had a whole armful of flowers and herbs tied together with bindweed and a straggle of wild strawberry—

'What do you think?'

'It's—colourful.'

She laughed. 'You mean inappropriate.'

Disorderly, colourful, inappropriate, wrong in every sense of the word—and yet with a curious appeal—a perfect description of Vianne Rocher, I thought, but did not say aloud. My eloquence—such as it is—is strictly limited to the page.

Instead I said, 'Armande would like it.'

'Yes,' she said. 'I think she would.'

Armande Voizin's is a family plot. Her parents and grandparents are there, and the husband who died forty years ago. There is a black marble urn at the foot of the grave—an urn she always greatly disliked, and a trough in which she would often slyly plant parsley, carrots, potatoes or other vegetables in defiance of the conventions of grief.

It is very like her now to persuade her friend to bring weeds—Vianne Rocher had told me all about the letter she received from Luc Clairmont,

37

and the note inside from Armande Voizin. Again, it is very like Armande to interfere—from beyond the grave!—to trouble my peace of mind in this way with memories of what once was. She says there is chocolate in Paradise. A blasphemous, inappropriate thought, and yet some hidden part of me hopes to God that she is right.

The children sat and waited on the side of the marble trough, which has now been replanted appropriately, with rows of neat French marigolds. I sense the hand of Caroline Clairmont, Armande's daughter—at least, by blood. I noticed a wisp of something—a weed—underneath the marigolds. I leant forward to pull it up, and recognized the impudent shoot of a baby carrot coming out of the ground. I smiled to myself and left it alone. Armande would have liked that, too.

When Vianne Rocher had finished at the graveside, she stood up.

'Now perhaps you could tell me,' she said. 'What exactly is going on?'

I sighed. 'Of course, Mademoiselle Rocher.'

I led the way to Les Marauds.

CHAPTER TEN

Sunday, 15th August

To understand, you really need to see for yourself what I'm talking about. Les Marauds, the slums of Lansquenet, if such an urban thing can be in a village of no more than four hundred souls. Once, it housed the tanneries that were Lansquenet's main source of income; and the buildings that line the riverbanks were all connected with that industry.

A tannery stinks and pollutes, and so Les Marauds was always a place apart, downriver from the village itself, existing in its own atmosphere of stench and dirt and poverty. But that was a hundred years ago. Now, of course, the tanneries and the brick-and-wooden houses are mostly converted into little shops and cheap dwellings. The river Tannes is sweet again, and children come here to paddle and play in the place where women used to scrub hides against a series of big, flat rocks worn hollow by decades of back-breaking work.

It's the place where the river-rats (political correctness dictates that we cannot call them gypsies any more) like to moor their boats and light their campfires on the bank, and cook pancakes on a griddle and play guitars, and sing, and dance, and sell cheap trinkets to our children, and tattoo their arms in henna, to the dismay of their parents and of Joline Drou, who runs the village school.

At least, that all *used* to be true. Now the children stay away, as do most of our villagers. Even the river-rats stay away—I haven't seen a houseboat arrive since Roux left four years ago. A different kind of atmosphere has settled on Les Marauds now; one that smells of spices and smoke, and sounds like a foreign country—

Don't misunderstand me. I do not dislike foreigners. Some do in Lansquenet, but I am not among them. I was quick to welcome the first few immigrant families—those Tunisians, Algerians, Moroccans, *Pieds-Noirs*, all now grouped together

39

under the collective name of *Maghrébins*—when they moved here from Agen, knowing that a village like ours, a village where people are set in their ways and have little to do with what is happening in the big cities, was likely to feel some resistance to the arrival of a group of folk so different from themselves.

They first came from Marseille or Toulouse; from the outskirts of cities so ridden with crime that they had escaped to quieter parts, taking their families with them; to Bordeaux, Agen, Nérac, and from there at last to Les Marauds, which the *municipalité* had designated as an area suitable for redevelopment, and where Georges Clairmont, our local builder, was more than happy to receive them.

That was almost eight years ago. Vianne Rocher had already moved on. Roux was still here, working on the hulk that would one day become his houseboat; living at the Café des Marauds, for which he paid by taking occasional work— mostly with Georges Clairmont, who knew a good carpenter when he saw one, and who was more than happy to pay less than the minimum wage to a man who never complained, always took cash and who dealt with all kinds of people.

Les Marauds was very different then. Health and Safety had not yet run mad among our local councillors and those derelict houses could quickly and cheaply be converted into homes and shops. There was already a shop selling fabrics there; another sold mangoes and lentils and yams. There was a café—no alcohol, but mint tea, and glass water-pipes of *kif*—that fragrant blend of tobacco and marijuana so common in Morocco. There was a market every week, selling strange and exotic

40

fruit and vegetables brought in from the docks at Marseille, and a little bakery, selling flatbread and pancakes and sweet milk rolls and honey pastries and almond *briouats*.

In those days, our *Maghrébin* community numbered only three or four families. All lived on a single street that some of our villagers (in their confusion over geography) came to call *Le Boulevard P'tit Baghdad*. Not that any of the newcomers had ever even *seen* Baghdad; most of them were secondor third-generation immigrants whose parents and grandparents had come to France seeking a better way of life. Their dress was varied and colourful; from the *djellaba*s and kaftans so typical of Morocco, to the hooded *burnous* cloak of the Arabs and Berbers, to modern European dress, usually with the addition of some kind of hat—a prayer cap, a Turkish cap, even a fez—according to their origins.

They were all of them Muslims, of course; they spoke Arabic and Berber among themselves; they went to the big mosque in Bordeaux and fasted during Ramadan. They looked to one man as leader and *imam*—this was Mohammed Mahjoubi, a widower of seventy who lived with his eldest son, Saïd, his wife, Samira, her mother and their teenage girls, Sonia and Alyssa.

Mohammed Mahjoubi was a simple man with a long white beard and a roguish eye, who could often be seen on his porch by the Tannes, reading, eating salted plums and spitting the stones into the river. His son Saïd ran a little gym, while his daughter-in-law looked after the house and cared for her aged mother. His granddaughters straddled two worlds, wearing jeans and a long-sleeved tunic

41

at school but more traditional dress at home, their long hair bound with coloured scarves.

In those early days, the place was alive with colour. It was in the market; the shops; the displays of food and rolls of silk. The Boulevard des Marauds was grandly named, but small, a single-track road through the slums of Lansquenet, its cobbles and paving stones looted by generations of river-gypsies, left to fall into disrepair by a series of local councillors who felt that their budget was better employed serving our community.

The *Maghrébins* didn't seem to mind. Many of them had already come from city slums and half-derelict flats. They drove battered old cars with no brakes or insurance; they didn't care about the state of the road. At first, their young people mixed with ours; the boys played football in the market square; the girls made friends with ours at school. A group of their old women learnt to play *pétanque*—and grew alarmingly good at it, beating our regulars several times. They were not quite a part of Lansquenet, but they were not outsiders either, and many of us felt that they contributed something to our village—a breath of other places, a scent of other cultures, a taste of the exotic—that was absent from all the other *bastides* along the Garonne and the Tannes.

Some people remained wary of the foreigners— Louis Acheron, among others—but most of us were happy enough to see Les Marauds gain a new lease of life. Georges Clairmont was among the best pleased—he was paid a good fee by the council, who subsidized the redevelopment project, and managed to make further profit by cutting every corner he could—the newcomers never noticed

42

if he used pine instead of oak, or slapped three coats of whitewash on a wall instead of five. His wife, Caro, was happy enough to accept the extra income, and turned a blind eye to the shocking state of the road. And the *Maghrébins* were friendly at first; I remember Joséphine Muscat bringing piles of sweet pastries from the place at the top end of the boulevard—the owner was Mehdi al-Djerba, born and bred in old Marseille, with a Midi accent you could cut with a knife—to serve to the patrons of her café. I also recall how she tried to repay them with the gift of a few dozen bottles of wine; how crestfallen she was to learn that *none* of the newcomers touched alcohol. (Later we found out that wasn't quite true; Mehdi al-Djerba has the odd drop, for strictly medicinal purposes, and one or two of the younger men used to sneak into the Café des Marauds when they thought folk weren't paying attention.) So, instead of wine, Joséphine brought planters filled with geraniums for them to put on their windowsills, so that all that summer the cobbled streets of Les Marauds were accented in scarlet. I remember the football matches between our boys and the *Maghrébins*, and how sometimes the fathers would come out to watch, each to their own side of the square, and solemnly shake hands at the end of the game. I even remember Caro Clairmont holding coffee mornings for the mothers and their children, all in the name of *entente cordiale*, as if she were a social worker from Paris instead of a little housewife from the provinces . . .

I say all this to prove to you, *père*, that these people were *not* unwelcome. I know that in the past I have been guilty of intolerance, and I have tried to make amends. When Jean-Pierre Acheron defaced the wall of Saïd Mahjoubi's gym, I was the one who intervened and made him scrub the graffiti off. When Joline Drou refused to teach Zahra Al-Djerba unless she removed her headscarf, I was the one who pointed out that a one-room primary school in Lansquenet is *not* a lycée in Paris—Joline herself wears a little gold cross, which, if we are to adhere strictly to the rules, should also be left at the schoolyard gate.

In short, you may find it hard to believe, but I respected the newcomers. I am not the kind of man who finds it easy to make friends, but I had nothing against the little community of Les Marauds—in fact, I thought that in some ways our own people could learn a few lessons from them. The *Maghrébins* were polite, discreet; they did not cause a disturbance. They were respectful to their parents, affectionate with their children; devout and modest in their ways. Any problem in the community—a family quarrel, a petty crime, an accident, a bereavement—was addressed by Mohammed Mahjoubi, whose status among the *Maghrébins* was that of priest and doctor and mayor and lawyer and social worker all rolled into one. His methods were not always conventional— there were some (Caro Clairmont among them) who believed him to be too old and too eccentric to be an efficient leader. But mostly, there was real affection for old Mahjoubi in the village. His word was law in Les Marauds, and no one questioned his authority.

Then came the first new development. Ever since his arrival, old Mahjoubi had been talking about converting one of the old buildings in Les Marauds into a mosque. As far as I understood

44

it, the plan was too expensive to make sense, even if a suitable building were to be made available. The big mosque in Bordeaux wasn't really so far away, besides which the entire population of Les Marauds still amounted to no more than a handful of families—maybe forty people or so.

The plans caused some discussion. There was opposition from across the river, with strenuous protests from staunchly Catholic families like the Acherons and the Drous. The thought of a mosque, not five minutes' walk away from our own church, seemed like a direct attack to them, a slap in the face of Saint-Jérôme, perhaps in the face of God Himself—

Old Mahjoubi asked me to intervene. I was, perhaps, less than sympathetic. I did not support the mosque idea, not because I was anti-mosque, but because it all seemed unnecessary—

But Mahjoubi refused to admit defeat. He, with the help of his son Saïd, adopted one of the old tanneries, and eventually, with funds from the Muslim community, and after much to-ing and fro-ing with the local authorities, with the help of Georges Clairmont (of course) and some volunteers from Les Marauds, what had been a derelict building right at the end of the boulevard became the village mosque instead, and the centre of the community.

Understand me, *père*, when I say that I have nothing against a mosque. Certainly, there were features which (as I had to point out) contravened local planning regulations. But these were very minor, and I only mentioned them in passing, to avoid unpleasantness later.

Certainly, the result was modest enough. A bland

45

old yellow-brick building with very little on the outside to indicate that it was a place of worship. Inside, a rather beautiful space, with a tiled floor and pale walls stencilled in gold. As a priest, I try to be sensitive to the beliefs of others, and I made a real effort to convey to the community of Les Marauds how much I admired their handiwork, and to make myself available if ever anyone needed help.

Even so, a shift had occurred. Somehow, during our interchange, old Mahjoubi had become defiant. He had always been a stubborn old man, and possessed of a curious levity that sometimes made it hard to know whether or not he was joking. His son Saïd was of a much more serious bent, and I sometimes wondered if it would not be better for the whole of Les Marauds if the father were to step down and leave the decision-making to his son.

Perhaps old Mahjoubi sensed this. In any case, his attitude seemed to have developed an edge. If ever I came to Les Marauds (which I still do, every day, out of a sense of duty), Mahjoubi never missed a chance to make some kind of comment. These were always good-natured, I am sure, but others may not have understood.

'Here comes Monsieur le Curé,' he would say in his thickly accented voice. 'Did you run out of sinners on your side of the river? Or are you here to join us at last? Have you learnt to smoke *kif*? Or is your incense heady enough?'

All in good humour, I know that; and yet there was something in his manner that seemed defiant, combative. His followers started to echo him, and before I knew it, almost overnight, Les Marauds had become hostile territory.

46

So—when did things begin to change? Hard to know for certain. Like looking in the mirror one day and seeing the first signs of old age: the wrinkles around the eyes; the way the skin around the jaw seems to slip out of alignment. There were a few new arrivals; friction within the community—nothing, when you looked at them, to justify my growing unease. But it must have been enough, *père*. Like the turning seasons, Les Marauds changed its colours, somehow. More of the girls began to wear black, with *hijab* scarves (so like a nun's wimple) completely hiding their hair and neck. The coffee mornings tailed off. Caro Clairmont had fallen out with one of her regular visitors, and after that the rest of them came less often, if at all. Saïd Mahjoubi extended his gym at the end of the Boulevard P'tit Baghdad—it wasn't a complicated affair, just a big, bare room with some weights, a spa pool and some running machines—and it became a meeting-place for all the young men of Les Marauds.

That was over five years ago. Since then, the community has grown. There have been more new arrivals—mostly relatives from abroad, coming to join their families. Last year, old Mahjoubi's granddaughter Sonia married a man called Karim Bencharki, who came to live in Lansquenet with his widowed sister and her child. Saïd Mahjoubi admired Karim, who was twelve years older than Sonia and had managed a business in Algiers, selling clothes and textiles. I was rather less certain. I had known Sonia since she was a child—not well, but we'd often spoken. She and her sister, Alyssa, had been bright, outgoing girls, who even played football with Luc Clairmont and his friends at

47

weekends. Married, Sonia changed; wore nothing but black; abandoned her plans to study. I saw her a couple of weeks ago, shopping at the market; she was veiled from head to foot, but there was no doubt that it was she.

The husband was with her, and the sister-in-law; standing between them, she still looked like a child.

I know what you are about to say. The community of Les Marauds is not my responsibility. Mohammed Mahjoubi is their *imam*—they look to him for guidance. But I couldn't help thinking about that girl. How much she had changed since she first arrived. Her younger sister had stayed the same—though the football games were a thing of the past—and it troubled me to see Sonia looking so very different.

But by then I had troubles of my own. There had been complaints from some of my parishioners about the tone of my sermons, which were felt to be old-fashioned and dull. Louis Acheron had taken offence at my treatment of his son (I had grabbed the Acheron boy, then sixteen, by the ear, before making him scrub the whitewashed wall of the gym that he had so recently adorned with a smiley face and a swastika) and since then, all the family had borne something of a grudge against me.

Acheron, an accountant, was on several of Caro's committees, and had worked with Georges Clairmont on a number of occasions. The families were friendly; their sons were very much of an age. Between them, they persuaded the Bishop that my old-fashioned attitudes were causing friction within the community. They even managed to suggest that I had some kind of a feud against old Mahjoubi and his mosque.

48

The Clairmonts and the Acherons started to attend Mass in Florient, where a new, young priest, Père Henri Lemaître, was proving increasingly popular. Very soon it became clear to me that Caro, who had once been one of my most devoted followers, had become a convert to Père Henri's charm, and was furtively but strenuously campaigning to have me replaced.

And then, one day six months ago, as I took my morning walk through Les Marauds, I noticed something irregular. Old Mahjoubi's mosque had somehow acquired a minaret.

Of course, this is not the custom in France. To build such a thing would have been considered needlessly provocative. But the old tannery had a chimney; a square brick chimney twenty feet high and maybe six feet in diameter. This chimney, like the rest of the building, had been freshly whitewashed and newly adorned with a silver crescent moon that gleamed in the early sunlight. And now I could hear an eerie sound amplified by the open flue; a voice half-singing in Arabic the *Azaan*, the traditional call to prayer.

Allahu Akhbar, Allahu Akhbar—

French law clearly states that any call to prayer must be made from *inside* the building in question, and without any form of amplification. In the case of the old tannery, a ladder had been fixed inside the chimney, so that the *muezzin*, the crier, could take advantage of the building's natural acoustics. Thus I could see old Mahjoubi had obeyed the *letter* of the law, but surely, I thought, this must have been a deliberate challenge. The role of *muezzin* was taken on mostly by Mahjoubi's son Saïd, and nowadays this call to prayer echoes all over Les

49

Marauds. We hear it five times a day, *père*, floating to us over the river, and sometimes I find myself (God forgive me) ringing the church bells morning and night especially loudly to compete.

And then, at about the same time, that woman moved into the shop. Karim Bencharki's sister and her child, a girl of eleven or twelve. They were no trouble, and yet at once trouble seemed to follow them. Nothing you could identify. No incidents, no arguments. I called on them, to introduce myself and to offer support if they needed it. The woman barely even spoke. Eyes lowered, head bowed, veiled from head to foot in black—I understood that my help was neither welcome, nor needed. I left her alone. She had made it clear that she wanted no contact with such as me.

But I always took care to greet her whenever we happened to cross in the street, though she never even nodded to me, or acknowledged my greeting in any way. As for the child, I rarely saw her. A little snippet of a thing, big eyes under her headscarf. I tried to speak to her once or twice. Like her mother, she never replied.

And so I watched from across the square, just as I had eight years ago, when Vianne Rocher moved into town. I expected to find at least a clue as to the woman's activities.

Why had she moved from her brother's house? Why had she chosen to live apart from the community in Les Marauds?

But the woman in black gave nothing away. There were no deliveries of goods; no tradesmen; no workmen; no family. She did have a number of visitors—all of them women, all *Maghrébines*, all of them with children. The mothers never stayed

50

long, but the children—all girls—often stayed for the day, sometimes over a dozen of them. I didn't recognize most of the girls, or even their mothers, dressed as they were, and it took me some time to realize that she was opening a school.

French schools—at least, the public ones—work on a strictly secular basis. No religious bias, no prayers, no symbols of faith of any kind. Girls like Sonia and Alyssa Mahjoubi had always managed to deal with this. But some of the other girls had not; and I was conscious that Zahra Al-Djerba, for instance, had never attended secondary school, but remained at home to help her mother. Our tiny village primary school had found a way to accommodate. But in the larger towns, like Agen, the problem of the headscarf remained. And now it seemed that Les Marauds had found itself a solution.

Most of the schoolgirls were dressed alike, in black, with scarves to cover their hair; little widows before their time, faces shyly averted. The *hijab* scarves, though mostly black, are all subtly different in style; some knotted, some pinned, some artfully draped, some wrapped around elaborate chignons, some demure as nuns' coifs.

The girls never talked to me, of course, but some of them occasionally shot curious glances at the church, with its whitewashed walls and its tall steeple and the statue of the Virgin teetering over the main door, and it strikes me how seldom we see them here now, on our side of the river. Within three months of its opening, I had counted fifteen *Maghrébine* girls, aged from ten to sixteen years old, coming to school in a single group; talking and giggling behind their hands as they crossed the

51

bridge into Lansquenet.

But by then Les Marauds was teeming with life—a hundred and fifty people or more, Moroccans, Algerians, Tunisians, Berbers—which, I suppose, is nothing to someone used to Paris or Marseille, but which, in Lansquenet-sous-Tannes, counts as half a village.

Why here? In our neighbouring villages there are no ethnic communities. Perhaps the presence of the mosque; perhaps the little school; perhaps the fact that a whole street was available for development. In any case, in less than eight years our new arrivals have multiplied like dandelions in spring, and in doing so have turned Les Marauds from a single colourful page to an entire foreign chapter.

Now I watched as Vianne Rocher took in the reality. The narrow streets have changed very little in two hundred years; but as for the rest, everything is different. The first thing to strike a visitor is the scent of incense mixed with that of fragrant smoke and unidentified spices. There are lines of washing hanging out between the balconies; men in long robes and prayer caps sit on their porches, smoking *kif* and drinking tea. There are no women among them. The women most often stay indoors; we rarely see them in the streets, and these days more of them wear black. The children, too, stay separate; the boys play football or swim in the Tannes; the girls help their mothers, look after the younger ones or cluster in giggling groups, to fall silent as soon as I appear. The sense of aloofness is palpable. It was more so today, of course; I imagine that after the fire in the shop, the village gossips have been at work.

Passing the row of little shops that line the

Boulevard des Marauds, we found them closed and shuttered. It was seven forty-five; the hot wind had dropped, and a couple of stars were beginning to show. The sky was a darkly luminous blue; with, on the western horizon, a stripe of startling yellow.

And then it began, as I'd known it would. The distant sound of the call to prayer. Distant, but clearly audible in the throat of the old brick tower: *Allahu Akhbar*—God is great.

Yes, of *course* I know what it means. Did you think that because I'm a Catholic I have no knowledge of other faiths? I knew that in a moment the streets would be filled with men going to mosque: the women would mostly stay indoors, preparing for the evening. And as soon as the moon was visible, there would be celebration; traditional foods from the homeland brought in for the occasion; fruits and nuts and dried figs; little deep-fried pastries.

Today is the fifth day of Ramadan, the Muslim month of fasting. It has been a long day. To go without food is one thing, perhaps; but to go without water on a day like today, when the harsh wind sweeps across the land, bleaching everything dry and white—

A woman, followed by a child, crossed the street in front of us. I could not see her averted face; but her black-gloved hands gave her away. It was the woman in black, I knew; the woman from the *chocolaterie*. It was the first time I'd seen her since the fire had gutted the house, and I was glad of the opportunity to check that she was being cared for.

'*Madame*,' I said. 'I hope you're all right—'

The woman did not even look at me. The face-veil that she always wears left only the narrowest letter-box through which to post my condolences. The child, too, seemed not to hear, and, reaching for her headscarf, tugged it a little closer, as if for added security.

'If you need any help—' I went on, but the woman had already passed us by, diving into a side street. By then, the *muezzin* had finished his chant, and the worshippers going to mosque had started to crowd the boulevard.

One of them I recognized, standing at the door of the mosque. It was Saïd Mahjoubi, old Mahjoubi's eldest son and the owner of the gym. A man in his forties; bearded; robed; wearing a prayer cap on his head. He does not smile often. He was not smiling now. I greeted him with a raised hand.

For a moment he just looked at me. Then he started towards us with a strutting, stiff-legged, nervous walk, like that of a cockerel ready to fight.

'What are you doing here?' he said.

I was surprised. 'I live here.'

'You live across the river,' said Saïd. 'And if you know what's good for you, you'll stay across the river.' A couple of other men had stopped, hearing Saïd's raised voice. I heard an exchange in Arabic, an urgent typewriter-clatter of sounds in which not a single word was intelligible to me.

'I don't understand,' I told him.

Saïd shot me a dark look and said something in Arabic. The cluster of men surrounding him telegraphed their approval. He moved a little closer. I could almost smell his rage. Now the voices in Arabic sounded hostile; aggressive. I was suddenly, absurdly convinced that the man was about to strike me.

Vianne took a step towards us. I'd almost

54

forgotten she was there. Anouk was watching cautiously; behind her, Rosette was chasing shadows in a nearby alleyway.

I wanted to tell her to stand aside—the man was angry enough not to care that a woman and her children were near—but her presence seemed to calm Saïd. Without saying anything, or even appearing to touch him, she made a sign with her fingers—some gesture of appeasement—and the man took a wary step backwards, looking suddenly slightly confused.

Had he realized his mistake?

Or did she whisper something?

If she did, I heard nothing. But in any case, the atmosphere, which had been close to violence, was gone. The incident—if there *had* been an incident—was averted.

'Perhaps we should go,' I said to Vianne. 'I'm sorry. I shouldn't have brought you here.'

She smiled. '*Did* you bring me here? Remember, I came to see Armande's house.'

Of course. I had forgotten. 'It's empty. It still belongs to the Clairmont boy. He didn't want to sell it—but I don't see him living there, either.'

Vianne was looking thoughtful. 'I wonder if he'd let us stay? Just for a few days, while we're here? We'd look after the place, clean it up, tidy up the garden—'

I shrugged. 'Perhaps. But—'

'Good,' she said.

Just like that. Decided. Almost as if she'd never been gone. I had to smile—and I am not a man who smiles easily or often.

I said: 'At least take a look at the house. For all you know, it's falling down.'

55

'It isn't falling down,' she said.

I had no doubt that she was right. Luc Clairmont would never have let his grandmother's house go to ruin. I surrendered to the inevitable.

'She used to leave the door keys under a flowerpot in the yard. They're probably still there,' I said.

I was not at all certain that I should be encouraging her to stay, but the thought of Vianne Rocher back in Lansquenet, even now, at this difficult time, seemed almost irresistible.

Vianne herself seemed unsurprised. Perhaps her life is always like this; solutions to her troubles offering themselves like suitors for her favour. Mine is as painfully intricate as a ball of razor-wire, where movement in any direction may cut. I wonder whether I shall be cut during this little interlude. I think it very likely I shall.

Vianne Rocher smiled at me.

'Oh, and one more thing—' she said.

I sighed.

'Do you like peaches?'

CHAPTER ELEVEN

☾

Sunday, 15th August

Les marauds. that's where trouble starts. Les Marauds, where it all began. That's where I first met Armande, walking by her little house. That's

56

where the trouble *always* starts; it's where the river-rats moored their boats; where Anouk used to play with Pantoufle along the reedy banks of the Tannes. And it's where Armande *told* me to go, if only I'd been thinking clearly.

There used to be a peach tree growing up the side of my house. If you come in summertime, the fruit should be ripe and ready to pick.

It was—an elderly peach tree, its limbs half calcified with age, its dagger-shaped leaves scorched by the sun. But she was right—the fruit was ripe. I picked three, still warm from the sun and downy as a baby's head. I handed one to Anouk, then Rosette. Then I gave one to Reynaud.

The scent of peaches was all around; a sleepy, end-of-summer scent that seemed to leave a glow in the air like a trace of sunset. Armande's little house is on a rise, slightly apart from the rest of Les Marauds, and from this vantage point we could see down towards the river. There were lights along the boulevard; they shone on the water like fireflies. Already we could hear the quiet sounds of the evening: voices; sounds of pots and pans; children playing in back yards; crickets and frogs by the water's edge as the birds fell silent.

Anouk had found the back-door key where Armande had always left it; but the door was already unlocked, like so many doors in Lansquenet. The gas and electricity have both been cut off, but there's Armande's range if we want to cook, and a pile of logs at the back of the house. There's linen in the cupboard and woollen blankets in lemon, rose, vanilla and blue. There's a double bed in Armande's room, a folding cot in the room upstairs and a sofa in the living room. I've stayed in

57

worse places.

'I really like it here,' said Anouk.

'Bam,' agreed Rosette affably.

'Then it's settled,' I told them. 'We'll stay the night, and talk to Luc in the morning.'

Reynaud was still holding his peach, looking stiff and awkward. His sense of correctness is so pronounced that he would rather have slept in a ditch than use an empty house without the formal permission of the owner. As for the peaches, I had no doubt that by his standards they too were stolen, and he looked at me with the same unease that Adam must have looked at Eve when she handed him the forbidden fruit.

'Aren't you going to eat that?' I said. Anouk and Rosette had finished theirs in greedy, luscious mouthfuls. It occurred to me that I had only once seen Reynaud eat—to him, food is a complicated business, as much to be feared as savoured.

'Listen, Mademoiselle Rocher—'

'Please,' I said. 'Just call me Vianne.'

He cleared his throat. 'I appreciate your not asking me the obvious question,' he said. 'But I think you should know that, until further notice, I have been relieved of my duties as priest of Lansquenet, pending an inquiry into the fire at the old *chocolaterie*.' He took a deep breath and went on. 'Of course, I need not tell you,' he said, 'that I am in no way responsible. I was not arrested. I have never been accused. The police simply came to ask questions. But for a man in my position—'

I could well imagine the scene, viewed from behind the shutters. All of Lansquenet's gossips must have been out in force that day. The shop, half burnt and derelict. The fire truck, an hour too late.

The police car parked outside the church. Or even worse—outside Reynaud's house, his little cottage on the Rue des Francs Bourgeois, with its neat beds of marigolds.

The Church owns the cottage, of course. The marigolds are Reynaud's responsibility. So like dandelions, in their way, and yet, to him, there is a world of difference between those sly, invasive weeds and the pretty little yellow blooms that grow with such military straightness.

'You didn't need to tell me that. I know you didn't light the fire.'

His mouth twitched. 'If only everyone were as certain. Caro Clairmont has been spreading the word like mad, while continuing to pretend sympathy, and hanging on to every word that my successor utters.'

'Your successor?'

'Père Henri Lemaître. The Bishop's new pet. An upstart with too many teeth and a passion for PowerPoint.' He shrugged. 'It's only a matter of time now. You know what they're like in Lansquenet.'

Oh yes, I do. I've been the subject of gossip myself, and I know how fast it spreads. I also know that, in the current climate, any hint of a scandal concerning a member of the priesthood must be seen to be dealt with. The Catholic Church has had too many scandals recently; and even if the police have no evidence to accuse him, Reynaud may end up being condemned by the court of public opinion.

He took another deep breath. 'Perhaps, Mademoiselle Rocher, if you are going to stay awhile, you might convey your—*doubts* to any of your friends among the community who seem to

59

take amusement from the situation. Joséphine, Narcisse—'

He broke off sharply and looked away. I stared at him in growing astonishment. The icy precision of his speech was still as apparent as ever, but there was no doubting the look on his face. In his oblique and diffident way, Francis Reynaud was asking for help.

I can barely imagine how difficult it must have been for him to ask. After everything that has happened here, to admit to himself that he needs someone—especially someone like me—

Reynaud's world is black and white. He thinks this makes things simple. In fact, all his black-and-white thinking does is harden hearts, fix prejudice and blind good folk to the harm they do. And if something happens to challenge the way in which they see the world, when black-and-white thinking at last dissolves into a million shades of grey, men like Reynaud are left floundering, grasping at straws in a hurricane.

'I'm sorry,' he said. 'What can you do? Forget I even asked.'

I smiled. 'Of course I'll help you if I can. But only on one condition—'

He looked at me bleakly. 'What's that?' he said.

'For pity's sake, will you eat that peach?'

FIRST
QUARTER

CHAPTER ONE

C

Monday, 16th August

Luc called round this morning. Reynaud told him we were here. He found us over breakfast— peaches and hot chocolate, served in Armande's mismatched crockery; ancient china translucent as skin, chipped at the gilded edges and hand-painted with the traditional designs of the Sous-Tannes; that tiny oblong of the Gers cut off from the rest by the river Tannes before it joins the larger Garonne. Anouk's bowl had a painted rabbit; Rosette's a clutch of chickens. Mine had flowers, and a name— *Sylvie-Anne*—painted on in curly script.

A relative, perhaps? It looked old. A sister, a cousin, a daughter, an aunt. I wondered what it would be like to have a bowl with my own name on it; given to me by my mother, perhaps, or handed down from my grandmother. But which name would it be, Armande? Which one of my many names?

'Vianne!'

A call from the open door jolted me from my reverie. Luc's voice has deepened, and he has lost his childhood stammer. But otherwise he looks the same: brown hair falling over his eyes, a smile that is at the same time open and mischievous.

He hugged me first, and then Anouk, and stared in frank curiosity at Rosette, who greeted him with bared teeth and a pert little monkeyish sound—

62

cak-cakk!—that first startled him, then made him laugh.

'I brought you some supplies,' he said, 'but it looks like you've finished breakfast.'

'Don't you believe it,' I said with a smile. 'The air gives us an appetite.'

Luc grinned and handed out fresh croissants and *pains au chocolat*. 'Since it's my fault you're here,' he said, 'feel free to stay as long as you want. Grand-mère would have liked that.'

I asked him what he meant to do with the house, now that he owned it outright.

He shrugged. 'I'm not sure. Maybe live in it. That is, if my parents—' He bit off the phrase. 'You heard about the fire, of course.'

I nodded.

'Accidents happen,' he said. 'But Maman thinks there's more to it than that. She thinks Reynaud lit the fire.'

'Does she?' I said. 'And what do you think?'

I remember Caro Clairmont; one of Lansquenet's most fervent gossips, she has always taken sustenance from the scandals and dramas of village life. I could imagine the covert glee with which she had welcomed Reynaud's disgrace; tempering those rumours with extravagant shows of sympathy.

Luc shrugged. 'Well, I've never liked him much. But I don't think he did it. I mean, he's cold and kind of stiff-necked, but he wouldn't do a thing like that.'

Luc was in a minority. We heard the rumour a dozen times more before the day was over. From Narcisse, bringing vegetables from his shop; from Poitou, the baker; from Joline Drou, the schoolteacher, who called by to see us with her son. In fact, most of Lansquenet seemed to be passing through Les Marauds today—with one surprising exception—as word of our arrival spread like dandelion seeds on the wind.

Vianne Rocher is back, they said. *Vianne Rocher is home at last—*

But that's absurd. I *have* a home. It's moored on the Quai de l'Elysée. I don't belong here any more than I did eight years ago, when Anouk and I first arrived. And yet—

'It would be so easy,' Guillaume said. 'You could fix up the old *chocolaterie*. A lick of paint, we could all lend a hand—'

I caught a flash from Anouk's eyes.

'You should see our houseboat in Paris,' I said. 'Right underneath the Pont des Arts, and in the mornings the river's all covered in mist, just like the Tannes.'

The flash subsided, veiled under long eyelashes.

'You ought to come and see us, Guillaume.'

'Oh, I'm too old for Paris.' He smiled. 'And Patch is used to first-class travel.'

Guillaume Duplessis is one of the few who do not believe in Reynaud's guilt. 'It's just a malicious rumour,' he says. 'Why would Reynaud burn down a school?'

Joline Drou was certain she knew. 'Because of *her*, that's why,' she said. 'That *burqa* woman. The woman in black.'

Anouk and Rosette had gone outside, and were beating a dusty carpet with a pair of old brooms. Joline's son, Jeannot, was with them—a lad of Anouk's age, whom I remembered from the days of the old *chocolaterie*. He and Anouk had been good

64

friends, in spite of his troublesome mother.

'Who is she?' I said.

Joline arched an eyebrow. 'Apparently, she's a widow, the sister of Karim Bencharki. I know Karim—he's very nice—he works at the gym in Les Marauds. But she's very different. Aggressive. Aloof. They're saying her husband divorced her.'

'You mean you don't know?' Joline is one of Lansquenet's most assiduous gossips. I found it hard to believe that she hadn't found out every detail of the newcomer as soon as she moved into town.

Joline shrugged. 'You don't understand. She never talks to anyone. She's not like the other *Maghrébins*. I don't even know if she speaks French.'

'You've never tried to find out?'

'It's not as easy as that,' said Joline. 'How do you even start to talk to someone who never shows their face? We used to be quite friendly with some of the women in Les Marauds. Caro used to invite a group of them to her house for tea. People think we're just rural folk, but we're *very* multicultural here. You'd be surprised, Vianne. I've even started eating couscous. It's really very healthy, you know, and not as fattening as you'd think.'

I hid a smile. Joline Drou and Caro Clairmont think they can enter a culture because they like eating couscous. I imagined those tea parties at Caro's house; the conversation, the little cakes, the china, the silver, the canapés. The well-meaning discussions, intended to promote *entente cordiale*. I winced at the thought.

'What happened?' I said.

Joline pulled a face. 'They stopped coming

round when that woman moved in,' she said. 'She's nothing but trouble. Walking around with that veil on her face, making people uncomfortable. Those women are all so competitive. It caught on like a fashion craze. Everyone started wearing it. Well, maybe not *everyone*, but you know. It drives men crazy, apparently. Keeps them guessing what's underneath. Makes their imaginations work overtime. Of course, Reynaud didn't like it. He's always been stuck in the past. He has no idea how to cope with a multicultural France. You heard about all that fuss with the mosque? And afterwards, with the minaret? And then, when that woman opened the school—' She shook her head. 'He must have cracked. That's all I can say. It wouldn't be the first time—'

'How many pupils were there?' I said.

'Oh, perhaps a dozen or so. God knows what she was teaching them.' She hunched a shoulder pettishly. 'Those *burqas* don't want to mix with us. They think we'll corrupt them with our loose morals.'

Or perhaps they're just sick of being patronized and misunderstood, I thought, but did not comment.

'Isn't there a daughter?' I said.

She nodded. 'Yes, poor little thing. Never plays with any of ours. Never talks to anyone.'

I looked out of the window, to where Anouk and Jeannot were sword-fighting with brooms while Rosette hooted encouragement. Living and travelling as we did for so long, my daughter and I have had more contact with different kinds of folk than anyone in Lansquenet. We have learnt to see to some extent beyond the layers in which we hide

66

ourselves. The *niqab*—or, as Joline wrongly calls it, the *burqa*—is only a layer of fabric. And yet, in the eyes of such as Joline it has the power to change an ordinary woman into an object of suspicion and fear. Even Guillaume, usually so tolerant, had little to say in defence of the woman from the *chocolaterie*.

'I always raise my hat when I meet her,' he said. 'It's what I was taught to do as a boy. But *she* never says as much as hello: never even looks at me. It's rude, Madame Rocher, plain rude. I don't care who anyone is, I always try to be polite. But when someone won't even *look* at you—'

I understand. It must be hard. But I have no moral high ground to take. For years I fled the Man in Black, seeing only my mother's fear and the black soutane of a hostile faith. For years I was like Guillaume and the rest, blinded by my prejudice. Only now do I see the truth; that my Man in Black is just a man, as vulnerable as any other. Is Lansquenet, with its Woman in Black, really any different? And could it be that under her veil, she too, like Reynaud, is in need of help?

CHAPTER TWO

☾

Monday, 16th August

Night was beginning to fall at last. The sky was veering from watermelon-red to a deep and velvety jewel-box blue. The wistful call of the *muezzin* sounded faintly across Les Marauds. At the same time, from across the river, the Lansquenet church bells began to ring, announcing the end of Mass. A dozen families had already invited us to dinner, had we wanted to socialize, but Rosette was already half asleep, and Anouk was glued to her iPod again. Both of them looked exhausted. Perhaps the fresh air; the change of scenery; the stream of friends and visitors. I set out a simple evening meal of olives, bread, fruit and cheese, with dandelion-leaf salad spiced with yellow nasturtiums. We ate mostly in silence, listening to the sounds of the night from the open window: crickets; church bells; frogs; evening birds; the ticking of Armande's old clock, with its grinning, parchment-yellow face. I noticed Rosette wasn't eating; just pushing olives around her plate like pieces in an elaborate game.

'What's wrong, Rosette? Aren't you hungry?'

'She misses Roux,' explained Anouk.

'*Rowr*,' said Rosette mournfully.

'We'll see him soon. You'll like it here,' said Anouk, hugging her. She looked at me. 'Joséphine didn't come. I thought she'd be the first to say hello.'

She was right. I'd noticed that. Of course, the café is open all day; Joséphine must have been busy. All the same, I thought she might have dropped by during her lunch break. Perhaps she didn't want to be around all those other people; people like Caro and Joline who only wanted to gossip and stare. Perhaps she was understaffed today, or meant to call at closing time. I hope so; of all those we left behind, perhaps Joséphine is the one I missed most; Joséphine with her soulful eyes and her air of stoic defiance.

'We'll go tomorrow,' I promised Anouk. 'Maybe she was busy today.'

We finished the meal in silence. Anouk and Rosette both went to bed. I stayed alone with a glass of red wine and wondered what Reynaud was doing now. I imagined him in his little house, watching the last of the sunset, listening to the church bells ring while his rival said Mass in his place. And then, because I was restless, I opened the door and went outside.

It smelt of dust and peaches. Crickets sang in the rosemary hedge. There are no streetlights in this part of town, but the sky, never totally dark, was enough to show me the path across the bridge into Lansquenet.

Below me, Les Marauds was coming alive. Lights shone around shuttered windows; people came and went in the street; the scent of incense and cooking rose from an open kitchen door. It all seemed very different from what it had been only hours ago: the dull, flat heat; the women in *hijab* scarves and *abayas* over their day clothes; the bearded men in their white robes; that cautious, watchful silence. Now there were voices; laughter; the sounds of celebration. Days are long during Ramadan. At the end of the day a simple meal comes as a feast, a glass of water a blessing. Stories are told; games played. Children stay up late into the evening.

A little girl in a yellow *kameez* ran across the boulevard, brandishing a long cane. It made a strident, whirring sound, and I recognized the local game of tying a large flying beetle to a stick with a piece of thread to make an improvised rattle.

Someone called out in Arabic. The child protested. A girl in a dark-blue kaftan came out. The child left the cane by the side of the road and followed the girl into the house. I wandered into Les Marauds, heading for the river. The bridge that links Les Marauds to the rest of Lansquenet stands at a kind of crossroads; this is where the tanneries stood, and where the village mosque now stands. On both sides, the walls of the old *bastide* remain, broken in places, a reminder to would-be intruders that Lansquenet protects its own.

The bridge is stone; rather low, the river dividing the village in two, like the halves of a sliced fruit. In winter, after the rain, the Tannes runs too high for any but the flattest of boats to pass. In autumn, if the summer has been especially hot, the river sometimes almost dries up, leaving banks of gritty sand divided by sparse rivulets. Just now, the river is perfect. Perfect for swimming; perfect for boats.

That made me wonder once again why Roux chose not to come. He spent four years in Lansquenet after Anouk and I left. So why would he stay in Paris now, loving the countryside as he does? Why has he chosen to stay on the Seine,

70

when the Tannes is so inviting? And I know Rosette misses him—Anouk and I miss him too, of course, but Rosette misses him in a special way, a way that the two of us don't understand. Of course, she still has Bam—who, in Roux's absence, has made his presence more than usually apparent; sitting on a stool by Anouk, his tail a gleaming question mark in the yellow lamplight.

Oh Roux, why didn't you come?

Roux dislikes technology; but I managed to persuade him to carry—if not to actually *use*—a mobile phone. I tried it now, but predictably it was turned off. I sent a text:

Arrived safely. Staying in Armande's old house. Everything fine, but some changes. May have to stay a few more days. We miss you. Lots of love, Vx

The act of sending a message home made Roux seem all the more distant. Home. *Is* it my home now? I looked across at Lansquenet; its little lights; its crooked streets; the church tower, white in the dusk. Across the bridge, the darker half; the streets lit only by house lights; the shadowy spike of the minaret, topped with its silver crescent, challenging the church tower that stands like an upraised fist in the square.

For a while I had thought that *this* was my home; that I might stay in Lansquenet. Even now, the word *home* still conjures up that little shop, the rooms above the *chocolaterie*; Anouk's bedroom in the loft, with its porthole window. And now I feel divided in a way I never was; half of me belongs with Roux; the other, here in Lansquenet. Perhaps because the village itself is now divided between two worlds; one new and multicultural, one as conservative as only the rural French can be, and I

71

understand it perfectly—

What am I doing here? I thought. Why have I
opened this box of uncertainties? Armande's letter
clearly said that someone in Lansquenet needed
help. But who is that person? Francis Reynaud?
The Woman in Black? Joséphine? Myself, perhaps?

My path had taken me past the house from which
the girl in the dark blue kaftan had come. The stick
with the captive beetle was lying by the side of the
road. I liberated the beetle, which buzzed at me
crossly before flying off, and paused to look at the
dwelling.

Like most of the houses in Les Marauds, it was
a low-roofed, two-storey building, part wood, part
yellow brick. It looked to be made from two houses
that had been knocked together; the door and
the shutters were painted green, and there were
window boxes on the sills in which red geraniums
were growing. From inside, I could hear voices;
laughter; conversation. I could smell cooking,
spices and mint. As I passed, the door opened again
and the little girl in the yellow *kameez* dashed out
into the street. She stopped as she saw me and
stared, bright-eyed; I guessed her to be five or six,
too young to be wearing a headscarf. Her hair was
in bunches, tied with yellow ribbon. She wore a gold
bracelet round one chubby wrist.

'Hello,' I said.

The little girl stared.

'I'm afraid I let your beetle escape,' I said, with
a glance at the discarded cane. 'He looked so sad,
tied up like that. Tomorrow, you can catch him
again. That is, if he wants to play.'

I smiled. The child continued to stare. I
wondered if she'd understood. In Paris, I'd seen

girls of Rosette's age who hardly spoke a word of French, even though they'd been born there. Usually, they'd mastered the language by the time they left primary school; though some families I'd known were reluctant to send their daughters to secondary school—sometimes because of the headscarf ban, sometimes because they were needed at home.

'What's your name?' I asked the child.

'Maya.' So she *did* understand.

'Well, I'm happy to meet you, Maya,' I said. 'I'm Vianne. I'm staying in that house up there with my two little girls.'

I pointed to Armande's old house.

Maya looked doubtful. 'That house there?'

'Yes. It belonged to my friend Armande.' I could see she was unconvinced. I said, 'Does your mother like peaches?'

Maya gave a little nod.

'Well, my friend has a peach tree growing up the side of her house. Tomorrow, if you like, I'll pick some and bring them to your mother for *iftar*.'

My use of the word made Maya smile. 'You know *iftar*?'

'Of course I do.'

My mother and I once lived in Tangier. A vibrant place in so many ways; filled with contradictions. I've always used food and recipes as a means of understanding those around me; and sometimes, in a place like Tangier, food is the only shared language.

'How are you breaking the fast tonight? Is there harissa soup?' I said. 'I love harissa soup.'

Maya's smile broadened. 'Me too,' she said. 'And Omi makes pancakes. She has a secret recipe.

73

They're the best pancakes in the world.'

Suddenly the green door opened again. A woman's voice spoke sharply in Arabic. Maya seemed about to protest, then reluctantly went back indoors. A female figure veiled in black appeared in the doorway as it closed—I raised a hand in greeting, but the door had already slammed shut before I could be certain whether the woman had seen me or not.

One thing I was sure of, though. The woman I'd just seen at the door was the same woman in *niqab* I'd seen by the church yesterday, and then again in Les Marauds. Karim Bencharki's sister, whose real name no one seems to know; the woman whose shadow stretches so far across these two communities . . .

Walking home along the Tannes, the calm was almost eerie. The crickets and birds had fallen still; even the frogs were silent.

On evenings like this, the locals say, the Autan wind is ready to blow; *le Vent des Fous*, the Mad Wind, that rattles windows, parches crops and stops people from sleeping. The White Autan brings dry heat; the Black Autan brings storms and rain. Whichever way the wind blows, change is never far away.

What am I doing in Lansquenet? Once more, I can't help wondering. Did the Autan bring me here? And which one will it be, this time? The White Autan, that keeps you awake, or the Black, that drives you insane?

CHAPTER THREE

Tuesday, 17th August

Bless me, father, for I have sinned. Of course, you're not here any more. But I need to confess to someone, *père*, and to do so to the new priest—Père Henri Lemaître with his blue jeans and his bleached smile and his new ideas—is absolutely impossible. The Bishop is equally so. He actually thinks I lit the fire. I will not kneel to these people, *père*. I will be damned before I do.

Of course, you're right. My sin is pride. I have always been aware of this. But I know that Père Henri Lemaître will destroy Saint-Jérôme's, and I cannot just stand by and watch. The man uses PowerPoint in his sermons, for God's sake, and has replaced the village organist with Lucie Levalois playing guitar. The result is undoubtedly popular— we've never had so many people coming from other villages—but I wonder what you'd think of it, *père*, who always used to be so austere.

The Bishop feels that, nowadays, worship should be more about fun than austerity. *We have to draw in the young*, he says—he himself is thirty-eight, seven years younger than I am, and he wears Nike trainers under his robe. Père Henri Lemaître is his protégé, and so, of course, can do no wrong. Hence his approval of Père Henri's intention to modernize Saint-Jérôme's, including display screens for his PowerPoint sermons, and plans to replace our old oak pews with something 'more appropriate'. By this I suppose he means that oak goes badly with PowerPoint.

But although I myself may deplore the loss, I will be in the minority. Caro Clairmont has been complaining for years about those pews, which are narrow and hard (Caro herself is neither). And of course, if they are taken out, her husband, Georges, will be the one to reclaim, restore and ultimately sell them, at an absurdly inflated price, in Bordeaux, to wealthy tourists looking to furnish their holiday homes with something nicely authentic.

It's hard not to get angry, *père*. I've given my life to Lansquenet. And for it all to be snatched away—and for such a reason—

It all comes back to that blasted shop. That blasted *chocolaterie*. What is it about that place that attracts trouble? First it was Vianne Rocher—then, Bencharki's sister. Now, even gutted and empty, it seems to be doing its best to provoke my downfall. The Bishop is certain, he tells me, that nothing links me to the fire. Hypocrite. You notice that he does *not* say that he believes in my innocence. What he says, very reasonably, is that, whatever the outcome of the investigation into my conduct, my position here has been compromised. Perhaps another parish, then, where my history is not known . . .

Damn his condescension. I will not go quietly. I refuse to believe that, after everything I have done for this community, *no one* here has faith in me. There must be something I can do. A gesture to earn myself some goodwill among my people and those of Les Marauds. Trying to talk with them has not helped; but maybe action will plead

76

my cause.

Which is why this morning I decided to go back to Place Saint-Jérôme and do what I could to make amends. The shop is structurally sound: it requires little more than a thorough clean, some tiles on the roof, some replacement wood and plasterwork and a few coats of paint to make it like new. Or so I thought; I also believed that if others saw me helping out, some of them would lend a hand.

Four hours later, I ached all over, and no one had even spoken to me. Poitou's bakery is opposite; the Café des Marauds just down the road, and no one had even thought to bring me as much as a drink in this crushing heat. I began to understand, *père*, that this was my penance—not for the fire, but for my arrogance in believing that I could win back my flock with a show of humility.

After lunch, the bakery closed; the sun-bleached square was silent. Only Saint-Jérôme's tower offered some relief from the sun; as I dragged pieces of charred debris from inside the shop on to the kerb, I lingered awhile in its shadow, then took a drink from the fountain.

'What are you doing?' said a voice.

I straightened up. Sweet Jesus. Of all the people I would rather *not* see—the Clairmont boy is no trouble, of course, but he'll tell his mother, and I would have much preferred him to see me surrounded by friendly volunteers, cleaning up the Bencharki place, instead of exhausted, filthy and sore, surrounded by nothing but burnt wood.

'Nothing much.' I shot him a smile. 'I thought we could show solidarity. You wouldn't want a mother and child to come back to a place like *this*—' I indicated the charred front door and the blackened

77

mess that lay beyond.

Luc gave me a guarded look. Perhaps the smile had been a mistake.

'All right, it makes me uncomfortable,' I confessed, dropping the smile. 'Knowing that half the village thinks *I* was the one responsible.'

Half the village? If only it was. Right now I could count my supporters on the fingers of one hand.

'I'll help,' Luc said. 'I've got nothing but time just now.'

Of course, his university term begins in late September. As I recall, he is studying French literature, to Caro's disapproval. But why would he want to help me now? He never liked me, not even when his mother was one of my devotees.

'I'll bring a van from the wood-yard,' he said, indicating the debris. 'First I'll help you clear this up, and then we can see what kind of supplies we're going to need.'

Well, I was in no position to refuse. After all, it was pride that got me into this. I thanked him and set to work again, dragging out the debris. There was far more of it than I'd thought, but with Luc's help, by the end of the day we had cleared out all the wreckage from downstairs.

The bells for Mass began to ring; the shadows lengthened in the square. Père Henri Lemaître, looking as if he'd stepped out of a refrigerated storage box just for priests, came sauntering out of Saint-Jérôme's, his soutane nicely pressed, his hair in a fashionably boyish style, his freshly laundered collar only a shade whiter than his teeth.

'Francis!' I hate it when he calls me that.

I gave him my most diplomatic smile.

'How good of you to do all this,' he said, as if I

78

had done it for him. 'If only you'd told me this morning, I could have put in a word after Mass—' His tone implied that he himself would have been more than happy to help, if only the burden of caring for *my* parish had not been thrust upon him. 'And, speaking of Mass—' He cast a critical glance at my sooty, sweating person. 'Were you thinking of attending this evening? I have a change of clothes in the vestry that I'd be more than glad—'

'No, thanks.'

'It's just that I notice you haven't been to Mass, or taken Communion, or attended confession since—'

'Thank you. I'll bear it in mind.'

As if I'd take the Host from him, and as for confession—well, *père*. I know it's a sin, but let's just say that the day I take a penance from him will be the day I leave the Church for ever.

He gave me a look of sympathy. 'My door is always open,' he said.

And then, with a last gleam of his toothpaste-commercial smile, he was gone, leaving me very far from serene, fists clenched behind my back.

That was enough. I called it a day. I went home before the crowd for Mass began to gather in the square. Those bells pursued me all the way, and when I arrived at my front door I saw that someone had tagged it in black aerosol. It must have been recent; I could still smell the paint fumes in the warm air.

I looked around; I saw no one but a trio of boys on mountain bikes at the end of the Rue des Francs Bourgeois. Teenagers, from what I could see; one dressed in a loose white shirt; the other two in T-shirts and jeans, all three wearing the chequered scarves that Arab men sometimes wear. They saw me and cycled off at speed towards Les Marauds, shouting something in Arabic. I do not know the language, but from their tone and their laughter I guessed it was probably not a compliment.

I could have followed them, *mon père*. Perhaps I should have done so. But I was tired and—yes, I confess—maybe just a little afraid. And so I went inside instead, and had a shower, and poured a beer, and tried to eat a sandwich.

But through the open window I could still hear those bells ringing for Mass, and beyond them, the voice of the *muezzin* carried over the river like a ribbon of smoke on the evening air. And I *would* have liked to pray, but somehow all I could think of was Armande Voizin, her snapping black eyes, her impertinent ways, and how she would have laughed at all this. Perhaps she sees me. The thought appals. And so I fetch another beer and watch the sun set over the Tannes, while in the east a crescent moon rises over Lansquenet.

CHAPTER FOUR

☾

Tuesday, 17th August

This morning, Rosette and I went off to find out what had happened to Joséphine. The shops were all shut in Les Marauds—a clothing store, a grocer's, a shop selling rolls of fabric—but we saw a little café there, staffed by a glum-looking man in a white *djellaba* and *taqiyah* prayer hat, polishing tables, who saw me look in and paused in his task just long enough to say, 'We're closed.'

I suspected as much. 'When do you open?'

'Later. Tonight.' He gave me a look that reminded me of Paul Muscat, in the days when he ran the Café des Marauds; a look that was both appraising and curiously hostile. Then he went back to his tables. Not everyone here is welcoming.

Cross man, signed Rosette. *Cross face. Let's go.*

Bam was at his most visible; a bright orange scribble of light at her heels. I saw a mischievous look pass over her face; the man's hat slipped and fell on to the floor.

Rosette made a crooning sound.

From the corner of my eye, I saw Bam do a somersault.

Hastily I took her hand. 'It's all right. We're going,' I said. 'This isn't the café we're looking for.'

But arriving at the Café des Marauds, instead of finding Joséphine, I found a sullen girl of about sixteen, watching TV from behind the bar, who told me that Madame Bonnet had driven down to Bordeaux to pick up a truckload of supplies, and might be back quite late.

No, there was no message, she said. Her face showed neither recognition nor curiosity. Her eyes were so heavily made up that I could barely see them, loaded as they were with shadow and mascara. Her lips were glossy as candied fruit, and her jaw moved placidly around a sizeable wad of pink gum.

'I'm Vianne. What's your name?'

She stared at me as if I were insane. 'Marie-Ange Lucas,' she said at last, in the same vaguely sullen

81

tone. 'I'm covering for Madame Bonnet.'

'Pleased to meet you, Marie-Ange. I'll take a *citron pressé*, please. And an Orangina for Rosette.'

Anouk had gone looking for Jeannot Drou. I hoped she'd have more luck finding him than I was having with Joséphine. I took our drinks on to the *terrasse* (Marie-Ange did not volunteer to bring them), and sat under the acacia tree, watching the deserted street that led over the bridge into Les Marauds.

Madame Bonnet? I wondered why my old friend, having gone back to her maiden name, should have chosen to keep the *madame*. But Lansquenet has its own way of imposing respectability. A woman of thirty-five or so, running her own business without the help of a man—such a woman cannot be a *mademoiselle*. I learnt this myself eight years ago. To these people, I was always Madame Rocher.

Rosette finished her drink and began to play with a couple of stones she had found in the road. It doesn't take much to amuse her; with her fingers she made a sign and the stones shone with a secret light. Rosette gave a little crow of impatience and made the stones dance on the table-top.

'Run off and play with Bam,' I said. 'Just stay where I can see you, all right?'

I watched her as she made for the bridge. I knew she could play for hours there, dropping sticks over the parapet and racing them to the other side, or just watching the reflections of the clouds as they sailed overhead. A shimmer in the hot air suggested the presence of Bam; I finished my *citron pressé* and ordered another.

A small boy of eight or so put his head around

82

the café door. He was wearing a *Lion King* T-shirt that came almost down to the hem of his faded shorts, and sneakers that gave every indication of having recently been in the Tannes. His hair was bleached by the sun, his eyes a sunny summer-blue. He was holding a piece of string, which, as it travelled into view from behind the angle of the door, revealed at its end a large, shaggy dog that had also recently been in the Tannes. Boy and dog stared at me with open curiosity. Then they both made a run for it, heading down the road to the bridge, the dog barking madly at the end of its lead, the boy skidding alongside, each step sending a small, contained explosion of road dust from under his grubby sneakers.

Marie-Ange brought me my second *pressé*. 'Who's that?' I said.

'Oh, that's Pilou. Madame Bonnet's son.'

'Her *son*?'

She gave me a look. 'Of course.'

'Oh. I didn't know,' I said.

She gave a shrug, as if to convey her total indifference to both of us. Then she collected the empty glasses and went back to watching her TV show.

I looked back at the boy and his dog, now splashing in the shallows. In the haze they looked gilded—the boy's hair in the sunlight, even that disreputable dog—caught in a matrix of diamonds.

I saw Rosette watching the boy and his dog with curiosity. She is a sociable little thing, but in Paris she tends to be left on her own; the other children won't play with her. Partly because she doesn't speak; partly because she frightens them. I heard Pilou call something to her from underneath

83

the bridge; in a moment she had joined him and the dog, and was splashing in the water. It's very shallow at that point; there's a bank of sandy, gritty stuff that might almost pass as a small beach. Rosette would be all right, I thought: I let her play with her new friends as I slowly finished my *citron pressé* and thought about my old friend.

So—Madame Bonnet had a son. Who was the father? She'd kept her name; she clearly hadn't remarried. Today, there was no one here but Marie-Ange; no sign of any partner. Of course, I had lost touch with my friends when I moved to Paris. A change of name, a change of life, and Lansquenet had been left behind along with so many other things that I had thought never to revisit. Roux, who might have told me the news, had never been good at writing letters, sending me picture postcards with nothing but a single-line scrawl from wherever he happened to be. But he'd lived in Lansquenet for four years: most of that time at the café itself. I know he despises gossip, but knowing how close I'd been to her, why on earth hadn't he told me that Joséphine had had a child?

I finished my drink and paid for it. The sun was already very hot. Rosette is eight, but small for her age; the boy Pilou may be younger. I wandered down towards the bridge, wishing I had brought a hat. The children were building a kind of dam across the sandy shallows; I could hear Rosette babbling in her private language— *bambaddabambaddabam!*—and Pilou giving orders, apparently in preparation for an attack by pirates.

'Forward! Aft! The cannons! *Bam!*'

'Bam!' Rosette repeated.

This was a game I knew very well; Anouk had played it with Jeannot Drou and their friends down by Les Marauds, eight years ago.

The boy looked up at me and grinned. 'Are you *Maghrébine*?'

I shook my head.

'But she talks foreign, doesn't she?' he said, with a sidelong glance at Rosette.

I smiled. 'Not foreign, exactly. But no, she doesn't speak much. She understands what you tell her, though. She's very clever at some things.'

'What's her name?'

'Rosette,' I said. 'And you're Pilou. What is it short for?'

'Jean-Philippe.' He grinned again. 'And this is my dog, Vladimir. Say hello to the lady, Vlad!'

Vlad barked and shook himself, sending a spray of water arcing over the little bridge.

Rosette laughed. *Good game*, she signed.

'What's she say?'

'She likes you.'

'Cool.'

'So you're Joséphine's boy,' I said. 'I'm Vianne, an old friend of your mother's. We're staying down in Les Marauds, in Madame Voizin's old house.' I paused. 'I'd love to invite you both. And your father, if he'd like.'

Pilou shrugged. 'I don't have one.' He sounded slightly defiant. 'Well, obviously I *do* have one, but—'

'You just don't know who he is?'

Pilou grinned. 'Yeah. That's right.'

'My little girl used to say that. My other little girl. Anouk.'

Pilou stared at me, round-eyed. 'I know who you

85

are,' he said. 'You're the lady from the shop, who used to make the chocolates!' His grin broadened, and he gave an exuberant little jump in the water. 'Maman talks about you all the time. You're practically a celebrity.'

I laughed. 'I wouldn't go that far.'

'We still hold the festival you started all those years ago. We have it at Easter, in front of the church. There's dancing, and Easter-egg hunts, and chocolate carving, and all kinds of other stuff.'

'Really?' I said.

'It's *awesome*.'

I remembered my own chocolate festival; the window display, the hand-lettered signs, Anouk at six, half a lifetime ago, splashing in the shallows in her yellow wellington boots, blowing her plastic trumpet while Joséphine danced in front of the church and Roux stood by with that look on his face, a look that was always half sullen, half shy—

I suddenly felt uneasy. 'She never mentioned your father *at all*?'

That grin again, as brilliant as sunlight on the river. 'She says he was a pirate, sailing down the river. Now he's on the high seas, drinking rum out of coconut shells and looking for buried treasure. She says I look just like him, and when I grow up I'll get out of this place and have adventures of my own. Maybe I'll meet him on the way.'

Now I felt more than uneasy. That sounded like one of Roux's stories. I'd always thought that Joséphine had something of a soft spot for Roux. In fact, there'd been a time when I'd thought maybe they'd fall in love. But life has a way of confounding our dearest expectations, and the futures that I'd planned for us both have turned out very differently.

Joséphine dreamt of getting away, and instead has stayed in Lansquenet; I promised myself never to go back to Paris, and Paris is where I came to rest. Like the wind, Life delights in taking us to the places we least expect to go, changing direction all the time so that beggars are crowned, kings fall, love fades to indifference and sworn enemies go to the grave hand-in-hand in friendship.

Never challenge Life to a game, my mother used to say to me. *Because Life plays dirty, changes the rules, steals the cards right out of your hands or, sometimes, turns them all to blank—*

Suddenly I wanted to read my mother's Tarot cards again. I'd brought them with me, as always, of course, but it has been a long time since I opened the sandalwood box. I'm afraid the technique has deserted me—or maybe that's *not* why I am afraid.

Back in Armande's house, which still smells of her scent—of the lavender she always kept pressed between her linens; of the cherries in brandy that even now line the shelves of her little pantry—I finally open my mother's box. It smells of her, just as Armande's house still smells of Armande; as if in death my mother has shrunk to something the size of a deck of cards, though her voice is as strong as ever.

I cut the cards and laid them out. Outside in Les Marauds, Rosette was still playing with her new friend. The cards are old, somewhat battered; the woodcut designs worn thin with frequent handling.

The Seven of Swords: futility. The Seven of Disks: failure. The Queen of Cups has a distant look; the look of a woman who has been

87

disappointed so badly and so often that she dares not hope again. The Knight of Cups, who should be a dynamic card, has suffered a little water damage; his face looks raddled and debauched. Who is he? He looks familiar. But he offers no answer to my question. In any case—

The cards are bad. I should put them away, I know. What am I doing here, anyhow? I almost wish I had never opened Armande's letter; that Roux had never delivered it; that he had thrown it into the Seine.

I check my phone. No message from Roux. It is more than likely that he hasn't checked his messages—he is as unreliable with mobile phones as he is with letters—but after what I've learnt today, I need that simple contact. It's absurd, I tell myself—I've never *needed* anyone. And yet I can't help thinking that the longer I stay in Lansquenet, the more precarious the thread that connects me with my new life—

Of course, we *could* go home tonight. It's very simple, really. What's keeping me here? Nostalgia? A memory? A handful of cards?

No, none of those things. What, then?

I put the cards back in their box. As I do so, one of them escapes and falls face down upon the floor. A woman holding a distaff, from which a lunar crescent unwinds. Her face is cloaked in shadow. The Moon. A card I've long associated with myself, but today she is someone different. Perhaps it is that crescent moon, so like the one above the mosque. Or maybe it's the shrouded face, which draws me back to the Woman in Black, that woman I have only glimpsed, but whose shadow stretches right across the river Tannes to Les Marauds, reeling me in, drawing me home . . .

Home. Oh, that word again. But Lansquenet is *not* my home. And yet, the pull of that word is strong. Do I even know what it means? Perhaps the Woman in Black can explain—that is, if I can find her.

Anouk is back from her day with Jeannot, with a cheery summer smile and sunburn across the bridge of her nose. I leave her here now with Rosette, whose little friend has gone home at last, taking his dog with him. However, I suspect we may see more of Pilou, and Vlad, and Jeannot in the next few days.

'Did you have a good time?'

Anouk nods. Her eyes are very bright. In spite of the difference in colouring, she looks very like Rosette today; her hair in exuberant ringlets from the damp wind on the Tannes. I'm glad she has found a friend in this place; even if he *is* the son of Joline Drou. I remember a bright-eyed little boy, diffident at first, but soon immersed in Anouk's extravagant games. His favourites were chocolate mice; he used to put them into fresh baguettes to make *pains au chocolat*. Now he must be Anouk's age; maybe a little older. He has broadened out since we last met, standing taller than either of his parents, although the illusion of maturity is belied by his adolescent slouch and the coltish, lolloping way he walks when he thinks no one is watching. I'm glad that Jeannot has retained something of the little boy he was. Too many people I know have changed, some beyond recognition.

Saint-Jérôme's clock strikes six o'clock. A good time to call on our neighbours. The men will still be at the mosque. The women are preparing *iftar*.

89

'I want to go out for a little while. Will you be all right?'

She nods. 'Sure. I'll make dinner.'

That means dried pasta again, I suppose, cooked on Armande's wood-stove. There's a jar of it in the pantry, though I dare not think how old it is. Anouk and Rosette love pasta above almost everything else; with a little dash of oil and some basil from the garden, they will both be happy. There are peaches, too; and brandied cherries and plums from Narcisse, and a *flan aux pruneaux* from his wife, and some *galette* and cheese from Luc.

I look towards the green-shuttered house. I promised Maya peaches. Anouk helps me to pick some. We put them in a basket on a bed of dandelion leaves. That's something I'd almost forgotten, living eight years in Paris: the scent of peaches on the tree, sunny and intoxicating; the slightly bitter scent of those leaves, like dusty pavements after the rain. To me it smells of childhood; of roadside stalls and summer nights.

What about the Woman in Black? Of course, I have no proof of this. But a part of me is confident that peaches are her favourites.

There was a time when I used to know *everybody*'s favourite. A part of me still does, although the gift my mother valued so highly has more than often been a curse. Knowledge is not always comfortable. Even power is not always good. I learnt that lesson four years ago, when Zozie de l'Alba burst into our lives like a hurricane in scarlet shoes. There is too much at stake for me to be truly happy riding the wind; too much responsibility in reading the script of the human heart.

Should I really be doing this? Can I make a

difference here? Or will the Woman in Black turn out to be my very own black *piñata*, filled with words that are best left unread, stories best left secret?

CHAPTER FIVE

☾

Tuesday, 17th August

I'd expected to find the Woman in Black. but instead, when I went to the green-shuttered house, an older woman opened the door. Late sixties; round-faced; plump; thick grey hair escaping from beneath a loosely knotted white *hijab*. She looked surprised to see me—even a little suspicious at first—but when I gave her the peaches and mentioned seeing Maya last night, her face broke into a broad smile.

'Ah, the little one,' she exclaimed. 'Always in trouble. So naughty, *hé*?' She spoke with the kind of indulgence only a grandparent can afford.

I smiled. 'I have a little girl too. Rosette. You'll probably see her soon. And my Anouk. I'm Vianne, by the way.'

I held out my hand. She gave my fingers the light press that counts as a handshake in Tangier. 'Your husband?'

'He's in Paris,' I said. 'We're only here for a few days.'

She gave her name as Fatima. Her husband was Mehdi al-Djerba. I remembered the name, though

91

vaguely, from something Reynaud had said the day I'd arrived: he'd said they ran some kind of shop; that they'd lived in Les Marauds for almost eight years; that Mehdi was from old Marseille and liked the occasional glass of wine—

Fatima gestured towards the door. 'Please, come in and have some tea—'

I shook my head. 'I don't want to intrude. I know you're very busy. I only came to say hello, and to bring the peaches. We have far too many, and—'

'Come in, come in!' Fatima said. 'I was only making food. I'll give you something to take home. Do you like Moroccan cooking?'

I told her I'd spent six months in Tangier while I was still in my teens.

The smile broadened still further. 'I make the very best *halwa chebakia*. With mint tea, or *qamar-el-deen*—you can take some home to your family.'

Such an offer cannot be refused. I know this from experience. Years of travelling with my mother have taught me that food is a universal passport. Whatever the constraints of language, culture or geography, food crosses over all boundaries. To offer food is to extend the hand of friendship; to accept is to be accepted into the most closed of communities. I wondered if Francis Reynaud had ever thought of this approach. Knowing him, he hasn't. Reynaud means well, but he isn't the type to buy *halwa chebakia* or to drink a glass of mint tea in the little café on the corner of the Boulevard P'tit Baghdad.

I followed Fatima into the house, making sure to leave my shoes at the door. It was pleasantly cool inside and smelt of frangipani; the shutters closed

92

since midday to guard against the heat of the sun. A door led into the kitchen, from which I caught the mingled scents of anise and almond and rosewater and chickpeas cooked in turmeric, and chopped mint, and toasted cardamom, and those wonderful *halwa chebakia*, sweet little sesame pastries deep-fried in oil, just small enough to pop into the mouth, flower-shaped and brittle and perfect with a glass of mint tea . . .

'No, really, I'll take them home,' I said, when she pressed me once more to accept tea and sweet-fried pastries. 'But you mustn't give me too many. You must be preparing for *iftar*.'

'Oh, we have plenty,' said Fatima. 'In this house, we like to cook. And everyone helps in the kitchen—' She opened the kitchen door on a semicircle of curious faces. I wondered whether one of these might be the Woman in Black, but dismissed the thought almost instantly. This, I knew, was a family.

There was Maya, on a little stool, preparing okra; and two young women in their late twenties that I guessed to be Fatima's daughters. One was in black, with the *hijab* neatly covering her hair and neck. The other wore an embroidered *hijab* over jeans and a silk *kameez*.

On a chair behind the door sat a tiny, very old lady, peering at me, bird-eyed, from a nest of wrinkles. Ninety or older, her fine white hair braided into a long, thin plait that was wrapped round her head half a dozen times, a yellow scarf falling loosely around her neck. Her face was like a shrivelled peach; her hands as crabbed as chicken claws. And as I stepped into the kitchen, hers was the voice that broke the silence, crowing shrilly in

93

Arabic.

'This is my mother-in-law,' said Fatima, smiling, with the same indulgent expression that she'd used when speaking of Maya. 'Come on, Omi, say hello to our guest.'

Omi al-Djerba gave me a look that reminded me oddly of Armande.

'Look, she brought peaches,' Fatima said.

The crow became a cackle. 'Let me see,' said Omi. Fatima held out the basket. 'Mmf,' said Omi, and shot me a smile as empty of teeth as a turtle's. 'That's good. You can come again. All these silly little things—these *briouats* and almonds and dates—how can I chew my way through these? My daughter-in-law is trying to starve me to death. *Inshallah*, she will not succeed and I shall outlive all of you!'

Maya laughed and clapped her hands. Omi pretended to snarl at her. Fatima smiled, with the air of one who has heard all this many times before. 'You see what I have to live with,' she said, indicating the others. 'These are my daughters, Zahra and Yasmina. Yasmina married Ismail Mahjoubi. Maya is their little girl.'

I smiled at the circle of women. Zahra—the one in the black *hijab*—gave me a shy smile in return. Her sister, Yasmina, shook my hand. They looked very much alike, I thought—although they were dressed very differently. I wondered for a moment whether Zahra was the Woman in Black, but the woman I had seen in the square—and later, at the door of the house—was taller, I thought, perhaps older, and more physically graceful beneath her robes.

I remembered enough of my Arabic to say:

94

'Jazak Allah.'

The women looked surprised, then pleased. Zahra murmured a polite reply. Maya gave a crow of laughter and clapped her hands again.

'Maya,' said Yasmina, and frowned.

'She's a sweet little girl,' I said.

Omi cackled. 'Wait till you meet my Du'a,' she said. 'Bright as a pin. What a memory! She can recite from the Qur'an better than old Mahjoubi. I tell you, if that girl had been a boy, she'd be running the village by now—'

Fatima gave me a comic look. 'Omi always wanted boys. This is why she encourages Maya to run wild. And to make fun of her grandfather.'

Omi winked at Maya. Maya grinned and winked back.

Yasmina smiled, but Zahra did not. She seemed less at ease than the others, guarded and uncomfortable. 'We should offer our guest some tea,' she said.

I shook my head. 'No, really, I won't. But thank you for the pastries. I have to get back anyway. I don't want my daughters to worry.'

I picked up my basket again, now filled with a selection of Moroccan sweetmeats.

'I've made these myself once or twice,' I said. 'But now I just make chocolates. Did you know I used to rent the shop, the one by the church, where there was the fire?'

'Did you?' Fatima shook her head.

'Well, that was a long time ago,' I said. 'Who lives there now?'

There was a barely perceptible pause, and the smile on Fatima's round face lost a little of its warmth. Yasmina looked down and began to

95

fuss with the ribbon in Maya's hair. Zahra looked suddenly anxious. Omi gave an audible sniff.

'That's Inès Bencharki,' she said at last.

Inès. *So that was her name*, I thought. 'Karim Bencharki's sister,' I said.

'Who told you that?' said Omi.

'Just someone in the village.'

Zahra shot Omi a sidelong glance. 'Omi, please—'

She made a face. '*Yar*. Perhaps another time. I hope you'll visit us again. Bring us some of those chocolates of yours. Bring your children.'

'Of course I will.' I turned to the door. Fatima accompanied me out.

'Thank you for the peaches.'

I smiled. 'Come and see us any time.'

The sun had set. Night would come quickly now. Soon, all over Les Marauds, people would sit down to break the day's fast. Stepping outside, I could already see people beginning to leave the mosque. A few shot me curious glances as I crossed the boulevard—it isn't usual to see a woman here, alone, especially one dressed as I was, in jeans and a shirt, my hair unbound. Most ignored me, with the deliberate averting of the eyes that in Tangier counts as respect, but which in Lansquenet might easily pass as an insult.

Most of the passers-by were men—at Ramadan, women will often stay behind to prepare *iftar*. Some were in white robes, a few in the vivid *djellabas*, the hooded robes that had been so common when my mother and I were in Tangier. Most wore *taqiyah* prayer caps, but some of the older men wore the *fez*, or the *keffieh* scarf, or even the black Basque beret. I counted a few women, too—most of them

96

in black *niqab*. I wondered if I would recognize Inès Bencharki among them. And then, with a jolt, I saw her: Inès Bencharki, the Woman in Black, walking along the boulevard with the measured grace of a dancer.

Other women walk together, talking and laughing among themselves. Inès Bencharki walks apart, bracketed in silence; shoulders straight; head held high; aloof in a capsule of twilit space.

She passed by close enough to touch. I caught a glimpse of colours from under her black *abaya*, and was suddenly, sharply reminded of that day on the Pont des Arts, of the woman I'd seen watching me; the kohl-darkened eyes above the *niqab*. Inès Bencharki's eyes are a different kind of beautiful; long as a lazy summer's day and innocent of make-up. She keeps her eyes lowered as she walks, and almost instinctively the others hold back to give her room. No one speaks to her in this crowd. No one even looks at her.

I wonder what it is about her that makes people so uncomfortable. Surely not the *niqab* she wears; there must be other women in Les Marauds who wear the veil without projecting that coldness, that air of isolation. Who is Inès Bencharki? Why does no one speak of her? And why do they maintain the pretence that she is Bencharki's sister, when Omi and the al-Djerbas clearly believe that she is not?

CHAPTER SIX

Wednesday, 18th August

It took me over an hour, Père, to scrub the black paint from my front door. Even then, the inscription remains, a negative of its former self, scoured into the paintwork. I'll simply have to repaint it, that's all. As if people didn't gossip enough.

I didn't sleep well last night. The air was too still, too oppressive. I awoke at dawn and opened the shutters to hear the distant call to prayer floating across from Les Marauds. *Allahu Akhbar.* God is great. I longed to ring the church bells, if only to drown out that echo and to wipe the grin from Mahjoubi's face. He knows that what he is doing is totally forbidden. He also knows that no local mayor will intervene on our behalf: the call is coming from *inside* the mosque, without amplification. Thus the letter of the law is technically satisfied.

Allahu Akhbar, Allahu Akhbar.

My hearing must be exceptional. Most other people don't even seem to notice the call to prayer—Narcisse, who is going deaf, claims it's my imagination. It is not; and on a day like this, so still that I can hear every ripple on the Tannes, every cry of every bird, the call of the *muezzin* cuts through the early morning like rain.

Rain. Now there's a thought. It has not rained at all this month. We all could use a little rain—to make the gardens flower, to wash away the dust from the streets, to cool down these infernal nights. But not today. The sky is clear.

I drank a cup of coffee and went up to Poitou's bakery. I bought a bag of croissants and some bread, and took them over to Armande's house, leaving the bag by the front door where Vianne Rocher would find it.

The streets of Les Marauds were silent. I guessed folk were having breakfast in the last half-hour before sunrise. I saw no one but a girl, all but her face concealed behind a dark-blue *hijab*, who darted across the main street just as I headed for the bridge. She glanced at me fearfully as I approached, then doubled back and disappeared down a side street opposite the gymnasium.

Saïd's gym. I hate that place. A mean, half-derelict building at the end of a mean little alleyway. It's always crowded with young men— never a white face among them—and you can smell the testosterone as you walk by the alley mouth. You can smell the *kif*, too—many of these young Moroccan men smoke it, and the police are reluctant to take action. In the words of Père Henri Lemaître, we have to be aware of cultural sensitivities. Presumably this also includes the girls who are kept from attending school and the occasional but persistent rumours of domestic violence within some of the families, which are sometimes reported, but never followed up. Apparently old Mahjoubi is in charge of such sensitive issues, which makes it unnecessary for the rest of us to take action, or even to notice these things.

The door of the gym was wedged open—on these

warm days it gets hot in there—and although I did not turn my head, I sensed the blast of hostility like invisible shrapnel. Then it was behind me again.

There. It's done.

I hate the fact that I am afraid of walking past that alleyway. I give myself the penance of walking past it every day, in the hope of beating my cowardice. In the same way, as a boy, I used to dare myself to go near the wasps' nest under the wall at the back of the churchyard. The wasps were fat and loathsome, *mon père,* and terrified me in a way that transcended the simple fear of being stung. I feel the same about Saïd's gym—that prickle of adrenaline, the sweat that stings at my armpits and gathers at the nape of my neck; the barely perceptible quickening of my step as I pass the place; the way my heart, too, quickens in fear, then slows in relief when the penance is done.

Bless me, Father, for I have sinned.

Ridiculous. I've done nothing wrong.

I arrived at the bridge into Lansquenet. From the parapet I could see old Mahjoubi on his terrace, sitting in the wicker rocking-chair that seems almost a part of him. He was reading—no doubt the Qur'an—but he looked up when he saw me and gave me an impudent little wave.

I returned the greeting with as much composure as I could. I will not allow myself to be drawn into undignified competition with this man. He grinned—even at that distance I could see his teeth—and I caught the brief sound of laughter from the half-open door of the house. The face of a small girl appeared at the door, topped with a yellow ribbon. His granddaughter, I believe, come to visit from Marseille. As I passed, the laughter redoubled.

'Hide the matches! Here comes Monsieur le Curé.'

Then a sharp command—*Maya!*—and the little face withdrew. In its place I saw Saïd Mahjoubi, glaring beneath his prayer cap. God forgive me, I almost prefer old Mahjoubi's mockery. Saïd continued to glare at me, openly hostile; menacing. The man thinks I am guilty, *père*. Nothing I say will change his mind.

Old Mahjoubi said something to his son in Arabic. Saïd replied in the same tongue, still without taking his eyes from mine.

I greeted him with a polite nod, to prove to him (and to his father) that I will not be intimidated. Then I quickly crossed the bridge back into friendlier territory.

See what I have to deal with, *père*? I used to know this community. People came to me with their problems, whether they went to church or not. Now Mohammed Mahjoubi is in charge—encouraged by Père Henri Lemaître, who, like Caro Clairmont, believes that phasing out the soutane, organizing multi-faith focus groups, holding coffee mornings, installing projection screens in the church and turning a blind eye to everything—to the *kif*-smokers; to the mosque, with its unsanctioned call to prayer and its illicit minaret—will bring the spirit of unity once more to Lansquenet-sous-Tannes.

He is wrong. There is only division now. Division in our own ranks; division between us and them. Mahjoubi's mosque, with its minaret, is not what really concerns me—in spite of what some people think, I still have a sense of humour. But the

101

hostility I feel every time I pass Saïd's gymnasium—
that is another matter. We must be tolerant of
other beliefs, says Père Henri Lemaître. But what
if the followers of those beliefs do not—*will* not—
tolerate *us*?

Back on my side of the river, I made my way back
towards Saint-Jérôme's. I'd arranged to meet Luc
there at nine; but somehow at seven thirty I found
myself standing once again outside the *chocolaterie*.

I went inside. It still smelt of smoke, but the
room was clear of debris. Yesterday, Luc and I
had barely glanced at the upstairs part, but the
fire's point of origin was easy enough to identify:
a letter-box, through which a wad of petrol-soaked
rags had been thrust, setting fire to the door, some
coats, a rug that was hanging on the wall and a
stack of wooden school-chairs.

It's really quite insulting, *père*. For them to
think that *I* did this—why, a child could have done
a better job. The fire was burning fiercely by the
time the Bencharki woman awoke, but there is a
fire escape at the back, and she and the girl got out
unhurt, while neighbours with hoses and buckets
worked together to put out the blaze.

You see, *père*. That's a community. You notice
that no one from *her* side was there. Les Marauds
might as well have been a hundred miles away that
night. The nearest fire station is thirty minutes'
drive away; in that time, the whole shop would
probably have gone up in flames.

Suddenly, I heard footsteps from the floor above.
There was someone in the house. Immediately I
thought of Luc; but what would he be doing there,
over an hour before our rendezvous? The sound
came again; a shuffling that I found distinctly

furtive.

'Who's there?' I said.

The shuffling stopped. For a moment there was silence. Then came a frantic patter across the bare floorboards and the sound of feet on the fire escape. *Children*, I thought immediately: children up to no good. I ran outside, hoping to intercept the culprits as they fled, but by the time I had opened the door, and fought my way through the mess of charred wood that was piled up in the garden, the trespassers had already gone. All I saw was a *Maghrébine* moving swiftly away down the lane; though whether this was a coincidence, or one of the intruders, I could only speculate.

I went upstairs to the bedrooms. There were two of them; one very small, accessible only by a ladder through a trapdoor. There was a little round window there; I remembered Roux putting it in. I stood on the ladder and peered inside. The damage looked relatively slight. A little grimy with smoke, perhaps, but otherwise almost habitable. A child's room, with a little bed and posters of Bollywood stars on the walls. There were books, too—mostly in French. As far as I could see, the intruders hadn't touched anything.

There came a sound from behind me. A woman said: 'What are you doing here?'

I turned. It was Inès Bencharki.

CHAPTER SEVEN

Wednesday, 18th August

I don't think I'd ever heard her voice. It was clear and barely accented, with, if anything, a touch of the North. She was in black, as always, covered to the fingertips. Her eyes, which for once were fixed on me, are a surprising shade of green, with lashes of unusual length.

'Madame Bencharki, good morning,' I said.

The woman repeated her question. 'What are you doing in my house?'

I found myself at a loss to reply. I muttered something about responsibilities to the parish and about cleaning up the village square, which made me sound as culpable as she no doubt believes me to be.

'What I mean is,' I went on, 'I thought that perhaps the community could help you fix up the place again. Waiting for the insurance people could take months, you must know that. As for the landlord, he lives in Agen, and it could be weeks before he even gets round to looking at the damage. Whereas if everyone just chips in—'

'Chips in,' the woman said.

I tried a smile. It was a mistake. Behind her veil, she might have been a pillar of salt; a block of stone.

She shook her head. 'I don't need help.'

'But you don't understand,' I said. 'No one would

ask you to pay for the work. It's just a gesture of goodwill.'

The woman simply repeated the phrase in the same flat, relentless voice.

I found myself wanting to plead with her, and instead replied in a brittle tone: 'Well, of course, it's your choice.'

The green eyes stayed expressionless. I tried the tentative smile again, but succeeded only in looking awkward and guilty.

'I'm really very sorry about what's happened,' I said. 'I'm hoping you and your daughter will be able to move back as soon as possible. How *is* the little girl, anyway?'

Once more, the woman said nothing. My armpits began to prickle with sweat.

As a boy at the seminary, I was once suspected of bringing cigarettes into school and was summoned to answer some questions by Père Louis Durand, who was in charge of discipline. I hadn't brought the cigarettes—although I knew the culprit—but my manner was so furtive that no one believed in my innocence. I was punished, both for the cigarettes and for trying to lay the blame on one of my comrades, and although I knew I was innocent, I felt the very same sense of shame that I did while addressing the woman in black; that sensation of utter helplessness.

'I'm sorry,' I repeated. 'If I can do anything to help—'

'You can leave me alone,' she said. 'My daughter and I—'

Then she stopped mid-sentence. Under the black robe her whole body seemed to stiffen and tense.

'Are you all right?'

105

She did not reply. And then I turned my head and saw Karim Bencharki standing there—who knows how long he'd been watching us.

He spoke a phrase in Arabic.

She answered in a sharp voice.

He spoke again, his voice a caress. I felt a pang of gratitude. I'd always seen Karim as an educated, progressive man, who understood France and French culture. Perhaps he could explain to Inès that all I was doing was trying to help.

At first sight, you wouldn't think Karim Bencharki was a *Maghrébin* at all. With his light skin and golden eyes he might be an Italian, and he dresses like a Westerner, in jeans and shirts and trainers. In fact, when he first came to Lansquenet, I thought the arrival of such an apparently Westernized and cosmopolitan member of the community might bring about a new integration between Les Marauds and ourselves; that his friendship with Saïd Mahjoubi might help me find a way to bridge the gap between old Mahjoubi's traditional ways and those of the twenty-first century.

I turned to him now in appeal. I said: 'As I was just explaining, Luc Clairmont and I have been trying to assess the damage caused by the fire. It's mostly superficial—really just smoke and water. It wouldn't take more than a week or so to make it habitable again. As you see, we have already cleared out most of the burnt wood and debris. A few coats of paint, some new wood and glass, and your sister could be ready to move back in—'

'She isn't going to move back in,' said Karim. 'From now on, she will be staying with me.'

'But what about the school?' I said. 'Won't you

106

be continuing?'

The woman spoke to her brother in Arabic. I do not know the language, but the unfamiliar syllables sounded harsh and angry—though whether this was my ignorance or whether it was truly so was not within my power to guess. Once again, I felt vaguely ashamed, and tried to compensate with a smile.

'I can't help feeling responsible for what has happened,' I told them. 'I'd really like to help, if I can.'

'She doesn't need your help,' said Karim. 'Now get out, or I'll call the police.'

'What?'

'You heard. I'll call the police. You think that because you're a priest you can get away with what you've done? Everyone knows you lit the fire. Even your people are saying so. And if I were you, I'd keep to the other side of the river from now on. The way things are, you might get hurt.'

For a moment, I stared at him. 'Are you trying to threaten me?'

And now, at last, came something to replace that feeling of guilt and shame. Anger flooded me, pure and cold; simple as spring water. I drew myself up to my full height—I am taller than either of them— and let out the frustration that has gathered in me over the past six or seven years.

Six years of trying to deal with these folk; of trying to make them understand; of lectures from the Bishop on community relations; of finding graffiti on my door; of having to fight my own flock; of old Mahjoubi and his mosque; of veiled women and sullen men; of ridicule and unspoken contempt.

I have tried so hard, *père*. I've tried so hard to be tolerant. But some things are intolerable. The

107

mosque I can just about tolerate, but the minaret? The *kif*-smokers? The gym, with its hostile atmosphere? The girls in *niqab*? The Muslim school, as if our own village school might teach their daughters something other than submission and fear?

Intolerable. *Intolerable!*

I do not remember all I said; or even how much I said aloud. But I was enraged, *père*. Enraged by their ingratitude as well as their hostility. But most of all by my loss of control; by the fact that, despite my intentions, if anyone in Les Marauds were still in doubt as to who had tried to burn down the school, I had just convinced them all that I was the one responsible.

CHAPTER EIGHT

☾

Wednesday, 18th August

Today, while Anouk was out with Jeannot, Rosette and I set out once again in search of Joséphine. We passed the green-shuttered house on the way, but, like the rest of Les Marauds, it looked closed and fast asleep. The mosque, too, was silent. Dawn prayers are over. Now is the time for rest and recovery; play for the children. Work starts late.

We walked to the end of the boulevard and made our way to the riverbank. There's a narrow walkway here along the Tannes, like a suspended boardwalk, where the half-timbered houses that line the street stand like drunken clowns on their stilts high above the river. Each house has its terrace: a wooden deck with a balustrade and a sharp drop to the water. Some of them are still safe; others have been closed off. Some are gardens, with pots of flowers and hanging baskets, with ropes of jasmine straggling down.

On a chair on one of these terraces sat an old man with a white beard, reading a book (I assumed it was the Qur'an), wearing a white *djellaba* and, somewhat incongruously, a black Basque beret.

He looked up as I passed, and raised a hand in greeting. I waved back and smiled. Rosette hooted amiably.

'Hello, I'm Vianne,' I told him. 'I'm staying in that house up there.'

The old man put down his book, which, to my surprise as I approached, I now saw was not the Qur'an at all, but the first volume of *Les Misérables*.

'So I heard,' the old man said. He had a slightly guttural voice, his accent an exotic blend of Midi and Medina. His eyes were dark, faintly bluish with age, and pixellated with wrinkles. 'I am Mohammed Mahjoubi,' he said. 'You already met my granddaughter.'

'Maya?' I said.

He nodded. '*Yar*. My youngest son Ismail's child. She says you brought peaches for Ramadan.'

I laughed. 'It wasn't quite like that. But I always like to say hello.'

The dark eyes crinkled appreciatively. 'Given your friends, that is surprising.'

'Do you mean Curé Reynaud?'

Old Mahjoubi showed his teeth.

'He's not a bad man, really. He's just a little—'

109

'Difficult? Intransigent? Stiff? Or is he just the arrogant weed that makes his bed on the dunghill and thinks he's the king in the castle?'

I smiled. 'He improves with acquaintance. When I first came to Lansquenet . . .' I told him a version of the tale, omitting what I had promised to keep secret. Old Mahjoubi listened, occasionally nodding and smiling encouragement, while Rosette added her own running commentary in hoots and signs and whistles.

'So—you came at the start of your Ramadan, to open a house of temptation? I see how that could be a problem,' he said. 'Your *curé* begins to have my sympathy.'

I feigned indignation. 'You're taking his side?'

Old Mahjoubi's smile broadened. 'You are a dangerous woman, *madame*. I see that much already.'

I smiled again. 'As to that,' I said, 'you went further, didn't you? I only opened a chocolate shop. You came and built a minaret.'

Now Mahjoubi laughed aloud. 'So, you heard that story. Yes, it took time, but we did it, *Alhumdullila*. And without breaking a single one of those complicated building regulations, either.' He eyed me. 'It stings him, does it not? To hear the call of the *muezzin* so close to his own place of worship? And yet, he rings those bells of his.'

'I can enjoy both,' I said.

He gave me an appreciative look. 'Not everyone here is so tolerant. Even my eldest son, Saïd, sometimes falls prey to that kind of thinking. I tell him: Allah judges. All we can do is watch and learn. And try to enjoy the sound of the bells if we cannot stop them ringing.'

110

I smiled. 'Next time, I'll bring you chocolates. I already promised some to Omi al-Djerba.'

'Don't encourage her,' he said, his eyes still bright with amusement. 'Already half the time she forgets that she's meant to be fasting for Ramadan. A bit of fruit doesn't count, she says. A little drink of tea doesn't count. Half a biscuit doesn't count. She's riding the devil's donkey.'

'I knew someone like that, once,' I told him, thinking of Armande.

'Well, people are the same everywhere. Is that your little girl?' He glanced at where Rosette was playing, now throwing pebbles into the Tannes.

I nodded. 'That's Rosette, my youngest.'

'Bring her to play with my Maya. She doesn't have any friends of her age. Just don't invite that priest of yours. And don't go feeding her chocolate.'

Walking back into Lansquenet, I wondered how such an affable old man could have fallen foul of Francis Reynaud. Is it the difference in culture? A simple dispute over territory? Or is there something else here, something closer to the bone?

We reached the end of the boardwalk, where it rejoins the boulevard. There I found a red door at the end of a little cul-de-sac, with a sign above it, black letters on white, that read: *CHEZ SAÏD. GYM.*

That must be Saïd Mahjoubi, I thought—old Mahjoubi's eldest son. Reynaud had told me about the place he had opened three or four years ago. An empty storage facility, converted as cheaply as possible into a sports hall and gymnasium. Through the door, which was slightly ajar, I could see exercise bicycles, running machines, racks of free

111

weights. A smell of chlorine and disinfectant and *kif* filtered through into the air.

The door opened, and three men in their early twenties came out, wearing sleeveless T-shirts and carrying sports bags. They did not greet me, but gave me the same vaguely aggressive look that I'd had from the man in the little café. I've seen it before in Paris, when we lived in Rue de l'Abbesse, and before that, in Tangier; it's not so much aggressive as faintly defiant, a challenge to the person they think I am. A woman alone, bare-headed; dressed in jeans and a sleeveless shirt. I am different; another tribe. Women are not welcome here.

And yet, old Mahjoubi welcomed me—even flirted with me, in his way. Perhaps because he is too old to see me as a woman at all. Perhaps because he is too secure in himself to see me as a threat.

The air is very close and still. The Autan must be almost due. Whether it is the Black or the White Autan, a breath of wind will bring relief. Today is the eighth day of Ramadan. Six more days till the full moon. I think of the Moon on my Tarot card, that woman with her distaff and yarn, and I wonder when she will show herself. Maybe when the wind blows.

Meanwhile, we have business elsewhere. I leave Les Marauds sleeping. From this distance it looks like a crocodile sprawled across the marshes, head almost buried in the reeds, twitching slightly in its sleep. Its spine is the Boulevard des Marauds; broad and grey and cobbled. Its jaws are the bridge, upturned at the corners. Its legs are the short, squat alleys that jut out of the boulevard at right

112

angles. And its eye is the mosque; half closed for now as the sun shines on the crescent moon that perches on the minaret. Is it dangerous? Reynaud thinks so. But I am not like Francis Reynaud, who sees every stranger in Lansquenet as a potential enemy. The men outside the gym are young; unsure of themselves and their territory. But the man to whom Les Marauds turns—Mohammed Mahjoubi—is different. I am sure that whatever problems Reynaud may have encountered in dealing with this community can be solved through humour and dialogue. As Mahjoubi told me himself, *people are the same everywhere*. Scratch off the paint, and what you find is the same, however far you go. I learnt that from my mother; from all the places we called home. And now, with the air like syrup and the Tannes so slow that it might be asleep, Rosette and I begin the climb up the narrow street into Lansquenet, all white and gleaming in the sun, with the church bells ringing morning Mass fit to wake a sleeping crocodile.

CHAPTER NINE

☾

Wednesday, 18th August

Arriving at the Café des marauds, I found Marie-Ange behind the bar again, chewing gum, watching TV and looking more sullen than ever. Today, purple eye-shadow, purple lipstick, and a purple streak in her hair. I hope the intended

113

recipient of all this glamour appreciates the effort.

I ordered a *café-crème*. 'Is Joséphine here this morning?'

The girl gave me a flat look. 'Sure she is. Who shall I say?'

'Tell her it's Vianne Rocher.'

I was expecting to find her changed. These things are so often inevitable. Grey hairs, laughter lines; kisses from the lips of time. But occasionally, someone changes so much that they can barely be recognized; and when Joséphine Muscat stepped through the bead curtain into the bar, it took me a moment to recognize my old friend in the woman who faced me.

It was not that she had aged. In fact, I thought she looked younger. She'd been a somewhat graceless woman when I first met her eight years ago; now she was pretty and self-assured, and her hair, which had been a dull mid-brown, had been changed to a smart blonde crop. She was wearing a white linen dress and a colourful necklace of little glass beads; she saw me at the *terrasse* and her face lit in a smile that I would have recognized however many years had gone by.

'Oh, Vianne! I didn't dare believe it!'

She hugged me tightly and sat down in the wicker chair opposite.

'I wanted to see you yesterday, but I had to work. You look wonderful—'

'So do you, Joséphine.'

'And Anouk? Is she here?'

'She's with Jeannot Drou. They always were inseparable.'

She laughed. 'I remember. So long ago. Anouk must be nearly grown up by now—' She broke off, suddenly subdued. 'You heard about the fire, of course. I'm sorry, Vianne.'

I shrugged. 'It's not my place any more. I'm only glad no one was hurt.'

She shook her head. 'I know. But the shop—it's always been yours in my mind. Even after you were gone. I'd always hoped you might come back, or at least that the people who rented it would be half as nice as you.'

'I take it they weren't?'

She shook her head. 'That horrible woman. That poor little girl.'

I'd heard those words from Joline Drou, but, coming from Joséphine, they surprised me.

'Why do you say that?'

She made a face. 'You'd understand if you met her,' she said. 'That is, if she deigned to talk to you. But she hardly talks to anyone here, and when she does, she's so *rude*—' She saw my doubtful look. 'You'll see. She's not like the other *Maghrébines*. Most of them are really nice—or were, before she came along. But then she arrived, and started everyone wearing the veil—'

'Not everyone,' I said. 'I've seen plenty of women without it.' I told her about my visit to the al-Djerba house, and my chat with Mohammed Mahjoubi.

'Oh, he's a sweetheart,' she said. 'I wish I could say the same for his son.' Mahjoubi has two sons, she says. Saïd, the eldest, who runs the gym, and Ismail, who married Yasmina al-Djerba.

'Ismail's OK,' said Joséphine. 'And Yasmina's lovely. She even comes here with Maya for lunch. But as for Saïd—' She pulled a face. 'Religion. He got it in a big way. Married his daughter at eighteen to a man he met on a pilgrimage. Since then I haven't had a chance to talk to either of Saïd's daughters. They used to come here all the time. They liked to play football in the square. Now they creep around like mice, draped from head to foot in black. I heard he fell out with his father about it. Old Mahjoubi doesn't approve of the veil. And Saïd doesn't approve of the way old Mahjoubi does things.'

'His choice of reading matter, perhaps?' I told her about old Mahjoubi's secret passion for Victor Hugo.

She smiled. 'For a priest, or whatever he is, he seems a bit eccentric. Apparently he tried to ban women from wearing the veil at mosque. Didn't approve of the girls' school, either. I don't think he likes that woman any more than the rest of us do.'

'You mean Inès Bencharki. Sonia Mahjoubi's sister-in-law.'

She nodded. 'That's right. Before she arrived, none of this would have happened.'

'None of what?'

She shrugged. 'The fire. That girls' school. Women wearing face-veils—in Paris, perhaps, but in Lansquenet? She was the one who started that. Everybody says so.'

Well, that's true, at least. I've heard this before from Reynaud, Guillaume, Poitou and Joline as well as from Omi al-Djerba. What is it about Inès that unites both Les Marauds and Lansquenet in dislike and suspicion?

Rosette, meanwhile, had been playing outside by the fountain in the square. It's not really a fountain—just a trickle of water that comes from an ornamental tap and splashes into a stone trough—but the sound of water is pleasant on a hot, still day like this, and from the *terrasse* of the Café des Marauds I could see Rosette darting in and out of the square of shade that was cast by Saint-Jérôme's tower, carrying water in her hands to splash across the cobblestones.

Now I saw the familiar shape of a boy in a *Lion King* T-shirt, followed by that of a shaggy dog, come round the side of Saint-Jérôme's and stop by the fountain.

Rosette gave a crow of welcome. *'Pilou!'*

By my side, Joséphine stiffened.

'That's my little Rosette,' I said. 'You'll meet her in a minute.' I smiled. 'We already met Pilou.'

For a moment I thought she looked furtive. Then her expression softened. 'He's terrific, isn't he?'

I nodded. 'Rosette thinks so, too.'

'That woman doesn't approve of him,' she said, with a glance towards the square. 'He tried to talk to her daughter once. She gave him such a mouthful! He was only being friendly.'

'Perhaps it was the dog,' I said.

'Why? He never does any harm. I'm sick of trying to be *sensitive*. I'm sick of that woman looking down her nose at me because my son happens to have a dog, because I don't wear a headscarf, because my café serves alcohol—' She broke off. 'I'm sorry, Vianne. Forget I spoke. It's just that—seeing you again—' Her eyes filled with tears. 'It's been too long. I've missed you so much.'

'I've missed you too. But look at you now—'

'Yes, look at me.' She wiped her eyes impatiently. 'Old enough to know better than to get all sentimental about the past. Another *café-crème*? On the house. Or would you rather have chocolate?'

117

I shook my head. 'The café looks great.'

'Yes, doesn't it?' She looked around. 'Amazing what a lick of paint and a bit of imagination can do. I remember what it used to be like—'

So did I: the yellowed walls, the greasy floor, the smell of old smoke that seemed to be part of the grain of the place. Now the walls are whitewashed and clean; the *terrasse* and the window-ledges are lined with red geraniums. A large and colourful abstract painting dominates the far wall—

She saw me looking. 'Pilou did that. What do you think?'

I thought it looked good, and said so. I also wondered why she had not said a word about Pilou's father. And then I thought of my little Rosette, who draws and paints so beautifully—

'You didn't remarry, did you?' I said.

For a moment she was silent. Then she gave me a luminous smile and said, 'No, Vianne. I never did. I thought one day perhaps I might, but—'

'What about Pilou's father?'

She shrugged. 'You told me once that Anouk was yours, and no one else's. Well, my son and I are like that. We're brought up to believe that there's someone there, a soulmate waiting for all of us. Pilou *is* my soulmate. Why would I need anyone else?'

She hadn't quite answered the question, I thought. Still, I told myself, there's time. Just because I once thought that Roux might fall for Joséphine, just because Pilou had said that his father was a pirate, just because the cards are bad, that doesn't automatically mean that my suspicions are justified. Even the fact that Joséphine hasn't mentioned Roux once, not even to ask me how he

118

is—

'Why don't you come over for dinner on Sunday? Both of you. I'll cook. Pancakes, cider and sausages, just like the river-rats used to make.'

Joséphine smiled. 'I'd like that. And what about Roux? Is he here too?'

'He stayed behind, with the boat,' I said.

Was that disappointment in the turn of her profile? Was that a furtive gleam of rose, hidden among her colours? *I should not spy on my friend*, I thought. But the urge was too great to combat. Joséphine has a secret desperate to reveal itself. The question is, do I *want* to know the thing that she is hiding? Or should I, for my own peace of mind, allow the past to stay buried?

CHAPTER TEN

Wednesday, 18th August

I spent the day in my garden, trying to forget that morning's scene in the old *chocolaterie*. I had already told Luc Clairmont not to come round as we had arranged; that the Bencharki woman was dealing with the repairs herself; but I could tell he had already guessed some of what had happened.

Damn the woman. Damn the boy. By now the news will be all over the village. It won't take long for Père Henri Lemaître to hear of it, and pass on the story to the Bishop. How long after that before I am officially replaced—moved to another parish, or worse, forced to leave the Church for good?

And so I spent the rest of the day digging in the hot sun, stopping every couple of hours for a break and a cold beer, but though my body was tired out by the time I'd finished work, my mind was no less agitated than it had been when I first began.

I do not sleep well nowadays. To tell you the truth, I never did. I find it increasingly difficult, and I often wake at four or five in the morning, soaked in sweat and feeling more exhausted than ever. Physical exercise sometimes helps, but this time, though I ached with fatigue, my mind remained alert, spinning with possibilities.

At one o'clock in the morning I stopped trying to fall asleep and decided to go for a walk instead. I may have had a few more beers than I had intended. In any case, my head ached. The night was cool and inviting.

I dressed in haste—a T-shirt, jeans. (Yes, I *do* possess a pair, for gardening, fishing and manual work.) No one would see me. The café was closed, and besides, Lansquenet folk rise early and go to bed accordingly.

It was dark out on the street. Streetlights are rare in Lansquenet. In Les Marauds there are none at all, and only a few house lights were visible across the bridge. There were more than I'd expected. Perhaps these people go to bed late.

I wandered down towards the bridge. It's cooler by the river. There is a stone parapet there that, even long after sunset, still retains the heat of the sun. Below it the river makes a series of small articulate sounds, half percussive, like the keys of some complex musical instrument.

I paused there, wondering whether I should

120

cross the bridge. I am not welcome in Les Marauds. Karim Bencharki has made that plain. And yet, Les Marauds draws me. Perhaps because of the river.

Suddenly, I heard a sound from the far bank of the Tannes. A heavy splash, like a log falling in. My head was still not entirely clear; the other side of the bridge was dark. It took me a moment to understand that there was someone in the water.

I called out. 'Is someone there?'

No reply. It occurred to me that this might be someone taking a late-night swim; perhaps one of the *Maghrébins*, who would not appreciate my interference. On the other hand, maybe a child had been playing too close to the water—

I ran to the other end of the bridge, where the Tannes runs deepest. I wondered if, in my fatigue, I might have somehow dreamt it. But then, I saw a blurry face appear for a moment and vanish again—

I kicked off my shoes and dived from the bridge. I am a competent swimmer. Even so, the cold water made me gasp and struggle for breath as I surfaced. The current, that had seemed so gentle from the parapet of the bridge, now demonstrated surprising strength, which, along with its collection of river debris—sticks and leaves and plastic bottles, cigarette butts, carrier bags and assorted junk—all conspired to drag me down.

I held my breath and followed the current. There was no sign of the figure I'd seen. I dived, but it was too dark. I came up gasping; dived again. I searched beneath the surface, combing the water with my hands, knowing I had only seconds before the victim—whoever he or she was—was swept away and vanished for good. It was almost hopeless,

I knew; and yet I knew I had to try.

Père, I am somewhat ashamed to confess that prayer never even occurred to me. My hand closed on a fistful of hair, then a fistful of fabric, and I pulled her to the surface, allowing the current to take us both a little further downriver, over rocks and jutting pieces of wood that lurked viciously just under the surface, until at last I reached the bank and hauled her on to the coarse sand—

City people often forget that moonlight can be surprisingly bright. Even a crescent moon is enough, in a place where there are no street-lamps, to make out a person's features. This was a girl, I realized, as I pulled back the scarf that hid her face. I knew her at once—after all, I'd seen her often enough in the square when she was a little girl, in jeans and an oversized sports shirt, playing football with the boys. A few years older now, of course; her face very pale in the moonlight; eyes closed, not breathing; her only spark of sentience that of a tiny diamond stud which blinked in one of her nostrils.

It was Alyssa Mahjoubi—Saïd's youngest daughter—lying dead on the riverbank at two o'clock in the morning.

CHAPTER ELEVEN

Thursday, 19th August

As pupils at the seminary, we attended a class on first aid. I still remember the embarrassment of having to practise mouth-to-mouth resuscitation on the instructor's dummy, a buxom lady he called Cunégonde, and the laughter of my classmates when I repeatedly failed to revive her.

But skills, once learnt, have a habit of resurfacing when needed most. I'd never had much success with Cunégonde, but with Alyssa Mahjoubi, desperation made me bold; I cupped my mouth over hers and tried to force the girl to breathe—and between pleading, invective and finally prayer, I managed to pummel and coax her back into the world of the living.

'Thank God. Oh, thank you, God.' By then I felt half dead myself. My head was spinning, my chest hurt, and though the night was mild, I was shivering.

Beside me, Alyssa Mahjoubi was coughing up river water. After a moment she sat up and looked at me with eyes that seemed to have swallowed the sky. I told myself she might be in shock. I tried to make my voice gentle.

'*Mademoiselle*—'

She flinched at that. I should have called her Alyssa. But people are often so sensitive—and God knows how many Islamic rules I had already broken in saving her life—that I thought it might be better to keep to the formalities.

I tried again. 'Are you all right?'

Once more, she flinched.

'Don't be afraid. You can talk to me. It's Francis Reynaud. Remember me?' Maybe she didn't recognize me without my collar and soutane. I tried a smile, with no response. 'You must have fallen in, somehow. Lucky I was here, eh? Can you stand? I'll take you home.'

She shook her head energetically.

'What? Shall I call a doctor?'

Once more, she shook her head.

'Is there a family member you'd like me to call? Your sister, your mother, perhaps?'

Again, that gesture. *No. No.* I was beginning to feel slightly desperate now, and Alyssa, too, was shivering.

I tried for a more jocular tone. 'Well, we can't sit here all night.'

No reaction at all from the girl. She simply sat on the riverbank, breathing hard, hugging her knees. She looked like a mouse rescued from a cat; uninjured; but dying from shock. That's what often happens with mice; they usually die anyway.

There goes my reputation, I thought. To be suspected of setting fire to a shop was bad enough; but if anyone saw me here, wet through, still smelling of beer and in the company of a young Muslim woman—a young, *unmarried* Muslim woman—showing every sign of mental disturbance, who, if she were to misunderstand the impulse that had brought me here, might in her confusion accuse me of assault, or worse . . .

'Please, Alyssa. Listen to me.' My voice was

sharper than I'd intended. 'You're cold. You'll catch your death here. You have to let me take you home.'

Again, she shook her head.

'Why *not*?'

Silence. The girl ignored me.

'All right,' I said. 'I won't take you home. But you can't stay here, either. I'll get your mother.'

No. No.

'Your sister? A friend?'

Once more: *No.*

My patience was deserting me. This was getting ridiculous. If the girl had been one of ours, I would have had no qualms about marching her home. But she was from Les Marauds, where I was *persona non grata* and where any hint of coercion would be taken very badly.

Equally unthinkable was to leave the girl unsupervised, even for the ten minutes or so it would take for me to run for the doctor. *A girl who can jump in the river once can always do it again*, I thought; and if Alyssa Mahjoubi were not entirely of sound mind, she needed someone to watch over her, at least until the crisis had passed. A hot bath; a change of clothes; a bed; perhaps a meal—

My own home was out of the question. I needed a woman to handle this. I thought of Caro Clairmont, who always used to get on so well with the community of Les Marauds, but the thought of trying to explain myself to her—to her, of all people—

Joséphine? She's a kind soul. And I knew she would be discreet. But could I ask a Muslim girl to stay in a place that serves strong drink? Joline Drou, the schoolteacher? But she was a crony of Caro Clairmont. *And* a gossip—by morning, everyone in Lansquenet would know about the scandal.

And then it came to me. Yes, of course! A place where Alyssa would be safe; where no one would even know where she was, and where she would be treated as if she were one of the family—

CHAPTER TWELVE

☽

Thursday, 19th August

It took me a long time to get to sleep. The sound of knocking woke me. An imperious rapping, first at the door, then against the shutters. Anouk and Rosette were sharing the bedroom; I had made my bed on the sofa, and as I struggled out of sleep, I was no longer sure where I was; suspended in a dreamcatcher's web between one life and the other.

The knocking became more persistent. I flung on a robe and opened the door. And there was Reynaud, looking stiff and defensive, with a young girl in a black *hijab* at his side. Both of them smelt of the Tannes, and the girl, who looked no older than eighteen or so, was shivering.

Reynaud started to explain, sounding as awkward as he looked. 'I'm sorry. She won't let me take her home. She won't say why she jumped into the Tannes. I've tried to get her to talk to me, but she doesn't trust me. None of them do. I'm sorry to burden you with this, but I didn't know what else—'

'Please,' I interrupted him. 'All that can wait till tomorrow.' I smiled at the girl, who was watching me with sullen-eyed suspicion. 'I have some towels in the back, and clothes I think will fit you. I'll get some water boiling, and then you can have a bath and change. There's no electricity yet—Luc said it might take a few days to arrange—but there are candles, the stove is hot, we'll get you warm in no time. As for you—' I turned to Reynaud. 'Please don't worry. You did the right thing. Try not to be so hard on yourself. Go home and get some sleep. The rest can wait till morning.'

Reynaud seemed to hesitate. 'But—you don't even know who she is.'

'Does it really matter?' I said.

He gave me one of his chilly looks. Then, surprisingly, he smiled. 'I never thought I'd say this. But, Mademoiselle Rocher, I'm glad you're here.'

And at that, he turned and walked away, stiffly, a little self-consciously. To anyone else he might have seemed a drab and disreputable figure as he set off down the stony path, limping a little (he was barefoot) before disappearing into the night. But I see more; I see the heart, even the heart that is hidden. I see more, and in his wake, the air was a shimmy of rainbows.

The
WHITE
AUTAN

CHAPTER ONE

☾

Thursday, 19th August

It took me until four o'clock to settle our unexpected guest into Armande's attic bedroom; a tiny, almost triangular space, in which a cot can only just fit. But it is clean and comfortable; and there is a little window at the apex of the triangle, which looks out over Les Marauds and catches the scent of the peach tree.

Anouk had woken up at the sound of voices in the hall, but Rosette can sleep through anything. We left her sleeping, while I made the bed and Anouk prepared hot chocolate with cardamom and lavender and valerian to help our guest sleep.

Washed and dressed in an old flannel robe that used to belong to Armande, her long hair carefully combed and dried, the girl looked even younger than I'd thought; sixteen, maybe seventeen, with dark espresso eyes that seemed to take up half her face. She accepted a cup of hot chocolate, but still refused to say anything, and although she was no longer shivering, she sometimes flinched, like a dreaming cat. She seemed curious of Anouk, and I left them together in the hope that the girl might prefer to talk to someone closer to her own age, but she did not; and finally, she went to sleep in front of the fire while Anouk sang the lullaby my mother used to sing to me:

V'là l'bon vent, v'là l'joli vent—

I carried the girl up to her room. She felt extremely light in my arms; lighter even than Rosette, and, like a child, she did not wake when I put her into bed. Anouk was full of questions, none of which I could answer, and finally I persuaded her to go back to bed and try to sleep. Sleep comes easily to Anouk; less easily to me. I made a pot of coffee and took it outside; dawn comes early at this time of year, and the sky was already luminous as I sat on Armande's garden wall and drank my coffee and listened for the sounds of Les Marauds coming to life.

Cockerels; geese; wild ducks on the Tannes; the morning percussion of small birds. The church clock striking five o'clock, very clear in the morning air; and then, as distant but equally clear, the sound of the *muezzin*, calling the faithful to prayer on this, the ninth day of Ramadan.

At nine o'clock, Reynaud arrived. Nine o'clock precisely, as if he had been waiting for a socially acceptable time to call. All in black, and collarless; hair slicked back fastidiously. I thought he looked tired, and wondered whether he had slept at all.

I gave him some coffee. He took it black and drank it standing up, by the wall. The sun was already pleasantly warm, releasing the scent from the roses that filled Armande's little garden; tumbling over the dirt path, capering over the trellis. They have not been pruned for eight years, and the flowers have almost gone wild, but the scent remains; a wonderful blend of Turkish delight and clean sheets in the wind. For a moment I said nothing, to allow Reynaud to enjoy the scent,

131

but he was impatient; anxious; on edge. I doubt whether he often takes time to sit and smell the roses.

'Well? Did she speak?' he said at last.

I shook my head. 'No, not a word.'

And now he told me his story; how he had rescued the girl from the Tannes; how she had refused to go home, or give any explanation for her erratic behaviour.

'I used to know her quite well. Her name is Alyssa Mahjoubi. Old Mahjoubi's granddaughter. She's just seventeen, a girl from a decent, honest family. I've talked to them a thousand times; they were always polite and friendly. There was never any trouble. Until Inès Bencharki arrived.'

That name again. Bencharki. The woman whose shadow lurks at the edge of every picture in this gallery; whose face remains as ill-defined as something glimpsed in a pack of cards.

'I know you don't believe me,' said Reynaud in a calm voice. 'Perhaps I even deserve it. But things have changed since you left us. Dare I say it?—*I* have changed.'

I wonder about that. *Has* he changed? Does anyone ever really change, deep down, where it matters?

I checked his colours. He means what he says. But self-awareness has never been one of Reynaud's qualities. I know him, and I know his kind: people with good intentions—

'I know what you're thinking,' said Reynaud. 'I *have* been guilty of prejudice. But in this case, I promise you—' He ran his hand through his slicked-back hair. 'Look,' he said. 'I won't pretend I was happy to find a girls' school at my door. We

132

already had a school of our own, and the girls would have been welcome there. And I won't pretend that I approve of all those young girls wearing the veil. I think it's wrong to make them ashamed, or afraid to show their faces. Whatever that woman's teaching them, it isn't healthy; it isn't right. But I've tried to be impartial. I've tried to keep my personal feelings out of it. I have a responsibility to the members of this community, and I've done my level best to avoid any kind of friction.'

I remembered what old Mahjoubi had said and smiled at the thought of the bells of Saint-Jérôme on one side of the Tannes competing with the *muezzin*; each one trying its best to drown out the echoes of the other. The friction had clearly been there from the start; but why blame Inès Bencharki? What had changed when she arrived? And how could Reynaud be so sure that she was the one responsible?

I asked the question. Reynaud shrugged. 'You have no reason to trust me,' he said. 'I know it's not the first time that I've blamed a woman and her child for causing trouble in Lansquenet.' I looked at him, and was surprised to see a gleam of amusement in his eyes. 'But I think you'll agree that I know something about my parishioners. I can tell when something has changed. And it started with Inès Bencharki.'

'When?' I said.

'Eighteen months ago. Old Mahjoubi's son, Saïd, met Karim on a pilgrimage. The next thing we knew, he'd moved here, and Saïd was arranging a marriage between Karim and his eldest daughter.'

'Sonia.'

'That's right. Sonia.' He finished his coffee and

put down the cup.

'What happened next?'

'For two weeks Les Marauds was nothing but celebrations. Cooking, talking, laughing, flowers. Dozens of bridal outfits. Caro Clairmont had a wonderful time, organizing multicultural days and who-knows-what and coffee mornings for the women. Joséphine was there, too; she used to be quite good friends with Sonia and Alyssa. She bought a fancy kaftan to wear to the wedding, from one of those little fabric shops on the Boulevard des Marauds. People came from everywhere: Marseille, Paris, even Tangier. And then—'

'The wind changed.'

He looked surprised. 'Yes,' he said. 'I suppose it did.'

That wind. He feels it too. Charged with possibilities; dangerous as a sleeping snake. Zozie called it the *Hurakan*, that sweeps everything ahead of it. For years it may be gentle—you may even believe it is tame—but anything can wake it up. A sigh, a prayer, a whisper—

'His sister arrived for the wedding,' he said. 'She wasn't supposed to stay for long. There wasn't room in the house, for a start. Old Mahjoubi didn't like her. But she came for a week and stayed for a month, and before we knew it she'd moved in for good and everything was different.' He sighed and went on: 'I blame myself. I should have seen it coming. But old Mahjoubi's sons were both so very Westernized. Ismail doesn't go to mosque except on special occasions, and Saïd was never radical. And as for Karim Bencharki, he seemed the most Westernized of all of them. And now look at the family. One girl married at eighteen, the other

134

jumping into the Tannes in the middle of the night. And that woman and her school, teaching the children God knows what in the name of religion—'

'So you think this is about religion?' I said.

Reynaud looked blank. 'What else could it be?'

Of course, he *would* believe that. Religion is his career, after all. He is used to dividing folk into tribes: Catholics, Protestants, Hindus, Jews or Muslims. There are so many tribes, after all; chosen tribes, lost tribes, warring tribes, converted tribes. Also, of course, football supporters; rock fans; political parties; believers in extraterrestrials; extremists; moderates; conspiracy theorists; Boy Scouts; the unemployed; river-gypsies; vegetarians; cancer survivors; poets and punks; each tribe with its multitude of smaller and smaller sub-categories, because, in the end, doesn't *everyone* really want to belong somewhere, to find their perfect space in the world?

I have never belonged to a tribe. It gives me a different perspective. Perhaps if I did, I too would feel ill at ease in Les Marauds. But I have always been different. Perhaps that's why I find it easier to cross the narrow boundaries between one tribe and the next. To belong so often means to exclude; to think in terms of *us* and *them*—two little words that, juxtaposed, so often lead to conflict.

Is this what has happened in Lansquenet? It wouldn't be the first time. Outsiders have never been welcome here. The smallest difference can be enough to make someone unwelcome; even folk from Pont-le-Saôul, just a few kilometres downriver, are still viewed with suspicion because they grow kiwis instead of melons; pink garlic instead of white; because they breed chickens instead of ducks and pray to Saint Luc and not Saint Jérôme.

'So what do you want me to do?' I said.

'I was hoping you might talk to the girl. Maybe get to know her.'

Of course, he does not want to be involved. I can understand that. His position in Lansquenet is already precarious; another hint of scandal and he could lose his job. I tried to imagine Reynaud in any other career but the Church, but could not quite picture it. Reynaud, working behind a bar; teaching schoolchildren; driving a bus; perhaps taking up carpentry. That made me suddenly think of Roux, and then, as abruptly, of Joséphine, and all that now lies between us.

'You weren't going to leave just yet?' he said. The tiny tremor in his voice betrayed his agitation. I thought again of Joséphine, and of that furtive look in her eyes, of secrets unspoken, of questions unasked. If I stay in Lansquenet, I will find out those secrets. It's a talent—or a curse—to see beyond the surface. But this time, I do not know whether I really *want* to see. There's always a price to pay for these things, and sometimes the price is much too high.

Yes, a part of me wants to leave. To leave today, without looking back; to run back to Paris and to Roux; to hide my face against that part of his shoulder that fits me so perfectly. Is that so hard to understand? I do not belong here any more. What do I care if Francis Reynaud has to leave the priesthood? And what do I care if Joséphine has a son who is eight years old, who likes to paint, who is fatherless? None of this has anything to do with me or with my family.

136

And yet—

Once more I glanced at Reynaud. His expression was carefully neutral. And yet I could see the tension in him; the rigid set of the shoulders, the appraising look in the cool grey eyes.

I sense that he will not be surprised if I refuse to help him. Reynaud is not the kind of man who understands forgiveness. To ask for help—and from someone like me—has already turned his world upside down. His dignity will not take more.

'Of course I'll stay,' I told him. 'Anouk and Rosette are enjoying themselves. And now that we have Alyssa, too—'

He let out a deep breath. 'Good.'

I smiled at him, and told myself that I was being over-sensitive. What's another week, after all? We've barely arrived, and Paris is always at its worst in August. Isn't that why we came here? To get away from the city heat? Now that we're here, we might as well stay and enjoy a few more days. At least until the Autan starts. Until we know which way the wind—black or white—is going to blow.

CHAPTER TWO

☾

Thursday, 19th August

When Reynaud had gone, I tried to phone Roux. reception is poor in Les Marauds. When I found a suitable spot, his mobile was turned off again, but I sent him a text:

May be staying another week. Is everything all right with you? Lots of things to talk about—if you turn your phone on! Love from all of us, Vianne x

I came back to the house to find Alyssa awake and dressed—not in last night's black *abaya* that I had washed and dried for her, but in a pair of Anouk's jeans and a yellow linen shirt, her *hijab* neatly back in place.

Anouk was up too, tousled and sleepy, and Rosette was having breakfast; hot chocolate and a dish of last night's pasta.

'The power is on!' bugled Anouk as I entered the kitchen. 'We have electricity! We have TV! I can charge my iPod!'

Good. That means hot water. Bucket showers are fine for a while; but after four years of living on a houseboat, taking showers with limited water— or at the local swimming pool—a real bath will be wonderful.

I turned to our guest. In Anouk's clothes, she looked no older than fifteen. She is rather slight of build, even slimmer than Anouk. I greeted her by name; she nodded, but did not answer me.

'I'd like to offer you breakfast,' I said.

The girl shrugged.

'Yes, I know. It's Ramadan. Tomorrow, if you're still here, we'll all have breakfast before dawn, and dinner after sunset. It won't be difficult for us, and you'll feel more comfortable.'

Once more Alyssa nodded, but this time I thought she relaxed a little.

'You've already met Anouk,' I said. 'Now let me introduce Rosette.'

Rosette glanced up from her hot chocolate and waved her spoon in greeting.

138

'She doesn't talk much either,' I said. 'But she's lots of fun.'

Rosette made a comic face and fingered a question in sign language.

'She wants to know if you like monkeys.'

Alyssa looked uncertain.

'You'll find that Rosette is very fond of monkeys. In fact, she's almost a monkey herself.'

Rosette crowed and sang a song in a series of wordless half-whistles. Alyssa gave a little smile, then lowered her eyes anxiously.

'That's enough. Give our guest some space. Perhaps you'd like to play outside, while Alyssa and I have a little talk. Who knows, maybe you'll find Pilou.'

'*Pilou!*' said Rosette exuberantly, and scampered outside to look for him. Once again, I told myself how good it was that she'd found a friend. She still misses Roux, of course, but Pilou has become important to her, even more important than Bam. I'm glad. Whatever doubts I may have about Pilou's absent father, the boy himself is a gift to us all.

I gestured to Anouk to stay; last night I felt that maybe she had made a connection with our young visitor. I took Alyssa's hand and smiled at her. Her fingers, I noticed, were very cold.

'I know you don't want to talk,' I said. 'That's fine. You'll talk when you want to. But there are things I need to know if I'm going to help you. Do you understand?'

She nodded.

'First of all, is there anyone you'd like me to call? Your mother, your father—'

She shook her head.

'Are you sure? No one at all? Just to tell them

139

you're all right?'

Once more, Alyssa shook her head. 'No. Thank you.'

It was a start. Only three words, but the silence was broken.

'OK. I understand. No one needs to know you're here. Curé Reynaud already knows, but he won't tell. You're safe with me.'

Alyssa gave a little nod.

Now for the difficult part, I thought. What makes a girl like Alyssa—a pretty girl from a loving home—want to throw herself in the Tannes?

'What happened last night, Alyssa?' I said. 'Do you want to talk about it?'

Alyssa gave me a blank look. Either she hadn't understood, or the answer was so obvious that she was unable to reply. I decided the questions could wait awhile—for another day, at least.

I tried for briskness and a smile. 'All right,' I said. 'Well, you're our guest, at least for now. This house belongs to Luc Clairmont. It used to be his grandmother's house.'

Once more, Alyssa nodded.

'You know him?' I said.

I remembered someone telling me—Reynaud, maybe, or Joséphine—that the Mahjoubi sisters had sometimes played football with Luc in the village square.

'Does he know I'm here?' said Alyssa.

'No one knows you're here,' I said. 'No one will see you indoors. There are books; television; a radio. Is there anything else you need?'

Alyssa shook her head.

'I think it would be better if we didn't alter our plans too much. Otherwise it may look unusual.

But I'll try to make sure that one of us—Anouk or I—is always around, in case you happen to need anything.'

Alyssa nodded, unsmiling.

I looked at Anouk, who, I knew, had planned to see Jeannot again today. She grinned at me. 'It's fine,' she said. 'We'll just sit here and watch daytime TV and sneer at all the reality shows.'

'Alyssa will love that,' I said, ruffling Anouk's hair. 'I'm sure *Estonia's Top Model* or *Women Who Can't Stop Eating Cake* will be a marvellous education. Alyssa, when you get tired of her, just tell her to leave you alone. OK?'

That glimmer of a smile again, like the edge of a crescent moon. There's clearly something about Anouk that appeals to Alyssa. I can't say I'm entirely surprised. My little stranger has always been good at attracting followers. Perhaps if I leave them together, Anouk will find out what I cannot.

I left them with instructions to keep an eye out for Rosette, and went back down into Les Marauds.

CHAPTER THREE

☾

Thursday, 19th August

I'd expected to find activity. instead, Les Marauds was lifeless; streets deserted; shops closed. It might have been six in the morning instead of almost ten thirty. The sun was hot, the air very still, with a kind of eerie clarity.

Only Saïd Mahjoubi's gym seemed open for business this morning. I wondered if he even knew that his daughter was missing. Surely, if he *had* known, he would have closed the gym for the day. But here it was business as usual, with nothing to suggest that a girl might have vanished overnight—

The red door opened. Two men came out. One was young, a teenager, in a sleeveless shirt and combat shorts. The other, in his thirties, was, quite simply, one of the most beautiful men I have ever seen. Graceful in that muscular way which hints at ballet, or martial arts; light olive skin; cropped black hair and a mouth of Oriental precision, drawn from a single voluptuous line . . .

'Can I help you, *mademoiselle*?'

For a moment, I was thrown. The last time I'd walked past the gym, I'd sensed an open hostility. But this man was different; he smiled at me, and I found myself the focus of a charm that was as potent as it was disarming.

Behind me, the teenage boy had gone. I was alone with the stranger. His eyes, beneath thick brows, were dark and soulful, glazed with gold.

'I'm staying here for a few days. I'm Vianne Rocher—'

'Hello, Vianne Rocher. I've heard about you. I'm Karim Bencharki.'

Once more, I was taken aback. *This* was Karim Bencharki?

Reynaud had said he was Westernized. Even so, I'd expected him to display some traditional features—a prayer hat, or at least a beard, like Saïd Mahjoubi. But *this* man might have been anyone, from any kind of background. I checked his colours. A flick of the wrist; a fork of the

142

fingers, nothing more. But he saw it; those eyes are acutely alert. I sensed a keen intelligence there; a deep and earnest intensity; and glossing over it all, that charm, which seems so easy and self-assured—

I confess—I was almost smitten. No one could have failed to respond to the warmth of those honey-glaze eyes. At least, no woman—though maybe Reynaud has filters through which he perceives these things. Certainly he never thought to mention the thing that would take me by surprise, then wring me like a wet rag and leave me stupidly speechless. It is a cheap kind of glamour, of course; and yet for some, it really works. Zozie de l'Alba was one of them; Karim Bencharki is another.

For a moment I struggled to find the words. At last I said: 'You've heard of me?'

The colours between my fingers crazed. Kaleidoscope colours, like pieces of glass spinning at my fingertips.

'Yes, of course. From my sister,' he said. His smile pinned me like a moth on a board. 'Another of Reynaud's lost crusades.'

'I'm not sure what you mean,' I said.

'Just that you're not the only one to get into trouble with the priest. He has quite a reputation where people like us are concerned.'

'People like us?'

'Undesirables. People whose faces will not fit, who don't keep to their side of the river.'

'We had a little encounter,' I said. 'Looking back, I don't think it was very wise of me to open a sweet shop in front of the church, right at the very beginning of Lent—'

143

He laughed at that. He has perfect teeth. 'My sister had the same problem,' he said.

'Didn't Reynaud approve of the school?'

'He never made any pretence of it. Right from the first, he was antagonistic. Inès remembers him standing there, in his black robe, watching. Every day watching, not saying a word, stiff with disapproval.'

I was struck by the similarity of his account to what Reynaud himself had said. That Woman in Black, never speaking—could it be that both sides of this conflict are jumping at shadows of themselves?

'Where is your sister living now?'

'With me, until the repairs are done. It's better she lives with her family.'

His words sounded both casual and proprietary, and I remembered the feeling I'd had at the al-Djerba house; the sense that Inès Bencharki might be more than just a sister. His first wife, perhaps? She has his name. Of course, she might have gone back to her maiden name. Still, Omi had hinted at something. But if so, why would Inès live alone? And why would Karim Bencharki lie?

'My sister has had a troubled life,' went on Karim in a gentle voice. 'Her husband died young, our parents are gone, she has only me to look after her. And now, just when she is beginning to make a fresh start, this happens.'

I said it was a pity.

'More than that,' said Karim. 'It is a scandal and a disgrace. And that priest is responsible. He should be made to pay. And he will.'

I decided against defending Reynaud in favour of finding out more. I said, 'You think he started

144

the fire, then?'

'No doubt about it,' said Karim. 'He has been linked with such things before. An incident with the river-folk in which a boat was set on fire. And then there was your shop, of course, and the way he tried to close you down. Madame Clairmont has told me all about it. The man thinks he is Mayor of Lansquenet.'

'*Caro* Clairmont?'

He nodded. 'Yes. She has been a great supporter of our little community.'

That didn't really surprise me. Caro Clairmont has always enjoyed making herself indispensable. Once one of Reynaud's Bible groupies, she has switched her allegiance to a younger priest, Père Henri Lemaître, whose attentiveness and boyish good looks make Reynaud's aloofness all the more distasteful. I imagine Karim, with his searchlight smile, must present a similar kind of appeal.

What was it that Reynaud said? That Caroline had fallen out with her regular coffee-morning group? Or is it just that she has always preferred the company of handsome young men?

'You are here with your daughter, is that right?'

I nodded. 'My daughters. Anouk and Rosette. Perhaps you've already seen them around.'

'If so, I would have remembered them.' His tone was almost flirtatious. Again, I was surprised at the ease with which he dispenses that charm of his—not a common skill, I guessed, among the men of Les Marauds. He moved a little closer, and I caught the scent of *kif*, mixed with something dark and sweet—chypre, perhaps, or frankincense—

I wondered if he was aware that his sister-in-law

145

was missing. These families are very close. Could Alyssa's parents have hidden their daughter's absence, even from Sonia and Karim?

Once more I checked his colours. Few people shine as brightly. Some people cannot help but shine, eclipsing everything in their path. Is this why Reynaud mistrusts him? Or is there another reason?

'I'd like to meet your sister,' I said. 'I've heard a lot about her.'

'Of course,' said Karim. 'But I think you should know my sister Inès is very shy. She keeps to herself. She does not—socialize.'

'But she has a daughter? What's her name?'

'Du'a. "A prayer" in Arabic.'

'How sad for her, to lose her father so young.'

A shadow came over his features. 'My sister has had a sad life. Du'a is all she has now. Her daughter, and of course her faith. Her faith means everything to her.'

The door to the gym opened then, and a man in a white *djellaba* looked out. I recognized one of the men I'd seen in Les Marauds the day I arrived, and knew this was Saïd Mahjoubi. He did not acknowledge me at all, but instead spoke to Karim in Arabic. I did not understand the words, but I was aware of their urgency, and of the way he glanced at me, quickly, sharply, before looking away.

'Excuse me. I have to go,' said Karim. 'Enjoy your stay here.'

And at that he turned and went back inside, closing the red door behind him.

Left alone, I returned to the boulevard. The late-morning sun was already high, and yet, away from the claustrophobia of the little alleyway, with its scents of chlorine and *kif* and sweat, I was conscious of a welcome sensation of freshness. It was nothing but a breeze, coming across the river, but it smelt of other places, and wild sage on the mountainside, and the peppery scent of the rabbit-tail grass that grows along the sand dunes and crazy-dances in the wind—and I realized what was different.

At last, the calm had broken.

The Autan had begun to blow.

CHAPTER FOUR

Friday, 20th August

Père Henri Lemaître called this morning. I had slept unusually late, and he caught me unshaven and just out of bed. How does he manage to do that, *père*? Does he have a special sense that tells him when I am vulnerable? In any case, he was at my door just as Saint-Jérôme's clock struck nine fifteen, his eyes shining almost—but not quite—as brightly as his teeth.

'Good heavens, Francis, you look terrible.'

I wish he wouldn't call me that.

'I'm perfectly well, thank you,' I said. 'To what do I owe this pleasure?'

He gave me one of those pitying looks and followed me into the house.

'Just checking on a colleague,' he said. 'The Bishop was asking after you.'

The Bishop. This gets better. 'Oh?'

'He thinks perhaps you need a rest. He mentioned you were looking unwell.'

'I thought I *was* having a rest,' I said, a little tartly. 'I'm certainly not overwhelmed by parish duties at the moment.'

That was true; for the past couple of weeks my work has been done by Père Henri Lemaître, who also happens to serve three other tiny villages with no appointed priest of their own. With fewer young men entering the priesthood and fewer people attending church, Lansquenet is unusual in having a resident *curé*, saying Mass twice a day and holding confession four times a week. Other villages have had to get used to hearing Mass only on Sundays, and sometimes having to travel to a different village to do so. No wonder church attendance is down. The Bishop and his kind would have us believe that priests are like kitchen utensils, all of us interchangeable. This may be true in Marseille or Toulouse. But here, people like to have their own church, their own priest for confession. They like to know that the word of God is not brought to them through some celestial telegraph, but through the lips of a man like themselves, a man with calluses on his hands, who knows and understands their lives. I wonder how many confessions Père Henri has heard in Lansquenet. I mean *sincere* confessions, not the kind that Caro Clairmont tells me to attract attention.

'Oh, mon père, I'm so afraid that I might have unwittingly caused offence. I was with Joline Drou the other day, we were shopping in Agen, and we'd stopped to look at summer frocks. You might have noticed I've lost some weight. Well, it's no crime to

148

want to look one's best, and the way some women let themselves go—anyway. I won't bore you, père.'

'*Quite.*'

'*Oh. Well—Joline had seen a dress she liked, and I happened to say that it wouldn't suit. I mean, it can't have escaped you,* père, *that Joline often chooses clothes that are* far *too young for a woman her age, not to mention the fact that she's getting just a* teeny *bit plump—I wouldn't say it to her* face, *but I wouldn't be a true friend if I let her make a fool of herself, and now I feel so guilty—*'

'*Enough. Two Avés.*'

'*But,* mon père—'

'*Please,* madame. *I don't have all day.*'

No. Diplomacy and flattery are not among my talents. I'm sure that Père Henri Lemaître would have dealt with her problem more sensitively. I am often impatient, often abrupt. I cannot hide my feelings the way Père Henri Lemaître hides his. I cannot feign interest or sympathy the way he does, or treat my flock as if they were anything but stupid sheep.

And yet I know them better than any priest from the city could. They may be sheep, but they are *my* sheep, and I have no intention of handing them over to Père Henri. How could he understand them, with his toothpaste smile and his winning ways? How could he know that Alain Poitou has become addicted to cough medicine, and doesn't want his wife to know? That Gilles Dumarin blames himself for allowing his sister to put their mother in Les Mimosas? That Joséphine Muscat used to steal, and still feels the need to do penance? That, following the death of his son, Jean Marron has thought of suicide? That Henriette Moisson, at eighty-five, confesses to me every week a theft committed when she was nine; that of a little sewing set she purloined from her sister, who died over sixty years ago, in a boating accident on the Tannes? That Marie-Ange Lucas is having internet sex with a boy she has never met, and wants to know if it is a sin? Or that Guillaume Duplessis still prays for the soul of a dog that died over eight years ago, and that I, God forgive me, allow him to believe that maybe animals *do* have souls, and will find a place in Paradise?

Whatever my faults, *père*, I know guilt. And I know that some problems cannot be solved by PowerPoint. Or even by a bishop, for that matter.

'You know why that is, Francis,' said Père Henri, bringing me back to reality. I had been so lost in my thoughts that it took me a few moments to recall what he had been referring to. He has taken over my duties because, according to him, at least, my office has been compromised by the rumours and gossip that have sprung up in the wake of the fire in the old *chocolaterie*. I suspect that this idea has come from Caroline Clairmont, a firm believer in progress, who sees in Père Henri Lemaître a kindred spirit as well as a possible rung on the ladder of her advancement. She has already seen what the man can accomplish in just two weeks. In six months, then, how much more could be done?

He followed me into the kitchen and sat down, uninvited.

'Make yourself at home,' I said. 'Would you like coffee?'

'Yes, please.'

'It's still my parish,' I told him, pouring coffee into two cups. He takes his with milk. I prefer black.

150

'I'm afraid I don't have any sugar.'

That smile again. 'No matter,' he said. 'I really shouldn't, anyway.' He patted his midsection. 'Have to keep an eye on the old tum, don't we, Francis?'

My God, he even *sounds* like Caro. I drank my coffee in one gulp and poured myself another. 'It's still my parish,' I said again. 'And unless I'm found guilty in some other court than that of gossip and conjecture, I have no intention of leaving.'

Of course, he knows that won't happen. The police have already spoken to me. There is no evidence at all to link me with the fire, and although the Lansquenet rumour mill continues to turn unabated, the rest of the world has lost interest.

Père Henri Lemaître gave me a look. 'It isn't as black and white as that. As I'm sure you must know, a priest must be absolutely beyond reproach. And in a delicate situation like this, where another culture is involved—'

'I have no problem with *other cultures*, as you put it,' I said, trying to keep my temper. 'In fact—' I bit off the rest of the phrase. In the heat of the moment I'd been dangerously close to revealing the events of the other night. 'If there has been antagonism,' I said at last in a calm voice, 'then it has been entirely from the community of Les Marauds, where old Mahjoubi has always done his utmost to provoke me.'

Père Henri Lemaître smiled. 'Yes, the old man was set in his ways. Different times, different styles. The new one, I think, will be easier.'

I looked at him. 'The new what?'

'Oh. Didn't you know? Old Mahjoubi's son Saïd is taking over his role at the mosque. It seems the old man had been causing concern for some time with his funny little quirks. Some people, it seems, were quite upset. Including you, of course,' he said, with yet another flash of his teeth.

I thought about that for a moment. It had never occurred to me that old Mahjoubi might also have had his detractors within Les Marauds. But can Saïd Mahjoubi bring the change Les Marauds needs?

'Saïd's a sensible man,' said Père Henri complacently. 'He understands his community. He knows how to lead, he's progressive, he's respected by everyone. I think we'll find him far easier to involve in dialogue than we did his father.'

People like Père Henri Lemaître never use the easiest phrase. It's always *involve in dialogue* instead of simply talking. And I couldn't help but suspect that maybe there was a hidden gibe against me in Père Henri's words. He has made it all too clear that he thinks I do *not* understand my community. I am *not* the most progressive of men, and after the fire at the old *chocolaterie* I think it is fairly safe to say that I am no longer the most respected. Is this his way of baiting me? Or simply his way of warning me that soon I too shall be replaced?

'The Bishop thinks you might benefit from a relocation,' he said. 'You've spent too long in Lansquenet. You've started to think of the place as your own. To impose your own rules, not those of the Church.'

I began to protest. Père Henri lifted a hand to silence me.

'I know you don't agree,' he said. 'But perhaps you need to examine your soul. Your soul, and perhaps your conscience.'

152

'My *conscience*!' I exploded.

He gave me one of his condescending looks. 'You know, Francis—may I call you Francis?'

'You already do,' I pointed out.

'I hope you'll forgive my frankness,' he said. 'But the Bishop—and others—have mentioned a certain arrogance in your dealings with—'

'Is *that* why I'm being disciplined?' My anger was almost too much to contain. 'And here I was, thinking it was for setting fire to a girls' school.'

'No one's saying that, Francis. And no one has said you're being disciplined.'

'Then what *are* they saying?'

He put down his cup. 'Nothing yet, not officially. I simply thought I'd warn you.' He shot me that smile of his. 'You're really not helping your case, you know. Perhaps God has sent you this trial as a lesson in humility.'

I clenched my fists behind my back. 'If he has, I'm sure he doesn't need *you* to help translate his meaning.'

I thought Père Henri bridled a little. 'I'm trying to be your friend, Francis.'

'I'm a priest. I have no friends.'

*   *   *

Yesterday was oppressively still. Today, a dry, abrasive wind blows. Tiny flecks of mica ripple and hang in the turbulent air; a scent, like that of old smoke, filters into everything. In the old *chocolaterie*, Luc Clairmont is making repairs. Scaffolding has been erected up the side of one wall; a sheet of plastic covers the roof. Now, with this wind, the plastic sheet rattles and creaks like an old ship's sail. In the street, women hold their skirts; papers fly; the sun is a disc of silver foil in a sky full of hectic dust. It is the White Autan, of course, so prevalent at this time of year. It usually lasts for a couple of weeks, and stories and sayings abound in its wake.

How I once hated those stories, those little fragments of paganism; seeding themselves like dandelions; invading the garden of our faith. Since then, I have learnt to tolerate, if not entirely trust them. We can all learn from stories, be they holy or profane.

Autan blanc, Autan blanc—

There's a saying in these parts that the White Autan can either send a man mad, or blow away his demons. It is an old wives' tale, of course. But, as Armande Voizin used to say, old wives are sometimes worth listening to.

Autan blanc, Autan blanc,
Autan en emporte le vent.

And now, as I watch Père Henri leave, head lowered into the scouring wind, I wonder briefly what it would take for the White Autan to blow *him* away.

CHAPTER FIVE

Friday, 20th August

Wind makes people excitable. Every schoolteacher knows that—yes, *père*, and every priest. The White Autan has so far brought a spate of quarrels, bursts of temper and petty acts of vandalism— three planters overturned in the square, graffiti on the scorched wall of the old *chocolaterie*—which suggests that this year the *Vent des Fous* has found its way into the collective brain, making fools of everyone.

Caro Clairmont is one of them. The wind brings out the worst in her. To me she is especially cloying, in that poisonous way I know too well; calling round yesterday to see if I needed anything, and managing before she left to deliver a number of barbed little shots—disguised as sympathy, of course—and to wish me well for the future.

'Why, are you going away?'

She looked slightly flustered. 'No, I—'

'Oh. I must have misunderstood.' I gave her my most vicious smile. 'Give my regards to your son, by the way. He's a fine boy. Armande would have been proud.'

Caro twitched. It is common knowledge in Lansquenet that she and Luc do not agree on a number of issues, including his choice of university and his decision to study literature instead of joining the family business, as well as the matter of Armande's house. Armande's will made it very

155

clear that the house belongs to Luc, but Caro believes it should be sold, and the money invested elsewhere. Of course, Luc will not hear of this, which has caused a certain tension in the Clairmont household. In any case, any mention of Luc or his plans is enough to bring on that twitch again. But satisfying though it is to needle Caro, it does not improve my position here. Père Henri Lemaître has done his work well, speaking of my situation (of course, in the utmost confidence) to all those women in Lansquenet who can most be trusted to spread the news.

Meanwhile, it has been two weeks since I last took confession. Even so, I hear things that Père Henri fails to notice. Henriette Moisson and Charles Lévy have fallen out over a cat, which technically belongs to Charles, but which Henriette feeds so often and so lavishly that it has attached itself to her. Charles resents this, and, the other day, trying his hand at investigative action, went so far as to hide himself in Henriette's back garden, in the hope of collecting photographic evidence of the animal's abduction, at which Henriette set up a scream that a *perverti* was spying on her, which roused the whole street—at least until the truth was discovered. The object of all this attention seemed quite unmoved by the disturbance, finishing the dish of minced steak that Henriette had prepared for him before going back to sleep on a cushion in front of the fire.

Henriette has already tried to confess to me a number of times. I tell her to ask for Père Henri Lemaître, but I don't think she understands.

'I looked for you at confession, *père*, but you were not in church,' she said. 'Instead I found some

156

perverti sitting inside the confessional! I told him if I saw him again I would call for the police—'

'That was Père Henri Lemaître,' I said.

'Why? What was *he* doing there?'

I sighed and finally told her that she could come round to my house if ever she needed confession. I also spoke to Charles Lévy, telling him that if he wishes to keep his cat, he should let it sleep indoors and feed it something more than scraps.

This morning I met him coming out of Benoît the fishmonger's with a small, wrapped package and a look of satisfaction.

'Monkfish,' he hissed at me as he passed. 'Let's see how she deals with *that*!' And then he was off, clutching his fish as if it were contraband. He does not know that Henriette has already bought some whitebait, as well as a leather collar inscribed with the name Tati. Charles calls his cat Otto, which Henriette tells me is a silly name for a cat, as well as being unpatriotic.

You see, *mon père*. In spite of all this, some people still speak to me. But Caro Clairmont, Joline Drou—the little set that Armande Voizin referred to as *Bible groupies*—are pointedly ignoring me. I saw Joline this afternoon crossing the square by Saint-Jérôme's, as I replaced the overturned pots and swept up the earth from the planters. I suspect one of the Acheron boys—I've seen them hanging around the square, and I am almost sure the graffiti on the *chocolaterie* wall is also their work: a spray-painted tag, which I must remove today before another one joins it.

Joline was on her way to the beauty shop with Bénédicte Acheron, who has (since their recent falling-out over the issue of Joline's new frock)

157

replaced Caro Clairmont as Joline's best friend. Both of them were dressed to the nines, their hair hidden under silk headscarves. Of course, this wind is disastrous to the feminine coiffure, and God forbid that either one should appear in a state of anything less than perfection.

I greeted her. She turned away. A priest should show some dignity. Perhaps it offends her to see me like this, in a T-shirt and a pair of old jeans, sweeping dirt from the pavement. Well, let her be offended. If Caro has not already done so, I imagine Père Henri Lemaître has already told her all about my terrible stubbornness, my refusal to confess, my lamentable insubordination and my ingratitude towards both the Bishop and Père Henri himself. I wondered as I watched her go (her high heels tapping the cobbles) if this was how Vianne was welcomed here, eight years ago—with sidelong glances; disdainful smiles.

Now, *I* am the outcast. *I* am the undesirable. The thought came to me so suddenly that I began to laugh aloud. It was a curious sound, *père*, the sound of my own laughter; and the thought occurred to me then that it was a sound I had not heard in twenty years.

'M'sieur le Curé? Are you all right?'

I must have let my eyes close. I opened them, and saw a boy holding a dog on a piece of string. It was Joséphine's boy, Jean-Philippe—she calls him Pilou—looking at me curiously.

Jean-Philippe Bonnet doesn't go to church. He and his mother are in a minority. And though she has never liked me, Joséphine has never been the kind of woman who uses gossip as currency. That makes her unique in Lansquenet; unique, if not

158

approachable. Her son is eight, with a sunny grin that some find almost infectious. His dog has been an annoyance ever since he acquired it, taking instant objection to a variety of everyday sights and sounds, including other dogs, nuns, church bells, bicycles, men with beards, the wind and most especially women in black, which always send the animal into a fit of barking. It was barking now, I saw. Probably that blasted wind.

'Yes, I'm fine,' I told the boy. 'Can't you shut that dog up?'

The boy gave me a pitying look. 'Not really,' he said. 'Vlad's a believer in free speech.'

'So I understand,' I said.

'But he's *very* corruptible.' The boy dug into his pocket and produced a biscuit. Vlad fell silent and raised a paw. 'There,' said Pilou. 'The price of peace.'

I shook my head and turned my attention to the graffiti on the *chocolaterie* wall. The wall needs a coat of whitewash. Even so, the colour will show if I do not scrub it clean. I'd brought a scrubbing brush and some bleach.

'Why are you doing that?' said Pilou.

I shrugged. 'Well, somebody has to.'

'But why *you*? It's not your house.'

'I don't like the way it looks,' I said. 'People shouldn't have to see graffiti on their way to church.'

'I don't go to church,' said Pilou.

'Yes, I know,' I told him.

'Maman says *you* don't, either.'

'That isn't the case,' I told him. 'I don't expect you'd understand.'

'Yes, I would. It's because of that fire,' he said.

159

Once more, I found myself on the edge of a precipice of laughter. 'Your mother taught you to speak your mind.'

'Oh yes,' said Pilou cheerily.

I scrubbed once more at the spray-painted tag. The paint has sunk into the porous wall, saturating the plaster. The more I scrubbed, the more tenaciously the pigment seemed to cling to the wall. I muttered a curse.

'That Acheron boy—' I said, with clenched teeth.

'Oh it wasn't *him*,' said Pilou.

'How do you know? Did you see something?'

'Nnn-hnn.' He shook his head.

'Then how do you know?'

'My friend says it's an Arabic word.'

'Your friend?'

'Du'a. She used to live here, before the fire.'

I looked at the boy with some surprise. How curious, that a boy like this—inseparable from his dog, living in the village café, surely a bad influence in every possible sense of the word—should be friends with Inès Bencharki's child.

'And what does Du'a say it means?'

Pilou shrugged and knelt down to adjust the makeshift lead on his dog's collar. 'It isn't very nice,' he said. 'Du'a says it means *whore*.'

160

CHAPTER SIX

☾

Saturday, 21st August

At last, a sign that all is not well among the streets of Les Marauds. I guessed as much when I saw Saïd the other day outside the gym, but now finally the rumour is free, whispering through Les Marauds like rain.

Have you heard?
Have you heard?

I heard it from Omi al-Djerba first. I met her as I walked with Rosette over the bridge into Lansquenet. She greeted me with a cackle, and waved to me to join her.

'Everything's going crazy here,' she told me in her cracked voice. 'Can you feel it? It's the wind. The wind sends everyone crazy.'

She smiled at Rosette, with petal-pink gums. 'Is this your little one here, eh? Does she like coconut macaroons?' She brought one out of the pocket of her embroidered kaftan. 'Delicious. We make them for Ramadan.' She handed one to Rosette, at the same time popping one slyly into her own mouth. 'This doesn't count,' she told me, seeing my surprise. 'It's only a bit of coconut. Besides, I'm too old to fast all day.' She winked at Rosette. *'Bismillah!'*

Rosette puffed out her cheeks and signed: *Monkeys like coconut too.*

'Well, of course,' said Omi, who seemed to have

161

understood perfectly. 'One more for your little friend.'

Rosette crowed with laughter, her mouth still full of coconut. Omi tweaked her marigold hair. 'They're saying Alyssa Mahjoubi has run away from home,' she said.

'Who is?'

'All the flapping tongues. Her mother says she's ill in bed, but no one has seen her for three days, and Reema Bouzana says she thinks she saw her at midnight on Wednesday, all alone and heading for the village.'

'Really?' I said.

'Of course, women talk. And Reema has always been envious of Samira Mahjoubi. Well, she has a daughter too—still unmarried at twenty-five, and with a tongue on her like a kitchen knife, while Samira's daughter has landed herself the best-looking man in Lansquenet—' Omi shot me a comic look. 'But Alyssa was always the restless one, and Sonia isn't saying a word. Still, maybe it's nothing, *inshallah.*'

I looked at her. 'That's not what *you* think.'

She laughed. '*I* think I've never seen Samira Mahjoubi take so many walks. Most of the time she's too full of herself even to walk to the market. Well, maybe she's trying to lose some weight. Or maybe she's thinking of buying up some of those empty houses along the river. Or maybe she's trying to find the girl before she causes a scandal—'

'But why would Alyssa run away?'

Omi shrugged. 'Who knows? These girls. They're all as mad as each other. But now, with Saïd in charge at the mosque, this isn't the time for his daughters to suddenly start asserting themselves.'

'Saïd's in charge at the mosque?' I said.

'*Hee*, didn't you know that?' Omi reached absent-mindedly into her pockets and pulled out another macaroon. 'Since the beginning of Ramadan. People were complaining that Mahjoubi was getting too old, that he was getting too many things wrong, that he was telling stories in mosque that aren't even in the Qur'an, that he wasn't in line with current affairs. Well, maybe that is true,' she said, popping the macaroon into her mouth. 'But I'd rather trust a wise man than a man with a handful of doctorates, and I still think that *that* old man could teach his son a thing or two.' She paused to tug her *hijab* into place. '*Hee!* This wind. This terrible dust. It whispers *waswaas* to everyone. My Zahra thinks the dust will get into her mouth and break her fast. It gives Yasmina headaches. And my little Maya can't keep still, she rattles around like a mad thing. No one sleeps. No one prays. Everyone jumps at nothing.' Once more Omi looked at Rosette. 'But you and I know better, eh? We say if the wind blows, saddle it up and ride it!'

Rosette laughed and signed: *Giddy-up!*

Omi smiled again. 'That's right. You don't have to talk. In a bag of walnuts, it's the empty one that makes most noise.' She looked across the street, where a trio of young women in *niqab* was passing by, talking and laughing. All three were in black, except for one, whose veil was tied with a neon-pink ribbon bisecting her face. I smiled and waved in greeting; the conversation stopped at once. I heard it resume when they had passed, although its pitch had dropped by then, and there was no more laughter.

Omi shook her head. '*Pff*. That was Aisha

163

Bouzana and her friends Jalila El Mardi and Rana Jannat. Silly gossips, all three of them. Rattling like empty nuts. Spreading their talk all over the village. Did you know that Aisha—she was the one with the pink stripe—was telling my Yasmina that Maya's name is not permitted, according to Islamic law? She says it's some kind of goddess name in some old pagan religion. As if she cared. It's just a way of attracting attention. Same as wearing the *niqab*. She never used to wear it before Karim Bencharki came here. None of those young women did. But all at once, when a handsome man happens to mention he likes *niqab*, suddenly dozens of them are wearing the veil and making eyes at each other.' She gave me one of her humorous looks. 'You're not saying *you* haven't noticed him yet? Looks like an angel? Lives at the gym?'

I nodded. 'Yes, I've noticed him.'

Omi cackled. 'You're not alone.'

'What about his sister?'

'Inès.' Her face was suddenly expressionless. 'We don't have much to do with her. She mostly stays in the house nowadays. She wasn't a popular teacher, either.'

'Why was that?'

The old woman shrugged. 'Who knows? But I must be going. My little Maya is waiting for me. We will be making pancakes. Oh, not for now, of course. But for later, we have *crêpes aux mille trous*, and *harira* soup, with lemons and dates. At Ramadan, everyone fasts, but we *think* about food all the time; we buy food, we prepare food, we offer food to our neighbours, we even *dream* of food—that is, if this wind allows us to sleep. I will bring some Moroccan sweets; some macaroons, and gazelle's horns, and almond meringues, and *chebakia*. And maybe then you can share with me the recipe for your chocolate.'

I watched her as she walked away, feeling a little puzzled that even Omi al-Djerba, with her cheery contempt for convention and what the neighbours might think of her, should still be so reluctant to talk to me about Inès Bencharki—

Rosette signed: *I like her.*

'Yes, Rosette. I like her too.'

She reminds me in so many ways of Armande, whose appetite for everything—food, drink, gossip, life—once scandalized her family. But Omi's family is different. Their love and respect increases with age. I cannot imagine the al-Djerbas ever thinking of doing what Caro Clairmont tried to do—to bully her mother into a home, or to keep her from seeing her grandchild.

The streets of Les Marauds were empty once more as I made my way back to Armande's house. Only a couple of people passed, and neither of them greeted me. But all along the Boulevard des Marauds I felt the windows watching me, and heard the whispers in the walls. *The wind cannot keep a secret*, as my mother used to say, and today the wind is telling me that Les Marauds is in distress. Is it because of Alyssa? Or is it some deeper, darker malaise? I look at the sky, which should be clear, but all I can see is that fine, bright dust. It makes Rosette sneeze; and every time she sneezes, Bam rolls in the dust and laughs at her.

She looked at me, bright-eyed. '*Pilou,*' she said.

'Not today,' I told her. 'But remember, he and Joséphine are coming to dinner tomorrow.'

She made a face. '*Rowr.*'

165

Roux.

I hugged her. She smelt of the river and of something sweeter, like baby soap and chocolate. 'I know you miss him, Rosette,' I said. 'I miss him too. All of us do. But we're having a good time, aren't we?'

She crowed emphatically and spoke a string of words in her personal language, from which all I caught was *Pilou* and *Vlad*, and (surprisingly) *awesome*. The scribble of red that is Bam today capered madly around her feet, all gilded and dusty with road-bronze.

I had to laugh. My little Rosette is a born comedian. For all her strangeness, my winter child can sometimes bring the sunshine.

'Come on,' I said. 'Let's get you home.'

And, shielding our eyes against the dust, we turned away from the river and started back up the steep hill towards the place I'd just called *home*, where the first of Armande's peaches were already beginning to fall.

CHAPTER SEVEN

☾

Saturday, 21st August

We came back on the tail of the wind, Rosette singing all the way: *Bam, bam BAM, bam badda-BAM—*

It's my mother's song, of course. Rosette doesn't really sing *words*, but she has her father's ear. She stamps her feet and claps her hands—

'Bam, bam BAM! Bam, badda-BAM!'

And the wind joins in; the blown leaves dance; autumn is coming early this year, and already the colours are turning. The linden trees are the first to go, shaking confetti into the sky. Rosette's hair is almost the same shade of red-gold as those falling leaves, which she stamps out like flames with her small bare feet.

Stamp, stamp, stamp. *'Bam, badda-bam!'*

From the cottage, I could sense Alyssa watching through the half-closed shutters. She has not spoken more than a few words to me since she first arrived here, but she seems easier with Anouk and Rosette, although she is still cautious. She has abandoned her *hijab*, and now wears her hair in two long plaits, which fascinate Anouk and Rosette. We take our main meal after sunset, so that she can observe Ramadan, but as far as I know, she has not prayed. Instead she watches TV and reads—

Not today, I decided.

I went to the other side of the house and looked at Armande's peach tree. I have already given some to Guillaume; some more to Poitou; some to Yasmina Al-Djerba; plus a *clafoutis* to Narcisse and his wife, and I'd promised a tart to Luc Clairmont, who is working to repair the *chocolaterie*, and another to Joséphine. Even so, there are too many left, and now, with the wind, they are falling.

'We have to gather the peaches today,' I said as I entered the kitchen. 'Armande would never forgive me if I let the wasps get to them.'

'Yay! Peach jam!' said Anouk, jumping up from the sofa.

I smiled. One of Anouk's most endearing traits is the way she flits so easily from childhood to

167

adulthood, light to shade, like a butterfly moving from flower to flower, unaware of the changing worlds. Today she is almost as young as she was the day we first arrived here.

Alyssa, so close to her in age, already seems so much older. What are her parents thinking now? Why has no one come looking for her? And how long can I keep her here before the news of her presence gets out?

'Did you know Armande?' I said. 'She was Luc's grandmother, and a friend of mine. I think you would have liked her. Not everyone did—she infuriated Monsieur le Curé—but she had a good heart, and Luc thought the world of her. She's the reason I came here. I promised I'd harvest her peaches.'

At last, the glimmer of a smile from the solemn little face. 'That sounds like my grandfather,' she said. 'He likes to grow things. He has a persimmon tree by his house. It's only ever given fruit once, but he cares for that little persimmon like it's his only son.'

This was by far the longest speech I had heard Alyssa make. Perhaps the contact with Anouk has helped her find her voice again. I smiled. 'Would you like to help?' I said. 'We're going to make some peach jam.'

'*Bam. Jam. Pam. Badda-bam!*' sang Rosette, picking up a wooden spoon and making it dance on the table-top.

Alyssa looked curious. 'Peach jam?'

'It's such an easy recipe. We already have everything we need. Jam sugar—that's sugar with pectin added, so that the jam sets properly—a copper pot, jars, cinnamon—oh, yes, and peaches,

168

of course.' I smiled. 'Come on. You can help us pick.'

For a moment, she hesitated. Then she followed me outside. It was quite safe; the house is secluded, and the peach tree invisible from the road. The Autan wind is merciless; already, the ground at the foot of the tree was covered with windfalls. Leave them more than a minute and the wasps will start to attack them, but windfall peaches are perfect for jam, and together we gathered more than enough in no more than ten minutes.

The copper pot belongs to Armande, though I have one very like it. It's large and shaped like a kettle-drum, with a hammered, uneven surface. Sitting on Armande's kitchen range, it looks like a witch's cauldron—not too far from the truth, I suppose, for what could be closer to alchemy than changing raw ingredients into something that makes the mouth water?

'*Bam, bam*,' went Rosette, drumming on the copper pot.

'Now, we have to prepare the fruit.'

I ran some cold water into the sink. We washed the peaches and took out the stones. A little bruising doesn't hurt; it makes the peach all the sweeter. And as we worked, our sleeves rolled up, the sweet juice running down our arms, the kitchen was filled with the sunny scent of peaches and sugar and summertime.

'*Bam. Jam. Bam-badda-bam*,' sang Rosette. In the slices of light and shade, she looked like a blurry bumblebee; Bam, in her shadow, a cluster of motes chasing into the rapturous air.

I saw Alyssa watching, a crease between her espresso eyes, and knew that she could see him

169

too. After three days, that doesn't surprise me. It doesn't usually take very long for people to start to notice Bam. Children are most susceptible; but even adults can see him, as long as they have an open mind. It begins as a trick of the light, a bloom like that on a bunch of golden grapes, and then, one day—

'*Jam! Bam!*'

'Why don't you take Rosette outside?'

Anouk gave me a comical look. Rosette is a plastic trumpet, too loud for me to hear whispers. And whispers are my business today; the whispers that Omi calls *waswaas*, or worry-whispers from Satan. But so far, Alyssa's whispers have been too timid for me to overhear. *Perhaps, if we were alone,* I thought, *with the everyday magic of making jam—*

At first, I did not try to make her speak. Instead I kept up a monologue that needed no reply from her; I talked about the recipe, and about Armande, and the chocolate shop; and Roux in Paris, and our boat, and Anouk, and Rosette, and the peaches.

'We're not going to cook the peaches today. Instead, we leave them overnight. A kilo of sugar to each one of fruit, minus the leaves and stones, of course. We slice them into the copper pan— copper's best for cooking because it heats up more quickly. We add the sugar. Then, with a wooden spoon, we crush the sugar into the fruit. Rosette likes this part best—' I smiled—'because it's messiest. And because it *smells* so good—'

I saw Alyssa's nostrils flare.

'Now we add the cinnamon,' I said. 'Sticks, not powder; broken in half. Three or four should do the trick—' The summery scent had turned autumnal; bonfires and Halloween. Cinnamon pancakes cooked outside. Mulled wine and burnt sugar.

'What do you think?'

'It's nice,' she said. The diamond stud in her nostril flared again, catching the light. 'What next?'

'We wait,' I said. 'We cover the pot with a cloth and leave the whole thing overnight. Then, in the morning, we light the range and stir as we bring the jam to the boil. It doesn't need to boil for more than four minutes, then we can put it into pots, ready for the winter.'

She looked at me quickly. 'The winter?'

'Of course, I won't be here,' I said. 'But jam is best in wintertime, when the nights are long and there's frost in the air, and every pot is like opening a little jar of sunshine—'

'Oh.' She sounded crestfallen. 'I thought perhaps you were going to stay.'

'I'm sorry, Alyssa. We can't,' I said.

'When?' It was almost a whisper.

'Soon. A couple of weeks, at most. But don't worry. We won't abandon you.'

'You'd take me with you to Paris?' she said. Suddenly her eyes were bright.

'We'll see. I hope I don't need to.' I turned away from the copper pan and looked at her directly. 'Whatever you're running away from, I hope we can find a better solution than that. Isn't there anyone you trust in Les Marauds? A family member? A teacher, perhaps?'

Alyssa flinched. 'No,' she said.

'But you *do* go to school, don't you?' I said. 'The little school opposite the church?'

Once more, Alyssa flinched. 'I did.'

There she is again, I thought. Inès Bencharki, the Woman in Black. I haven't even mentioned her name, yet once more her shadow is strong enough to eclipse even this little gleam of light. Is *this* what Alyssa fears so much? What is she trying to escape?

'Wouldn't you miss your family if you went to Paris? Your parents? Your sister?'

Silently, she shook her head. The bright look of hope that had been in her eyes had dimmed once more to a sullen flame.

'Your grandfather, then. I know you'd miss *him*.' It was a tentative shot, but there'd been a genuine note of affection in her voice as she spoke about old Mahjoubi and the persimmon tree.

She turned away. I saw a tear gather and roll down the side of her face. She looked very young at that moment; younger even than Anouk, and almost without thinking I reached out to take her in my arms. She stiffened, then relaxed, and I felt her sobbing against my shoulder, sobbing almost soundlessly, her hands clenched around her elbows.

I let her cry. It sometimes helps. Around us, the scent of peaches was almost too intense to bear. Outside, the wind rattled the windows. When the Autan wind blows, the farmers of this region strip their fruit trees of their leaves, to avoid giving too much purchase to the gusts that tear at the trees, shaking the ripening fruit from the boughs. This may seem cruel to an outsider, but the alternative is broken branches and a ruined harvest. There's a time to coddle fruit trees, as my friend Framboise used to say, as well as a time to strip them back. Children are not so different. Neither benefits from an excess of sensitivity.

I held her until I sensed that her sobs were close to subsiding. Then I said in a quiet voice, 'Alyssa. What happened the other night?'

172

She looked at me.

'I'd like to help. But I wish you could tell me what's happening. Why does a girl like you decide she doesn't want to live any more?'

For a moment I thought she wouldn't answer. Then she said in a halting voice, 'Someone once told me: *When Ramadan comes, the gates of Paradise are opened, and the gates of hellfire are locked and the devils shackled.* That means that if a person dies during the month of Ramadan—'

She paused and looked away again.

'They wouldn't go to hell?' I said.

'I guess that sounds pretty crazy to you.'

'Because I'm not a Muslim?' I said. 'Well, I'm not a Christian either, and I don't believe in hell. But I don't think you're crazy. Just sad and confused.'

Alyssa sighed.

'It's all right. Whatever it is may seem hopeless to you, but there's always a solution. I promise you we'll find it. You don't have to deal with this alone.'

She gave a little nod. 'But you can't tell anyone else,' she said. 'No one in my family. No one at all. You promise?'

'I do.'

She sat down at the table, tracing with her fingertips the scars on the wooden surface. Outside, the wind redoubled, making the old eaves whisper and creak. The wind makes Rosette talkative; I hoped today it might do the same for Alyssa.

'You can talk to me,' I said. 'Whatever it is, I bet I've seen worse.'

'Worse?' said Alyssa.

I thought of all the places I'd seen; of all the years I'd travelled. Over those years I have seen

173

so much; the death of my mother; the loss of my friends; a million casual cruelties; as many flashes of sweetness.

I've watched the sun rise over mountains where no human being has ever trod and seen it go down over cities where every inch of space is filled with people, pushing and fighting each other for life. I've given birth. I've been in love. I've changed beyond expectation. I've seen people die in alleyways; seen others survive impossible odds; known happiness and darkness and grief, and the one thing I'm still sure about is that life is mystery; life is change; it's what my mother called magic, and it's capable of anything—

I started to tell Alyssa. It's hard to put these things into words. For the first time since I arrived here, I wished for my *chocolaterie*; the scent of melting chocolate; the silver pot on the counter; the cups; the ease of talking without words. I have no desire to challenge her faith. But Ramadan excludes me. It means I cannot offer her the kind of comfort I know best: the square of chocolate on the tongue, childhood's magic cure-all—

Suddenly, there came a sound, a scratching at the window. Maybe a bramble or a branch, tapping in that restless wind. But when I looked up, I saw a face looking in from behind the half-closed shutters; a round nose pressed against the glass, a pair of dark eyes, widening in recognition—

It was Maya.

CHAPTER EIGHT

☾

Saturday, 21st August

Alyssa had fled upstairs the moment the child had appeared at the window. But Maya had already seen her. Too late to think of an excuse; I went to the door and opened it.

'Maya,' I said.

She smiled up at me. The White Autan was in her eyes, her wild hair, her flushed cheeks. She was wearing a pair of dungarees and a T-shirt with a daisy motif. Under her arm she was carrying a knitted toy that might have been a cat, or a rabbit, and which had clearly been much loved, if somewhat the worse for the experience.

'You said I could play with your little girl.'

'Rosette,' I said. 'She's gone outside. Would you like me to call her?'

She peered in through the door. 'I saw my cousin Alyssa in there.'

I nodded.

'Is she hiding?'

'Yes.'

'Why?' said Maya.

I looked at her. 'Can you keep a secret?' I said.

'Mmm-hmm. Can I tell Omi?'

I shook my head. 'No, Maya. You can't. Not Omi, not Jiddo—your grandfather—just let's keep it a secret, shall we?'

'Not even Du'a? She's my best friend.'

175

Once more, I shook my head. 'No, you mustn't tell anyone. Alyssa's staying here with me. She doesn't want anyone else to know.'

'Why?' said Maya.

'She doesn't want anyone to know that, either.'

'Oh,' said Maya. 'Can I stay, too?'

'I don't think that's a good idea. But you can come back any time you like. As long as you don't tell anyone. And if you're very, *very* good—'

She took a step inside the house. 'What are you making?'

I told her.

'Oh. Can I try some?'

'Of course you can, when it's ready. You and Rosette can label the pots. Would you like that?'

'Can Du'a come? She's bigger than me. She can keep a secret, too.'

I sighed. This was getting complicated. But Maya, I knew, was only five, and perhaps Du'a might be able to keep her from talking. Besides, I was still curious about Inès Bencharki's child; perhaps, if I got to meet her, I might find out more about her mother.

'Where is Du'a now?' I said.

'At home, with her mother, doing chores. She only comes out when her mother sleeps.'

'Where do they live?'

'With Sonia, of course. But Amma says I can't play there. So Du'a and I, we play somewhere else. We have a place, a special place—' She stopped. 'But that's our secret.'

I noticed that as we were talking, Alyssa had come down to sit on the stairs. She sat there in silence, hugging her knees, her pale face pinched with tension.

'I won't tell anyone you're here, Alyssa, I *promise*,' said Maya.

Alyssa hesitated a moment longer, then seemed to relax a little. 'All right. How's everyone?'

Maya shrugged. 'OK, I guess. Everyone's looking for you, though. My *jiddo* and my Uncle Saïd aren't talking at all any more. Omi says they're both as bad as each other, but I don't know. And Omi is making *tamina* cake for *iftar* tonight. She says it's OK to taste it to see if it's done. But my *jiddo* says she tastes it *too* much. Half of it is already gone.'

I smiled, imagining the scene. I wondered if the quarrel between old Mahjoubi and Saïd was about the leadership of the mosque; Omi had already hinted at a conflict between them. It seems ironic, doesn't it, that both Reynaud and old Mahjoubi should be in the same situation, replaced by someone younger, someone more open to new ideas?

I said as much to Alyssa when Maya had gone. She looked surprised.

'Is *that* what you think? If so, you're wrong. My grandfather isn't the problem. *He* doesn't think we need to live in the Middle Ages. *He* doesn't tell me what to do, or what to wear, or who to be friends with. *He* doesn't go crazy if I talk to a boy from the other side of the river—'

She broke off abruptly, looking away.

'Is that what your father does?' I said.

She gave that characteristic half-shrug so common to adolescent girls. 'I dunno.'

I said nothing more. Already, this was progress. Instead I turned my attention back to the copper of peach jam, releasing its autumnal scent. Peach is perhaps the most perfect fruit for making jam:

177

sweet, yet firm; the golden flesh turning to a darker burnt-orange with cooking. My method allows the pieces of fruit to stay intact during the process, while retaining all the flavour. Today, we will leave the sugar and peach mixture to steep under a sheet of muslin; tomorrow, we will cook it, then ladle it into clean glass jars to put away for the winter.

There's something very comforting about the ritual of jam-making. It speaks of cellars filled with preserves; of neat rows of jars on pantry shelves. It speaks of winter mornings and bowls of *chocolat au lait*, with thick slices of good fresh bread and last year's peach jam, like a promise of sunshine at the darkest point of the year. It speaks of four stone walls, a roof, and of seasons that turn in the same place, in the same way, year after year, with sweet familiarity. It is the taste of home.

'There.' I covered the pan with the muslin sheet. 'Tomorrow we'll put it into jars.'

Alyssa nodded. 'OK.'

I knew better than to try to resume our earlier confidences straight away. Maya's interruption had broken the connection I'd made. But there *was* a connection; and I am sure that, with time, I can make it again. For now, we have guests to prepare for; a menu to plan, baking to do. Whatever Alyssa's secret may be—

Like the peaches, it will keep.

CHAPTER NINE

Sunday, 22nd August

Père Henri Lemaître is busy today. Morning Mass in Lansquenet, then Florient, Chancy and Pont-le-Saôul. With Lansquenet added to his list of parishes, he has cut down on weekday services in some of the smaller communities, but Sunday Mass is still a priority everywhere along the Tannes. Standing here on the bridge now, I can hear the bells from their steeples borne to me on the Autan wind—Saint-Jérôme's double carillon, the twin bells of Florient's Sainte-Anne, the cracked and characteristic sound of Chancy's little chapel bell. With so much activity in the air, it seems wrong for me to be idle; more so to be here without my soutane, looking like a tourist.

And yet I will not hide, *mon père*. Let the flock think what they please. Walking to church in their Sunday suits, hats crammed down against the wind, the women in their high-heeled shoes on the uncertain cobbles, they look at the same time a little shamefaced and oddly triumphant; unruly sheep who know that the dog has a thorn in his paw. I know what they're thinking. *Reynaud has earnt his comeuppance. Serves him right for thinking that he could be above the law.*

It is only a matter of time now till word comes from the Bishop. Perhaps he will send Père Henri Lemaître with the news of my relocation—perhaps to another village where my reputation is intact; perhaps to an inner-city parish in Marseille or Toulouse, to teach me the value of community relations and interracial *entente cordiale*. In any case, Père Henri insists, this is *not* a punishment. It is merely the Church's way of deploying its human resources where they are most needed. It is not up to the priest to decide where and how he will be deployed. A good priest should have the humility to make whatever sacrifice the Church demands; to look into his soul and uproot the weeds of selfishness and pride. And yet, *mon père*, you understand, I've lived in Lansquenet all my life. This is where I belong; this place, with its cobbled streets and crooked rows of houses. This countryside, with its marquetry of little fields and strip-farms. This scouring wind; this river; this sky. This wholly unremarkable place—except to those who call it home.

I told Père Henri the other day, *a priest has no friends*. In good times, he has followers; in bad times, only enemies. Set apart by his calling, his vows, he has to be more than human; every day walking the tightrope of faith, knowing that if he falters, those who applauded yesterday will turn upon him in a pack today, wallowing in his disgrace, overjoyed to see him brought low.

The sheep are almost ready to turn. Few people greet me this morning. Guillaume Duplessis was one of them, and so was Henriette Moisson; but Charles Lévy looked furtive, and Jean Poitou, of whom I'd thought better, pretended to be talking to Simon Cussonet when he passed by on the way to church. Everyone ignores me in his or her particular way. Louis Acheron is contemptuous;

180

Joline Drou regretful, but firm. Georges Clairmont is sheepish and guilty; Caro sweetly triumphant.

Everyone knows he did it, of course. They'll never manage to prove it, but—

Do you really think he'll go?

Oh, yes. It's only a matter of time. He's always been so difficult. Do you remember, when Vianne Rocher—

Shh! Be quiet! Here he comes.

They file past the bridge towards the church, faces lowered into the wind. The weather is turning again; the sky has veered from blue to mackerel-grey. I hear their voices, carried downwind, echoing the sound of the bells:

He looks so different without his soutane.

What's he doing, staring like that?

The Autan must have driven him mad.

Well, Caro, perhaps it has. But at last I feel very empty—as if my head were full of seeds that the wind has blown away. I thought I was necessary to this place; that, whatever else happened, Lansquenet would always be my kingdom, my parish, my refuge, my home. People called me *Father*. And now—

'*Mon père?*' A voice at my shoulder. 'Can I offer you a drink?'

Joséphine doesn't go to church. I've always known the reason. She, unlike Caro Clairmont, has never made a secret of her dislike of me, which makes it all the more perverse of her now, when most of the village shares her opinion, that she should choose to seek me out and offer hospitality.

Maybe she feels sorry for me. Wonderful. That's all I need. To be pitied by Joséphine Bonnet, to be taken home like a stray dog—

181

I turned and saw her smiling. 'I thought you could use a coffee.'

'Do I look so terrible?'

She shrugged. 'I've seen you look better. Listen, I've baked an apple tart. Perhaps you'd like to try a slice? On the house?'

I gritted my teeth. All the same, I knew she meant well. She has no reason to like me, or to offer me sympathy, and yet she offers it openly, in defiance of Caro and her poisonous toadies. Of all those I have offended here, I'd thought Joséphine the least likely to show me any compassion, and I found myself unexpectedly moved.

'You're very kind.'

I followed her home. Not *quite* like a dog, perhaps, but feeling almost as humble. *The Bishop would have approved*, I thought. But Vianne Rocher would have laughed at the joke.

She served the tart with whipped cream, the coffee with a splash of cognac. With her round face and cropped blonde hair she looks nothing like Vianne Rocher, and yet she has something of her style. That way of waiting quietly; of smiling with her eyes. I ate. I was hungrier than I'd expected. Over the course of the past few days I thought I had lost my appetite.

'I'm supposed to be having dinner with Vianne,' she said. 'I hoped maybe you'd come along, too.'

I shook my head. 'I don't think so, thanks.'

'I'd be so happy if you would.'

I looked at her suspiciously. Was this a trick to humiliate me? She did not seem to be making fun. Instead I thought she looked concerned; hands moving restlessly in her lap as they had in the days before Vianne Rocher. In those days, Joséphine

Muscat was as much of an outcast as I am now; a sad, inarticulate woman whose kleptomaniac tendencies she confessed to me every week, just as Paul-Marie confessed his regular abuse of her.

Perhaps that's why she hated me. Because I knew her secret. Because I was the only one who knew her husband beat her, and allowed him to pay for it in *Avés* instead of intervening. Since then, she has not been to church. God did not protect her. More importantly, neither did I—bound hand and foot by my vows and the secret of the confessional.

And yet, today, the old Joséphine was back—or at least, the ghost of her. These days, she looks so self-assured that no one but I can see the truth; the perpetual crease between her eyes; the way she looks to the left when she speaks to me, like a child telling a lie. *There's something on her mind*, I thought; something she would like to confess. Something to do with Vianne Rocher—

'Listen, Joséphine,' I said. 'I appreciate the gesture, but I really don't need to be rescued. Not by Vianne, and not by you. I can look after myself.'

She blinked. 'You think *that*'s why I invited you?'

No doubt about it; she was sincere. Something was troubling Joséphine which had nothing to do with me, or my current predicament.

'Is there something wrong?' I said. 'Have you quarrelled with Vianne?'

'Oh, *no*! She's my dearest friend—'

'Then what is it?' I asked her, more gently than I might have done with someone like Caro Clairmont. 'Why don't you want to see her?'

I'll admit, this was a long shot. But Joséphine flinched, and I knew I'd hit home.

'It's not that I don't want to see her,' she said.

183

'But—people change.' She gave a sigh. 'I don't want to disappoint her.'

'Why do you think you would?' I said.

'We had so many plans, she and I. She did so much to help me. I owed her everything, and then—' She raised her eyes to mine again. '*Curé*, I need a favour,' she said.

'Anything,' I told her.

'It's been eight years since I last went to church. Somehow it didn't feel right any more. But now you're here, I wonder if—you could take my confession?'

That came as a surprise. I faltered. 'Surely, Père Henri would be—'

'Père Henri doesn't know me,' she said. 'He doesn't care about any of us. We're just another village to him, another step up the ladder to Rome. You've been here for ever, *mon père*.'

'Not quite for ever,' I told her drily.

'But will you do it?'

'Why me?' I said.

'Because you understand, of course. Because you know how shame feels.'

In silence, I finished my *café-cognac*. She's right, of course. I know it well. That Scylla to the Charybdis of pride, it has been my companion for many years. Its voice is always in my heart, reminding me of my failings, while pride stands by with a flaming sword, barring my way to forgiveness.

Two words. *Forgive me*. That's all it takes. And yet, I have never spoken them. Not in the confessional, not to a relative, not to a friend. Not even to the Almighty Himself—

'Will you, *mon père*?'

'Of course I will.'

CHAPTER TEN

☾

Sunday, 22nd August

Maya came back this morning to help Alyssa finish the jam. She and Rosette spent a messy half-hour labelling the glass jars and decorating the labels—Rosette with her favourite drawings of rabbits, monkeys and flying snakes; Maya with less practised but all the more exuberant pictures of various kinds of fruit, including pineapples, strawberries and, improbably, coconuts (these are for Omi, she explains), with the word PEECH (or sometimes CHEEP) in capitals on every one.

At five, making friends is easy. It begins with a shy kind of circling, like two little curious animals. Language is no barrier; culture and colour, irrelevant. Rosette puts out a hand to touch the golden bangle around Maya's wrist; Maya is equally fascinated by Rosette's red, curly hair. Five minutes later, they are at ease; Rosette signing and chattering in her private language, Maya, who seems to understand, watching her with round, bright eyes.

I noticed that Bam, always curious, had moved in to inspect the newcomer. I can see him quite clearly today, like something glimpsed against the sun. Long tail, whiskery face, eyes alight with intelligence. Maya sees him too, I think; but of

185

course, she's only five.

After they'd finished the labels, the two of them went out to play while Anouk went off to meet Jeannot Drou, leaving Alyssa and me to complete the task of filling the jars. Alyssa was silent this morning, her face bland and expressionless, and when I tried to draw her out I found her unresponsive.

Perhaps it's the prospect of Joséphine coming for dinner tonight. Alyssa's presence in the house makes entertaining difficult, but to cancel at short notice might attract too much attention. Alyssa can always hide in her room—besides, I have my own reasons for wanting to talk to Joséphine.

'She has a son,' I said. 'Eight years old, and she never told me.'

Alyssa was using a wet rag to wipe the jars as I sealed them. Each one topped with a cellophane square, fastened with an elastic band, like a string of paper lanterns filled with a mellow golden light. The smell of hot sugar and cinnamon was like a caress over everything.

'Who?' said Alyssa.

I realized I had spoken my thought aloud. 'My friend,' I told her. 'Joséphine.'

My friend. In their way, the words are almost as unfamiliar as *home*. Friends are the ones we leave behind, so my mother taught me; even now, I invoke the word with a kind of reluctance, as if it were a genie that, once released, might be dangerous.

'What happened?' said Alyssa.

'She reinvented herself,' I said.

Well, yes. I suppose that's what it was. Joséphine reinvented herself. How could she not, after all? I

186

am myself a mistress of reinvention. I taught her my technique. And now, for the first time, I understand why my mother never looked back; why she never revisited the places she and I once loved.

'The trouble with people is, they change. Sometimes beyond recognition.'

'Is this what happened with your friend?'

I shrugged. 'Maybe it was,' I said.

The copper pot was empty. Together, we'd filled every jar in the house. I cook when I am restless; I like the simple recipes; the preparing of ingredients; the knowledge that if I follow the rules the dish will never disappoint. If only people were like this. If only the heart was as simple.

'What did she do?' said Alyssa, looking into the copper pot. She ran her finger along the rim as if to lick it; then hesitated. 'I mean, to reinvent herself? What did she do?'

Good question, I thought. When I called the other day, she seemed so glad to see me. And yet, I've been here over a week—

'It's hard to explain,' I told her. 'There are so many things that have stayed the same. She looks a little different—she's cut her hair and dyed it blonde—but underneath she's still Joséphine, impulsive and warm-hearted and sometimes a little crazy, but there's something about her that's different somehow—'

'Maybe she has something to hide.'

I looked at her inquiringly.

'Sometimes, when you feel that way, you just can't face being with your friends. It's not that you don't want to see them, but you know you can't talk to them, either.' She put her finger into her mouth and sucked it. '*There*. I broke my fast. What would

187

my mother say if she knew?'

'I'm sure your mother wouldn't care. They all just want to know you're safe.'

Fiercely, Alyssa shook her head. 'You don't know my mother. People think my father's the tough one, but that isn't true. My mother would rather see me dead than have me bring shame into the family.'

I said, 'I'm assuming this isn't about you licking a jam pot before the sun sets.'

Alyssa gave a reluctant smile. 'I suppose you think that's stupid.'

I shook my head. 'No, not at all.'

'But you don't believe in religion.'

'You're wrong. I believe in lots of things.'

'You know what I mean—'

'Of course I do.' I made her sit down at the table. Between us, the rows of jam jars shone like Chinese lanterns. 'I've met a lot of believers, one way or another. Some of them were honest and good; others used their religion as an excuse to hate other people, or to impose their own rules—'

Alyssa sighed. 'I know what you mean. My mother's obsessed with little things. But she never wants to hear about the things that are really *important*. It's always *don't sleep on your stomach*, or *don't wear make-up*, or *don't talk to boys*, or *don't wear that, don't eat that, don't say that, don't go there*. My grandfather says Allah doesn't care what you eat or what you wear as long as your heart's in the right place and as long as we care for each other.'

'I like your grandfather,' I said.

'Me too,' said Alyssa. 'But since he and my father fell out, I don't see him much any more.'

'Why did they fall out?' I said.

188

'My grandfather doesn't like *niqab*. He said the girls shouldn't be wearing it in school. He doesn't like Sonia wearing it. She never used to wear it before.'

'So why does she wear it now?'

She shrugged. 'Maybe she's like your friend,' she said. 'Maybe she has something to hide.'

I thought about what Alyssa had said as she and I prepared for tonight. The pancakes would be easy, but the batter, made to an old recipe, with buckwheat flour and cider instead of milk, needed to rest for a couple of hours. Eat them on their own, or with salted butter, or sausages, or with goat's cheese, onion marmalade, or duck *confit* with peaches. I remembered making them for Roux and the river-gypsies, the night their boats were set on fire. I remember it so well; the column of sparks from the bonfire leaping up like a firecrake; Anouk, dancing with Pantoufle and Roux—Roux as he was then, laughing, telling jokes, long hair tied back with a piece of twine; barefoot on the jetty.

Joséphine wasn't there, of course. Poor Joséphine, in the tartan coat she wore whatever the weather; hair designed to hide her face and the bruises that so often settled there; poor, suspicious Joséphine, who trusted no one, least of all the river-gypsies, who did as they liked, and travelled all over the river, reinventing themselves as they pleased wherever they moored their houseboats. Later, when she had escaped from Paul-Marie and his abuse, she began to understand the price of that freedom; Roux's boat, gutted and burnt; his friends moving on without him; the hatred of our village folk for those who abide by their own rules, see stars more often than streetlights, who do not pay taxes, or go to church, or fit into the community. An outcast herself, she warmed to that. Childless, he brought out the mother in her. I thought they could be more than friends, and yet—

You wanted him yourself. Where's the harm in that, Vianne?

The voice is not that of my mother this time, or even of Armande Voizin. It's the voice of Zozie de l'Alba, who sometimes still reappears in my dreams. Zozie de l'Alba, who saved my life because she wanted it for herself; Zozie, the free spirit, the stealer of hearts; and her voice is harder for me to ignore than all my other whisperers.

You wanted him. You took him, Vianne. Joséphine didn't stand a chance.

Because Zozie, for all her guile, traded more in truths than lies. She showed us reflections of ourselves; showed our secret faces. There's darkness in everyone, I know that; I've fought against it all my life. But until Zozie, I'd never known how much darkness I carried inside; how much selfishness and fear.

The Queen of Cups. The Knight of Cups. The Seven of Swords. The Seven of Disks. My mother's cards; their dreamy scent; their faces, so familiar.

Is Joséphine the faded Queen? *Should* Roux have been her Knight? And am I the Moon, unstable, two-faced, spinning her web between them?

At three o'clock in the afternoon, Anouk and Rosette came home, with Pilou, all laughing and breathless from the wind.

'Pilou has a kite,' said Anouk, while Rosette echoed her words exuberantly, in sign language. 'We flew it downriver, the three of us and that

190

crazy dog. Honestly, what a mutt. At one point he actually *jumped* into the river, trying to grab hold of the kite's tail, and we all ended up having to drag him out, which is why Rosette has weed in her hair and everyone else smells of wet dog.'

'That isn't fair,' protested Pilou. 'Vlad is *not* a mutt. He is a highly intelligent, highly trained Kite Retriever, descended from the fabled Fishing Dogs of ancient China.'

'*Dog fish,*' said Rosette. '*Fish dog. Kite fish.*' And she did a little dance with Bam around the kitchen.

Alyssa had fled upstairs again as soon as she heard the dog barking.

Anouk said: 'It's all right. It's only Vlad. You can come out. He won't bite you.'

For a moment, I was sure Alyssa wouldn't come downstairs. But finally curiosity overcame her shyness. She came to sit on the landing, looking down through the banisters. Pilou shot her a passing glance, but seemed more interested in the basin of pancake batter on top of the stove.

'Is that for tonight?' he said.

'That's right. Do you like pancakes?'

Pilou nodded vigorously. 'Cooked outside, on an open fire, like the river people used to make. With sausages and cider, of course.'

'Did you see much of the river people? I thought they'd stopped coming here,' I said.

'They did, when I was little,' he said. 'Too much trouble in Les Marauds. I guess my father went with them.' He shrugged and went back to his investigation of what was cooking in the oven.

Once more, I thought of the Queen of Cups. I searched for Roux in Pilou's face, but saw nothing I recognized. Curly hair, bleached by the

191

sun; round face; snub nose. An air of Joséphine, perhaps, in the eyes, but nothing of Roux—and yet, like Rosette, he loves to paint.

I remembered the abstract painting in the bar at Joséphine's, and the look in her eyes when she spoke of Pilou's father. Except that she *hadn't* spoken of him, I remembered suddenly; she had simply said that Pilou was hers, and no one else's. It's what I used to say myself when people asked about Anouk's father; and yet, to hear it from Joséphine troubles me—more, perhaps, than it should.

'When's your birthday?'

He looked surprised. 'The seventeenth of December. Why?'

Rosette's is the twentieth of December. So close. So very close. But what would it matter anyway, if what I suspect turned out to be true? Roux doesn't care that Anouk is not his. Why should *this* be different? And yet, the thought that Roux might have known, might have hidden that knowledge for eight years—four of which he'd spent right here in Lansquenet, working on farms and on his boat, renting a room from Joséphine—

The Knight of Cups has something to hide. His face is marbled with shadows. The Queen holds her cup too languidly, as if it contains something that sickens her. The children have gone upstairs, with Vlad. They are surprisingly silent. I leave them to their game and go out with my phone into Les Marauds.

Once more, there is no message from Roux. His phone is turned off. I write:

Roux, please get in touch! I need—

Of course, I didn't send it. I've never *needed*

192

anyone. If Roux wants to get in touch, he will. Besides, what would I say to him? I have to see him face to face. I have to read his colours.

The weather is turning. I felt it before, talking with Omi in Les Marauds. The wind is as strong as ever, but now the angel-faced clouds have dirty feet. A drop of rain falls on to my face as I reach the top of the hill—

The Black Autan is on its way.

The BLACK AUTAN

CHAPTER ONE

Monday, 23rd August

Well, of course I can't tell you what she said. Confession—be it official or not—is a secret that cannot be betrayed. But she was pale as the Host when she finished her story, and nothing I could say seemed to give her comfort.

'I don't know what to tell her,' she said. 'She was so proud of what I'd become. The world was opening up for me. I was ready to spread my wings. And now, I'm just like everyone else. Living in the same place, running my café, getting old—'

I said I didn't think she looked old. She shot me an impatient glance.

'All the things I hoped to do. All the places I hoped to see. She reminds me of all that, she did it *all*, and it makes me feel—' She clenched her fists. 'Oh, what's the *use*? Some people spend the whole of their lives sitting waiting for one train, only to find that they never even made it to the station.'

'You did your duty,' I told her.

She made a face. 'My *duty*.'

'Well, yes. Some of us have to do that,' I said. 'We can't all be like Vianne Rocher, moving from place to place all the time, never belonging anywhere, never taking responsibility.'

She looked surprised. 'You disapprove.'

'I didn't say that,' I told her. 'But anyone can run away. It takes something more to stay in one place.'

'Is that what *you*'re going to do?' she said. 'Will you defy the Church, and stay?'

I pointed out, rather tartly, that this was supposed to be her confession, not mine.

She smiled. 'Do *you* ever confess, Monsieur le Curé?'

'Of course,' I lied. Well, not *quite* a lie. After all, I confess to *you*. 'We all need someone to talk to,' I said.

She smiled again. She smiles with her eyes. 'You know, you're easier to talk to when you're not in your soutane.'

Am I? I find it harder, somehow. The uniform of office makes everything so simple for me. Without it, I feel anchorless, a single voice in the multitude. Does anyone really care what I say? Is anyone even listening?

*　　　*　　　*

We found Vianne in the garden, trying to light the barbecue. She was wearing jeans and a sleeveless blouse, her long hair tied with a yellow scarf. She had managed to find a relatively sheltered place out of the wind, but the air was sultry with unshed rain, and the little paper lanterns that she had hung around the garden had mostly blown out.

She greeted Joséphine with a kiss, and smiled at me. 'I'm glad you've come. You'll stay for dinner, won't you?'

'No, no. I only came to—'

'Don't give me that. You'll be telling me you're too busy with your parish duties next.'

I had to admit that I was not.

'Then eat with us, for heaven's sake. Or don't

you *have* to eat?'

I smiled. 'You're very kind, Mademoiselle Ro—'

She punched me on the arm. *'Vianne!'*

Joséphine said: 'I'm sorry, Monsieur le Curé. If I'd known she was going to be violent, I wouldn't have brought you along.'

Vianne laughed. 'Come in and have a glass of wine. The children are inside.'

I followed both of them into the house. I found myself feeling both puzzlement and something else, something I could not identify. But it was good to sit by the stove in Armande's old kitchen, a kitchen that now seemed more than usually crowded, due to the presence of four children and an unruly dog, playing some kind of boisterous game around the kitchen table.

The game, which seemed to involve a great deal of shouting, some coloured crayons, barking from the dog, pieces of drawing paper and lots of exuberant miming from Rosette, was enough to disguise my entrance for a few minutes, and gave me time to recognize Alyssa Mahjoubi among them—Alyssa Mahjoubi changed almost beyond my recognition; in Western dress—a blue shirt and jeans—her hair cut into a lopsided bob at the level of her jaw. Most striking of all, she was laughing—her small, vivid face lit up with the excitement of the game, all memory of her escapade apparently gone from her thoughts.

I was sharply reminded of the fact that, at seventeen, Alyssa is still very much a child—even though, at much the same age, her sister was already married. At seventeen, balanced on that precarious walkway between adolescence and adulthood, the world is a crazy obstacle course;

paved one day with broken glass, the next with apple blossom. Close enough to touch Eden, yet all we want is to leave it behind. I caught Vianne's expression and wondered if she too was thinking the same thing. Her daughter is only fifteen, and yet there is a wildness in her eyes, a promise of roads to be travelled, of sights to be seen. What was it Joséphine said? *Some people spend the whole of their lives sitting waiting for one train, only to find that they never even made it to the station.* Anouk is at the station. I sense that any train will do.

She turned, as if she had read my thought. 'Monsieur le Curé!'

Everyone turned. For a moment Alyssa looked startled, then a little defiant.

I said: 'I haven't told anyone. And I won't, unless you want me to.'

She looked away with a shy smile. It is a characteristic gesture that she shares with her sister; a dipping motion of the chin, a turn of the head slightly to the left, a lowering of the eyelashes, now echoed by the gentle sweep of the newly bobbed hair across her face. She is extraordinarily beautiful, in spite of—perhaps because of—her youth. It makes me slightly uneasy, as feminine beauty so often does. As a priest, I am not meant to notice. And yet, as a man, I always do.

'I'm reinventing myself,' she said. 'I let Anouk and Rosette cut my hair.'

Anouk grinned. 'It's a bit shorter on one side,' she said. 'But I still think it looks pretty cool. What do you think?'

I said I was no judge. But Joséphine embraced her and said: 'You look adorable.'

Alyssa smiled. 'You did it, too. You reinvented

199

yourself,' she said.

A shadow flickered across Joséphine's face. 'I did? Who told you that?'

'Vianne.'

Once more, that look; like a cat's paw of wind on the surface of the Tannes. 'I suppose you could say that,' she said. 'Now, what about those pancakes?'

The cry from the children that greeted this was enough to mask the awkwardness, at least from Alyssa, although I thought Vianne might have sensed something, somehow. She has a curious affinity with secrets unspoken, stories untold. Her eyes, which are dark as espresso, can sift the shadows of the human heart.

I looked around the living room. Something has changed here since Vianne arrived, which I cannot identify. Is it the light from the candles that stand on every surface, or the little red sachets for good luck that hang from the frame of every door? Could it be the incense that burns—the creamy scent of sandalwood—or the smell of scorching leaves from outside, or the pancakes fried in butter, or the spiced sausages on the barbecue?

'I hope you're hungry,' said Vianne Rocher.

Unexpectedly, I was. There was rain in the wind, and so we stayed indoors for the meal, though Vianne cooked most of it outside, where the smoke would blow away cleanly.

There were pancakes, of course; and sausages; and duck *confit* and goose-liver terrine; and sweet pink onions, fried mushrooms with herbs, and little *tomme* cheeses rolled in ash; and *pastis gascon*, and nut bread, aniseed bread, *fouace*, olives, chillies and dates. To drink, there was cider and wine and *floc*, with fruit juices for the children and even a dish of leftovers for the dog, which later curled up by the fire and slept, occasionally twitching its tail and muttering vague obscenities between its teeth.

Outside, the Autan wind gained strength, and we began to hear the rain smacking against the window glass. Vianne threw more logs on to the fire; Joséphine wedged the door closed and Anouk began to sing a song I'd heard a long, long time ago, a sad old song about the wind and how it always takes its due:

V'là l'bon vent, v'là l'joli vent—

She has a sweet, untrained little voice; and seems surprisingly ready to sing, without a trace of self-consciousness. Rosette joined in with her usual zest, and Pilou accompanied them both by drumming on the table-top with more enthusiasm than skill.

'Come on, Alyssa,' said Anouk. 'Join in with the chorus.'

Alyssa looked awkward. 'I can't sing.'

'Neither can I,' said Anouk. 'Come *on!*'

'I mean, I *can't*. I don't know how.'

'Everyone can sing,' said Anouk. 'Just like everyone can dance.'

'Not in our house, they can't,' she said. 'Well, at least, not any more. I used to sing when I was small. Sonia and I both used to do that. We used to sing along and dance to music on the radio. Even my grandfather did, before—' She lowered her voice. 'Before *she* came.'

'You mean Inès Bencharki?' said Vianne.

Alyssa nodded.

That woman again. 'Her brother is very protective,' I said.

'He's not her *brother*,' Alyssa said. There was a world of scorn in her voice.

I looked at her. 'Who is she, then?'

She shrugged. 'No one really knows. Some people say she was his wife. Some say she's his mistress. Whatever it is, she still has some kind of hold over him. Before the fire, he used to go to her house all the time.'

I looked at Vianne. 'Did you know this?'

'It had crossed my mind.'

I drank some wine. 'How is it,' I said, 'that you get to know more about this village in a week than I've managed to do in years?'

I must have sounded resentful. Perhaps I was; it's my job to know what happens in my parish. People come to *me* to confess—and yet, in that chocolate shop of hers, Vianne Rocher heard more than I ever did. Even the *Maghrébins* talk to her. In eight years, nothing has changed.

I drank more wine. 'That woman,' I said. 'I *knew* she was hiding something. Looks so pious under that veil, behaves as if every man in the world wants nothing more than to rape her on sight, looks down her nose at everyone, and all the time—'

'You don't *know* that.'

'If even her people think so—' I said.

'It's still only rumour,' said Vianne Rocher.

I supposed she was right. Damn her, *mon père*, why does she so often have to be *right*?

'What about the child?' I said.

'Du'a,' said Alyssa. 'She's a lovely little girl. She's never known her father. She says he died when she was a child—I think she really believes it. Karim doesn't seem to care about her. He doesn't even talk to her. Aisha Bouzana says *she* heard that

202

Inès isn't her mother, that she stole Du'a as a baby because she couldn't have children herself.' Alyssa lowered her voice and went on: 'I've even heard some people say that Inès isn't a woman at all, but some kind of Jinn, an *aamar* who whispers *waswaas* into children's minds and delivers them to Shaitan.'

This was a very long speech from a girl I'd hardly ever heard speak more than a few words at a time. Perhaps the presence of her friends; the absence of supervision. I noticed she hadn't eaten much— just a pancake and some fruit—and, of course, no wine at all. Even so, her face was flushed, and she sounded almost intoxicated.

'You don't really believe that,' I said.

She shrugged. 'I don't know what I believe. Omi al-Djerba says there are *amaar* everywhere. They live among us. They even look like we do. But inside they are not human, and all they want is to hurt us.'

'I know exactly what you mean,' said Anouk, leaning forward. 'She called herself Zozie de l'Alba, and she pretended to be our friend, but really she wasn't a person at all, just something without a shadow—'

'That's enough, Anouk,' said Vianne. She put a hand on Alyssa's arm. 'If people are so suspicious of Inès, then why do they send their children to her?'

Alyssa shrugged. 'They weren't, at first. And everyone loves Karim, of course.'

I made a face.

'You don't?' said Vianne.

Alyssa looked away. 'No.' Even in the firelight, I thought her face looked flushed. I saw Vianne watching her curiously, but she did not pursue the

203

topic, shifting instead to another one so deftly that only I noticed. We spent the rest of the evening discussing unrelated matters, and so pleasantly that I was surprised when I looked at my watch and saw that it was already past midnight.

I glanced at Joséphine and said: 'I've stayed too long. I have to go.'

'Pilou and I will walk with you.'

Outside, the wind was still strong, scented with the river and peppered with fat, stinging droplets of rain, like wasps in the slipstream of summer. Pilou was holding his dog's leash, and Vlad hurled abuse at the racing sky and tried to chase the fallen leaves along the path to the river. Les Marauds was still wide awake; there were lights in every window, and strands of coloured fairy lights were strung across the narrow streets, tumbling like fireflies in the wind.

Saïd's gym was shut, of course. Still, I felt that sting of unease. There are places that can do that, *père*; where even bricks and mortar seem to echo with hostility. I walked Joséphine and her son back home to the Café des Marauds, then took the Rue des Francs Bourgeois towards my little cottage.

I did not hear them following me. All I could hear was the wind's steady roar, and beyond it, the roaring of the Tannes. Besides, I had drunk more wine than I am accustomed to, and I was feeling strangely disconnected. Above me, the sky raced from light to dark as clouds flashed across the big, bright moon, making the shadows leap like jacks across the walls and houses. I was tired, but not yet sleepy. Too many thoughts were in my head. Alyssa Mahjoubi; Vianne Rocher; Inès Bencharki; Joséphine—

Suddenly I became aware of movement behind me. A double shadow moving in; a hint of tobacco mixed with *kif*; two figures in the moonlight, their faces hidden behind chequered scarves—

The first blow hit me in the shoulder, and it took me entirely by surprise. There is no crime in Lansquenet. Most people leave their doors unlocked. The only violence we tend to see is the odd case of domestic abuse, and fist-fights between our local boys. There hasn't been a burglary in over ten years, or a mugging—

This was what went through my mind as I fell. The rest is somewhat blurry. I know I was struck a second time with something I guessed was a length of wood, and, as I dropped to my knees in the road, someone punched me in the face and said: 'Pig. You deserve all that's coming to you.'

What came was a volley of punches and kicks. I had no means of fighting back. I was already on the ground; all I could do was curl up and try my best to protect myself. Blows hammered into my ribs and back. My sense of disconnection grew; I could feel the pain, but a part of me seemed to be watching from somewhere else.

'Pig,' said the voice. 'This is a war. We warned you to keep out of it. If you interfere again, we'll make you wish you were never born.'

And then, with a last well-aimed kick to the thigh, where that long muscle, the *rectus femoris*, I think, can be made to spasm and cramp with such agonizing precision, my unknown attackers fled into the night, leaving me breathing the dust of the road and hearing the rush of blood in my ears louder than the roar of the wind.

I stayed where I was till the cramps had died

down, and I could move my legs again. I was muddy; my shirt was torn. My heart was a crazy cavalcade. I have never been in a fight, not even as a schoolboy. I had never been struck in anger before, or even suffered a bad fall.

They say you know instinctively if ever you have a broken bone. As it turns out I have several. Not that I knew it then, *père*; I was ablaze with adrenaline; if my legs had been working properly I would have had no hesitation in pursuing my assailants back to Les Marauds (where, if I had found them, they would in all probability have beaten me worse than before). As it was, my anger was analgesic enough in itself to delay the pain of two broken fingers, a cracked rib and, of course, my damaged nose, which in the light of day now looks all the more impressive for the bruising around my eyes.

Who were my assailants? I had no way of knowing. The scarves they wore might have belonged to any man in Les Marauds, and their voices had not been familiar. Why had I been targeted? There had been no attempt at robbery. Was this revenge for the fire at the school? It seemed the likeliest reason. But who had set them up to it? And what did they mean by *This is a war*?

Carefully, I picked myself up, the adrenaline buzzing uselessly in my veins. The rain was falling steadily, and now, at last, I was starting to hurt. My house was only down the road, and yet the walk seemed endless.

A shaggy dog ran across my path, then stopped and came over to sniff at my hand. I recognized Pilou's dog.

'Go home.'

The dog wagged its tail and began to follow me.

'Vlad, go home.'

The animal ignored me. Arriving at my front door, I found it once more at my heels, wagging its tail and panting.

'Go home,' I repeated, more sternly. 'You are mistaking me for that *other* Francis, the one who likes animals.'

The dog looked at me and barked.

I cursed softly under my breath. By rights I ought to take the dog home. But it was late; it was raining; the dog's barking would wake the neighbours, and besides, I didn't want Joséphine and her son to see me in my current state.

'All right, you can come in,' I said. 'But you sleep in the kitchen. And no barking!'

The dog, who seemed to have understood every word, promptly followed me up to my room. I was too tired to argue. I left my discarded clothes on the floor and fell into bed immediately; and when I awoke too early, in pain, I found the dog sprawled across my bed. I know I should have objected, *mon père*; but secretly I was weak enough to feel a kind of gratitude for the presence of another being, and I patted the dog on the head before falling once more into fitful sleep, lulled by the roaring of the wind.

CHAPTER TWO

Monday, 23rd August

When I awoke I could barely move. My muscles had stiffened during the night, and every part of me was at war with every other part. A hot shower helped a little, but even so I was so stiff that it took me fifteen minutes to dress, and the fingers of my right hand were so painful and swollen that I could not even tie my shoelaces.

I made some coffee and fed the dog. There was very little to eat in the house. But after seeing my bruised face in the bathroom mirror, I thought it best to stay indoors—unless I wanted to give Caro and her coffee group the best piece of gossip they'd had in years.

The question of the dog remained. I did not want to set it free, so I phoned the café, hoping to get the answering machine.

Instead, Joséphine picked up. I explained about the dog and suggested she send Pilou to collect him.

'Why don't you come over for breakfast?' she said.

'I—no. I'm busy this morning,' I lied. I am not a very good liar, *père*.

She must have heard it in my voice, because she asked: 'Are you all right?'

'Of course.'

'You really don't sound it,' said Joséphine.

I gave an inward curse. 'Well—no. There was an incident. Last night, as I was coming home.'

'What kind of incident?'

I shook my head in exasperation. 'It was nothing. Forget it,' I said. 'Just send your son to collect his dog. I don't have time to bring it myself.'

I hung up, feeling agitated. I was unsure of why this was. Perhaps the approaching full moon, which so often inflames the susceptible. A priest gets to know these things, *mon père*. A full moon often brings trouble. Tempers flare as it reaches its peak; sensitivities increase. Lovers quarrel; neighbours fall out; ancient grudges are recalled. Tomorrow, Père Henri's confessional will be full of petty complaints. Surprisingly, the thought gives me a measure of amusement. This time, these things are not my concern. Leave them to Père Henri Lemaître. Perhaps then he will understand what he has to deal with here.

I had tethered the dog to the gate-post. There came a knock at my front door. Through the half-closed shutters, I was dismayed to see not only Pilou but also his mother on the step, collars drawn up against the rain. Joséphine was wearing wellington boots and a black raincoat that must once have belonged to Paul; Pilou, a parka several sizes too large for him.

Joséphine knocked again.

I opened the door a centimetre.

'The dog's outside!'

'Can I come in?'

'Ah—I'd rather you didn't,' I said.

'Just for a minute,' she said, and walked in. 'My God, Francis, what *happened* to you?'

I gave a hiss of exasperation. 'Didn't I tell you

not to do that?'

'What happened?' she repeated. Her face was suddenly very white. Behind her, on the doorstep, the boy looked up at me with open admiration.

'*Awesome!* Were you in a fight?'

'No.'

He looked disappointed. Joséphine turned to him and said: 'Pilou, I want you to take Vlad home. Tell Marie-Ange to mind the bar for me. Then bring me the first-aid kit from my room, the big one, with the red cross on the lid—'

'I really don't need help,' I said.

She made an inarticulate sound and threw her raincoat on to a chair. Underneath it, she was wearing a powder-blue sweater and a black skirt. Her short blonde hair was spiky with rain. She looked both concerned and furious.

'Francis Reynaud, if you don't tell me what happened *immediately*, I shall tell *all* my customers that you got into a fight in my bar and *I* had to knock some sense into you!'

'All right, all right.'

I told her. She listened in disbelief.

'You're saying this was about the fire?'

I shrugged. 'What else could it be about?'

'But *you* didn't burn down the girls' school.'

'I think many people would disagree.'

'Then they're idiots, all of them. Now just sit still and let me take a look at you.'

I spent the next half-hour in a state of profound embarrassment as Joséphine used her first-aid kit to see to my various injuries. The woman is impossible. There was nothing I could say or do to prevent her from interfering. Arnica cream, suture strips, tape around my fingers and ribs—

210

'Since when were you a qualified nurse—*ouch*!'

'Don't pull away,' she said. 'When I was married to Paul-Marie, I soon learnt all there is to know about black eyes and broken bones. Take off your shirt.'

'But, Joséphine—'

'I said, take off your shirt, Monsieur le Curé. Or would you rather I called Dr Cussonet and let him spread the news all over the village?'

I submitted, though with bad grace. When she had finally finished, she said: 'There. Isn't that better?'

I shrugged. 'I hurt all over.'

'Ingrate.' She smiled. (Did I mention she smiles with her eyes?)

'Thank you, Joséphine,' I said. 'I'm very grateful for your help. And I'd appreciate it if you didn't mention this to anyone else. I'm hardly in a strong position with the Bishop already, and if he hears about *this*, well—'

She looked at me. 'Your secret's safe. I'm good at keeping secrets.' And then, with a final, mischievous smile, she leant over and kissed me on the cheek, and was gone into the rain like a dream of summertime.

*   *   *

Bless me, Father, for I have sinned. Well, at least, I *would* have sinned, if I'd had the chance. Perhaps the stressful events of last night; perhaps the touch of her hands on my skin. It has been so long, *mon père*, since a woman touched me. It makes me ashamed to think of the times she hid her bruises as I do now; the sunglasses on cloudy days; the coats

211

that served as armour; the times she shut herself in her room with 'migraines' that lasted days at a time.

Is that why she helped me, *père*? Because she knows what it feels like to be a victim, to feel ashamed? I do not deserve her kindness. I knew Paul-Marie was violent, but as long as he came to confession what could I do? I could not intervene. Vianne Rocher did that. Vianne Rocher, who arrives with the wind and rings the changes for us all . . .

That wind. Why does it blow? Why does there have to be change, *mon père*? We were happy before—well, at least most of us were satisfied. Why do things have to be different?

The White Autan brings madness, they say; the Black Autan, chaos and despair. Not that I believe in those tales. But somehow the wind has changed again, and for the first time in my life, *père*, I can feel its dark appeal. Lansquenet has disowned me, from both sides of the river. The Church has disowned me, or at least is likely about to do so. This is when the voice of the wind is at its most seductive. The wind that travels light, the wind that goes wherever it wants to go . . .

212

CHAPTER THREE

☾

Tuesday, 24th August

Still more of this squalling, ratcheting rain. for two days it has barely stopped. It rattles down the guttering; shimmies down the windows; pixellates the air and keeps us prisoners indoors. The Black Autan is on the rampage like a gang of delinquents, tearing the leaves from the chestnut trees; turning umbrellas inside out; tugging on hats, wrecking coiffures; scrawling its crazy graffiti all along the river.

Anouk and Alyssa spend most of their time playing music and watching TV. Rosette has been drawing monkeys again, though today she has moved on to elephants. All three seem happy enough, even though they are penned indoors. *I* am the one who is restless, looking out of the window, watching the raindrops race down the glass and waiting—for what? I really don't know.

This afternoon, I went to find Joséphine. I wore Armande's old raincoat and a pair of rubber boots. But she wasn't at the Café des Marauds, and Marie-Ange told me she didn't know when she would be back again. Outside, the streets were sparse and sad. The sky was dark as November. Passing the church, I noticed that the door of the old *chocolaterie* was slightly off the catch, and was making a forlorn percussive sound, signals in forgotten code.

Bat-bat-bat. Bat-bat. Bat-bat.

It is not my house any more. I am not responsible. And yet, there are ghosts in that old house; ghosts that now jostle and cry for attention. Of course, I know how to banish ghosts. But these are the ghosts of myself and Anouk; of Roux, of Reynaud; of Joséphine. And Armande, my dear old friend; her apple-doll face creased into a thousand wrinkles; Armande perched on a bar-stool, her long black skirt hiked up to reveal the tail of a bright red petticoat; Armande drinking chocolate through a sugar straw; Armande reading poetry with Luc in Caro's absence.

I looked around. The square was clear. The plastic sheeting that covers the roof rippled against the scaffolding. Work has begun on restoring the place, but in this weather it cannot go on. The place would be empty, I told myself. Empty, but teeming with glamours and ghosts.

Bat-bat-bat. Like an eyelid. Like a wink from an open grave. *Come inside, Vianne*, it says. *We're all here. Your old friends. The Man in Black; your mother; your past. And the air is bitter like chocolate and sweet with regret, like incense. Try me. Taste me—*

I went inside.

Someone has tried to clean things up. The debris has been removed, the walls scrubbed down ready for repainting. If I look in a certain way, I can almost see those ghosts now, the woman and her six-year-old walking into the empty house; the carpet of grey dust; the look of sadness and neglect. It looks like that again now; and this time there is no one to part the shadows with a blast from a plastic trumpet; or to bang on a pot with a wooden

214

spoon and shout, *Evil spirits, get thee hence*.

Still, I can see how that could change. The walls painted yellow and stencilled in blue; a counter, maybe a couple of stools. The air smells of smoke, now stale and damp; but throw open the windows and doors, burn a bundle of sage and scrub the floorboards with a mixture of baking soda and lavender oil—

Evil spirits, get thee hence. Yes, I could do it so easily. A house reflects its occupants; and this one recognizes me. How easily it could take us back; how easily could the past be reclaimed.

Bat-bat.

The house is restless. It twitches and stirs. Floorboards creak; doors slam; broken windows whisper. And now, upstairs, on the second floor, from the crow's-nest where Anouk once had her room, the sound of footsteps on bare wood.

That was no ghost. I called: 'Who's there?'

There was a silence, and then a face appeared at the top of the ladder that led to Anouk's little attic room. A small brown face edged in black; dark eyes wide and anxious.

'Did I frighten you?' I said. 'I'm sorry, I didn't think there'd be anyone home. I used to live here, long ago, before you and your mother moved in. I used to run a chocolate shop. Maybe you've heard the story.'

The child did not move. Under the *hijab*, she looked about twelve.

'You must be Du'a,' I told her. 'I'm Vianne. Is your mother here?'

She shook her head.

'That used to be my daughter's room. Does it still have the little round window, like a porthole, in the roof? She used to look through it at night and pretend she was on a pirate ship.'

Du'a nodded cautiously. Behind her, a soft, scuffling noise. Maya's face appeared alongside hers, sweet as a chocolate button.

'It's Vianne!' said Maya. 'Come on up! We thought it was Du'a's *memti*.'

I looked at Du'a. 'May I?' I said.

Du'a still looked hesitant.

'It's all right,' said Maya. 'She knows how to keep a secret. She's been looking after Alyssa for *ages*, and she hasn't told anyone. Come on up, Vianne, and see!'

I climbed up the ladder through the trapdoor. It still smelt of smoke, but now I could see that the damage here was minimal. The room has not changed much since Anouk was here; a few shelves of books, a little bed, a desk with a computer, some toys, a couple of posters on the walls of singers that I did not recognize. And, sitting on cushions on the floor, three more children—Pilou among them—and a cardboard box from which came a series of scuffling, whining sounds.

'Why, hello, everyone,' I said. 'I wasn't expecting a party.'

Pilou grinned. 'Meet Du'a,' he said. 'Maya you already know, of course. And these two—' he made an inclusive gesture—'are Karine and François.' The two children looked at me cautiously. François, the elder, looked about twelve. Karine was maybe Maya's age. Both were in jeans and T-shirts. I guessed that they were siblings.

'What's going on up here?' I said.

'Desperate goings-on,' said Pilou. 'Piracy. *Contraband—*'

216

'Stop it, Pilou,' said Du'a. Her voice was soft, but authoritative. She looked at me. 'He sometimes gets carried away,' she said.

I looked inside the cardboard box. Two black-and-white puppies looked back. They must have been about five weeks old. Plump, snub-nosed and playful, they were climbing over each other in their eagerness to get out of the box, making happy snarling sounds.

'I see.' I picked up a puppy, which promptly bit my finger.

'It's OK. He does that,' said Pilou. 'I'm going to call him Biter.'

'Who do they belong to?' I said.

'No one. *Us*,' said Maya, at once.

'So *this* was your secret?' I smiled at her. 'I have to say, you've kept it well.' I saw that Du'a looked anxious, and said, 'Don't worry. It's safe with me.'

She gave me a look of suspicion. Under the black *hijab*, her face was small and sharp and angular. Her eyes were very striking, ringed with concentric circles of gold.

'Monsieur Acheron was going to drown them,' she said. 'François and Karine brought them here. That was just before the fire. Since then, we've been looking after them here. Luc knows, because he's been working here. But no one else does. Except you now.'

'They're so *cute*,' said Maya. 'And no one lives here any more, so no one cares whether the angels can get into the house or not.'

'Angels?' I said.

'It's in the Qur'an. My Omi says if there's a dog in the house, then the angels can't come in.'

'You mean the *cat* can't come in,' said Pilou.

217

'It's not a cat,' said Maya. 'It's *angels*.'

'You mentioned Monsieur Acheron.' I looked at François and Karine. 'Would that be Louis Acheron?'

François nodded. 'He's our dad. He'd have a fit if he knew we were here. He doesn't like *Maghrébins* any more than he likes puppies. Says if they want to live in France, they ought to live the way we do. Says they're dragging the country down into socio-economic collapse.'

I smiled. 'Then it's best you don't tell him,' I said. 'What about your mother, Du'a? Does she know where you are?'

Du'a shook her head. 'She thinks I'm babysitting Maya.'

'And *your* mother, Maya?'

'She thinks I'm at *hers*, of course.' Maya patted the puppy. 'I like coming here. It's nice. There are toys. I'm not supposed to have toys.'

'That's true,' said Pilou earnestly. 'Do you know that their religion says you can't have plushies, or Barbie dolls, or even action figures?'

'I have them at home,' Maya said. 'My Little Pony and Disney Princess. But here I'm not supposed to. *Memti* made me leave them behind. Except for this.' She pulled an object from under her arm. I recognized the same knitted toy that she had been holding when I last saw her; a porridge-coloured thing with ears, which might have been a rabbit. 'This is Tipo. He's my friend. My Omi made him for me.' She frowned. 'My Uncle Saïd says animal toys are *haram*. I heard him tell my *jiddo*.'

'Can you believe that?' said Pilou. 'I mean, why would God care about that kind of thing?'

I said: 'It's sometimes hard to understand why

218

other people believe what they do.'

'But—*plushies?*' said Pilou, in disbelief. 'And music—did you know that's a sin, too? And dancing, and wine, and sausages—'

'*Sausages?*' echoed François.

'Well, actually, most kinds of *charcuterie*,' corrected Pilou knowledgeably. 'But you *can* still eat Haribo. Or at least, the Muslim kind. Which tastes just the same as the regular sort, but you can only get it in special places, like in Bordeaux, at, like, ten Euros a bag or something.'

Pilou and the Lansquenet children exchanged awed looks at the thought of Muslim Haribo.

I turned towards Du'a. 'Where are you staying now?'

She shrugged. 'With my uncle and auntie,' she said.

'Karim and Sonia?'

She nodded.

'And do you like your new aunt?'

She made an odd little half-shrug. 'She's all right. She doesn't talk much. I liked Alyssa better.'

I noticed she used the past tense. 'Liked? You don't think she'll come home?'

Again, that little half-shrug. In fact, it is not so much a shrug as a kind of oscillation of the head and shoulders; a gesture as natural as thought; intricate as a dance movement.

I said: 'Why did Alyssa run away?'

She tilted her head. 'It was *zina*, my mother says.'

I wanted to ask what kind of a sin would cause a young girl to take her own life, but for a woman there is only one. *Zina*, a word that sounds almost as if it might be a name—perhaps a kind of flower, but one that blooms only to sicken, and must be

219

torn up before it spreads. My mother and I did not stay long in Tangier, but it was long enough for me to understand. A single mother and her child were objects of contempt and shame; even now they have few rights; twenty years ago, they had none. As Westerners, my mother and I were something of an exception. Few people actually *welcomed* us, but we were different enough—and respectful enough of their faith—to slip through the net of their judgement. But women who had abandoned *hayaa*—that complex word that means both *modesty* and *shame*—were given little sympathy. My mother knew several of these unmarried mothers, cast out from their families, unable either to work or to claim social security benefits for children born out of wedlock. She never got to know them well— the gulf that separated us was still too deep for that—but even so, I managed to gather scraps of information. One had been promised marriage by a man who left her when he discovered that she was pregnant. Another had been raped by a group of men who told her as they raped her that she was a whore, who deserved nothing else. My mother cried when she heard the tale—my mother didn't cry easily, but the girl was only nineteen, and when we met her was working long hours in a fish-canning factory, where she also slept. Her baby—a girl— had died soon after it was born. She had named her Rashillah. My mother never understood how a faith that claimed to teach forgiveness could become such a relentless wall of ice against the poorest and most vulnerable members of the community. We thought we'd seen prejudice in Rome, in Paris, in Berlin, in Prague, but that was nothing compared with Tangier, where disgraced women lined up outside the mosques to beg, while their virtuous sisters ignored them, eyes averted, faces veiled, modest and implacable.

That was the sin, my mother said, as we slipped through the hot, white streets in the sun, with the souks and the *muezzin* vying for attention under the clashing, pitiless sky. *That* was the sin, the averted gaze; that brief, dismissive gesture. We'd seen it so often before, she and I: in Paris, outside Notre-Dame; in Rome, at the gates of the Vatican. Even here in Lansquenet, in the eyes of people like Caro Clairmont, I've *always* recognized that look— that look of sanctified contempt adopted by the righteous.

'There are worse things than *zina*,' I said.

I thought Du'a looked slightly shocked.

'Does Alyssa have a boyfriend?'

Du'a nodded. 'She used to,' she said. 'She talked to him on the internet. But then her father took the computer away, and so I let her use mine instead. At least, I did until the fire.'

'Oh. I see.' An internet friend. Anouk does not have a computer. At home, she spends hours in the internet café on the Boulevard Saint-Michel, talking with her friends—or most often with Jean-Loup, who uses virtual media to compensate for his all-too-frequent trips to hospital. 'Is this someone she knows in real life? Someone from the village, perhaps?'

Once more, Du'a nodded. 'Maybe. I think so. She never said.'

'I see.' And suddenly I did. It explained everything. The football games in the village square; the coffee mornings with Caro Clairmont that had so suddenly come to an end; Caro's disillusionment with the Les Marauds community; the coolness that had arisen between the village and the Boulevard P'tit Baghdad.

In Caro's world, tolerance means reading the right kind of newspaper; occasionally eating couscous and calling oneself a liberal. It does not extend to allowing her son to fall in love with a *Maghrébine*. And as for Saïd Mahjoubi, to whom people look for spiritual guidance; a man who defines himself by his faith—

I left the children to their game. Children are strangely accepting. Even the Acheron children exist below the radar of parental prejudice. It doesn't take much to make them forget the differences between them. A cardboard box with puppies inside; a hiding-place in an abandoned house. If only the world were as simple for us. But we have the uncanny knack of focusing on *difference*; as if excluding others could make our sense of identity stronger. And yet, in all my travels, I have found that people are mostly the same everywhere. Under the veil, the beard, the soutane, it's always the same machinery. In spite of what my mother believed, there is no magic to what we do. We see because we look beyond the clutter of what others see. The colours of the human heart. The colours of the soul.

It was still raining as I came out. A hard, fat rain, that spackled the ground like firecrackers in the wind. And now I know what I have to do. I think I knew it from the start. From the day I first arrived and saw her standing in the sun, motionless, veiled to the eyes, watching the crowd like a basilisk.

I made a call from my mobile phone. Not to Roux, this time, but to Guy, who supplies my chocolates. This time, my order was modest, just a box or two of couverture chocolate and a few utensils. But as my mother always said, *on some days, only magic works*. It isn't a grand kind of magic, no; but it's all we have, and I need it now.

Then I headed back into the rain in search of Inès Bencharki.

CHAPTER FOUR

☾

Tuesday, 24th August

In Les marauds the streets were deserted. The Black Autan was out in force. The sky had acquired a sulphurous look, and against it the raindrops were almost black. The few birds that still braved the wind were tumbled like pages of newspaper along the barricade of trees that grow on the riverbank. The air smelt salty, although the sea is over two hours' drive away, and in spite of the rain and wind it was warm; a vaguely unpleasant, milky warmth, as if something were festering. And from every window, every pair of shutters, came that sensation of being watched; an all-too-familiar feeling, remembered from so many places along the road.

Here, people are wary of strangers, I know. Children are warned against us. The way we dress, our accent, even the kind of food we eat— everything marks us as different; potentially hostile; dangerous. I remember taking Anouk to school when we first arrived in Lansquenet; the way the mothers looked at us, taking in every difference. The brightly coloured clothes; the shop; the child; the absent wedding ring. Now, I almost belong here. Except in Les Marauds, of course, where every centimetre of space is crossed with invisible tripwires; every one a broken rule, an inadvertent transgression.

Still, there is one house, I know, where I am not a stranger. Perhaps because of the peaches; or perhaps because the al-Djerbas were here when Les Marauds was still part of Lansquenet, and not a population apart.

I made my way to the green door. At my feet, the drains were an orchestra and the gutters spouted exuberantly. My hair was plastered to my face; even through Armande's old raincoat, my shirt and jeans were wet. I knocked, and seemed to wait a long time before Fatima came to open the door. She was wearing a blue sequinned kaftan and a harried expression. On seeing me, her face assumed a look of concern.

'Vianne! Are you all right? You must be soaked—'

In seconds, I was in the house, sitting on cushions in front of the fire, while Yasmina ran to fetch towels and Zahra prepared some mint tea. Omi was in the living room, resting on a low couch, and from the kitchen came the smell of something cooking; coconut and cumin seeds and cardamom and rising dough—bread, I guessed, for that evening's *iftar*.

Omi gave me her turtle grin. 'You promised to bring me chocolates.'

I smiled. 'Of course. I'm awaiting supplies.'

'Well, hurry. I won't live for ever.'

'I'm sure you can hang on for a week.'

Omi laughed. 'I'll do my best. And what are you doing, Vianne Rocher, running about in the rain like this?'

I mentioned Inès Bencharki.

'*Khee.*' Omi snapped her toothless jaws. 'And why do you want to bother with *her*?'

I drank my tea. 'She's interesting.'

'Interesting, you call it? *Yar.* I say the woman is trouble.'

'Why?'

Omi shrugged. 'It's her nature. There's a story about a scorpion that wants to cross a river. She talks a water-buffalo into carrying her across on his back. Halfway across, she stings him. Dying, the buffalo says, "But why? If I die here, then you drown too." And the scorpion says, "I'm a scorpion. My friend, I thought you knew that."'

I smiled. I know the story. 'Are you saying Inès is a scorpion?'

'I'm saying some people would rather die than give up the chance to sting,' she said. 'Believe me, nothing good will come of befriending Inès Bencharki.'

'But *why*?'

'That's what the buffalo said.' Once more, Omi gave an impatient shrug. 'Some people can't be helped, Vianne. And sometimes people leave a trail behind them that poisons everyone who crosses it.'

Believe me, Omi, I know that trail. I've crossed it myself a few times. Some people leave poison in their wake, even where they try to do good. Sometimes I lie awake at night, wondering whether I am one of them. What has my gift ever *really* achieved? What have I given to the world? Sweet dreams and illusions; transient joys; promises by the

225

quarter-pound. But my path is littered with failures; with pain and disappointment. Even now, do I really believe that chocolate can change anything?

'Omi, I need to see her,' I said.

She looked at me. 'I suppose you do. Well, wait until your hair dries, at least. And drink some more of this mint tea.'

I did as she said. The tea was good, bright green and smelling of summer. As I sat there, a black cat walked in and draped itself, purring, across my lap.

'Hazrat likes you,' said Omi.

I stroked the cat. 'Is he yours?'

She smiled. 'A cat belongs to no one,' she said. 'He comes and goes, like the Black Autan. But Du'a gave him a name, and now he comes here every day because he knows there is food.' She pulled out a coconut macaroon from her pocket. 'Here, Hazi. Your favourite.'

She broke off a piece of the sweetmeat and held it out towards the cat. Hazi extended an elegant paw and snagged the piece of coconut before settling down to eat it with every sign of enjoyment.

Omi finished the macaroon. 'Hazrat Abu Hurairah was a famous *Sahabi*. He was known as "the kitten man" because he was very fond of cats. My little Du'a named this cat after him. She says he is a stray, but I think he simply prefers the food here.'

'Who wouldn't?' I said with a smile.

'Well, my daughter-in-law's cooking *is* the best in Les Marauds. Don't tell her I said that.'

'You're very fond of Du'a,' I said.

Omi nodded. 'She's a good little girl. Well, maybe not so *very* good, but she always knows how to make me smile. And she helps with my little

226

Maya.'

'Maya sounds like a handful,' I said.

'Yes, well, she lives in Toulouse,' said Omi, as if this explained everything. 'Yasmina comes for Ramadan, but the rest of the time we don't see her. She doesn't really like it here. She says the life is too quiet for her.'

'I think she underestimates us.'

Us. Now why did I use that word? But Omi seemed not to notice. She gave me a comic look. '*Yar.* Plenty going on round here. And I've heard *you* have a visitor.'

I kept a straight face. 'We have nothing but visitors. The other night it was Joséphine, who keeps the Café des Marauds. But we've had half of Lansquenet dropping in at different times.'

Omi gave me another look. Under the sparse, expressive brows, her eyes are milky-blue, like veins. 'You must think I was born yesterday. As if anything could happen in this village without me knowing about it. Still, if you want to play secrets—'

'It isn't my secret to give away.'

Omi shrugged. 'That's fair, I suppose. But—'

'What's all this about secrets?' That was Fatima, coming back into the living room with Zahra and some Moroccan sweets. 'Has my Omi been whispering?'

'On the contrary,' I said. 'Omi is always *very* discreet.'

Fatima laughed. 'Not the Omi *I* know. Now, try some of these. I have *halwa*, and dates, and macaroons, and rosewater candies and sesame snaps. No, no, not *you*, Omi—' she said, laughing, as Omi reached for the dish. 'It's Ramadan, remember?'

227

'I must have forgotten,' said Omi, and winked.

I noticed that Fatima was looking distracted. 'Is everything all right?' I said.

She nodded. 'It's my Yasmina's father-in-law. Mohammed Mahjoubi. He isn't well. He has moved in with us while Ismail and Yasmina are here. He prefers it to living with Saïd.'

Omi made a rude noise. 'Say rather he cannot bear to be so close to that woman,' she said.

Fatima tutted. 'Omi, please—'

But I was watching Zahra, so different from Yasmina, and yet so very like her. It was not the first time I had noticed her unease where Inès Bencharki was mentioned.

'What do *you* think of Inès?' I said, addressing Zahra.

She looked alarmed at the question. In her black *hijab*, pinned in the traditional style, she looks both older and younger than her sister. She also seems painfully shy, and when she speaks, her voice is oddly atonal.

'I—think she's interesting,' she said.

Omi squawked. 'Well, seeing as you practically *live* in that house—'

Zahra coloured. 'Sonia's my friend.'

'Sonia, is it? I thought you went there to make sheep's eyes at that young man.'

Now Zahra's cheeks were on fire. She seemed about to leave the room—

I stood up. 'Well, that's lucky,' I said. 'I was about to ask if someone could show me where Inès Bencharki lived. Perhaps you could do that, Zahra? I know it's raining—'

'Of course I will.' There was no expression in the girl's voice, but her eyes were grateful. 'I'll get your

228

coat. It's almost dry.'

As she left, I heard Fatima say, 'Omi, you're too hard on that girl.'

Omi cackled. '*Life* is hard. She needs to learn. She'd drown in a glass of water.'

I smiled. '*Jazak Allah*,' I said. 'And thanks for your hospitality. Next time, I'll bring chocolate. As soon as my supplies arrive.'

At the door, I collected my shoes. Zahra was waiting with my coat. 'Don't pay attention to what she says,' she said in that odd, atonal voice. 'She's old. She's used to speaking her mind. Even when her mind runs on a single broken wheel.' She opened the door. 'It isn't far. I'll show you.'

There are no house numbers in Les Marauds. It's one of our eccentricities. Even the street names are unofficial, although now that the area has been redeveloped, that too may change in time. Reynaud tells me Georges Clairmont has been campaigning to have the place designated as some kind of a heritage site (with himself as the main contractor, of course), but there are too many villages like Lansquenet along this part of the river, too many charming little *bastides*, too many old tanneries and picturesque stone bridges and medieval gibbets and statues of mysterious saints for our local officials to care very much about a single street of wood-and-wattle houses, already half eaten away by the Tannes. Only the postman seems to mind if street names and numbers are absent here, and if someone chooses to fix up one of these derelict houses and live there in defiance of planning regulations, no one is likely to stop them, or care much one way or the other.

Zahra had put on her *niqab* to walk me to

the Bencharkis' house. Beneath it, her face was unreadable. It makes her bolder, more confident. Even her posture is different. She turned to me as we walked and said:

'Why do you want to see Inès?'

'I used to live in her house,' I said.

'That's not a very good reason.'

'I know.'

'She draws you, doesn't she?' she said. 'I know. I can tell. You're not the first. We've all had dealings with Inès in some way or other. When she first came here and opened the school, it seemed like such a good idea. We'd had nothing but problems with the village school, and that Drou woman who wanted the *hijab* banned. And Inès's brother was so friendly with the Mahjoubis, and it all seemed so perfect for a while.'

We had reached the end of the boulevard. Beyond that, the houses were derelict. The last house had a red door.

'That's where the Mahjoubis live. Karim and Sonia live there, too.'

'But not Inès?'

She shook her head. 'Not any more.'

'Why not? Wasn't there space?'

'That's not why,' said Zahra. 'In any case, you'll find her *there*—' And she pointed to some fig trees growing by the water's edge, where an old jetty rises above a Gothic tangle of tree-roots. It's where the river-rats moored their boats, in the days when they still came every year, and now I saw it: a riverboat, low in the water and painted black, moored in the shelter of the trees.

'The boat? She's living there?' I said.

'She borrowed it. It was already here.'

230

I know. I recognize that boat. Too cramped for two adults, it might just take a single woman and her child. As long as they didn't need too much space, or bring too many possessions—

I didn't think that would be a problem for Inès Bencharki. But—

'What about Du'a?' I said.

'We look after her most of the time. She helps out with our little Maya. Sometimes she stays with Inès, sometimes not. She comes to our house for *iftar*.'

'But why a boat?'

'She says it feels safe. Besides, no one has claimed it.'

That doesn't surprise me. Its owner has not been here in over four years. But why would Roux leave his boat here if he didn't mean to return?

Unless it wasn't meant for him, but for someone else—

Someone else?

A single woman and her child. Roux's reluctance to come here with me, although I know he stays in touch with some of his friends from Lansquenet. Joséphine's reluctance to talk to me about the father of her son. Four years ago, when Roux was still here. Pilou must have been four years old. Old enough to travel, perhaps. Old enough for Joséphine to think about moving upriver . . .

Did Roux ask her to leave with him? Did she refuse? Did he change his mind? While he was in Paris with me, was she waiting in Lansquenet, waiting for him to come back to her?

So many unanswered questions. So many doubts. So many fears. The seasons change; lovers and friends are blown away like leaves on the wind. My

231

mother never stayed with a man for more than a couple of weeks. She said: *Only children stay true, Vianne.* For years I followed that motto. Then, along came Roux, and I told myself there was an exception to every rule.

Perhaps I was wrong, I told myself now. Perhaps *this* was what I came here to learn.

'Are you all right?' It was Zahra.

'Thanks.' I turned towards her. 'Tell me, Zahra, what made you start wearing *niqab*, when your mother and your sister don't?'

Her eyes looked startled under her veil.

'Was it Inès?'

'In a way, perhaps. Well, anyway, that's where she is.' Zahra looked at the black houseboat. 'But I don't think she'll talk to you.'

She left me standing in the rain at the end of the Boulevard des Marauds. The sky had darkened still further—I doubted whether we would see even a glimpse of the full moon that night. I heard the church tower strike four o'clock; as heavy and as ponderous as the air. I looked at Roux's boat, so silent, so still, moored along the riverbank, and thought of Inès Bencharki. Omi had called her a scorpion trying to cross a river. But in the story the scorpion drowned.

Just then, in my pocket, my mobile rang. I pulled it out; looked at the screen. The caller's number flashed up.

Of course. Who else would it be?

It was Roux.

CHAPTER FIVE

Tuesday, 24th August

Nothing stays secret for very long. Not in Lansquenet, anyway. I haven't been out of my house for two days, but already the whispers have started. I can't lay the blame on Joséphine, or even on Pilou. I know. It started this morning, when Charles Lévy came round again to complain about his missing cat.

Through the tiniest crack in the door, I told him that I was feeling unwell. But Charles Lévy was undeterred. Kneeling on the doorstep, he addressed me through the letter-box, his voice shaking with suppressed emotion.

'It's Henriette Moisson, *père*. She takes my Otto into her house. She feeds him, and she calls him Tati. Doesn't that count as abduction, or false imprisonment, or something?'

I answered him from behind the door: 'Don't you think you're taking all this a little too personally?'

'The woman has stolen my cat, *père*. How else should I take it?'

I tried to explain. 'She's lonely, that's all. Perhaps if you tried to talk to her—'

'I *have* tried! She denies it! She says she hasn't seen the cat. She claims she hasn't seen him for days, but the whole of her cottage smells of fish—'

My head was aching. My bruised ribs hurt. I was in no mood for this.

233

'Monsieur Lévy!' I yelled through the door. 'Did not the Good Lord tell us to *love thy neighbour as thyself*? Am I mistaken, or did he mean us instead to complain as much as we possibly can about our neighbours and, using the most flimsy of excuses, spread discord throughout the neighbourhood? Would Jesus have begrudged a lonely old woman the occasional use of his cat?'

There was a silence from outside. Then a voice came through the slot: 'I'm sorry, *mon père*. I didn't think.'

'Ten *Avés*.'

'Yes, *mon père*.'

After that, word quickly spread that Monsieur le Curé was taking confession through his letter-box. Gilles Dumarin came calling next, ostensibly to ask about a donation to the church flower fund, but in fact for advice about his mother. Then came Henriette Moisson, for absolution of a sin committed when I was not yet in embryo. Then Guillaume Duplessis, to ask me if I needed anything. Then Joline Drou, to report to Caro that something strange was going on. Then Caro herself, disdaining pretence, who flatly accused me (through the door) of having something to hide.

Sitting on the doormat, I said: 'Caro. Go away. Please.'

'Not until you tell me what's going on,' said Caro in a ringing voice. 'Have you been drinking? Is that it?'

'Of course not.'

'Then open the door!'

When I refused to comply, she left, but returned this evening with Père Henri. I considered pretending to be out, but when Caro came to the

234

window and started peering through the shutters, I knew that this time she would not give up.

I opened the door.

'Good heavens, Francis!'

Yes, *Henri*. I know what it looks like. Most of the damage is superficial, of course, but even so, it is impressive. For a moment I found myself taking a certain enjoyment in their expressions of disbelief. But the Bishop needed nothing more than the smallest excuse to send me away; and now, it seems, he has found it. Of course, I am not at fault here, says Père Henri (implying the opposite), but this attack on my person proves that I can no longer claim credibility in Lansquenet. For the good of my flock, as well as for my own safety (he says), I am being transferred to another parish. It may take a week or so to arrange, but already the wheels are in motion. An inner-city parish, I am told, where I may improve my social skills, preach to a wider audience and learn to understand the needs of a multi-faith community.

Of course, I am not fooled for a moment. I know I am being punished. Perhaps the Bishop does not know how much. To him, all priests are the same, like pawns. But I have lived in Lansquenet nearly all my life; to send me away is to tear out some essential part of me. I know I haven't always been as open or as obedient as perhaps I should have been. I may have been resistant to change; defiant to authority. My dealings with the river-folk have not always been cordial. I am sometimes impatient with my flock, even more so with the *Maghrébins*. In short, I have treated Lansquenet as my personal fiefdom, making up rules as I went along, playing the role of dictator and judge. But all the same, to

235

send me away—

Night is beginning to fall. I hurt. Outside, I can hear the Black Autan screeching in triumph as it bears the sound of the *muezzin* over the water towards me.

Autan blanc, emporte le vent.
Autan noir, désespoir.

And now, for the first time, I feel afraid. No, *mon père*; I feel despair. The wind that has blown so often for me now has me by the scruff of the neck. It chased away the river-rats; it closed down Vianne's *chocolaterie*. I thought the wind was on my side; that I would stand here like a rock; immovable and resolute—

But tonight, the wind is at my door. I am no longer immovable. No one wants me here any more. And now I am afraid, *mon père*, that *I* am the one to be blown away.

CHAPTER SIX

☾

Tuesday, 24th August

His voice was startlingly close, as if he were standing just metres away. My heart gave a sudden, rolling lurch, like a wave so laden with debris that it is close to collapsing. *Trust Roux*, I thought fiercely. Of all the times he could have phoned to give me reassurance, for him to finally do so now seemed

236

curiously typical.

Quickly I took shelter alongside one of the old tanneries. 'Roux. Where have you been?' I said. 'I left you all those messages—'

'I lost my phone.' I could hear his shrug. 'Was it something important?'

I almost laughed. What could I say? How could I tell him my thoughts, my fears, my growing conviction that he had lied, allowing me to believe for four whole years that we could be a family—

'Vianne?' He sounded wary. I reminded myself that he always sounds wary on the phone. I wished I could see his eyes. Better still, I wished I could see his colours.

I said: 'I talked to Joséphine. She has a son. I never knew.'

A shutterclick of silence.

'Roux. Why didn't you tell me before?'

'I promised her I wouldn't.'

He makes it sound so simple. And yet, behind the screen of words, a thousand writhing shadows. 'So—do you know the boy's father?'

'I promised I wouldn't tell you.'

I promised. For Roux, that's more than enough. To him, the past is irrelevant. Even I have only the barest knowledge of where he came from, who he is. He doesn't talk about his past. He may even have forgotten it. It's one of the things I love about him, his refusal to allow the past to have any purchase over him, and yet, it makes him dangerous. A man without a past is like a man without a shadow.

'Did you leave a boat here?' I said.

'Yes. I gave it to Joséphine.'

Again, that shutterclick pause, as if a screen had fallen between us.

237

'You gave it to Joséphine? Why?' I said.

'She was talking about getting away,' said Roux, in a careful, toneless voice. 'She wanted to travel for a while, go upriver, see the world. I owed her for everything she'd done—putting me up for the winter, giving me work, cooking for me. So I gave her the boat. I reckoned I didn't need it any more.'

Now I could see it all in my mind, clear as scrying with chocolate. And the worst of it was that I'd known all along in some deep, hidden part of my heart, the place where my mother speaks to me.

So, you thought you could settle down? Do you think I didn't try? People like us don't do that, Vianne. We cast too long a shadow. We try to keep possession of what little joy and light we have, but everything gets lost in the end.

He said: 'When are you coming back?'

'I'm not sure yet. There's something I have to do first.'

'What is it?' He sounded so close. I imagined him sitting on deck, in the sun, with maybe a can of beer at his side, with the Seine at his back like a stretch of beach and the silhouette of the Pont des Arts black against the summer sky. I saw it all so clearly, like something in a lucid dream. But, as in many of my dreams, I felt disconnected from the scene, moving away uncontrollably, backwards into darkness.

'I think you should come home,' said Roux. 'You said you'd only be a few days.'

'I know. It won't be long now. But there's—'

'Something you have to do. I know. But Vianne—there'll *always* be something. And then there'll always be something more. That bloody village is like that. And before you know it, you'll

238

have been there six months and you'll be picking out fabric for curtains.'

'That's ridiculous,' I said. 'I'll only be a few more days.' I thought of the phone call I'd made to Guy, and of my order for chocolate supplies. 'Well, call it a week,' I amended. 'Besides, if you miss me, you could come here.'

A pause. 'You know I can't do that.'

'Why not?'

Another, longer pause. I could sense his frustration. 'Why don't you trust me?' he said at last. 'Why can't it ever be simple?'

Because it *isn't* simple, Roux. Because, however far you stray, the river brings you home in the end. And because I see more than I want to see, even when I'd rather be blind—

'Is this because of Joséphine? *Don't* you trust me?'

'I don't know.'

Once more that silence, like a screen full of jumping shadows. Then he said: 'OK, Vianne. I only hope it's worth it,' and I was left with the sound of the sea in my ear, like the surf through a seashell—

I shook my head. My face was wet. The cold had numbed my fingertips. This is my fault, I told myself. I shouldn't have summoned the wind that day. It feels so harmless, doesn't it, so effortless and natural? But the wind can change at any time; and these little things we build for ourselves are swept away in front of it.

Did Armande see this coming? Did she guess about Roux and Joséphine? Could she have guessed that her letter-bomb would blow my life with Roux apart? That's what happens, I suppose,

239

when you open a letter from the dead. Better by far to never look back; like Roux, to cast no shadow.

Still, it's far too late for that. I imagine Armande knew that, too. Why did I come back to Lansquenet? Why must I face the Woman in Black? For the same reason the scorpion stung the buffalo, knowing it would mean both their deaths. Because we have no choice, she and I. Because we are connected.

The rain had stopped, but the wind had reached that tremulous point of intensity where it plucks at the telephone wires and *keens*—giving the Black Autan a voice: a voice, and maybe a message. *What did you* think *would happen, Vianne? Did you think I'd let you go? Did you think I'd let you belong to someone else for ever?*

I left the Boulevard des Marauds and made my way on to the old jetty. That's where the black houseboat was moored, surrounded by those bare-rooted trees. It's sheltered by the riverbank, but just a few metres further out the Tannes has become a surging, unruly animal; its sleek surface ramshackle with debris; deadly assemblages of branches and detritus, snarled together with cable and wire. To swim in there now would be more than unwise; even the shallows are treacherous. If Alyssa had jumped from the bridge last night instead of six days ago, she would never have survived: nor would Reynaud, for that matter. I moved a little closer. I called out: 'Madame Bencharki?'

I knew she was home; I could feel her eyes. I took another step forward. The wind whipped my hair into my face; the ground at my feet was waterlogged.

'Inès?'

I imagined her watching me, hidden away; watching with feral, suspicious eyes. I wished I'd thought to bring a gift; but the peaches are almost gone, and besides, I had no idea what kind of approach would work with her. Beneath her many veils Inès hides as many different faces: to Omi, a scorpion; to Zahra, a friend; to old Mahjoubi, a subversive; to Alyssa, a figure of dread—

And to Karim?

Once more, I called. This time I thought I heard movement from inside the houseboat. The tiny door to the galley opened. A woman in *niqab* appeared.

'What do you want?' Her voice is low and barely accented; and yet, there is something discordant about it, like music played in the wrong key.

'Hello, I'm Vianne Rocher,' I said, and held out my hand.

She did not move. Her eyes above the square of cloth were as blank as buttons. I started to say what I had prepared; that I had once lived in the *chocolaterie*; that I was staying in Les Marauds; that I wanted to help her and Du'a.

Inès listened without a word. Standing on the low deck, she seemed to be walking on water. Behind her, a fine spray arose from the Tannes. She might have been a ghost—or a witch.

'I know who you are,' she said at last. 'You are a friend of the priest, Reynaud.'

I smiled. 'He and I go back a long way. But we weren't always friends. In fact, he once tried to drive me out of town.'

Her eyes showed no expression. Her hands, gloved in black, stayed at her sides. Her feet, too, were hidden beneath her *abaya*—in fact, but for

241

those expressionless eyes, she might have been a trick of the light, with nothing beneath her *niqab* but air.

'Some people are saying he lit the fire. That isn't true,' I told her. 'Reynaud's a good man, in spite of his faults. He isn't a sneak or a coward. The person who lit that fire is both. And now they're letting him take the blame—'

'Is that why you came? To plead his case?'

'I thought you might need help,' I said.

'Thank you, I don't.' Her voice was flat.

'You're living on a *boat*,' I said.

'So what?' said Inès Bencharki. 'You think living on a boat is hard? Believe me, I have known much worse. This country is easy compared with mine. Easy, and soft, and lazy.' Her voice had risen in contempt; her eyes had narrowed above the veil. And now I could see her colours at last, flaring in the sullen light, giving her plain black *abaya* a brilliant lining of moiré silk. I reached for her thoughts instinctively; came back with a plundered handful. A basket of scarlet strawberries; a pair of yellow slippers; a bracelet of black jet beads; a woman's face in a mirror. And silks; embroidered, coloured silks; gauze like misted spider's web; chiffon scattered with crystals; wedding-dress white; saffron-gold; mulberry-purple; forest-green—

So much colour; bewildering. Without it, you might never have guessed that she and Karim were related; but scratch the surface, and there they are, those colours that cannot be concealed.

She flinched. It was as if I had touched her in some forbidden, intimate way. Her eyes widened in outrage, and now I could see their colour, too—a

242

green so dark it might almost be black, into which a droplet of gold has dissolved.

She said: 'Stop that!'

I held out my hand. 'It's all right, Inès. I understand.'

She laughed, a jangly, discordant sound. 'Is that what you think? That you understand? Because you see a little more than all these other blind people?'

'I came here for a reason,' I said. 'I had a letter from the dead. It told me I was needed here. And then I saw *you*—'

'And you thought—what? Poor, downtrodden Muslim woman in *niqab*, victimized by the *kuffar*? Poor, frightened widow, will welcome any offer, however patronizing, of friendship—or of chocolate? Yes, I know all about you, *Vianne*—' she went on, seeing my look of surprise. 'I know how you came here eight years ago and charmed everyone into loving you—yes, even that odious priest. You think I haven't heard all that? You think Karim hasn't told me? That woman from the café, she talks about you all the time. So does the old man with the dog, and the baker, Poitou, and the florist, Narcisse. They make you sound like an angel come down from *Jannat* to save us. And now, Fatima al-Djerba and her mother have caught it too—ah, how they all love the chocolate woman, who thinks that because she once went to Tangier she understands our culture—'

I listened to her in silence, stunned by the depth of her contempt. Whatever I'd expected from our first encounter, it wasn't this; this opening of the floodgates, this outpouring of venom. *A scorpion*, Omi had said. And now I was drowning, and the worst of it was that I had no one to blame but

243

myself. The buffalo in the story is as much a slave to its nature as the scorpion is to hers; and didn't a part of me *want* to be stung, to prove what I've always secretly known? That nothing lasts; that magic can fail; that everything we work for and love comes back to the same blank wall in the end—

Was *this* the lesson I came here to learn? Is *this* why I came back to Lansquenet?

'I know you're hiding Alyssa,' she said.

I shivered, feeling suddenly cold.

'You think I don't hear? You think I don't see? You think because I wear *niqab* I don't pay attention the way you do? You think because you can't see me, I don't notice *every*thing?'

'It's nothing to do with *niqab*,' I said. 'And I'm not *hiding* Alyssa. She's staying with me of her own accord, until she decides what she wants to do.'

Inès made a harsh sound in her throat. 'I suppose you think you're helping,' she said.

'Someone had to help,' I said. 'She was trying to kill herself.'

She fixed me with her green-gold gaze. Beneath the *abaya* she is graceful, poised and straight as a dancer. From the beauty of her eyes, I knew she must be striking.

'You think like a child,' she told me. 'A child sees a baby bird fall from the nest. She picks it up and takes it home. One of two things happens next. The baby bird dies almost at once; or it survives for a day or two, and the child takes it back to its family. But the scent of human is on it now, and the family rejects it. It dies of starvation, or a cat kills it, or the other birds peck it to death. With luck, the child will never know.'

I felt myself flush. 'This isn't the same. Alyssa

isn't a baby bird.'

'Isn't she?' said Inès. 'You'll be telling me next she's kept her fast and she *hasn't* cut her hair.'

'Did Maya tell you that?' I said.

'I don't need a child to tell me. You think you're the only one who sees things?'

I thought of what Alyssa had said: that Inès Bencharki was an *amaar*, an evil spirit in human form, sent to corrupt the innocent. I've heard that accusation before—more than once—on my travels. People with insight—people like us—are often seen as sinister. My mother called herself a witch. That was her style; I never did. That word is overburdened now with history and prejudice. Those people who say that words have no power know nothing of the nature of words. Words, well placed, can end a regime; can turn affection to hatred; can start a religion, or even a war. Words are the shepherds of lies; they lead the best of us to the slaughter.

I said: 'My mother was a witch.'

She laughed and said: 'I should have guessed.'

And at that she turned and went back inside—behind her, that glimpse of colours, like the twist in the eye of a marble—and then the door closed behind her and I was left standing at the side of the Tannes, with the black wind screeching in the wires and the rain beginning to fall again.

CHAPTER SEVEN

✝

Wednesday, 25th August

Midnight, and the rain has stopped. The sky is cloudy agate. The August full moon—the one which, according to folklore, *père*, is causing all our problems—is all in rags, a supplicant on the night's horizon. I cannot sleep. My fingers hurt. My mind is all static and restlessness. I can already feel tomorrow like an avalanche ready to fall; the telephone calls, the visitors, the poised inevitability of a life about to be toppled.

Outside, the wind is relentless. It tugs at me like an eager child. It strikes me how few possessions I have—the cottage belongs to the Church, as does all the furniture, most of the books, and the pictures. A canvas rucksack with a broken strap—the one I took with me to the seminary more years ago than I like to think—would easily take everything I own. Aside from my priest's clothes, which of course I would leave behind, what do I have? A couple of shirts; a pair of jeans, three T-shirts, socks and underwear. A thick, hand-knitted sweater that I wear in winter, when it's cold. A scarf. A hat. A toothbrush. A comb. The copy of Saint Augustine you gave me when I was a boy. My father's watch. Your rosary, with the green glass beads; a cheap thing, but I am fond of it. A brown envelope of photographs, papers and documents. Some money. Not much. Forty-five

246

years, neatly packed up in a single rucksack.

Now why did I do that, *père*? It's absurd. I'm not going anywhere. For a start, I have nowhere to go. It's the middle of the night. It's raining. And yet, I can see myself stepping out, rucksack on my shoulder. Leaving the key in the front door, closing the gate behind me. Going down the deserted street in my coat and walking boots, feeling the sky above my head. The sky must feel different to a man who has no home to go to. The road, too, must feel different. Harder on the feet, somehow. My boots are well worn and comfortable. I can walk for hours before I need to think about what to do next.

Mon père, that sounds so attractive. To know that every step I take takes me further from Père Henri Lemaître. To have no responsibility, no choices to make but where to sleep, what to eat, whether to turn right or left. To abandon desire and to offer myself to the randomness of the universe—

Randomness?

Well, yes, *père*. Of course, I know God has a plan. But in recent years I've found it increasingly hard to believe that the plan is running as smoothly as He intended. The more I think about it now, the more I see God as a harried bureaucrat, *wanting* to help, but crippled by paperwork and committees. If He sees us at all, *père*, it is from behind a desk piled high with accounts and works-in-progress. That's why He has priests to do His work, and bishops to oversee them. That is why I bear Him no grudge. But try to juggle too many balls, and this is what happens. Some go astray.

The wind has cleared my head, somehow. History is filled with the stories of men who abandoned conventional life for a life on the road.

247

My namesake, Saint Francis, is one of them. Maybe I'll go to Assisi.

I must have slept a little, *père*. I awoke feeling stiff. My rucksack was propped against the front door. For a moment, clinging to sleep, I couldn't remember leaving it there. Then I remembered, and felt afraid. The certainties of the past few hours were slipping away as daybreak approached. First thing in the morning, I usually go to Poitou's, for croissants or *pain au chocolat*. Today, I did not. I don't want Poitou talking about me all over the village, and besides, to go to the bakery at this stage would be almost like tempting myself to stay, when I had already decided to leave.

I made coffee and toasted a piece of stale bread. It smelt better than it tasted, but it was enough to remind me how hungry I'd been. I am not as good at going hungry as I once was, *père*. I no longer keep my Lenten fast. If I left, I told myself, I'd have to get used to hunger. Saint Francis ate roots and berries, of course. I suppose they must have sustained him. But I would find it difficult to go without my breakfast croissant.

I looked at the sky. It was still dark. Dawn was more than an hour away. I did not want to be seen as I left, especially not by the people of Les Marauds as they arose for morning prayers. I knew I would have to pass their way if I wanted to follow the river. That seemed the most sensible plan, at least until I had covered enough ground to guarantee I wouldn't meet anyone who would recognize me. A clean break, I told myself; no explanations, no goodbyes. Not even to Vianne, or Joséphine—

Especially not to Joséphine.

I finished my breakfast. Time to go.

248

I washed the dishes in the sink. I watered the plants. I stripped the bed. I loaded the bedclothes into the washing machine on a medium cycle. I put on my boots and raincoat. I hoisted my rucksack on to my shoulder by its one unbroken strap. I turned off the lights.

I said: 'Goodbye.'

Then I stepped out into the dark.

CHAPTER ONE

Wednesday, 25th August

I kept to the side streets in Les Marauds. I'd forgotten how early these people rise. Already the lights were on all the way down the boulevard; warm and coloured squares of light in yellow, red, blue, green. *So this is what it feels like*, I thought. *To be an outsider*. It pleased me, somehow. The thought was almost romantic. Perhaps to be an outsider is simply to know how to look at things from the outside. I checked my watch. Six o'clock. Soon, the *muezzin* would call. I planned to be out of Les Marauds by then. Avoiding the boulevard and the gym, I took one of the little alleyways that lead to the old jetty. There, boats were often moored, back in the days of the river-rats, but now no one uses it any more. There's a towpath here by the river, once used for dragging barges upstream; I knew if I followed it far enough it would lead me to Pont-le-Saôul, where I could take a bus to Agen, and from there—

To Paris? London? Rome?

A multitude of highways, leading me further and further from home, spiralling out like a spider's web to every corner of the map—

I tried not to think too hard about what I was about to do. *One step at a time*, I thought. *One foot in front of the other*. The river had risen again, I saw. At this rate, I thought, the banks will burst and flood the Boulevard des Marauds.

Les Marauds is used to flooding, of course; the riverside houses are built on stilts to accommodate the rise and fall of the Tannes. But the houses are old; the original wood has been bleached and warped and twisted by time; some reinforced with metal struts that have rusted and corroded over the years. Each year brings them closer to collapse. To restore them would cost a fortune. One day, maybe, one winter's day, those struts will give way, and that row of crooked houses that makes up the Boulevard des Marauds will come crashing down into the Tannes, one against the other, gathering momentum like a row of deadly dominoes, leaving nothing but a deadfall of wood and broken plaster.

Would that be such a bad thing?

In any case, *père*, it is no longer my concern. I am done with Lansquenet. I have decided what I must do. Let the river decide the rest.

It was then that I saw a houseboat moored against the jetty. Well away from the slipstream, tucked into the riverbank like a sleeper into the crook of his elbow. River-gypsies? Surely not. Their time is long gone. And yet I could see smoke coming out of the chimney—smoke or steam, I wasn't sure which. There was a light in the window. Someone was home.

Instinctively, I made for the trees. A screen of them stands between the river and the end of the boulevard, and I had no wish to be seen. Whoever was living in that boat was no longer any business of mine. I would join the towpath another way.

But just as I reached the stand of trees, I saw a figure heading my way. A slender figure in black, head to toe, a veil across her features. You'd think

253

they'd be impossible to tell apart; but I knew her from the way she moved. It was Sonia Bencharki.

She must have been running, I suppose. She almost ran into me as I approached. I could hear her breathing, ragged and fast; her eyes above the black veil were wide with alarm and astonishment. I feared she might scream.

I said: 'It's all right. Sonia, it's me. Francis Reynaud.'

If anything, I thought her alarm increased. She gave a tiny, strangled cry.

I said: 'I was taking a walk, that's all. I didn't mean to frighten you.'

Of course, my story failed to explain the rucksack on my shoulder. But the last thing I wanted right now was any kind of attention. Why was Sonia here at all? By the river—alone, at this time?

'Sonia,' I said. 'Is anything wrong?'

She made a sound at the back of her throat.

'Please,' I said. 'I can't leave you like this. Does your father know you're here?'

'No.' Her voice was a whisper.

I thought of Alyssa. This wasn't fair. All I wanted was to leave. *Mon père*, I thought: *why make it so hard? How many obstacles must God put in my way?*

She is not my responsibility. Alyssa is not my responsibility. Inès Bencharki is not my responsibility. Everything bad that has happened to me over the course of the past few weeks has been the result of my interfering with matters that are not my responsibility. Well, this is where it ends, I thought. Les Marauds has its own priest. Let him deal with the flock himself.

And then I smelt the petrol. My God, had she been *bathing* in it?

'What were you doing here?' I said, more harshly than I'd intended. 'Why do you smell of petrol? Were you going to burn yourself?'

She started to whimper. 'You don't understand—'

'We're going to get your father,' I said, taking hold of her by the wrist. 'It's up to him to sort this out.'

'No. No.' She shook her head so hard that the whole of her body followed suit. The can of petrol that she had been carrying under her robe fell to the ground.

The frustration I had felt over the past few weeks had reached the point of combustion. Anger made me pitiless. I know, *père*. I'm not proud of this.

'What *is* it with you people?' I said. 'First your sister, then you! Are you crazy? Do you want to die? Do you *really* believe that if you die during Ramadan, God will give you a free pass into Paradise?'

She looked at me blankly. 'I don't want to die.'

'Then *what*?'

Her reply was inaudible.

'Then *what*?'

She winced at my raised voice. 'I wanted Inès to go away.'

That woman again. 'Who the hell is she? And how has she managed to somehow infect the whole of Les Marauds with her insanity?' I stopped. 'Hang on a minute,' I said. 'How exactly did you propose to make her go away?' I indicated the petrol can. 'Sonia, what were you planning to burn?'

Sweet Jesus. The penny dropped. It felt like repeated blows to the head. The houseboat. The petrol can. Sonia. The school. The graffiti in

Arabic. *Whore*. The act that sent my world crashing down, that has made me a pariah, both in Les Marauds and Lansquenet, that has cost me my reputation, my pride—

'*You* lit the fire,' I told her. 'Why?'

'I wanted her to leave,' she said. Her voice was like tiny metal tacks being hammered into a piece of wood. 'I want her to go away for good. Back to wherever she came from. She was never supposed to stay. She only came for the wedding. If she goes, then Karim will be mine all the way through, the way he was supposed to be. But for as long as she's around—'

'You could have killed someone,' I said. 'Inès, or her daughter, or one of the people who came to help—'

She shook her head. 'I was careful,' she said. 'I lit the fire at the front of the house. The fire escape is at the back. And I threw stones at the windows, to make sure they were awake.'

For a moment I was speechless. That it should be *Sonia* who had tried to burn down the school— Sonia, whom I'd always liked, who used to play with the boys in the square and drink *diabolos* at Joséphine's—

'Have you any idea of the harm you've done? You do know everyone blames *me*?'

'I'm sorry about that,' she said.

'Oh, so that excuses it?' Anger made me intemperate. My voice ripped into the silence like fire. 'Arson, attempted murder, and lies?'

Surprisingly, she did not cry. I'd rather expected her to, *père*, but her voice was as small and as hard as before. 'I'm four months pregnant, Curé,' she said. 'If he divorces me now, I'm alone. I get

256

nothing. He can stay here or go back to Morocco if he likes. I have no rights. Do you understand?'

'Why would he divorce you?' I said.

'He will if he finds out I lit the fire. I told you before. He worships Inès. And don't expect my father to help. He loves Karim like a favourite son. My mother—she thinks he's an angel come down from *Jannat* to save us all. And as for Inès—'

She looked away. The *muezzin* began the call to prayer. It's really quite a musical chant, taken out of context. The chimney of the old tannery provides a resonant platform from which to harangue the faithful. *Hayya la-s-salah. Hayya la-s-salah.* In moments, the streets will be busy again. So much for my quiet exit.

She said: 'He goes to her at night. I hear him getting out of bed. He comes back smelling of perfume, and *her*. I know it's her. I can feel it. I can see and feel and hear everything, and yet I can't speak. She's bewitched him. He's under her spell. We both are.'

This is ridiculous, père, I thought. *I have forsaken the way of the cloth, and here I am taking confession again.* 'There are no witches,' I told her. 'Have you spoken to Karim?'

'No.'

'Why not?'

'I tried,' she said. 'But he just gets angry. Then my mother and father say that I'm not being obedient. They say I should be more like Inès, modest and respectful.'

'What about your grandfather? Have you tried confiding in him?'

For the first time, I saw a smile in her eyes. 'Dear Jiddo. But he doesn't live with us any more, and so

257

I don't see him as often. My father and he had an argument; my father says he's a bad influence. And Jiddo doesn't like it that my father has taken his place at the mosque. He lives with the al-Djerbas now, my Uncle Ismail's family. They're saying he's ill. That he's going to die.'

'I'm sorry,' I said. I realized I was; Mohammed Mahjoubi has been here for years. In spite of our disagreements, I have always considered him an honest man. If he dies, he will leave a space in this community. I wish the same were true of me.

'Go home,' I said. 'And change your dress. That one reeks of petrol.'

She looked at me uncertainly. 'You won't tell Karim, or my father?'

'No. As long as you leave Inès alone. Whatever is between you, you should solve it honestly. That means openly, with words, not with dangerous pranks like this.'

'You *promise* you won't tell them?'

'As long as you stop this nonsense right now.'

She gave a sigh. 'All right.'

'Two *Avés*.'

She looked at me in surprise.

'Joke.'

I think you need to be a priest to really see the humour, *père*. But she smiled with her eyes. I like that.

'*Jazak Allah*, Curé,' she said.

Then she quietly crept away.

258

CHAPTER TWO

☾

Wednesday, 25th August

I slipped from one dream to the other all night, and awoke at dawn to the tiny sound of the front door closing on the latch. I sat up on my sofa-bed, and saw a shadow through the glass; a figure in a black robe, features hidden behind a scarf.

'Alyssa?'

I turned on the lights. She was by the door, only her eyes visible behind the tightly folded scarf. But it wasn't Alyssa. Now I could see that this was a much slighter figure; hidden, not under an *abaya*, but under a black coat much too big for her.

'Du'a?'

She turned to look at me. Her small, expressionless face was pale. She said in a strangely adult voice: 'I need to talk to Alyssa.'

I stood up and pulled on my robe. 'Of course. Is anything wrong?'

She gave me a look. It is the same look that Anouk, at nine, used to give me when I said something she considered particularly obtuse.

I said: 'I'll get her.'

She followed me up to Alyssa's little bedroom. I found Alyssa already awake, watching the rain through the window. She jumped to her feet when she saw Du'a, and there followed a rapid interchange in Arabic, from which I caught practically nothing but the word *Jiddo*—

259

grandfather—and a general sense of urgency. Alyssa listened intently, occasionally breaking in with a comment or a question.

Then she said: 'I have to go.'

'What's wrong?'

'It's Jiddo. He's ill. He says he wants to see me.'

Now I remembered Fatima telling me old Mahjoubi was ill. In my haste to find Inès, I hadn't paid much attention. I recalled something about a disagreement with Saïd—or was it Inès?—and that old Mahjoubi had come to stay with the al-Djerbas for a while. I thought of the one occasion on which I'd had a chance to speak to him. I'd liked the roguish look of him and his mischievous humour. Whatever his illness, I told myself, it must have come on very quickly.

'What's wrong with him?'

She shrugged. 'No one knows. He doesn't say. He won't see a doctor. He won't even eat. Just reads his book, or sleeps all day. He's asking for me. I have to go.' She hesitated. 'Come with me? Please?'

I smiled. 'Of course. Let me get dressed.'

We set off five minutes later under the slow and steady rain. Alyssa was wearing her *hijab* again, and her face looked small and angular beneath the folds of fabric. Les Marauds smells even more strongly now of the sea at low tide; a brackish scent that reminded me of harbours and journeys and beaches at dawn, with footprints in the black mud and children digging for cockles. The Tannes has broken its banks overnight, flooding one end of the boulevard; forming a kind of shallow lake, in which the mosque, with its white minaret, is reflected like a mirage. A little more of this, I

260

think, and the houses on the street will flood, from the cellars upwards, water pouring in from the sewers and drains and filling the houses, one by one.

Fatima did not comment when the three of us arrived. Instead she simply waved us inside, tidied away our clothes and shoes, and showed us into the front room. Zahra and Omi were already there, dressed for the mosque, sitting on cushions and playing a game that looked like chequers, but was not. Maya was in the kitchen with her mother, but came out when she heard us. No one seemed surprised to see me.

'How bad is it?' said Alyssa.

Omi shook her head. 'Who knows? He came to us five days ago. Said he preferred to stay with us. Since then, he hardly talks, doesn't eat, doesn't even go to mosque. Just sits and reads that book of his and looks out of the window. It's almost as if he has given up hope, now that Saïd has taken his place. But if *you* talk to him, perhaps—' She shrugged. '*Inshallah*. It's worth a try.'

Alyssa said nothing for a while. She seemed to be thinking furiously. 'Does anyone else know I'm here?' she said.

Fatima put a hand on her arm. 'I promise, we haven't told anyone. But nothing stays secret here for long. People talk. People guess.'

'Has anyone else been here?' she said. 'Sonia? My father? Karim?'

'No. Saïd says we shouldn't indulge the old man. Says no one is to visit him unless he agrees to come back home.' Fatima sighed and shook her head. 'They're both as stubborn as old mules. Neither one will give way. Mehdi's with the old man now. I'm

261

sure he'll be glad to see you both.'

She led us up the narrow stairs. Old Mahjoubi's room is an attic bedroom at the back of the house, overlooking the river. A single triangular window lets in the daylight; the eaves are low and made of ancient timber, bleached pale and eaten by woodworm. Old Mahjoubi was sitting there, a tartan blanket over his knees. His face was pale and sunken. Beside him, on the bedside table, the third volume of *Les Misérables*, with a bookmark just past the halfway point. Standing next to him was a man I took to be Fatima's husband, Mehdi; grey-haired, with a little paunch, and a humorous face, now pouchy with concern.

I stayed at the door. Alyssa went in and flung her arms around her grandfather. In Arabic, she addressed him; urgent, staggered sentences spoken in a low voice. Of course I didn't understand; but as she spoke the old man's face took on a little more animation; reflecting for a second or two a vestige of the personality I'd seen just a few days earlier.

'Alyssa,' he said in a papery voice. His eyes turned slowly to look at me. 'And Madame Rocher. Isn't it? The one who brings peaches for Ramadan?'

'My friends call me Vianne,' I told him.

'I owe you a debt.' He lifted a hand. An oddly courtly gesture, like an old king conferring favour. 'On behalf of my little Alyssa.'

I smiled. 'You owe me nothing,' I said. 'If anything, Monsieur le Curé is the one who deserves the credit.'

He nodded. 'So I understand. I hope you can pass on my thanks to him.'

Alyssa was kneeling on the rug beside the old

262

man's chair. His hand, as sallow and misshapen as a piece of driftwood, came to rest on the girl's head. He said something gently in Arabic, in which I caught the word *zina*, and nothing else.

Softly, Alyssa began to cry. 'I don't want you to die, Jiddo. You have to see a doctor.'

Old Mahjoubi shook his head. 'I will not die, I promise you. At least not until I have finished this book. And remember, it is a *long* book, and all in French, and the print is small, and my eyes are not as good as they were—'

'Don't make jokes about this, Jiddo. You have to take more care of yourself. Eat some food. See a doctor. There are lots of people who need you here.'

Old Mahjoubi sighed. 'Is that so?'

'Of course there are,' I told him. 'Some of them may not admit it to you. But the people who refuse your help are often the ones who need it most.'

I thought the old eyes brightened at that. 'You are speaking of my son Saïd.'

I shrugged. 'Do you think he's good enough to take your place without guidance? Or—' I quoted a Moroccan proverb—'if, at noon, he says it is night, will you say: *Behold, the stars?*'

He looked at me appreciatively. 'Madame, I think I liked you best when you were just bringing peaches.'

I quoted another proverb: 'A nod is enough for a wise man. A fool may need a kick up the—'

He gave a crack of laughter. 'You know a lot of our sayings, *madame*. Do you know the one that goes: *A wise woman has much to say, and yet is most often silent?*'

'I never said I was wise,' I said. 'All I do is make

chocolates.'

He looked at me then, with eyes that seemed to be nothing but shine under a webwork of wrinkles. 'I dreamt of you, Madame Rocher,' he said. 'When I tried to perform *istikhaara*. I dreamt of you, and then of her. Take care. Stay away from the water.'

Alyssa looked concerned. She said: 'You should get some rest, Jiddo.'

He smiled, and the focus returned to his eyes. 'See how she nags at me, this child? *Alhumdullila*, I hope you will come again. Remember what I told you.'

He was clearly very tired now. I put my hand on Alyssa's arm. 'We should let him rest, if he can. Perhaps you can see him tomorrow.'

She looked at me. 'Oh, Vianne. Do you think—'

'We'll come back tomorrow. I promise. For the moment, let him sleep.'

Reluctantly, she followed me downstairs into the living room. Maya was playing chequers with Omi, the cat, Hazrat, clasped in her arms.

'Is Jiddo better now?' she said, looking up as we came in. 'Memti says he's too tired to play, and Omi always cheats.'

'I do *not* cheat,' said Omi. 'I am old, and therefore infallible.' She gave me her toothless, crumpled smile. 'How was the old man? Did he talk to you?'

'A little.'

'Good. You should come again. Bring him some of your chocolate.'

I nodded. 'Of course.'

'Don't leave it too long.'

*   *   *

264

Walking home in the rain, I asked: 'Alyssa. What's *istikhaara*?'

She looked surprised. 'Oh, that,' she said. 'It's a way of asking for guidance. We pray, and then we go to sleep, and we dream of the answer to our prayer. It sometimes works, but not every time. Dreams aren't always easy to understand.'

Like the cards, I thought to myself. Images layered in meaning. *Stay away from the water*, he'd said. The scorpion and the buffalo.

Why did the old man dream of me? What kind of guidance does he seek? Was he trying to warn me to stay clear of Inès Bencharki? And if so, is it already too late? Has the scorpion stung me?

'Why did you jump in the river?' I said. 'Was it because of Luc Clairmont?'

The eyes jerked upwards. 'Luc?'

I smiled. 'Du'a told me about him. How you've been meeting him online, how you're afraid someone will find out—'

She stared at me blankly. *'Luc?'* she said.

'You used to play football with him in the square. It's all right. I understand. Your parents were different in those days. Les Marauds was different. But I know Luc. He has a mind of his own. If he loves you, he won't be put off by family disagreements. He'll stand up to his parents, the way you stood up to yours. It'll be all right. I promise you. And if you love him, how can it be wrong?'

I'd expected her to look different. To cry, perhaps; to express relief. But her expression did not change; her face was as blank as new-baked bread. Then she suddenly started to laugh;

265

unhappy, jagged laughter that cut through the air like shrapnel.

'Is *that* what you think?' she said at last. 'That I'm in love with Luc Clairmont?'

'Aren't you?' I said.

She laughed again.

'Then who is it, Alyssa?' I said. 'And why is it *zina*?'

'I thought you could *see* things,' she said with contempt, sounding so like Inès that it hurt. Beneath the tightly pinned *hijab*, she looked so much older than seventeen; at that moment she could have been thirty, or older. 'I thought you were different from everyone else. But you don't really see anything. No one here sees *anything*.'

She started to cry, a hacking sound as painful as her laughter. I tried to put my arms around her, but she pushed me away.

'Please, Alyssa.' I tried again. This time, she did not push me away, but her body was rigid in my arms. 'Please, won't you tell me what's wrong? I don't pretend to know everything, but I don't judge. I'll promise you that.'

For a long time, I thought she would not reply. We simply stood there in the rain, listening to the sound of the Tannes, and the wind tearing the leaves from the trees. Then she took a deep breath and looked at me unswervingly.

'You were right about one thing. I *am* in love. But not with Luc.'

'Then who?'

She sighed. 'Haven't you guessed? I thought you might have figured it out. You've seen him, after all. Everyone's crazy about him. Sonia, my mother, Zahra, Inès—' She gave me an unhappy smile.

266

'That's why I wanted to die,' she said. 'I'm in love with Karim Bencharki.'

CHAPTER THREE

☾

Wednesday, 25th August

She told me the whole story then, speaking in fierce little phrases. We sat in the shelter of the trees at the end of the Boulevard des Marauds, and she gave me her full confession.

'He was so beautiful,' she said. 'All of us were in love with him. When he arrived, we expected him to be some kind of a boring scholar. Our father talked so much about him, but he made him sound so *dull*, you know? And then he came, and suddenly all the girls wanted to catch his eye. Well, you've seen him, haven't you?'

Eyes like wild honey; voice like silk. 'Oh, yes. I've seen him.'

She shrugged. 'My sister was crazy for him. She'd made such a fuss before they met. Said she didn't want to get married, said they couldn't make her. Even planned to run away. And then she saw him, and everything changed. She couldn't stop talking about him then. And Aisha Bouzana; Jalila El Mardi; Rana Jannat—all making eyes at him, gossiping behind Sonia's back, saying she wasn't serious; saying she wasn't a good Muslim girl. They even brought up those football games we used to have in the village square. It made our mother nervous—imagine the scandal if he pulled out! But Karim didn't seem to care. He made friends with everyone. Helped Saïd fix up the gym; all the men started going there. It was a place to go for them, a friendly place. And then *she* came.'

'Inès,' I said.

She nodded.

'She didn't arrive with Karim?'

Alyssa shook her head. 'Not then. She turned up for the wedding, though. She's his only family. And he loves her, he's so *protective* of her—' She made a sound of disgust. '*Khee!* She wears the *niqab* all the time. In the house. Even with my father. Pretending to be so virtuous. But her eyes are evil. You must have seen *that*.'

Once I would have told you that I don't believe in evil. Now, of course, I know better.

I thought of Inès Bencharki; the look of contempt in her long dark eyes; the colours she tries so hard to hide. Is a scorpion evil because it has no other choice but to sting? I handled our first meeting badly, I know. I let her take me by surprise. I blundered in, eager, well-meaning, naïve. In short, I behaved like an amateur. Next time, things will be different.

I said: 'I don't think she's evil.'

Alyssa shrugged. 'You don't know her. When she was in charge of the school, all the girls were afraid of her. She never smiles, never laughs, never takes off her *niqab*. She's the reason so many girls are wearing it now—well, that and because Karim always says that a woman in *niqab* is a queen—'

'He seems devoted to her,' I said.

She made a face. 'That's right. He is. She's the only woman he really loves. I don't know what he

268

sees in her. She must be very beautiful. Or maybe she's a witch, an *amaar*. All I know is, she isn't his sister.'

'How can you be sure?' I said.

'Because I know,' said Alyssa. 'Because of the way he looks at her. Or rather, *doesn't* look at her. When she's there, he's different. *Everybody*'s different. She's like the bitter drop in the broth that changes the taste of everything.'

'Zahra al-Djerba likes her,' I said.

'Zahra wants to *be* her.' Alyssa's voice was scornful. 'She never used to be like that; talking politics; wearing *niqab*. But she copies everything Inès does now. Says we need to reclaim what's ours. She does it to impress Karim. Not that he'd ever notice *her*.'

'Tell me about Karim,' I said.

She sighed. 'I'm cold. Can we go home?'

'Of course we can. We can talk on the way.'

Like so many victims, she blames herself. She must have encouraged him somehow. Perhaps by wearing Western dress, to which he was unaccustomed. If she had worn *niqab*, or even proper *hijab*, she says, then it would never have happened at all. But Alyssa was young and naïve; used to playing with boys in the square; listening to music; watching TV. She never saw it coming. And when she did, it was too late; *zina* was in the room with them both.

'At first, we never even touched,' she said. 'We only talked in private. Even then, I knew it was wrong. Karim wanted to help me. But when he tried to pray with me, all I could think of was his face, and the way he moves, and his mouth, like a peach—'

He'd been having problems with Sonia, she said. Sonia had found sex painful at first, and hadn't wanted to try again. Karim had been feeling lonely and hurt. He'd confided in Alyssa because she and Sonia were so close, but by then their friendship had deepened, and had started to veer towards something else.

'The first time we kissed, it was terrible. Karim blamed himself. Not me at all. He would have moved away at once, except that he would have had to explain to my sister what had happened. Instead we gave *du'a* for guidance, and tried not to be alone together. Karim spent all his time at the gym. I started to wear *hijab*. But it wasn't easy. We were living in the same house. I thought if I dressed differently, said my prayers more often, tried to be more serious, then maybe things would change back. But by then there was something inside me that didn't really *want* to change. And then, one night, he came to my room.'

That was just four weeks ago. Since then, it had happened twice more. Once when they were alone in the house, once more at the back of the gym. Both times he had begged for forgiveness, and Alyssa had blamed herself.

Then, Inès had intervened.

'Inès?'

Alyssa nodded. 'Yes. Maybe he told her. Maybe she guessed. But somehow, Inès knew everything.' She shivered. 'She was very calm. She told me to stay away from Karim, or she would tell my parents. She would tell my sister. And Sonia was three months pregnant. What would that kind of news do to her? And then she looked at me over her veil and said, *Do you think you're the only one? Do you think it hasn't happened before? Do you think he can ever belong to you when he already belongs to me?'*

We were approaching Armande's house. All the lights were on inside. It looked like a Chinese lantern; cheery and festive and welcoming. I guessed Anouk and Rosette must be up.

Alyssa looked at me warily. 'You won't tell anyone else?' she said.

I shook my head. 'Of course not.'

She gave a fierce little nod. 'Now you see why I had to get away. She told me herself—he belongs to her. She has him in her power. And ever since, she's been watching me. Watching, waiting to catch me out. She never talks to me. But she hates me. I can see it in her eyes.'

'Why did she stop living with you?'

Alyssa made a face. 'Jiddo wasn't happy that she always wore *niqab* in the house. He doesn't like the *niqab*, he thinks it's wrong for girls to wear it nowadays. He quarrelled with my father about it. And he doesn't like Father spending so much time at the gym. Holding court, he calls it. Anyway, he moved out, and so did Inès, soon afterwards. She said she didn't want to be the cause of a family argument. But by then it was too late anyway. She had poisoned everything.'

We were standing in Armande's front porch. The rain had stopped, at least for a time. Even the wind had calmed a little, and I wondered if the Black Autan was finally coming to its end.

'I'm sorry I shouted at you,' she said. 'I was ungrateful. I owe you so much.'

I smiled. 'You don't owe me anything. Now get inside before you catch cold.'

Inside, Anouk and Rosette were toasting

croissants for breakfast. A pan of hot chocolate stood on the stove. It smelt of vanilla and spices. Alyssa took off her *hijab* and ran her hands through her damp hair.

'Can I have some of that?' she said.

'Of course. But what about Ramadan?'

She gave a wry little smile. 'I've already broken too many rules for a cup of hot chocolate to make any difference. My *jiddo* says that the rules of Islam have become a veil that hides the face of Allah. People are afraid to look. All they care about is the surface.'

I poured her a cup of hot chocolate. It was good—far better than I'd expected from the ancient jar of cocoa powder in Armande's little pantry. I mentioned the difference to Anouk.

'Oh, yes!' she exclaimed. 'The delivery came. I put it downstairs, where it's cooler.'

Good. I'd hoped it would arrive. A box of chocolate-making supplies: some blocks of couverture; packets of cocoa; boxes, rice paper, ribbons and moulds. By no means a large delivery; but enough to fulfil my promises.

'I thought we could start with some truffles,' I said.

'Sure,' said Anouk. 'Can we all help?'

'That's what I was hoping.'

Rosette looked up from her breakfast and hooted. Even she knows how to make truffles; rolled in cocoa powder and stored in boxes lined with rice paper, they are the easiest chocolates to make. You don't even need a sugar thermometer; only a good sense of timing and a nose for the moment when sugar turns and cries out for a spoonful of cream; some cinnamon; a dash of

272

Cointreau—

'I promised Omi al-Djerba I'd make her some of my chocolates. I promised old Mahjoubi, too. And then there's Guillaume, and Luc Clairmont—'

'And Joséphine and Pilou,' said Anouk.

'Pilou!' trumpeted Rosette.

'And some for Jeannot, of course.'

Anouk gave me a bright and open smile. 'Of course!'

I know what that means. One more thing to complicate our return to Lansquenet: one more obstacle on the way back to our home in Paris. I have been so concerned with my own affairs that I have paid less attention to Anouk, but I know from her carefully cheery response that Jeannot Drou has been more on her mind than she would like to admit to me. The Black Autan has brought that, too; the shadow of something I knew was there, but would rather not face at the moment. I know what I was like at fifteen. But then, it has taken me twenty years to scale the wall between sex and love. I was too young. Anouk is too young. I never listened. Neither will she.

I returned to the chocolate. Chocolate is safe. Chocolate follows specific rules. If it burns, it's because we failed to follow the directions properly. Love is random, centreless; striking out like pestilence. For the first time since Alyssa arrived, I feel a kind of sympathy for Saïd and Samira Mahjoubi. They have already lost one daughter. They are close to losing another. And as I work on my truffles, measuring, grating the chocolate, melting it slowly in the pan, adding the Cointreau drop by drop, I wonder: do they feel the same? Did they watch as Love stole their daughter away,

273

drawing her inexorably into another's orbit? Or were they so preoccupied that they never saw it coming?

I must see Joséphine again. I must see Inès Bencharki. I must find definite answers to the questions that keep me here. In the steam that rises from the pot, I can see their faces now; Joséphine's eyes looking out at me from over Inès Bencharki's veil; the Queen of Cups in her black robe, draining the bitter draught to the dregs—

The fumes from the mixture are pungent and rich; scented with citrus and cinnamon. For a moment it makes my head spin; carnival colours turn in the smoke. Scrying with chocolate is an uncertain business, closer to dreams than to the truth, more likely to throw up fantasies than anything that I can use. It flutters like dark confetti, each piece an ephemeral fragment, gleaming for a second and then going out like a blown spark. For a moment I think I see Roux; then I recognize Reynaud, walking, head lowered, by the Tannes. Reynaud as a vagrant, unshaven and pale, carrying a rucksack with a broken leather strap. What does it mean? Why Reynaud? What role does he play in this?

The chocolate mixture is ready now. Ten seconds longer, and it would burn. I take the copper pan off the heat; in moments the steam will dissipate. With it, the colours and that hint of something momentous to be revealed. Maybe I'll call on Reynaud today. Or maybe I'll make it tomorrow. Yes, maybe tomorrow would be best. After all, there's no urgency. Reynaud is not my main concern. Other people need me more.

CHAPTER FOUR

Wednesday, 25th August

I should have left at that moment, *père.* but the streets had already started to fill with people on their way to the mosque. And so I stayed watching among the trees, the boulevard on one side, the river on the other. I could still see that houseboat tucked into the river bend, just like in the days of the river-rats, and now that I knew who was living there, conflicting emotions tore at me.

The river people have always been a source of contention in Lansquenet. They pay no taxes; they go where they like; they work as and when they need to. Some are more honest than others, but it's easy enough to break the law when tomorrow you'll be gone; when you have no community to protect, no loyalty to anywhere. That's why I don't like the river-folk: because they do not contribute; because they have chosen to cut themselves off from the mainstream of society. It's the same reason I hate the *niqab*—I can say this to you, *père*, because you don't report to the Bishop—I hate the *niqab* because it allows the wearer to sever links with the rest of us; to scorn even the simplest connections that bring two cultures together.

A smile, a simple greeting, *père*—have *you* ever tried saying hello to a woman in *niqab*? Even these are denied us. I've tried so hard to be sensitive. To learn to accommodate their beliefs. But there is nothing in the Qur'an instructing women to hide their face. No, *père*. They choose to reject us. Our efforts to understand their ways have not been reciprocated.

Look at Inès Bencharki. All I've ever done was try to make her feel at home. And look how *that* turned out, eh? Well, she is Père Henri's responsibility now. He is welcome to her. Let him try where I have failed. I am free of her at last.

All this was going through my mind as I watched the last of them enter the mosque. The streets were deserted; at that moment I could have left without being seen. Instead, I made for the jetty.

I know, *père*. It was unreasonable. I could leave without saying goodbye to my friends. I could leave without informing the Bishop. But I could not leave without seeing *her*—a woman who, since her arrival, has never even shown me her face, or spoken to me unless it was absolutely necessary. Why am I drawn to her like this? Sonia said she was a witch. I told her there was no such thing. I lied, *père*. I've known witches.

I moved a little closer to the houseboat tethered by the bank. The rain had lulled to a fine mist, and I could see a filament of smoke coming out of the chimney. She might have been back in her house by now, if she had allowed me to help with repairs. Instead, she threw me out like a thief. She may even be responsible for setting those men on to me the other night. What was it they said again? *This is a war. Keep out of it*—

But now I know who lit the fire. I could clear my name at last; one word to the Bishop and I could be reinstated. Père Henri Lemaître and Caro Clairmont would be forced to eat their words. The

276

whole of Lansquenet would know that I have been unjustly condemned.

But that would mean betraying a trust. Sonia Bencharki *confessed* to me. Not officially, of course. But it *was* a confession, nevertheless. Therefore, it is sacrosanct. Even if I managed to talk to Inès, I would not be free to tell her the truth. Better to leave with the last of my pride intact. Better to do it now. And yet—

That houseboat, like a coffin moored along the riverbank. That woman, in her veil, so like the dark screen of the confessional. What do I hope to hear from her now? Or am *I* the one who needs to confess?

I moved a little closer. The Tannes was pebbled with shots of rain. The black houseboat shone sleekly in the greenish light of dawn. I must have been standing there for a long time, because at some point, in the distance, I remember being aware of the sound of the worshippers leaving prayers and making their way home through the streets.

No movement yet from the houseboat. Nevertheless, I knew she was in there. I picked up a stone and threw it. It hit the deck and bounced twice.

For a moment, there was silence. Then a door opened. The woman emerged. I could tell she hadn't seen me; she squinted out from the doorway. She did not look at all afraid; she was clearly expecting someone.

Karim Bencharki, perhaps? Either way, it was none of my business. Still I watched from between those trees; feeling both guilty and strangely exhilarated. The furtive, voyeuristic joy of being outside and looking in; the knowledge that I was unobserved—

The woman came out on to the deck. She moves like a dancer when she is alone; her steps are almost silent. The wind caught at her black robe, bringing a partner into the dance. Underneath, I saw something bright; a sudden flash of turquoise.

That surprised me a little, *père*. I'd imagined her black all the way through, like a twist of charred paper. She lifted her arms into the air as if the wind might lift her up. And then she reached round the back of her head and untied the strings of her face-veil—

I did not see her face, *père*. She was facing the water. But I could see the black flag of the *niqab* fluttering at her fingertips. If only she would turn round—

I know, *mon père*. All I can say is that at that moment the Black Autan must have driven me mad. I called out her name. She started to turn. And then I heard a sound behind me, and something—perhaps a coat or a scarf—was flung around my head. At the same time I was pushed forward, and I fell awkwardly on to my knees, with the weight of my assailant on my back. Something—an arm—angled around my neck. I tore at it without success. I couldn't breathe. I started to choke. Dark chrysanthemums bloomed across my vision.

A medium level of pressure a pplied to the carotid artery can bring unconsciousness in under ten seconds. Death follows within a minute if the pressure is not released.

And now, here comes the Black Autan: cold; rushing; pitiless. It fills my head; consumes me;

278

sweeps me away into darkness.

Autan blanc, emporte le vent.

Two more seconds—
And I'm gone.

CHAPTER FIVE

☾

Wednesday, 25th August

It was already after noon by the time we left the house. This was partly because of Rosette, who, having helped make the truffles, wanted to help deliver them, leading the way in her red rubber boots, splashing in every puddle and singing at the top of her voice—'*Bam bam BAM, bam badda-BAM!*'—while Anouk stayed indoors with Alyssa and I tried to marshal my erring thoughts.

I fought the temptation to phone Roux. There's nothing more he can tell me. Besides, if what I suspect is true, it is I, not Roux or Joséphine, who have been at fault in this affair. My mother was right: I was never supposed to build my life around one man. I never needed Roux. I should not have interfered.

The wind is losing momentum. But the rain continues, relentless. Today it is a warm rain; mild and warm as mother's milk. I think of Inès Bencharki; of Omi and Alyssa's belief that she is Karim's mistress. Is this what I am to Joséphine? A scorpion, a witch who has poisoned her life?

I should leave today, I know. I should go home while I still can. But isn't it too late for that? Already I am too involved in the life of Les Marauds. I cannot abandon Alyssa, and the problem of Inès Bencharki remains. Besides, I promised to help Reynaud salvage his reputation. In less than two weeks I have become entangled in half a dozen secrets, from Du'a's hideaway in the loft to Omi eating macaroons in defiance of Ramadan. But Lansquenet is like that. It looks so inoffensive, with its crooked little houses with the hollyhocks against the walls. But this is only a device to draw in the unwary. Like the sundew that draws in the fly with its many honeyed strands, it pulls me in and keeps me here, making those connections—

Pilou was fishing from the bridge as I crossed into Lansquenet. Vlad was with him; both were wet through, but with the insouciance of small boys and dogs everywhere, neither seemed to care much.

'I've made some chocolates,' I said. 'Want to try one?'

Pilou grinned. He has a most engaging smile, though even with my new knowledge I cannot see any of Roux in him. He has his mother's eyes, though; and her restless energy, although he has none of her awkwardness. A bright and happy little boy, and yet, if my suspicions are right, I have stolen his father.

I chose him a milk chocolate truffle. 'I think you'll like these best,' I said.

I did *not* say that his favourites would be my strawberry and black pepper squares, because I don't have the time or resources to make special chocolates for everyone. But all boys like milk chocolate best. He ate it with noisy appreciation, while Rosette watched him eagerly.

'Wow, these are amazing,' he said. 'You really made them?'

'It's what I do.' I smiled at him. 'Is your mother home?'

'Dunno,' he said. 'I think she went to see the *curé*.' Pilou grinned at my look of surprise. 'She brings him *pains au chocolat*.'

'*Pains au chocolat*?' I said.

I know Reynaud and Joséphine have mostly resolved their differences, but the vision of my old friend bringing Reynaud breakfast seems as bizarre as that of the *curé* encouraging her advances. It's the kind of thing Caro might have done—before the fire at the school, that is. But now—

I suddenly realized I hadn't seen Reynaud since Sunday night. Last week, he called by every day to bring us bread from the bakery. I'd assumed that for the past three days the rain had kept him from his morning walk. Now I remembered what I'd seen when I was making the chocolates—that vision of Reynaud, walking alone—

'Is he all right?' I said to Pilou.

'I'm not supposed to tell,' he said.

'Tell me what?'

Pilou shrugged. 'I think he got into a fight,' he said. 'With some of the people in Les Marauds. Du'a says there are bad people there. People who blame him for the fire. Anyhow, he's staying home. At least until things calm down.'

That explains it. 'Oh, I see. Maybe I'll take him some chocolates.'

It took us the rest of the afternoon to honour all my promises. A box of truffles to Narcisse, who has been so generous with gifts of fruit and vegetables. Another to Luc, who lent us this house, and without whom we might never have come here at all. A third to Guillaume, with strict instructions *not* to feed the chocolates to his dog: and with each visit those sundew filaments wrap tighter around the two of us, making it harder for us to leave, cocooning us in sweetness.

Rosette signed: *I like it here*.

Of course she does. It's so comforting. So different from Paris, with its sour suburbs and faceless crowds.

Can we stay? Can Roux come too?

Oh, Rosette. What can I do?

I got to the Café des Marauds just as the church bells rang four o'clock. Joséphine was behind the bar, and welcomed us with hot chocolate. She looked delighted to see us, but there was something in her colours that told me she was uncomfortable. I gave her a box of truffles; darkest chocolate rolled in white, the kind that I call *Les Hypocrites*.

She tried one. 'These are *wonderful*. You haven't lost your touch at all. Think of what you could do if only you—' She bit off the end of the phrase so hard that I heard her teeth click together.

If I what? Moved here for good? Is that what she was trying to say? And why does the thought alarm her?

I smiled. 'Just keeping in practice,' I said. 'Besides, I thought you'd like some.'

The café was not crowded; only a few tables were occupied. Behind the bar, I saw Marie-Ange peering out through the bead curtain that led into the back room. I drank my chocolate. It was good. Not quite as good as mine, but still—

She glanced towards the bead curtain, where Marie-Ange was beckoning persistently.

'I'm sorry, Vianne. I have to go. There's something I have to deal with.'

'Anything wrong?'

She shook her head. Her smile was all surface brilliance, hiding unease beneath the waterline. 'No, no. Please finish your chocolate. But you know—it's always so busy—'

Once more, I looked around the quiet café. Two youngsters drinking *diabolo-menthe*; Poitou having his afternoon snack before the bakery opens again; Joline Drou and Bénédicte Acheron, drinking black coffee and watching the street. Neither said anything to me, but I could see them watching Rosette, who had migrated under the table to play with Bam, hooting softly to herself. For a moment I wondered if Rosette might be the cause of Joséphine's discomfort; some people are uneasy when faced with what is unusual, and clearly Joline and Bénédicte found her vaguely disturbing—

Or it is because of her father?

I held out the box of chocolates. 'Why don't you try my *Hypocrites*? I can tell they're your favourites.'

Joline looked flustered. 'I—I don't eat chocolate.'

Bénédicte gave me a superior look. A faded blonde with a sugary smile and too many accessories, she thinks of herself as Caro Clairmont's natural successor. 'I don't think you'll find many women here do,' she told me. 'We have to watch our figures, don't we?'

'Yes, don't we?' I said, and smiled.

Her colours flared a bilious green. Under the table, Rosette began to sing in her strangely birdlike voice.

'What a sweet little girl you have,' said Bénédicte in a syrupy tone. 'What a pity she doesn't talk.'

'Oh, she sometimes talks,' I said. 'It's just that she waits to have something to say. It's a pity everyone isn't like that.'

'Excuse me, *madame*.' A voice at my back. I turned and recognized Charles Lévy, who lives down the Rue des Francs Bourgeois, not far from where Reynaud lives. Not one of my regulars, but a pleasant old man nevertheless; always neat and scrupulous. At his side was Henriette Moisson, a very elderly lady I recognized from the *chocolaterie* days. In her hand she was holding a pink cat collar adorned with a heart-shaped metal tag and was looking bewildered and anxious.

'I wonder if you could help,' said Charles. 'We're looking for Monsieur le Curé.'

Joline said: 'But it's Wednesday. You know he doesn't do Wednesdays.'

Charles Lévy gave her a look. 'No, not Père Henri,' he said. 'I'm looking for Curé Reynaud.'

Joline raised an overplucked eyebrow. 'Reynaud? Why do you want him? Everyone knows he's crazy.'

'He seemed perfectly sane when I saw him on Sunday,' I said.

'Well, Caro saw him yesterday. She thinks he's having a meltdown. It was only a matter of time, she says. He's always been the type, you know.'

Charles ignored her and addressed me again. 'I believe you are friends with Monsieur le Curé,' he said. 'I was speaking to him about my cat. My

284

Otto, whom Madame Moisson has partly adopted. I am fond of my cat, *madame*. But Curé Reynaud made me understand that perhaps her need may be greater than mine. However, Otto has now disappeared, and Madame Moisson suspects me.'

Henriette gave him a scornful look. 'My Tati would never run away.'

'He's a *cat*,' said Charles. 'Of course he would. And if you called him by his *name*, which he understands, and *responds* to—'

'Otto. That's a *Boche* name,' said Henriette contemptuously.

'My grandfather was German,' said Charles.

Henriette made a scornful sound. 'No wonder the cat doesn't want to stay. You'll be telling me he took this off by himself next!' She held out the pink collar. I saw that the heart-shaped metal tag was inscribed with the name *TATI*.

'I found it by the river,' she said. 'My Tati *loves* his collar.'

'By the river?' I frowned. 'Would Otto—or Tati—be a black cat with a little white smudge on the side of his nose?'

'You've seen him!' said Charles.

'I think I have. Although in Les Marauds I believe he goes by the name of Hazrat, and has developed a passion for coconut macaroons.'

Henriette gave a wail. 'No! Les Marauds? Those *Maghrébins*! A cat isn't safe in their neighbourhood. They'll make my Tati into cat kebabs—'

I assured her Tati was an honoured guest, and promised to bring word of him soon. Henriette was not entirely reassured, but consented to eat a truffle. Charles joined her, sitting down only when Henriette was comfortably seated.

'Thank you, Madame Rocher,' he said, softly, to avoid being heard by Joline and Bénédicte. 'I've tried Monsieur le Curé's house, but he won't talk to anyone any more, not even through his letter-box.'

'His *letter-box*?'

'Oh yes,' said Charles. 'He's been taking confession. He's not allowed to take it in church. Not now Père Henri's in charge.'

'That *perverti*,' said Henriette. 'Do you know he was hiding in the confessional when I last went to church? He was even dressed as a priest, *pardi*!'

'Père Henri *is* a priest,' said Charles.

'You'd have thought a *perverti* like that wouldn't be allowed,' said Henriette.

Charles took another chocolate, apparently to calm his nerves. 'You see what she's like?' he hissed at me. 'The sooner we find Otto, the better. He seems to calm her down, somehow.'

'I'll find him. I promise,' I told them both.

But their words had reawakened my doubts. Something was wrong with Francis Reynaud. Staying indoors for fear of attack; taking confession through his letter-box; appearing to me through a chocolate haze; behaving so uncharacteristically that Caro Clairmont had managed to spread the rumour that he was going mad—

I gathered up Rosette and Bam and what was left of my chocolates. The sense of unease that was nagging at me had now become an imperative. I made my way to Reynaud's cottage on the Rue des Francs Bourgeois and knocked at the door. No answer. The shutters were open; looking inside, I saw no sign of anyone. I tried the door again. No reply. Then I turned the doorknob.

The door was not locked. That in itself was not

much of a surprise. Lansquenet has barely any crime; even now, most people don't bother to lock their doors. There was a thief, a few years ago; so Narcisse was telling me. One of the Acheron cousins, I think; but since he was caught, there has been no one.

The house was empty. I knew it at once. The sound is subtly different. It smelt very slightly of burnt toast, and of rooms left unaired since the previous day. I went into the bedroom and saw the bed, neatly stripped, with the pillows heaped on the mattress. Everything was scrupulously neat; everything clean and squared away. The plants had been recently watered; no dirty plates in the kitchen; the plastic bowl in the sink turned carefully upside down. In the scullery, I found a load of clean, dry washing in the machine: it still smelt fresh, as if it had been put there some time that morning. The bathroom was as bare as the kitchen; no towels on the towel rail; no toothbrush on the glass shelf.

Could Reynaud have gone away?

I moved back into the living room, where Rosette was playing quietly. The sound of her game and of the clock that was ticking above the mantelpiece was all the life there was left in the place. Some people leave a part of themselves in the house where they once lived; but there is no trace of Francis Reynaud; no footprint; no shadow; not even a ghost.

'Where has he gone?' I said aloud.

Rosette looked up and hooted at me.

'Bam!' It's an invitation to play.

I shook my head. 'Not now, Rosette. I'm thinking. Where would he go, without telling us?'

The river, signed Rosette at once, as if the answer were obvious.

The river. The thought of it made me feel cold. Swollen now by a week of rain, it must be getting treacherous. And hadn't old Mahjoubi warned me it was dangerous? I had a sudden, disquieting image of Reynaud standing on the parapet, looking into the water.

Could it be that Caro was right? Could Reynaud have suffered some kind of a nervous breakdown? Could the stress of the past few weeks have driven him to suicide? Surely not. He isn't the type. And yet—

People change, my mother's voice whispers from the darkness. *After all, you changed, didn't you? You, and Roux, and Joséphine—*

Now it was Armande's voice: *You tried to save me, didn't you? Just as you did your mother. All the same, we both died.*

'Bam!' said Rosette. '*Bam bam, badda-bam!*'

That's right, Rosette. You tell those ghosts. Tell them all to leave us alone. This is just the Black Autan, working its way into my head, giving me unquiet thoughts, making me question my common sense. Reynaud has probably gone for a walk. We'll see him in the morning. Besides, we have more chocolates to deliver in Les Marauds; coconut truffles for Omi; rose and cardamom for Fatima and her daughters; chilli for old Mahjoubi, that warms the heart and brings courage. And one more package, for Inès; tied with a red silk ribbon. The gift that crosses all cultures; that brings a smile to the sourest face; that pulls back the years and takes us to a simpler, sweeter time. Last time I tried to approach her, I failed. I came unarmed and

unaware. This time will be different.
This time I'm bringing her favourites.

CHAPTER SIX

Wednesday, 25th August

I cannot have been unconscious for long, but I awoke in darkness. My head hurt, and so did my back; I guessed that whoever had brought me here had not been especially gentle.

Where was *here*? With care, I sat up. A cellar of some kind, perhaps: the floor was flagged; that cellar smell. It was cold and smelt of damp, of mildew and things gone to rot.

Near by, I could hear the river: its throaty, rushing, roaring sound, charged with floodwater debris, and rolling like a juggernaut.

I called: 'Hello?'

No one answered.

I could have called again, but did not. I guessed that my attacker might be one of the men who set upon me the other night. If so, did I want to meet him again?

I tried to explore my surroundings. Feeling my way in a darkness that felt as vast as a ballroom, I found some empty wooden crates, some broken plaster, damp cardboard; bundles of ancient newspaper, and beyond that, at last, a dozen stone steps, leading up to a locked door. There was no doorknob on my side. I slammed against it with my fists. No one came. The door was strong. The sound of my fists against the wood was barely audible above the sound of the river.

Mon père, I know it sounds absurd. But at first I was not afraid. In fact, I found it hard to believe that I was even here at all; easier by far to think that this was all some kind of dream brought about by stress, fatigue or the pain of my still-throbbing fingers. It is only now that fear has moved in, like the unwelcome guest who gradually takes over the entire house. I see that the darkness is not quite complete; a dim rectangle of daylight frames the door at the top of the steps, and high up the far wall there is a grille, like that of the confessional, through which filters a pallid glow.

Now, as my eyes adapt to the dark, a kind of perspective begins to emerge. I find I can see shapes now, and the menacing glint of water. The floor is built on a pronounced slope; the lower end is flooded, which makes me guess that this must be one of the derelict tanneries. As the water levels rise, the cellar will fill with alarming speed. I've seen it happen more than once by the river in Les Marauds; it's one of the principal reasons that most of the buildings along the boulevard are condemned.

Approximately an hour ago, a thin rivulet of water began to trickle out of a pipe in the wall. Since then, the trickle has grown, becoming a puddle of water that streams almost silently down the wall and pools in sinister fashion in the far corner of the room. In an hour, the puddle has crept almost halfway across the floor.

Who has done this? Why am I here? Is it an attempt to intimidate me? I will admit that I am

290

afraid. But mostly, *père*, I am angry. That someone should do this to me—to *me*, a representative of the Holy Catholic Church—

Of course, you might say that I walked away. I tried to evade my duty. I left like a criminal in the night, leaving no word of my intentions. With hindsight, maybe that was a mistake. No one will know I am missing. Perhaps in a few days' time, someone will think to drop by the house. But how would they know where to look for me? And how high will this water rise?

I suppose you would say it serves me right. I never should have tried to leave. A priest cannot simply walk away from God, or from his calling. Although God does not speak to me as you do, *père*, and over the years I have found myself wondering whether this calling of mine is not simply another way of trying to impose order upon a world grown increasingly strange and chaotic. But without the Church, I am defenceless; my current predicament proves it. Like Jonah, I have been swallowed up into the belly of something too large and too alien to tackle alone.

I dragged the crates against the far wall, making a kind of pyramid. Climbing on to this, I found that I could now just see out through the grille. There isn't much to see, *père*: nothing but a brick wall. It must be an alley, flooded now that the Tannes has broken its banks. It smells vaguely of piss, *père*, overlaid with chlorine and disinfectant; in the distance, I can also smell *kif*, and spices, and something cooking. The alley must be very small; perhaps one of the connecting passages—barely a metre or so in width—that link the street with the riverside. Even in good weather, they are not often used. My chances of being heard by a passer-by are insignificant.

And now I am hungry—hours have passed, and my stomach is protesting that I have missed at least one meal. I eat some of the food I brought with me in my rucksack—unfortunately, that's not very much; I was planning to buy supplies as soon as I left Lansquenet. A couple of tins of tuna in oil; some bread left over from the previous day. An apple. A bottle of water. I force myself not to eat it all.

But now that my need has subsided, I find that my fear has become all the more acute. I try the door at the top of the steps every twenty minutes or so, as if it might open miraculously, although I know it to be locked. It's cold in here—much colder than the air outside—and I am already shivering. I find the oversized sweater that I packed inside my rucksack and put it on under my coat. The wool is coarse, but comforting. If I close my eyes, I find that even the sound of the water has a soporific effect. I might be at sea; the sound of the Tannes comes to me from a distance. At sea, on my way to a new world; a childhood fantasy long abandoned by the time I went off to the seminary.

This is what happens, Francis Reynaud, to boys who run away to sea.

That's your voice, *mon père*. I know. You're right. I should ask God's forgiveness. And yet, I cannot help but feel a kind of exhilaration. Perhaps this is why I cannot pray. I do not feel repentance.

Once more, I consider the sea-monster, which has swallowed me so efficiently. Are you right to blame me? Is this my punishment for running away? Or could it be that all my life I was *already*

292

living inside the beast, unaware of the world outside?

CHAPTER SEVEN

Wednesday, 25th August

I must have slept. How long, I don't know. but when I awoke, night was falling, and even the small square of daylight that appeared around the grille had faded to a reddish glow. My body was stiff and my muscles hurt from lying on the stone floor. Even so, *mon père*, I slept. I must have been exhausted.

I checked the view of the alleyway from my position on the crates, noting as I did that the puddle was much deeper now, soaking into my walking boots.

The wind had died down, and the rain had stopped. Standing on the pile of crates, face pressed up against the grille, I found that the smell of cooking had become more pronounced. Of course. These people eat after sunset, sometimes at midnight or later.

I considered crying out for help. Maybe someone would set me free. After all, how long could my captors hope to perpetuate this ridiculous state of affairs? The more I thought about it now, the more this looked like a prank gone wrong, a joke that someone had taken too far.

The water coming from the pipe in the wall

continues unabated. Perhaps it is the outlet to a disused system of gas pipes—whatever it was, the rising Tannes has channelled it in my direction. There is no way to stop up the pipe, as I found to my cost when I made the attempt; all I managed to achieve was to wet my clothes a little more.

I stood on the crates and called for help.

No one came. There was no response. My voice sounded barely audible in the belly of the whale.

I called until my voice was hoarse. Five minutes; maybe ten. I could smell something like baking bread; like sauces rich with spices and oil; like rose petals and roasting lamb and chickpea pasties and chestnuts.

'Help me! I'm *here*! It's Francis Reynaud!'

By now I was dizzy with shouting. I would have been grateful to see anyone—even my attackers, *père*—rather than face this solitude. The knowledge surprised me a little. I have never had so little taste for my own company. Even the face of Père Henri Lemaître would be manna in this wilderness.

'Help me! *Please!*'

I was unsure whom I was addressing. Maybe you, *mon père*—or God. In any case, nobody answered, and in the end I left my post and returned to the steps—soon to become the only part of the cellar untouched by the rising water—wrapped myself in my overcoat and tried to go to sleep again. I may have done so; or maybe I simply lapsed into a kind of dull lethargy, from which I was roused some time later by a thudding sound above my head.

Boom, boom, boom, boom.

The sound was persistent and rhythmic, like a distant bassline.

Boom, boom, boom, boom.

Music? No, I don't think so. The community of Les Marauds is not a place where music abounds. Besides, that regular pounding has something organic about it; a barely perceptible unevenness, like that of an erratic heart. Perhaps it is the heart of the whale, *mon père*, as it dreams of further conquests.

And then it suddenly hit me. At last, *mon père*, I know where I am. That sound, like that of a giant heart, is the sound of a treadmill.

My cellar is underneath the gym.

CHAPTER EIGHT

☾

Wednesday, 25th August

The sunset was spectacular as we crossed into Les Marauds. The rain has finally stopped, and the result is this glorious sunset; dramatic layers of lemon and rose under an ominous sheet of slate. By the time I crossed the river again, every house was crimson; every window illuminated in gold leaf. And behind them, the Tannes; lustrous and rich; sleek and shining and silken.

I could see Inès Bencharki's boat moored in the shelter of the trees. A light was shining from inside, and a filament of pale smoke beckoned from the chimney. I took out my last batch of chocolates; a handful of dark and light truffles rolled in spiced cocoa powder. There's cardamom, for comfort; vanilla seeds for sweetness; green tea, rose and tamarind for harmony and goodwill. Sprinkled with gold leaf, they look like tiny Christmas baubles; prettily scented; perfectly round—how could she resist these?

Rosette had made for the water at once. Bam enjoys swimming, apparently. Rosette can swim as well as Roux, and has no fear of the water. A pointed stick serves to test the depth as well as to fish out any debris that might be promising. As I approached the jetty I saw that she had already rescued several sticks, a champagne cork and a doll's head, which she had placed on top of the pile like a cannibal's trophy.

'Don't go in the water, Rosette.' Across the gilded surface, Bam ricocheted like a skimming-stone.

'What's that in the water?'

A voice at my side. I turned and saw Maya watching us from one of the little passageways connecting the riverside to the street. There must be half a dozen of these along the Boulevard des Marauds; narrow for an adult to use, but just right for a five-year-old. Maya was wearing bright pink wellingtons and a sweater with the shape of a frog knitted into the pattern. Under her arm she was carrying Tipo, the unidentified knitted toy from which she seems inseparable.

I said: 'That's Bam. Rosette's special friend. Not everyone can see him, though. I think he must like you, Maya.'

Maya's eyes grew rounder. 'Is he a Jinni? My *jiddo* says there are Jinn everywhere. Some of them are friendly. Some of them are *shayteen*.'

I smiled and said, 'He's a monkey. Rosette doesn't have many friends back home.'

296

'I wish *I* had a monkey. Where did he come from?'

I tried to explain. 'It's something my mother taught me to do. It's like a kind of magic. Anouk has a special friend, too. But hers is a rabbit. His name is Pantoufle.'

Maya's lip protruded. 'I wish *I* had an animal friend.'

'Well, you can, Maya,' I said. 'All you have to do is close your eyes, and imagine one.'

Maya screwed her eyes shut so hard that the whole of her body shook. Rosette grinned and poked her.

Maya giggled. '*Stop* it, Rosette.' She opened her eyes and grinned back. 'Let's see if my Jinni's here yet,' she said, and both of them raced across the boardwalk, bouncing along in their wellington boots like two brightly coloured rubber balls.

I followed them. 'Don't fall in,' I said. 'That jetty could be slippery.'

Rosette just laughed and started to sing: '*Bam bam bam! Bam badda-bam!*'

Soon, Maya had joined her, with more enthusiasm than skill, both of them stamping out the rhythm on the boards of the jetty. They made so much noise that in the end the door of the houseboat opened and Inès Bencharki looked out.

'I thought perhaps you'd like to try some of my chocolates,' I told her. 'I've taken some to Fatima. I'd promised some to her mother, too, and to your father-in-law.'

She dipped her head in acknowledgement. Today her black *niqab* was trimmed with a single silver stripe. It gave her face definition; underlined those beautiful eyes.

I handed her the chocolates in a twist of rice paper. 'Try one,' I said. 'They're your favourites.'

'Are they now?' Her voice was dry.

Well, of course, it's hard to tell when someone is so hard to read. But she took them, albeit reluctantly.

'It's after sunset,' I told her. 'And don't they *smell* just marvellous?'

She held up the twist of paper. Behind the veil, I guessed the scent would not be as pronounced. She said, in her half-musical, half-grating voice: 'Forgive me. My sense of smell is not good.' I saw her glance at Rosette and Maya at the mouth of the little passageway.

'That's my little Rosette,' I said, sensing her curiosity.

Inès spoke to Maya in Arabic.

Maya looked mutinous, then pulled a face.

Inès spoke in a sharper voice, too quickly for me to understand.

Maya stamped her pink boot and whispered something in Rosette's ear. Then she ran off down the passage between the houses, pausing only to wave at Rosette as she reached the corner.

'What did you say to her?' I asked Inès.

'Only the truth. That it's dangerous to play here on the jetty. Her mother does not know where she is. She should not be out here alone.'

'She wasn't alone. She was with me.'

Inès said nothing.

'Isn't the truth that you disapprove of Maya playing with Rosette?'

Inès made the same gesture—the same half-shrug, half head-tilt—that Alyssa often makes to indicate ambivalence.

298

'There's nothing wrong with Rosette,' I said. 'She's friendly, she loves everyone. And Maya has no friends of her own—'

'Maya has been spoilt,' said Inès, her voice surprisingly gentle. 'Just as Alyssa and Sonia were spoilt. If parents let their children play with *kuffar* children, go to their homes, play with their toys, pet their dogs, they should not be surprised when their daughters turn away from their families and their sons are led astray—'

'Maya's only five years old,' I said.

'And soon she will have to learn to wear *hijab*. And the children at school will call her names, and ask her why she does not eat *haram* food, or listen to their music, or wear the same clothes as they do. And even if her parents are what you like to call *tolerant*, and let her play with toys, and cut her hair, and watch cartoons on television, she will still be a *Maghrébine*—not one of *them*, but one of *us*.'

I don't often get angry, but this time I was. Anger like a smokeless flame; blue, almost invisible. 'Not everyone here is like that,' I said.

'Maybe not,' she told me. 'But there are more than enough who hate to compensate for those who do not. Even here in Lansquenet. Do you think I can't hear what they say about me? *Niqab* does not make me deaf, or blind. In Marseille, men used to follow me about and ask me what I looked like. One day, in the supermarket queue, a woman tried to pull off my veil. Every day I would hear someone say, *You don't belong here. You're not French. You're antisocial. You hate the* kuffar. *You won't eat our food. You sympathize with terrorists. Why else would you hide your face?*' Her voice had grown harsh. 'Every day I hear someone say that soon *niqab* will be outlawed. What does it matter to them what I wear? Must I give up *everything*?'

She stopped, a little breathless. In her colours I saw surprise. Perhaps she is not accustomed to speaking so freely to strangers. She lifted the twist of paper with the chocolates inside.

'You're right,' she said. 'These do smell good.'

I smiled. 'You can try them later. I'll leave a packet for Du'a.'

'You know my daughter?'

'We've met,' I said. 'She seems quite a lonely little girl.'

Once more, I saw her colours change. Surprise gave way to the blue tones of sorrow and regret. She said: 'We have had to move around more than I intended. It is good for Du'a to live here. She has no family at home.'

'I'm sorry about your husband,' I said.

Her colours flared like the sunset.

'We're not as different as you might think,' I said. 'I used to move around a lot. First with my mother, then with Anouk. I know what it's like to never belong. To have everybody looking at you. To have people like Caro Clairmont looking down their noses because there is no *Monsieur* Rocher—'

I sensed she was listening closely. I knew I had made a connection. *It may be a cheap kind of magic*, I thought, *but it always works*. It always works. In her hand the rice-paper twist releases its battery of scents; bitter chocolate melted with cream and sweetened with vanilla seeds, scented with roses as red as your heart. *Try me. Taste me. Test me.*

And then she raised her eyes to mine. I saw myself, reflected. For a moment I was haloed in gold against the illuminated sky.

And then she said, without dropping her gaze: 'Mademoiselle Rocher. With respect, we have nothing in common. I am a widow—unfortunate, but hardly reprehensible. I have been forced to travel abroad by circumstances beyond my control. I have a child, whom I have brought up in modesty and obedience. You, on the other hand, are an unmarried woman with two children, no faith and no proper home. And that, in our culture, makes you a whore.'

And at that she extended her gloved hand and gave me back my chocolates, and went back into the houseboat, just as the bells began to ring for Mass across the water, and I was left holding the paper twist, stupidly, uselessly; with the tears beginning to burn my eyes as if the sky were raining fire.

CHAPTER NINE

☾

Wednesday, 25th August

A whore. Is that what she thinks of me? of course, I've been called worse things, but never with such cold intent. *A scorpion*, said Omi. Yes, that's what she is—poison, poison through and through. I dropped the chocolates on to the deck and almost ran back to the boulevard. I felt as if I were drowning; as if I were tied to a block of stone, sinking into the indifferent Tannes.

Well, what did you expect, Vianne? said a voice

301

inside my head. *It's only chocolate, after all. A second-rate, mean kind of magic, when you could have had the Hurakan—*

That voice, so like my mother's, but without any of my mother's warmth. It's the voice of Zozie de l'Alba, that still sometimes talks to me in dreams. She would never have allowed sentiment to get in her way. She is impervious to blows; poison slips right through her.

You're weak, Vianne, that's your problem, she says, and secretly I know she's right. I am weak because I care too much what other people think of me; because I want to be needed; because even a scorpion who lives to sting can expect me to hold out a helping hand—

That's just stupid, Zozie says. *Anyone would think you* wanted *to be stung.*

Is that true? Am I fooling myself? Am I drawn by failure? Was my impulse to help Inès simply an urge towards self-harm?

I took Rosette home through streets that now seemed thick with contempt and hostility. We walked past the gym, where a huddle of men in prayer hats and *djellabas* were talking in lowered voices. The conversation stopped as we passed, then resumed as we went by.

Back home, I made dinner for everyone— home-made soup and olive bread; baked rice pudding and peach jam—but I was too restless to eat anything. Instead I drank coffee and sat by the window and watched the lights on the boulevard, and felt homesick for Roux, and our houseboat with my little *chocolaterie* in it, and Nico, and my mother, and all those simple, familiar things that aren't so simple any more.

302

Roux was right. Why am I here? It was a mistake for me to come; a terrible, ruinous, stupid mistake. How could I have ever believed that chocolate could solve anything? The ground beans of a South American tree; some sugar; a pinch of spices. Sweet conceits, no more substantial than a handful of powder on the wind. Armande said Lansquenet needed me. But what have I done since I arrived but kick open doors that should have stayed shut?

Roux asked me to come home last night. Roux, who never asks for anything. If only he'd asked a week ago, before all this. Now it's too late. Nothing has turned out as I planned. My trust in him has been broken; my friendship with Joséphine compromised. Even Reynaud, whom I promised to help, has come to grief since I came here. Why did I stay? To help Inès? She clearly doesn't want my help. And as for Rosette and Anouk—well. Is it fair to bring them here, to let them make friends—and maybe more—knowing that it cannot last?

There's something different about Anouk. I've sensed it over the past few days. Today she is excessively bright; yesterday she was moody. Her colours are like the autumn sky, veering from grey, to purple, to blue, all in the space of an instant. Is she hiding something from me? Is something preying on her mind? With Anouk, it's so hard to know; although I suspect that Jeannot Drou may have something to do with it. The furtive glances; the innocent airs; the time spent on her mobile phone, texting, or searching Facebook. And now, this new, almost fey Anouk; this stream of chatter; this girlish glow like that of a latent fever. All the more reason not to stay. And yet, perhaps—

At nine o'clock, a knock at the door. I opened

303

it to see Luc Clairmont, out of breath and slightly embarrassed. I didn't need to read colours to know that Caroline had sent him.

He came in, declined coffee and sat down at the kitchen table. Alyssa, who had fled upstairs, came quietly back down again. Of course, she looks very different now, with her short hair and cast-off jeans. But whatever she says about not loving Luc, it is clear to me that he loves *her*. His face lit up when he saw her; his eyes were almost as wide as Rosette's.

She said: 'Don't tell anyone I'm here.'

'O-OK.' He gave her a sideways look from under his overlong fringe. The stutter that he has mostly outgrown made a brief reappearance. 'Have you left home?'

Alyssa shrugged. 'I'm nearly eighteen. I can do whatever I like.'

Now I saw envy in Luc's eyes. Leaving Caroline Clairmont will be no simple achievement. Although he is older than Alyssa and already has a house of his own, his mother still casts a long shadow, and he has not yet escaped it. Some people never do—trust me, Luc, I should know.

He gave me an apologetic look. 'My mother says you were at Reynaud's house.'

I said: 'Yes, I was. But he wasn't home.'

'Well, that's the problem,' Luc went on. 'He hasn't been seen since yesterday. My m-mother just checked his house. He's not home. She phoned Père Henri. He hasn't seen him either. She thought he might be here w-with you.' That little ghost-stutter was back in his voice. He looked profoundly uncomfortable. 'I didn't really want to ask, but people are getting worried, and—'

304

'No, Luc.' I shook my head. 'I haven't seen him either.'

'Oh. But I mean—where would he go? It isn't like him just to disappear. And without even telling anyone? It doesn't make *sense*—'

Actually, it makes perfect sense. I know exactly how he feels. We have tried and tried, he and I, and still Lansquenet defies us. We are not so very different, after all, Reynaud and I. We both feel the pull of the Black Autan. We both have known disappointment here, and sadness, and betrayal. That vision of Reynaud I saw when I was making the chocolates—I took it as a diversion, when all the time I was seeing the truth almost as it was happening—

'Why would he leave?' I said it aloud. 'Because he can't face it any more. Because he thinks he's let you down. He tried to help, but it made things worse. He thinks you'll be better without him. And maybe he's right—' I realized I was no longer speaking entirely for Reynaud. 'Some things—some *people*—can't be saved. There's a limit to what goodwill can do. We can only be what we're *made* to be, not what others expect, or hope—' I broke off, seeing Luc staring. 'What I mean is,' I went on, 'sometimes walking away is best. I should know. It's my speciality.'

He looked at me, incredulous. 'Is that really what you think?'

'I know it's hard to understand, but—'

'Oh, I *understand* just fine.' Suddenly, he was furious. 'You're the queen of walking away, aren't you, Vianne? My grandmother said you'd leave, and you did. Right on cue, just like she said. But she was sure you'd be back some day. Even wrote

305

you a letter. And now, here you are again, saying that sometimes walking away is best. You think any of this would have happened if you'd stayed here in the first place?'

I stared at him in astonishment. Could this really be Luc Clairmont? Little Luc, who'd once had a stammer so pronounced that he could hardly finish a sentence? Luc, who'd read Rimbaud's poems in secret when his mother was in church?

A voice in my head gave a gleeful chuckle. Not my mother's voice, this time, or even Zozie's, but Armande's voice, which made it very hard to dismiss. *That's my boy. You tell her*, it said. *Sometimes even a witch needs that.*

I tried to ignore it. 'That's not fair. I *had* to leave,' I told him. 'My journey wasn't finished, Luc. I had to try to find myself.'

'And did you?' He was still furious.

I shrugged.

'I didn't think so.'

* * *

His words stayed with me long after he'd left and the children had all gone to bed. Of course it's ridiculous and unfair. Francis Reynaud is not a child. He must have his reasons for leaving. And yet, that inner voice persists: *You think any of this would have happened if you'd stayed here in the first place?*

If I'd stayed in Lansquenet, Roux would never have left Joséphine. The fire in the *chocolaterie* would never have happened. Reynaud would never have been accused. We would have made friends with the *Maghrébins*—Inès Bencharki and her

306

brother would never have found a foothold in Les Marauds.

I texted Roux:

I'm sorry. I meant to come home. But I don't even know what that means any more. Too many things are happening here. I'll try to call again. V.

I wondered if he would understand. Roux, like Rosette, lives for the present, and has no patience with *what-if* or *if-only*. Places have no hold on him; he makes his home wherever he wants. If only I could be like Roux, and leave the past where it belongs.

But the past is never far from my thoughts; regret never more than a blink away. When I was a child, I liked gardens; the tidy rows of marigolds; the lavender bushes along the walls; the nicely tended vegetable plots with their rows of cabbages and leeks and onions and potatoes.

Yes, I'd have liked a garden. Even a handful of herbs in a pot. My mother said: *'Why bother, Vianne? You make them grow, you water them, and then one day you have to move on. There's no one left to care for them. They die. Why try to make them grow at all?'*

All the same, I always tried. A geranium on a window-ledge. An acorn underneath a hedge. A scatter of wildflowers along a stretch of roadside verge; something that might take root and grow, and still be there if I came by again—

I remembered Reynaud in his garden, grimly fighting the yearly invasion of dandelions that poke their green tongues from the flowerbeds, the vegetable patch, the neatly trimmed lawn. If he stays away, in a month his garden will be overgrown. Dandelions will march across the

307

garden path, invade the lawn, and scatter regiments of parachutes into the grey and turbulent air. Lavender will grow spidery through the gaps in the garden wall, and ivy will sink its tendrils between the loosened blocks of stone. In the flowerbeds, anarchy. The ranks of dahlias will fall, and the morning glories will blow their trumpets in triumph as the weeds begin to take over.

Reynaud, where *are* you?

I tried the cards. But they were as indistinct as before. Here comes the Knight of Cups again; the Eight of Cups; despair; debauch. *Is* the Knight of Cups Reynaud? His face is in shadow, too raddled to tell. The cards, which were cheap to begin with, are badly stained with handling. And now comes his partner, the Queen of Cups; and between them, the Lovers—Joséphine and Roux?—and the Tower, broken and tumbling. Thrown dice. Destruction. Change. But who rings the changes?

You do.

The
KNIGHT
of
CUPS

CHAPTER ONE

Thursday, 26th August

I must have slept again, *père*, because I dreamt. I do not dream often—it is a habit I seem to have lost—but this time my dreams were like locusts, swarming all over me, picking me dry, and the world was filled with the sound of their wings. I awoke feeling stiff and exhausted. My ribs still hurt, and my injured hand was swollen and throbbing fiercely. I wished I had brought some painkillers with me, but of course I had left them at home.

Home. Oh, what a fool I've been. To think that I could try to outrun the shadows that pursue me. To be like Vianne Rocher, to go wherever the winds blow. That's where I made my mistake, *père*. Oh, God, for the chance to take it back.

The little pale square around the grille had reappeared again. It was daylight. The trickle of water from the pipe has now reached the top of the lowest step. I finished the last of my supplies and examined my position, which, on the whole, does not look good.

I must have been here a day and a night. In that time, no one has come, either to explain the reason for my imprisonment or (better still) to ensure my release. I was hoping that, in the light of day, whoever did this might get cold feet, decide that I have been punished enough and simply let me go on my way. This has not happened, and now

I begin to wonder whether my assessment of the situation has not been overly optimistic. How long am I to be kept here? Why am I a prisoner? More importantly, who has made himself judge and jury over me?

Above me, the sound of the treadmill maintains a steady heartbeat, occasionally joined by the sound of other fitness machinery. I had no idea that Saïd's gym was such a hub of activity. Of course, I knew it was popular, but I never suspected the number of men who use it as a meeting-place. Over time, I have learnt to distinguish the voices of the different machines; the thumping of the treadmill, the *creak-thump* of the rowing machines; the *ack-ack-ack* of the bicycles; the purposeful nearly-there *thud* of the weights. There are classes, too; I can hear them, the scuffling of many feet on the floor above punctuated by muffled cries of encouragement. Keep-fit? Martial arts? Difficult to say for sure, but from what I can hear, half the male population of Les Marauds is there, stamping their feet more or less in time, presumably wholly unaware of my presence here, in the bilges.

I tried calling for help again. No one heard me. No one came. For half an hour, the sound of activity stopped completely and I guessed that it was time for prayer. During that time, I heard noises; scuffling noises in the walls. Rats, I imagine. The cellars are infested with them. Then the treadmill began again.

I stood on the crates and looked outside. The rain has stopped for the present. The view was as dull as yesterday, a brick wall, skirted with litter; dandelions between the stones. I prepared to call

311

for help again—

And saw a small, round, curious face staring at me (upside down) from between a pair of pink wellington boots. Espresso-dark eyes blinked in surprise.

'Are you a Jinni?' said Maya.

CHAPTER TWO

☾

Thursday, 26th August

After a restless night's half-sleep, I went out to check if Reynaud had come home. I was not alone in this. In the Rue des Francs Bourgeois, I found Caro Clairmont holding court outside Reynaud's back door, with Joline and Bénédicte. It soon became clear that Caro viewed Monsieur le Curé's disappearance as suspicious, maybe even sinister.

'I think Père Henri would do well to check the parish accounts for the past few months,' she was saying as I arrived. 'Say what you like, there's no smoke without fire, and with everything that's been happening—' She shot me a disapproving glance. I suppose my presence also counts as an unusual happening. Her blue eyes, pale and powdery, lingered on me like chalk dust. 'Of course, if he's somehow involved with that girl—'

'What girl?' I said.

She gave a tight little smile. 'One of the girls from Les Marauds,' she said. 'According to Louis Acheron, he was seen last week, around midnight, with a girl by the side of the bridge. A *Maghrébine*, by all accounts.'

I shrugged. 'So what?'

'So, who *was* she? Louis says she was wearing a veil.'

'Half the women in Les Marauds wear a veil,' said Charles Lévy, who was watching from over his garden fence.

'But do half the women in Les Marauds have midnight meetings with Monsieur le Curé?' Caro's voice was like *baba au rhum*.

'Maybe they do.' It was Bénédicte. 'I've heard that Joséphine Muscat has been getting awfully friendly with him.'

Caro and Joline both glanced at me.

'Well, it wouldn't be the first time,' said Caro.

'What do you mean?'

She gave that syrupy smile again. 'She's *your* friend. Why don't you ask her? As for Reynaud, his behaviour has been—shall we say, *irregular*. There's something going on, I'm sure. I've called Père Henri. He'll know what to do.'

I left them to wait for Père Henri and headed for the Place Saint-Jérôme. If anyone knew where Reynaud had gone, I guessed it might be Joséphine. But Caro's comment had struck a nerve.

It wouldn't be the first time.

Of course, she has never liked Joséphine. And an unmarried mother in Lansquenet is always the subject of gossip. I ought to know better by now than to let Caro's gossip trouble me. But all the same, could she have known the truth about Pilou's father?

I found the café empty. Even the bar was deserted. I called Joséphine. No answer.

313

Marie-Ange must be on her break. I felt a childish pang of relief. *Now I won't have to see her.* Then I saw movement from behind the glass bead curtain dividing the bar from the living quarters at the back.

'Joséphine?' I called again.

'Who wants her?' said a man's voice.

'It's Vianne,' I said. 'Vianne Rocher.'

For a moment there was silence. Then the bead curtain parted, and a grey-haired man in a wheelchair emerged. For a moment I didn't recognize him. All I could see was that wheelchair, and the wasted legs tucked neatly beneath a stretch of tartan blanket. Then, I saw him: the dark eyes; the handsome, brutal features; the smile; the muscular arms emerging from the sleeves of a denim work-shirt.

'Hello, you interfering bitch.'

The man was Paul-Marie Muscat.

CHAPTER THREE

☾

Thursday, 26th August

I felt as if he'd punched me. Not because of what he'd said, but the shock of his appearance. His face has not altered very much. His grey hair is shorn to a stubble, showing the contours of his scalp. He has lost weight, and the coarseness that once characterized his features has been refined to a kind of severe beauty. But his expression is the same: appraising; vaguely hostile; suspicious, and yet coloured with a kind of trollish good humour.

'Surprised to see me, eh?' he said. 'I heard you were back in Lansquenet. I don't suppose the bitch mentioned me. She wouldn't. I'm not good for business.'

I held his gaze. 'If you mean Joséphine, then no, she didn't mention you.'

He laughed harshly and lit a Gauloise. 'She doesn't like me smoking in here. Doesn't like me drinking, either. Whisky?'

I shook my head. 'No, thanks.'

He poured himself a double from a bottle standing on the bar. 'I built this place out of nothing,' he said. 'I ran it like clockwork for six whole years. Of course, she likes to pretend it's hers, and that she doesn't owe me a thing. Why would she? I only gave her my name, looked after her, paid for her clothes, lived with her moods. But as soon as we hit a rough patch, she threw me out like a stray dog.' He gave another joyless laugh and blew smoke out of his nostrils. 'I guess I have you to thank for that. Giving her ideas. Well, I hope you're happy now.' He took a drink of his whisky. 'Because I'm *right* where you wanted me.'

I looked at him. 'What happened to you?'

'What do you care? Or am I one of your causes, now that I'm only half a man?'

I checked his colours. They were, as I'd expected, as muddy as they'd always been, shot through with the same angry flashes of smoky red and burnt orange. And in the smoke were glimpses of life; a row of optics above a bar; something burning by the side of a road. *This* was my Knight of Cups, I knew: this angry, broken, contemptuous man.

'You always went for the damaged ones. The hopeless cases. The river-rats. That old bitch Armande. And Joséphine—' He gave his mean and hateful laugh. 'I guess she must have surprised you, too. Who'd have thought she had it in her? Throws me out of my own house, threatens me with the police, then when I come back six months later, just to pick up a few of my things, she's shacked up with that redhead of hers, and he's building her a boat. Oh yes, *and* she's pregnant. Happy days.' He gave a drag on his Gauloise and chased it with the last of the whisky. 'Of course, you'll know all about that,' he said, giving me his cheerless grin. 'Tell me, was it one at a time, or both together? Either way, he must have been something pretty damn special for *both* of you to be—'

'Shut *up*, Paul,' said a harsh voice from behind me.

I turned and saw Joséphine standing there, her face pale with anger.

Paul gave another humourless laugh and stubbed out his cigarette into his glass. 'Oops, here comes the ball and chain,' he said. '*Now* I'm in trouble.' He gave Joséphine a broad, hateful smile. 'Vianne and I were just catching up. Old friends, lost loves, a little glass of whisky—and how was *your* morning, my lovely one?'

'I said, shut *up*,' said Joséphine.

Paul shrugged. 'Or what, my love?'

Joséphine ignored him and turned to me. 'I was meaning to tell you, really I was. I just didn't know how to do it.' Her face was no longer pale, but red, and for almost the first time since I arrived I felt I really recognized the sad, awkward, inarticulate Joséphine of eight years ago; the Joséphine who

316

stole chocolate from me because she couldn't help herself.

A wave of sorrow washed over me. What happened to Joséphine Bonnet, who had such big, brave dreams? I thought I had freed her from Paul-Marie. Now I find that she is still as much of a prisoner as she ever was. What happened? And is this my fault?

She shot me a look. 'Let's go for a walk. Suddenly, I need some air.'

Paul grinned and lit another Gauloise. 'Knock yourself out.'

*   *   *

I followed Joséphine outside. For a time she seemed unwilling to talk, and we simply walked; past the church; through the square; down the cobbled street towards the river. When we reached the bridge, she stopped and looked over the parapet. Below us, the rushing water was the colour of milky tea.

'Vianne, I'm so sorry—' she began.

I looked at her. 'It's not your fault. I went away. I left you both. I was selfish. What did I *think* would happen?'

She looked confused. 'I don't understand—'

'I know about Pilou,' I said.

She looked at me blankly. 'Pilou?'

I smiled. 'He's a fine boy, Joséphine. You're right to be proud of him. I would be, too. As for his father—'

Her face crumpled. 'Please. Don't.'

I put my hand on hers. 'It's all right. You didn't do anything wrong. It was me. I was the one who

317

brought you together. I was the one who went away.
And then, when Roux came to Paris, I was the one
who ignored the signs—'

She looked at me curiously. 'Roux?'

'Well—isn't that what you meant?' I said. 'That
Roux is Pilou's father?'

She shook her head. 'It's worse than that.'

'Worse?' *How could it be worse?* I thought.

She sat down on the parapet. 'I really wanted to
tell you,' she said. 'But I couldn't think how to do
it. You were so proud of what I'd done, leaving my
husband, running this place, even though in the end
I never managed to catch that train—'

'You had Pilou,' I reminded her.

Joséphine smiled. 'Yes. Pilou. All this time I've
lied to him because I couldn't bear the truth. Just
as I've lied to you, Vianne, because I wanted you to
think I'd made something better of my life—'

I started to speak, but she stopped me. 'Please,
Vianne. Let me go on. I wanted you to be proud
of me. I wanted Roux to be proud of me. In my
dreams I was just like you, a free spirit, going where
I liked. No ties, no family. Paul was gone. You'd
already left Lansquenet, and I was making plans
to go. And then, I found out I was pregnant.' She
stopped, and her face took on a curious expression,
part tender, part sorrowful. 'At first I couldn't
believe it,' she said. 'I thought I couldn't *have*
children. We'd tried for so long, Paul and I, and
then, as soon as he went away—' She shrugged. 'It
couldn't have come at a worse time. I was all set up
to go. But Roux persuaded me to stay at least until
the baby was born. And then, when I saw him—'

'You fell in love.'

She smiled. 'That's right. I fell in love. And when

318

Pilou was old enough to ask, I told him his father was a pirate, a sailor, a soldier, an adventurer—anyone but Paul Muscat, a wife-beating coward who ran away as soon as I stood up to him.'

I stared at her. 'Paul-Marie?' I said. '*He*'s Pilou's father? But I thought you and Roux were—'

She shook her head. 'That never happened,' she told me. 'It might have done, if things had been different. But he and I were only friends. Even then, I think he belonged to you. But when Paul-Marie came back and found that Roux had been staying here, and that I was pregnant—'

'You let him think the baby wasn't his?' I said.

She nodded. 'I couldn't bear it. He would never have let me go, not if he'd known, not Paul-Marie. I was eight months pregnant when he came back, and—oh, Vianne, it was ugly.'

'I can imagine.'

Yes, I could; Paul-Marie, red-faced with rage; Roux, trying to protect her; and Joséphine, clutching at the single poor handful of straw that might build her any kind of defence. Paul had been drunk and aggressive, demanding his *rights*, as he called it—his share of the café's takings; the few possessions he'd left behind. He'd jumped to the conclusion that Roux was the baby's father, and Joséphine had let him believe it, rather than try to tell him the truth.

'What happened next?'

'The usual. He smashed up the bar, called me some names, and then drove off on his motorbike. Later, the police came round and told me he'd had an accident.'

Paul had been taken to hospital. Joséphine was his next of kin. When she'd learnt he would never

319

walk again, she had allowed him to come back home. What else could she do? It was partly her fault. Her lie had set in motion the chain of events that had brought him to this, and although she could never tell him the truth, she could not escape her responsibility. He had no job, no savings. She had given him a room of his own at the Café des Marauds and a permanent tab at the bar. A part of her had somehow hoped that he would recover the use of his legs, but he never had. She blamed herself. And here they were, eight years down the road; chained together by circumstance, with that lie growing bigger between them every day. Poor Paul-Marie. Poor Joséphine.

And then, the realization came. In my concern for Joséphine, I'd failed to see the essential thing. Roux never betrayed me. He wasn't Pilou's father. He may have been fond of Joséphine, but when it came to a choice, he chose me. All my suspicions, all my doubts, were nothing but *waswaas*, after all; *whispers of Shaitan*, as Omi says, brought to me on the Black Autan. But why don't I feel happier? A weight has been lifted from my heart. And yet I still feel it, even though I know it isn't there any more; a dark and whispering presence where once there was nothing but sweetness . . .

Why can't you trust me? Roux said. *Why can't it ever be simple?*

Perhaps that's the difference between us, Roux. You believe life can be simple. For others, perhaps—but not for me. Why didn't I trust you? Perhaps because I always felt that you were never mine to keep, that sooner or later the wind would change . . .

I pushed the thought aside. It could wait.

320

Joséphine still needed me.

I put my arms around her and said: 'It's all right. It wasn't your fault.'

Joséphine smiled. 'That's what Reynaud said.'

'You told him?' I was surprised at that. Joséphine had never been a regular churchgoer, and the idea of her confessing her closely guarded secret—and to *Reynaud*, of all people—seemed wholly out of character.

She smiled. 'Yes, isn't it strange?' she said. 'But I had to tell *someone*, and—he was there.'

I thought I understood it now. It was in her colours; her flushed face; the sad and hopeful look in her eyes. *The Lovers*. Why hadn't I seen it before? The Queen of Cups and her crippled Knight were Joséphine and Paul-Marie. But those Lovers—

Joséphine and Reynaud?

Could it be true? They seem at first glance an unlikely pair, and yet they have some things in common. Both are damaged individuals; solitary and secretive. Both have been victims of Lansquenet's busy web of gossips. Both have qualities of which they are not entirely aware; stubbornness; strength of mind; a refusal to let the enemy win.

'You like him, don't you?'

She looked away.

'Do you know where he is?' I said.

Once more, she shook her head. 'He just disappeared. I don't know where. But *she* has something to do with it.' She jerked her head in the direction of the old *chocolaterie*. 'That woman. Those people in Les Marauds.'

Little by little, the story came out. The graffiti on

Monsieur le Curé's door; his misplaced attempt to fix up the *chocolaterie*; the violent attack on Sunday night and the warning that he'd been given.

This is a war. Keep out of it.

A war? Is that how they see it? And who are the warring factions? The church? The mosque? The veil? The soutane? Or is it simply Lansquenet's traditional war against the outsider; the river-rats; the outcasts; and now, the people of Les Marauds, a name that means *The Invaders*, although in reality it is only a corruption of the word *marais*, or *marshland*, built as it is so close to the Tannes, and subject to regular flooding—

Once more, I considered Reynaud. Could someone have frightened him away with threats of further violence? That seems unlike Monsieur le Curé. He is as stubborn as I am myself. And he is a rock, unmovable; the wind has never shaken him.

So—where is he? Someone must know. Someone must have seen him go. If not here, then in Les Marauds, where the road leads to join the *autoroute*. I thought of what I'd seen in the smoke, the day I made the chocolates: Reynaud, alone, with his rucksack, walking along the riverbank.

Is this a vision of things to come, or has it already happened? And where is he now? Asleep in a ditch? Beaten to death in an alleyway? I never thought I would ever care what happened to Francis Reynaud. But faced with these possibilities, I find that I do. I care very much.

'We'll find him,' I said, as much to myself as to Joséphine, who was listening. 'We'll find him and we'll bring him home. Wherever he's gone. I promise we will.'

She gave her sad and hopeful smile. 'When you

322

say things like that, I almost believe that anything is possible.'

'It is,' I said. 'Now come with me.'

We crossed the bridge into Les Marauds.

CHAPTER FOUR

Thursday, 26th August

I looked into the bright brown eyes that peered at me from behind the grille. I wondered what she could see of me—not much, by my guess—a pallid blur, an upheld hand glimpsed through slices of shadow. My first instinct was to cry out for help, but the girl was very young, and I feared she might run away if I startled her.

'Maya. Don't be afraid,' I said in the gentlest voice I could manage.

She knelt to look closer inside the grille. I could see her knees on the gritty stone, and her socks above the pink wellingtons.

'Are you a Jinni?' she repeated. 'Jinn live in holes.'

'No, Maya, I'm not.'

'So what are you doing down there?' she said. 'Did you do something bad? My *jiddo* says if you do something bad, the police can put you in prison.'

'No, I didn't do anything bad. Someone locked me in here.'

The eyes grew rounder. 'You *are* a Jinni. You know my name and everything.'

I made my voice persuasively soft. 'Please, Maya. Listen to me. I'm not a Jinn, and I haven't done anything bad. But I *am* a prisoner. I need your help.'

She made a face. 'A Jinni *would* say that. Jinn always lie.'

'Please. I'm not lying.' I heard the urgent sting in my voice and made an effort to soften it. 'Please, Maya. Help me. Don't you want to help me?'

Maya nodded doubtfully.

'All right.' I drew a deep breath. I had to think this out carefully. Of course I could have asked Maya to fetch one of her parents, but as yet I had no idea who was responsible for my incarceration, and the thought of having to explain myself to a group of *Maghrébins* who believed that I had set fire to their school was a little daunting, to say the least. But there was someone in Les Marauds who I knew would help me, if only I could get to her.

I reached out to Maya with my voice. 'Do you know Vianne Rocher?'

She nodded. 'Rosette's *memti*,' she said.

'That's right,' I told her. 'Go and find Vianne. Tell her I'm here. Tell her Reynaud's here, and needs help.'

She seemed to consider this for a while. 'Is that your name?' she said at last.

'Yes.' Oh, God, give me patience. 'Please. I've been down here since yesterday. The water's rising. And there are rats.'

'Rats? *Awesome!*' Clearly the child has been spending too much time with Jean-Philippe Bonnet. I took another deep breath. *Breathe, Francis. Concentrate.*

'I'll give you anything you like. Toys, sweets. Just

tell Vianne.'

She hesitated. 'Anything I want?' she said. 'Like three wishes or something? Like in *Aladdin*?'

'Anything!'

Once more, the child seemed lost in thought. Then she came to a decision.

'OK,' she said, and jumped to her feet. The candy-pink wellingtons shot into view. Tears of gratitude stung my eyes—or was it simply the dust from the street?

'My first wish,' said Maya through the grille, 'is for you to make my *jiddo* well again. I'll think of the other two later. Bye-bye, Jinni. See you soon.'

'No, wait!' I said. 'Maya! Please! Listen to me!'

But the candy-pink boots had already gone.

I cursed to myself in Latin and French and climbed down from the packing crates. And then, just at that moment, as I stood ankle-deep in cold, filthy water, thinking that my situation could not possibly get any worse, I heard footsteps behind the cellar door.

Quickly I moved away from the crates. Then came the sound of a key in the lock. For a moment I considered surprising my captors and rushing the door, but this was only fantasy. In my current physical state, even a woman would have had no difficulty in pushing me back down the cellar steps.

The door opened. Three men appeared. Even in silhouette I recognized Karim Bencharki. The other two were younger men, I guessed two of the boys from the gym. Both of the boys were carrying torches, and Karim had a canister in his hand. I caught the smell of petrol.

'You people never learn,' said Karim.

I was still inside the whale.

CHAPTER FIVE

Thursday, 26th August

'This is a misunderstanding,' I said. 'Let me out, and I'll explain.'

Karim dropped the petrol can. I could tell by the sound it was empty. 'Explain this, Monsieur le Curé. You had it when we caught you spying on my sister.'

'That isn't tr—' I began to say. Then I remembered Sonia. That must be her petrol can. She'd dropped it when I accosted her. But she had confessed to me. How could I tell her husband?

'I wasn't spying on her,' I said. It was a lie, and sounded it. 'I was going to talk to her.'

'Is that why you were hiding behind a tree?'

I started to tell another lie, but knew as I did so that it wouldn't work. Some people are natural liars, *père*: I am not among them. I tried another tack. I said: 'Let me ask you something, Karim. How long do you think you can keep me locked in here? Let me go right now, and I promise I won't take any action against you.'

Looking at that in retrospect, I suppose I might have sounded just a little arrogant. One of the younger men spoke to Karim. Karim replied, sounding impatient. There followed a brief, rapid interchange in Arabic.

I started to feel nervous. 'Look, you have to believe me,' I said, addressing Karim directly. 'I never tried to burn down the school. I've never attacked your sister. I've always tried to help her.'

Against the light in the doorway, Karim's face was unreadable. But I sensed the hostility coming from him like static from a radio. Once more, he spoke to his friends. Then he spoke to me again.

'What have you done with my sister-in-law?'

I was taken aback. 'What?'

'Alyssa Mahjoubi. Where is she? And why was she with you a week ago?'

I took a deep breath. 'She's safe,' I said. 'But that has nothing to do with me. She's staying with a friend. Her choice. I had nothing to do with it.'

Karim gave the tiniest of nods. 'I see. But Madame Clairmont says you were seen with a young woman at night, by the river.'

'It wasn't like that—' I began. *God*, I thought, *that sounded weak*. 'I happened upon her by accident. She was in trouble. I helped her. That's all.'

'Just as you helped my sister?'

I opened my mouth, but said nothing.

'Monsieur le Curé,' said Karim. 'You have a reputation here. On more than one occasion, you have expressed your contempt for outsiders. Even your Père Henri says this. You are an intolerant man. You like to be in authority. You tried to stop the mosque from being built. You often speak out against the *niqab*. You once even tried to vandalize a chocolate shop that was opened in defiance of your religious traditions. I already know that you broke into her house last week. And now, we catch you sneaking around her boat with a can of petrol, on the very day you try to leave town—'

I started to laugh out of sheer nerves.

327

'You think it's funny?' said Karim.

'No. Of course not. But you're wrong.'

Karim gave a scornful laugh. 'I don't think your Père Henri would agree. Now tell us where Alyssa is, and what you were doing here yesterday.'

I should have tried to stay calm, *mon père*. But instead I began to feel angry. 'I don't have to justify myself, to you or anyone else,' I said. 'Things were fine here till you arrived, you and your sister. Since then I've been threatened, assaulted, accused and kept down here against my will. I won't let you intimidate me. As for Alyssa, I understand. You're worried. Of course, she's too young to leave home. And when you let me out of here, I promise we'll all sit down together and try to find a solution—'

Once more Karim and his companions exchanged words in their guttural Arabic. Then he turned to me again.

'Excuse me, Monsieur le Curé. I have a lot to do today. When I return, I hope we can talk.'

When I return? My heart sank. I realized how much I'd been counting on the fact that he would let me go.

'I don't see what you think you can gain from keeping me here. Do you think you can make me confess? To *what*? Your sister-in-law's in no danger, Karim. She's staying with Vianne Rocher.'

A pause. 'With Vianne Rocher?'

'That's right. Now—'

'What did she tell you?'

'Nothing at all. Now will you let me out of here?'

A longer pause. 'I can't,' he said.

'Why not?' My anger had grown. 'What the hell do you want from me?'

Karim took a step closer to me. Now I could see

328

his face clearly, and I saw that what I had taken for calm was a quiet though nonetheless violent rage.

'My sister, Inès, has gone missing,' he said. 'She and the child have been missing since I caught you yesterday, trying to burn the boat in which she and her daughter were sleeping. Of course, we could have called the police. But how sympathetic would they be? And so we will keep you here, *curé*, until you give us the answers we need. *Inshallah*, I am very much hoping that next time you will tell the truth.'

And at that he and his companions left, closing the door behind them. I heard the sound of a key in the lock.

I cursed, both in French and in Latin. And then I sat down on the steps and waited and hoped for Maya's return, and wondered what I had done to God to make him punish me like this, thinking of coffee and fresh croissants, as above me the treadmill and running machines resumed their infernal pounding.

CHAPTER SIX

☾

Thursday, 26th August

Our first port of call in Les Marauds was the one place I thought I could be sure of finding a warm reception. But arriving at the al-Djerbas' house, we found the dark-green shutters closed, and when Zahra opened the door she looked uneasy behind her *niqab*.

'I'm sorry, my mother's out,' she said.

I explained we were looking for Reynaud, and asked if she had seen him.

She shook her head. Behind the veil, her colours were shot with turbulence.

'How were the chocolate truffles?' I said. 'Did Omi like her coconut?'

'Omi is also out,' Zahra said.

I could see she was still looking troubled. Behind the veil her eyes were moving from me to Joséphine. 'You're sure you haven't seen Reynaud? Or heard anything?'

She shook her head. 'He is a friend of yours, is he not?'

'Yes,' I said. 'I suppose he is.'

'Curious, that such a man should be the friend of such as you.' Her voice was flat, giving nothing away, but under the veil she was all fire; her colours flared and shimmered.

'It wasn't always the case,' I said. 'In fact, you might say we were enemies. But that was a long, long time ago. Both of us have changed since then. And I found that the fear inside me belonged to *me*, and not to him, and only by letting it go could I be completely free.'

She thought about that for a moment. 'You people. I don't understand you at all. Always talking about freedom. Where I come from we believe that no one can ever truly be free. Allah sees everything, controls everything.'

'Reynaud thinks that, too,' I said.

'But you don't?'

I shook my head.

'What about Shaitan?'

I shrugged. 'I think there are plenty of human causes for the wrong that people do without bringing the devil into it. And I was brought up to believe that we should learn to control our own lives, write our own rules, and accept the consequences.'

She made a small, ambivalent sound. 'How different from what we are taught,' she said. 'But if there are no rules, then how do you always know what to do?'

'I don't think *anyone* always knows,' I said. 'Sometimes, we make mistakes. But to follow rules without thinking, to do as we're told, like children—I don't think *that* idea comes from God. It comes from those who use God as an excuse to make others obey them. I don't think God cares what we wear, what we eat; I don't think He cares who we choose to love. And I don't believe in a God who wants to test people to destruction, or to play with them like a little boy with an ant farm.'

I thought she might comment on that, but as she began to speak there came a sudden commotion behind her, and Maya came bounding out, carrying Tipo under her arm.

She looked at me with interest and said: 'Is Rosette with you?'

'Not today.'

She pulled a face. 'But I'm so bored! Can't I go out and play with Rosette? There's something I want to show her.' She gave Zahra a mischievous look. 'A secret. Just for me and Rosette.'

Zahra frowned. 'Maya, be good. Jiddo isn't feeling well.'

The brown eyes widened. 'But I—'

Zahra said something in Arabic.

331

Maya pulled another face. 'He misses the cat,' she told me. 'When he lived with Uncle Saïd, the cat always came to sit with him. Maybe if we *brought* the cat—'

Zahra looked impatient. 'It's nothing to do with the cat,' she said.

I saw a quarrel looming and intervened before it could erupt. 'Why don't I take Maya?' I said. 'Then you can all get some rest. I know exactly what it's like to have a little girl in the house.' I could see that Zahra was tempted. 'Don't worry. She'll be with Rosette. I'll bring her back before *iftar*.'

I could see her still considering it. Then she gave a sharp little nod, like a bird pecking at a nut. 'All right,' she said. 'And now I must go. Thank you for coming to see us, Vianne.'

And at that the green door closed again, and the three of us were left outside, with the wind still whistling in the eaves, and the long shadow of the minaret reaching across the sunny street like the needle of a sundial.

Joséphine gave me a doubtful look. 'I thought you said they were friends of yours.'

'They are.' I was puzzled. 'Zahra seems a little upset. Perhaps she's worried about old Mahjoubi.'

As we walked back down the boulevard, Maya running ahead of us, jumping in the puddles, I explained about the old man's illness, and the estrangement between him and the rest of his family. I did not mention his warning to stay away from the water, or his dreams of myself and Inès. We passed the gym. As always, the door was slightly open and the scent of chlorine filtered through to mix with the scent of Les Marauds, that compound of dust, *kif*, cooking and the river. I noticed that

332

Maya hurried past the mouth of the alley, but lingered in front of a passageway leading on to the boardwalk. An adult might have had difficulty passing between the buildings, but for Maya it would have been easy.

'That's where my Jinni lives,' she said, indicating the passageway.

'Really?' I smiled. 'You have a Jinni?'

'Uh-huh. He gave me three wishes.'

'Oh. And does he have a name?'

'Foxy!'

'That's nice.'

I had to laugh. She reminds me so much of Anouk at five, with her vivid face and her brilliant smile, bouncing around in those bubblegum boots. Anouk, my little stranger, who unexpectedly one day came back from the woods with a rabbit called Pantoufle, which only the privileged few could see.

'Kids, eh?' said Joséphine.

'Pilou's very good with Rosette. You'd think he had a sister.'

She smiled. She lights up at his name. 'You've seen what he's like. Sweet through and through. You understand why I did what I did? I couldn't stand to share him with Paul. Not when you know how Paul would have tried to fill his head with his own ideas.'

That was probably true, I thought. And yet, the boy is Paul's only son. Who knows how fatherhood might have changed him?

She read my expression. 'You think I was wrong.'

'No, but—'

'I know,' she said. 'It preys on me, too. At least it does when I'm feeling weak. When I'm strong I know better. Pilou deserves better than

Paul-Marie.'

'You say he changed your life, Joséphine—doesn't Paul deserve the same chance?'

Stubbornly, she shook her head. 'You know what he's like. He'd never change.'

'Anyone can change,' I said.

As we reached the end of the street I wondered if that was really true. Some people cannot be mended. But what had it done to Paul-Marie, to share a home with the little boy he believed was the son of a rival? I thought of his bright and baleful eyes, the rage and hopelessness of his mouth. He looks like an animal caught in a trap, snapping at anyone who comes close. Of course, I am not naïve enough to believe that a man like Paul-Marie would melt at the news that he has a son. But doesn't he deserve a chance? And what has that lie done to Joséphine?

We reached the end of the boulevard. The last time I had come this way, Inès Bencharki's houseboat had been moored alongside the jetty. Now, I noticed, it had gone; only a neat little coil of rope remained to show where it had been. I saw Joséphine's eyes widen. Yes, of course, the boat was hers, although she rarely used it.

'You mean that woman was living there?' she said, when I began to explain. 'How dare she break into *my* boat? And where the hell has she taken it?'

I didn't know. I stood on the jetty and scanned the riverbank. There was no sign of the black houseboat, either on the side of Les Marauds or on that of Lansquenet. Could Inès have left for good? There are only a few safe places here to moor a riverboat of that size, and right now, with the floodwater, the swollen Tannes is at its least forgiving. In addition, Joséphine's boat has no working engine, so the best Inès could hope for would be to drift with the current downriver, and maybe find another place in Chavigny or Pont-le-Saôul. Why had she gone? Had she taken Du'a? And when—if at all—did she mean to return?

And then I saw something on the bank, half trodden into the muddy grass. It was a necklace, I thought at first; a little string of green glass beads, connected by a silver chain. Perhaps Du'a had dropped it, I thought as I picked it up—and then I saw the crucifix at the end of the chain—

'It's a rosary.'

Joséphine came to look. 'This belongs to Reynaud,' she said. 'I've seen it on his mantelpiece. What do you think he was doing here? Do you think *he* took my boat?'

I shook my head. 'I have no idea. I assumed Inès had.' Could she still be in Les Marauds? If so, did she know where he was?

I tried asking Maya, to no avail. She seemed more concerned about Du'a than about the boat's disappearance, mostly because of the puppies that she and the others were keeping in the old *chocolaterie*.

Joséphine raised an eyebrow. 'What?'

Maya clapped a hand to her mouth. 'I wasn't supposed to tell,' she said. 'Snappy and Biter. We're hiding them there. Monsieur Acheron wanted to drown them.'

'You think Du'a might still be there?'

Joséphine shrugged. 'It's worth a try.'

CHAPTER SEVEN

☾

Thursday, 26th August

We arrived at the old *chocolaterie* to find it outwardly derelict. Sheets of thick plastic covered the door, the windows and a part of the roof. A crudely painted wooden sign across the door said: *DANGER. KEEP OUT.*

Inside, however, was a frenzy of activity. Behind the door, we found Luc Clairmont, Jeannot Drou, Anouk, Rosette, Pilou and, most surprisingly, Alyssa; along with Vlad; a stepladder; some pots of emulsion; sponges, rollers, brushes and the cardboard box with the puppies inside. Between them, they had managed to paint most of the kitchen, the landing and what had once been the front of the shop in a cheery shade of primrose, while on one wall I could see an unfinished mural beginning to take shape; a mostly abstract tangle—with the occasional animal shape hidden inside the pattern—very like the one in the Café des Marauds. Pilou was clearly the creative force behind this, though the others were working equally hard, while also managing to transfer paint liberally on to themselves, their clothes and Vlad, who seemed to be joining in with verve, if not with efficiency.

As we entered, everyone froze, except for Vlad, who, recognizing a friend, set off a volley of barking.

Luc started to explain. 'I said I'd do some work

on the house. Just to repair the damage. Then I found all *this*—' he indicated Pilou and the box of puppies. 'I thought that while they were here, they might as well make themselves useful. And so I brought in a few supplies, and—' He broke off with a sheepish grin. 'Things kind of took over from there,' he said.

'I can see that,' I told him, trying to curb Vlad's enthusiasm.

Pilou admitted that Vlad had been more of a hindrance than a help, although he maintained that a guard dog was essential to protect the work-in-progress.

'So. What do you think?' said Anouk. She was standing next to Jeannot Drou. Both of them were covered in paint; yellow handprints adorned Jeannot's T-shirt, while Anouk's face bore a similar print right across one cheek. 'Did we do OK, Maman?'

For a moment I could hardly speak. To see the place like this again—brightly if not expertly painted; filled with the sounds of activity; all of its shadows and whisperings driven out by their laughter—

Evil spirits, get thee hence. I smiled at her. 'I think you did.'

She looked relieved. 'I knew you would. Luc came to find us. I thought it would be OK if we all came together.'

I looked at Alyssa curiously. She was wearing a straw hat to protect her hair from the wet paint, and seemed to have cast off her troubles as easily as her *hijab*.

'It turns out no one notices me unless I wear *hijab*,' she said. 'I walked right past Poitou's bakery,

337

and no one even looked at me.'

'We got in through the fire escape,' said Pilou. 'No one knows we're here. Except for you two, and Sputnik—'

'Sputnik?' I said.

'My cat,' said Pilou.

'Your what?' said Joséphine.

Pilou gave his summery grin. 'I caught him in here the other day, trying to steal the puppies' food. Biter bit him.'

'Oh. I see.'

'Do you want to help, Vianne? I could use some help with the mural. And Rosette keeps wanting to paint monkeys on everything, and we haven't even started on the bedrooms—'

I said: 'Not today. I'm looking for your friend Du'a and her mother.'

I explained to them what had happened. As I'd expected, no one had seen Inès or her daughter since yesterday. But why did she leave so suddenly, and without even telling anyone? And what about Monsieur le Curé? No one seemed to know.

We left them to their painting and went back outside into the square. Rosette had joined Maya, and both of them ran out of the shop and into the sun, where Poitou, sitting outside the church, was moodily eating a cheese baguette. He looked surprised to see us.

'What are you doing in there?' he said. 'Don't you know that's the *burqa* woman's place?'

'That's who I was looking for.'

He pulled a face. 'Good luck with that. Isn't she staying somewhere in Les Marauds?'

'I think she might have gone,' I said.

'I haven't seen her here in days.' A sudden

338

thought occurred to him. 'Maybe she ran off with Monsieur le Curé. He was working here last week, you know. Cleaning up the mess he made.' He laughed uproariously at this, though Joséphine and I did not. The thought that Reynaud's departure might be linked with the disappearance of Inès Bencharki's boat was not entirely implausible. After all, we'd found his rosary not twenty paces from where it was moored. *Could* Reynaud have taken it?

Joséphine didn't think so. 'I think that woman took it,' she said. 'Maybe she fixed the engine. Or maybe she steered it downriver, or maybe she sold it to someone else. Honestly, if she has, I don't care. It would be worth it, to see her gone.'

'So Karim was right. She *has* disappeared.'

I turned and saw an unwelcome sight: Caro, approaching purposefully across the little square, with her husband, Georges, looking sheepish, in tow. Père Henri was with them. He gave me a flashy, meaningless smile and patted Maya on the head.

Maya shot him a dark look. 'My Jinni doesn't like you,' she said.

Père Henri looked startled.

'My Jinni lives in a hole,' she said. 'He has rats. He's given me three wishes.'

Père Henri's smile broadened grotesquely. 'What an original child,' he said.

'A pity she's allowed to run wild,' said Caroline, looking meaningfully at Rosette. 'With everything that's been going on in Les Marauds recently, I would have thought that the last thing people wanted would be for their children to be running about all over the place without proper supervision.'

Rosette made one of her noises—an impudent little popping sound. At the same time, one of Caro's stiletto heels stuck in a crack between the cobbles. Caro tried to dislodge it, but the heel was stuck fast.

'Rosette!' I said.

Rosette gave me an innocent look and made the popping sound again. Caro's heel was released so abruptly that the shoe went flying off into the square. Père Henri ran to retrieve it.

Maya and Rosette exchanged looks and giggled.

'You spoke to Karim?' I asked Caro. 'He told you his sister had left Les Marauds?'

She nodded. 'He's a good friend of ours. A very nice man; progressive; polite; totally non-political, unlike old Mahjoubi. If only they could all be like him.'

'I didn't know you were so close. What about his sister?'

'Inès. If you ask me, he's better off without her.'

It was almost what Joséphine had said.

'Why?'

Caro pulled a face. 'The woman's a liability. She's alienated everyone. Karim's been trying so hard to help to bring the community into the twenty-first century. Look how supportive he's been of his sister—*not* the most stable of characters— and of that poor child of hers. He was the first one to understand why old Mahjoubi needed to be replaced; he was the one who made the gym into what it is today. Before he came, the place was just a concrete box with a few running machines in it. Now it's a social club; a meeting-place; a place for healthy young men to go instead of drinking alcohol.' She arched her eyebrows at Joséphine. 'If only *our* boys had something like that.'

'They used to play here,' said Joséphine. 'I remember your Luc playing football with Alyssa and Sonia.'

Caro made a scornful noise. 'You don't understand their culture,' she said. 'You can't expect boys and girls to mix. It's not what they're used to, and it can lead to all kinds of trouble.' She gave her icing-sugar smile. '*You* should bear that in mind,' she said.

'Why?' said Joséphine softly.

'Well, *your* boy seems very friendly with Inès Bencharki's daughter. And having seen what happens when the children of two cultures mix—' She broke off abruptly, looking annoyed, and I wondered if she was thinking of Luc. 'What I mean is, we have to be *sensitive*,' she finished, glancing sharply at Georges, who so far hadn't spoken a word. 'Some people just aren't compatible with *our* kind of community.'

'People like Inès?' I said. 'Or maybe Alyssa Mahjoubi?'

Caro stiffened visibly. 'Obviously, you know more about it than I do,' she said. Then, turning to Père Henri: 'Come on, *mon père*. We have work to do.'

At which she and her entourage proceeded past us into the church, where, in Reynaud's absence, even now the ancient pews are being removed to make way for practical plastic chairs, and video screens are soon to arrive to herald the entry of Saint-Jérôme into the twenty-first century.

CHAPTER EIGHT

☾

Thursday, 26th August

Joséphine was furious. 'How could they do that to Reynaud? They know how much he loves this place. They'd never dare if he was *here*—'

That was certainly true, I thought. Like old Mahjoubi, Francis Reynaud is not a friend of the new ways. Not for the first time, I wondered how two men with so much in common should have become such enemies.

'Come home with me,' I said to her. 'We'll make some chocolate and talk. There's nothing we can do here, anyway.'

And so we went back to Armande's house, and I made hot chocolate with cardamom, and put in a batch of peach pastries, ready in twenty minutes, using the freshly made peach jam and a splash of whipped cream with Armagnac. Rosette and Maya helped, rather messily, in the kitchen, Rosette singing her wordless song, Maya joining in solemnly with improvised lyrics of her own while tapping the table with a wooden spoon.

'Home-made jam—'

'*Bam badda-bam*—'

'Vianne's peach jam for Ramadan!'

Joséphine couldn't help laughing. 'And here I was thinking boys were the most fun.'

'We should take some of these to my *jiddo* tonight,' said Maya, when the pastries were done.

'He can eat some for *iftar*. My Jinni has put magic inside to make him feel all better.'

'I hope so,' I said.

Not *magic*, precisely; but we all have our secrets. A whisper; a sign; a pinch of spice. The turn of a friendly card. A song.

Maya smiled. 'It'll work,' she said. 'It's one of my three wishes.'

Well, Maya. Perhaps it will. Stranger things have happened. I already know from my visit to him that old Mahjoubi's affliction has nothing to do with disease. Its cause is *waswaas*: those whispers that creep into the mind and bring troubled dreams, depression, despair. The quarrel with his son. The fact that he is no longer regarded as a suitable leader. Alyssa's departure, in such mysterious circumstances—all these must have contributed to the old man's sudden decline.

'We'll bring some when I take you home. Alyssa wants to see him too. I'm sure that, between you, you'll make him well.'

'Foxy will do it,' said Maya.

At five o'clock, Anouk came back with Pilou, Luc, Jeannot and Alyssa; all in excellent spirits and splashed with paint from head to foot. I sent them to wash and change their clothes, and put in another batch of peach pastries, while Vlad lay in front of the kitchen stove, smelling strongly of fresh paint, and dreamt, and twitched his busy paws. Then I made some more chocolate, with extra sugar, marshmallows and cream, and we sat around Armande's scarred old kitchen table, eating and drinking and laughing, as if we'd lived there all our lives instead of not even a fortnight.

'The shop looks fabulous,' said Anouk. 'Nearly

343

as good as it was before. Now all it needs is a new sign—'

I looked at her. She glanced at Jeannot. 'That is, if anyone wanted to make it a *chocolaterie* again. It wouldn't be so difficult. All you'd need would be to put in a counter, and some glass display cabinets, and maybe a couple of tables and chairs—'

Rosette signed: *I like it. I drew monkeys on the wall.*

'It was just a thought,' said Anouk. 'But I don't think it's a school any more.'

Oh, Anouk. Oh, Rosette. Things are never as simple as that. We were never meant to stay: never meant to settle here. We've lived in Paris longer than anywhere else I've ever been. To give that up, to admit defeat, is totally unthinkable.

And then, there's Roux. What would he say? He has tried so hard to build us a life, to find some kind of common ground between his gypsy lifestyle and our own. To leave it now—and for Lansquenet—would be the worst kind of rejection. Would he survive it? Could he adapt? Can a river-rat ever change? Would I even want him to try?

A knock at the door put an end to my thoughts. Joséphine went to answer it. Perhaps she thought it might be Reynaud—

It was Karim Bencharki.

He pushed his way past Joséphine as if she were a curtain, and I was suddenly reminded of Paul-Marie, eight years ago, drunk and enraged, trying to force open the *chocolaterie* door. His colours crazed; his face was flushed; he was still as handsome as ever, but shining now with a new light, a dangerous light, like wildfire.

Alyssa saw him and froze at once. For a moment

344

the strategy almost worked. In that cramped room, her hair cut short, she looked so unlike her usual self that he might even have missed her. The golden eyes moved fitfully over a half-dozen upturned faces. Then they widened a little as they settled on Alyssa.

'So it's true. You *are* here.' Then he turned to me and said, 'I'm very sorry, Madame Rocher. I didn't mean to barge in like this. I don't know what she's been telling you, but Alyssa's been missing for several days. Her family has been—'

'Who told you she was here?' I said.

'It doesn't matter. They were right.' Once more, he addressed Alyssa: 'What were you thinking, running away? Don't you know your mother and father are frantic?'

Alyssa answered in Arabic.

He broke in: 'Never mind. Come home.'

Alyssa said nothing, but shook her head.

'Come on, Alyssa. Get properly dressed. Your mother's going crazy—'

'I don't care. I'm not going back. And it's not up to you to order me to.'

A rattle of furious Arabic, through which his hectic colours flared. He took a step towards her. Alyssa shrank back, protesting, while Karim's voice rose angrily.

'Stop that! Leave her alone!' It was Luc. 'She's staying with Vianne. She's perfectly safe. Whenever she wants to come h-home—' Again, I could hear the ghost of his childhood stammer begin to resurface in his voice, but his gaze was steady enough, and he sounded surprisingly adult. 'When she's ready to go back, she will. But it's up to her to make her choice.'

For a moment Karim held his gaze. Clearly he didn't remember Luc, who has spent most of the past two years away at university. Then he took another step. Vlad began to growl softly. Karim gave the dog a wary look.

'Keep your dog under control.'

Alyssa said something in Arabic.

Karim glared at her and took a step back. 'This is ridiculous,' he said. 'Do you *want* to make an exhibition of yourself?' He glanced contemptuously at Luc. 'Is *he* the reason you ran away? What lies have you told these people?'

Luc said: 'I think you should l-leave.'

Karim took a closer look at Luc. Then he said: 'I know your mother. Madame Clairmont, isn't it? She has been very supportive of us. I wonder what she'd think if she knew about your interference.'

For a moment Luc was taken aback. Then he spoke up again, this time without the trace of a stammer: 'This has nothing to do with her. This is *my* house. Alyssa's my guest. And Pilou's dog gets nervous around people who try to threaten my guests.'

I saw surprise in Karim's eyes. In fact, little Luc had surprised us all. The passive, sullen little boy with the stammer has finally escaped his mother's dominant influence.

Alyssa was watching attentively, her face alight with the look of someone who has just worked out the answer to a previously unsolvable question. There were still traces of yellow paint in her hair and on her face. She looked incredibly young and almost heart-wrenchingly beautiful.

Karim made a gesture of protest. Now he looked more hurt than angry, as if this were the first time

that anyone had resisted his charm. He looked at
Joséphine in appeal.

'Madame Muscat—'

She shook her head. 'I knew a man like you
once,' she said. 'But Vianne showed me a long time
ago that I didn't have to run away to take control
of my own life. Alyssa knows that now, too. She has
friends who care for her. She doesn't need you, or
any man, to tell her what to do any more.'

Karim looked around for support, and found
none.

'I'll give your regards to my mother,' said Luc.

Karim turned and made for the door, with a
final, dangerous glance that took in Anouk, Rosette
and myself. 'Be careful,' he said. 'This is a war.
Don't get caught in the crossfire.'

CHAPTER NINE

☾
Thursday, 26th August

The sun was low. soon it would set. It was almost
time to take Maya home. I'd promised to bring
some pastries, too, and to take Alyssa to see her
jiddo. We said goodnight to the others. Once more
Alyssa put on her *hijab*. As they said goodbye,
I caught a look between Anouk and Jeannot—
something bright in their colours, like the promise
of secrets to come. Then, the rest of us packed up
a box of chocolates and the freshly baked peach
pastries and headed towards the al-Djerba house.

347

Alyssa was silent all the way there. Anouk was also silent, checking for messages on her mobile phone. Maya and Rosette ran ahead, playing some kind of noisy game, in which the names *Bam* and *Foxy* seemed to be a recurrent theme. I could see Bam quite clearly, bouncing intermittently across the cobbled boulevard, but so far Foxy has yet to show himself. Presumably Maya can see him. I wonder if Rosette can, too.

We arrived at the green-shuttered house and knocked. Maya's mother opened the door. She was wearing a yellow *hijab* over jeans and a silk *kameez*. Her pretty face brightened when she saw us.

Maya bugled: 'Vianne has brought cakes. We made them! I helped!'

Yasmina smiled. 'I'm glad you're all here. I was just making dinner. Come in!' She said something quickly, aside to Alyssa. Alyssa nodded and went upstairs. 'Please, come in and have some tea. My mother and sister are both here.'

We followed her into the front room, where Fatima and Zahra were sitting with Omi on cushions on the floor. Zahra was wrapped in a brown *djellaba* and her customary *hijab*. Fatima was sewing. Omi looked up as I came in with an expression so unlike her usual look of concentrated naughtiness that I was suddenly sure old Mahjoubi had died.

'What's wrong?' I said.

Omi shrugged. 'I was hoping perhaps my Du'a was with you.'

I shook my head. 'I'm sorry, no.'

'Her mother has taken her,' Fatima said. 'Karim is in pieces.'

'Really?' I said. 'I had no idea they were so

close.' I did not mention Karim's visit to Armande's house, but Zahra must have heard something in my voice, because she gave me a searching look. Fatima did not notice.

'Karim is devoted to Du'a,' she said.

Omi made a scornful noise. 'That's why he never speaks to her, or even bothers to *look* at her if she happens to be in the room.' She looked at Fatima defiantly. 'She may have you wrapped around her thumb, but that woman is not who she says she is.'

'Omi, please,' Zahra said. 'Hasn't there been gossip enough?'

Omi ignored her. 'I know these things. I may be old, but I'm not blind. I say that woman is Karim's first wife, and Du'a is their daughter.'

Hastily, I intervened. 'I brought supplies,' I told them. 'Home-made peach jam pastries. I hope you'll try them when you can.'

'I'll try one now,' said Omi.

'Omi, *please*—'

I held out the box. She looked inside. 'So *this* is your magic, Vianne,' she said. 'It smells like the flower fields of *Jannat*.' She gave Rosette her turtle smile. 'And you helped make these, little one?'

'We all did.' That was Anouk. 'I've been making chocolate since I was five.'

Omi's smile broadened. 'Well, if these don't bring the old man downstairs—'

'He'll come,' Maya said. 'I asked my Jinni to make him well.'

Omi looked surprised. 'You did? Your Jinni, eh?'

Maya nodded earnestly. 'He promised me three wishes,' she said.

I said: 'Rosette has an imaginary friend. I think

349

Maya wanted one, too.'

'Oh. I see. And what next? Let me think. Maybe he'll turn you into a princess. Or make me young and thin again. Or give you a magic carpet made of tiny butterflies, that can fly you anywhere in the world without ever needing a passport—'

Maya gave her a stern look. 'That's just silly, Omi,' she said.

Omi cackled. 'Then it's a good thing I have you to keep me sensible.'

But in defiance of Omi's pessimism, it was less than ten minutes later that Mohammed Mahjoubi appeared at the door, looking shrunken, but fully dressed in his white *djellaba* and prayer hat. Alyssa was with him, clear-eyed; relieved.

On seeing me, he inclined his head. '*Assalaamu alaikum*, Madame Rocher. Thank you for bringing Alyssa once more.' He held out his hand to Alyssa, who took it, and spoke with her softly in Arabic. Then he addressed the whole room in his heavily accented French.

'I spoke to my granddaughter yesterday. She promised to consider my words. And today, *Alhumdullila*, she has decided to come home with me. Life is too short and time too precious for foolish quarrels to intrude. Tomorrow, I will speak to my son. Whatever has happened between us, I am still his father.' He gave the shadow of a smile. 'And you, my little Maya,' he said. 'What have you been doing today?'

'*We*'ve been making pastries. Magic ones, to make you well.'

'I see. Magic pastries.' The smile seemed to brighten slightly. 'Well, don't say that to your Uncle Saïd. I don't think he would approve, somehow.'

350

'I hope you will join us for *iftar*,' said Fatima to the rest of us. 'We have more than enough. You are welcome.'

And so we sat down on the brightly coloured cushions, the men on one side, the women on the other. Mehdi al-Djerba joined us, with Yasmina's husband Ismail, who looks very like his brother Saïd, though without the beard, and in Western dress. Mohammed said prayers. Alyssa was quiet, but seemed content. I was amused to see Maya showing Rosette the right way to eat—*this is how we do it, Rosette, and sit up straight on your cushion*—while Bam followed suit, sitting comically straight, gleaming in the shadows.

We began with dates, the traditional way of breaking fast at Ramadan. Then, harissa and rose-petal soup, with *crêpes mille trous*, saffron couscous and roast spiced lamb. Almonds and apricots for dessert, with *rahat loukoum* and coconut rice. Then the pastries we had brought, and chocolates for everyone.

Mohammed Mahjoubi ate little, but accepted a pastry from Maya. 'You *have* to eat one, Jiddo. Rosette and I helped make them!'

He smiled. 'Of course. How could I not? Especially if they are magic.'

Omi had no hesitation. The absence of teeth does not trouble her; she simply lets the chocolate melt. 'This is better than dates,' she said. 'Here, pass me another.'

It isn't *really* magic, of course. But food that has been made with love *does* have special properties. Everyone praised the truffles, and the pastries were soon finished.

By this time Mohammed was looking tired, and

351

announced that he was going to bed.

'Goodnight,' he said. 'It has been a long day. There will be another tomorrow.' He gave Alyssa a speaking look.

'But it's still *early*—' Maya said. 'And you promised to play chequers with me—'

'It's almost midnight,' Omi said. 'And magic chocolates go only so far. Old people are easily tired.'

'*You*'re not tired,' Maya protested.

'I'm indestructible,' Omi said.

Maya gave the matter some thought. 'We need the cat,' she said at last. 'Hazi will make Jiddo happy again. I'll ask my Jinni to see to it.'

Yasmina smiled. 'You do that,' she said.

While Yasmina put Maya to bed, Zahra went to prepare mint tea; I joined her in the kitchen while the others talked next door. She took off her veil as she made the tea; I noticed she was looking concerned.

'You're still worried about Inès.'

She shrugged. 'If I am, I'm the only one.'

'You think something might have happened to her?'

Once more, she shrugged. 'Who knows?' she said. 'Maybe she just got tired of everybody gossiping.'

'Do *you* believe she's Karim's first wife?'

She shook her head. 'I know she is not.'

She sounded very certain of this. 'Do you believe she's his sister?' I said.

She looked at me. 'I know who she is. But it is not for me to say.'

The tea was strong and fragrant. Zahra uses fresh mint, two generous fistfuls, brewed in an ornate silver pot so large that it requires both hands to lift it. Steam bloomed from the rosebud spout like a cartoon genie.

That made me think of Maya's Jinni. Does Maya see her animal friend as Anouk and Rosette see theirs? I have to say, I'm a little surprised that so far I haven't seen a glimpse of him. Children's imaginations are very powerful, and I have always been sensitive. But now, in the steam, I found myself catching traces of something else; a pattern like that of frost-feathers on a frozen windowpane. I moved a little closer. The scent of mint enveloped us both.

'Zahra. Please. I want to help,' I said, and reached out very delicately—not with my hands, but with my thoughts. It's a trick that sometimes provides insights, though most of the time it offers me nothing but shades and reflections.

A basket of scarlet strawberries; a pair of yellow slippers; a bracelet of black jet beads; a woman's face in a mirror. Whose face is that? Have I seen it before? Or is it the face of the Woman in Black? If so, she is even more beautiful than the gossips would have us believe. And she is young; absurdly young; with the unconscious arrogance of youth, the look of one who does not believe that she will ever grow old, or die, or give up her illusions. Anouk has that look. I once had it myself.

I tried to shape the scented steam, to comb it with my fingers. Its end-of-summer fragrance was clean and sweetly nostalgic. I saw my mother's cards again, saw them in my mind's eye; the Queen of Cups, the Knight of Cups, the Lovers and the Tower—

The Tower. Broken and lightning-struck, it

353

looks far too slender to ever have been any kind of stronghold. A spire as thin as a shard of glass; decorative; windowless. Who—or *what*—is the Tower?

Of course, we have two towers here. One is the tower of Saint-Jérôme's; that squat whitewashed rectangle with its stubby little spire. The second is the minaret; the disused chimney, now crowned with a silver crescent moon. Which is the Tower on the card? The church spire or the minaret? Which one has been lightning-struck? Which will stand, and which will fall?

A third time, I tried to read the steam. The scent of mint grew stronger. And now once again I could see Francis Reynaud walking along the riverbank, deep in thought, rucksack in hand, shoulders bowed against the rain. And there was something at his feet; a scorpion, black and venomous. He picked it up. And I thought: if Inès is the scorpion, could *Reynaud* be the buffalo? And if so, am I already too late to save them both from drowning?

I saw Zahra watching suspiciously. 'What are you doing?'

'Trying to understand,' I said. 'Your friend is missing. *My* friend, too. And if you know anything that might help—'

'I don't,' said Zahra. 'This is a war. I'm sorry you're mixed up in it.'

I looked at her. 'What kind of a war?'

She shrugged and retied her face-veil. Behind it, her colours skipped and danced. 'A war that we can never win; between women and men; old and young; love and hate; East and West; tolerance and tradition. No one really wants it, but there it is. It's no one's fault. I only wish things were different.'

She held out the silver teapot. 'Here, take this. I'll bring the cups.'

'Zahra. Wait. If you know anything—'

She shook her head. 'I have to get back. I'm sorry about your friend.'

CHAPTER TEN

✝

Thursday, 26th August

It rained twice during the night. The first time, I heard the sound of the rain in the alley above my cell, and wished I had saved some drinking water from the bottle in my rucksack. The second time, the broken pipe began to trickle floodwater again, and I knew that the river was rising once more. Nevertheless, I managed to sleep a little, in the dry space at the top of the steps, wrapped up in my overcoat. My feet are wet and freezing. I would sell my soul for a hot bath.

My watch has stopped. Maybe the damp has interfered with the battery. But between the *muezzin* and the machines and the distant sound of Saint-Jérôme's chime, I find that my sense of time passing is reasonably accurate. This is why I can be certain that it was between ten and eleven o'clock that the door to my cellar was unlocked, and Karim Bencharki came in, alone. A strong scent of *kif* accompanied him. He looked angry and agitated.

He shone his flashlight into my eyes and said: 'Reynaud, for the last time, what have you done

355

with my sister?'

I told him I didn't know where she was. But Karim was too angry to listen.

'What did you tell her? What did you say? What were you doing that morning?'

I told him: 'I didn't say anything. I don't know where your sister has gone.'

'Don't lie. I know you were spying on her.' His voice had acquired a razor-blade edge. 'What did you see by the river? What lies has Alyssa told you?'

'Please.' God, I hate that word. 'This is all a dreadful mistake. Let me out, and I'll do all I can to help. Just let me go.'

He looked at me. 'You must be hungry and thirsty by now.'

'I am,' I said. 'Please let me go. Let me go, and we'll sort this out. If Inès is missing—'

'What did you see?'

'I told you. I saw nothing. Why?'

He made a sound of frustration. 'Hah! Ever since she came here, you've never left my sister alone. Spying on her from the church. Asking questions. Pretending to help. What has she told you? *What do you know?*'

'Nothing at all. As far as I know, your sister hates me as much as you do.'

I could tell he didn't believe me. Why? What is he so afraid of? What secrets are they hiding? I remembered what Sonia had told me. *He goes to her at night sometimes. She's bewitched him. He's under her spell.* At the time, I dismissed it as jealous fantasy. The woman's his sister, after all. But—what if she were not, *père*? What proof do we have of *who* she is?

356

'She isn't your sister, is she?' I said.

A pause. 'Who told you that?'

'I guessed.'

Another, longer pause. Then Karim seemed to make a decision. He turned off the flashlight, leaving me to squint at his face. 'I will give you one more chance,' he told me in a new, cool voice. 'Next time I come, I will bring my friends. The friends you met on Sunday night, by your house, in the village. And you will tell me everything. Otherwise—' Karim's voice grew even cooler and more distant. 'We can make it look like an accident. We can make it look as if you drowned. Any marks on your body would seem to be the work of the river. No one would know. No one would care. You're not the most popular man around here. No one would even look for you.'

And at that, he closed the door again, leaving me in darkness.

Of course, he was trying to frighten me. I know that, *père*. I'm not afraid. Karim is not a murderer. He may well be responsible for last Sunday's attack on me, but that's not the same as murder. Still—

No one would know. No one would care. No one would even look for you. That at least is true, *père*. If I disappeared for good, would anyone really miss me?

An hour or so later, the cellar door opened again. I leapt to the foot of the steps at once, fully expecting to see Karim and his friends standing there. Instead, a woman, veiled in black, appeared in the narrow doorway.

'If you try to get out, I shall scream.' Her voice was unfamiliar. But so few of those women ever speak (except among themselves, of course) that I

357

hadn't expected to recognize her. She was young, though: that I could tell. Her French was almost unaccented.

I looked up at her bleakly. The water was up to my ankles. 'What do you want?'

I saw that she was carrying a cardboard box.

She said: 'I have brought water and food. I will leave it at the top of the steps. If you hide the wrapping, Karim and the others will not know I was here.'

'Karim doesn't know?'

She shook her head. 'I thought you would be hungry.'

'Then let me out,' I said urgently. 'Please! I swear—'

'I am sorry,' she said. 'I only came to bring the food.'

The food turned out to be some kind of soup in a styrofoam cup, and some bread, olives and dried figs wrapped in a piece of waxed paper. There was water too, in a plastic bottle, and some kind of pastry. When the woman had gone, I ate and drank everything, and hid the papers and the box inside one of the empty crates.

I must get out of here, I thought; before Karim and his friends come back. The woman in black who brought me food—*could* that have been Sonia? Perhaps. But surely I would have recognized her. Does she even know I am here? If so, she must feel guilty. Perhaps that's why she brought the food. Perhaps, next time—

If there *is* a next time. Perhaps that was my last meal. The last meal of the condemned man. If only Maya would come back—

Sweet Jesus. Am I so desperate? And yet,

she's all I have now. My last, precarious thread of hope lies in the hands of a five-year-old. Will she remember her promise, *père*? Or has she already forgotten the game?

CHAPTER ELEVEN

☾

Friday, 27th August

Another night, with no answers. My mother's cards are no help at all. I made chocolate for the children and drank mine out of Armande's bowl; creamy, rich and very sweet. If only Armande were here now. I can almost hear her voice. *If heaven is half as good as this, I'll give up sin tomorrow.* Dear Armande. How she would laugh to see me like this, so concerned about Francis Reynaud.

He can look after himself, she would say. *Let him wander. Do him good.* And yet, every instinct screams at me that Reynaud is in trouble. I thought Inès Bencharki was the one I was meant to save; but I was wrong. *Reynaud* was the one. Reynaud was the one from the very start.

What was it Armande's letter said? *Lansquenet will need you again. But I can't count on our stubborn curé to tell you when that happens.*

No, because men like Reynaud never ask; never rely on anyone. Did he try to help Inès? Has he been stung by the scorpion?

Père Henri has reported him missing, but the police are proving unhelpful. There is nothing to indicate that Monsieur le Curé has been the victim of foul play; in fact, wasn't it Père Henri himself who suggested that he take a leave of absence? As for the rumour that Reynaud left town because of new evidence concerning the fire at the old *chocolaterie*, there seems to be nothing to support this, much to Caro's disappointment.

I dropped by the church. It was empty, but for a stack of new chairs and a couple of visitors sitting in front of the confessional. I recognized Charles Lévy and Henriette Moisson, and wondered if they, too, were looking for our missing *curé*.

'He hasn't really gone,' said Charles, when I asked the question. 'He wouldn't leave us. Where would he go? Who would look after his garden?'

Henriette Moisson agreed. 'Anyway, he has to take confession. He hasn't done it for ages. I won't talk to that other one—the *perverti* who hides in the church. He's a shifty one.'

'That's Père Henri Lemaître,' said Charles.

'*I* know that,' said Henriette.

Charles sighed. 'She gets confused. I'd better take her home.' He turned to Henriette and smiled. 'Come on, Madame Moisson,' he said. 'Let's get you home. Tati's waiting.'

Joséphine has no news, either. I called by the café to find Paul-Marie, pallid and unshaven, looking at the same time both wretched and curiously triumphant.

'Oh, hooray, it's the cavalry. Come to set the world to rights? Heal the sick? Cure the lame? Oh, wait—' He gave a humourless grin. 'I guess your special powers must be playing up today, because as far as I can see, we're still in a world of shit.'

'I never claimed I had powers,' I said.

360

He gave a snarl of laughter. 'You mean there's things you *can't* do? Because if you believe that bitch I married, you can practically walk on water. And as for that brat of hers—'

'Pilou.'

'Well, according to him, you're a cross between Mary Poppins and the Sugar Plum Fairy. Magic chocolates, invisible pets, you've got it all, haven't you? What next? A cure for Aids? I'd settle for a working pair of legs—oh yes, and maybe a blowjob.'

I said: 'Pilou's an imaginative boy. I think he and Maya and Rosette might have been playing some kind of game.'

Paul-Marie made a sour face. 'Is that what you call it? *Imaginative?* Playing around by the river all day with a pair of sissy little girls? *You* might call it imaginative. I say get him some proper friends— and by that I mean *boys*, real French boys, not that scum from Les Marauds—'

I did not rise to the bait. Paul Muscat is one of those men who love to provoke a reaction. Instead I said: 'Where's Joséphine?'

He shrugged. 'She took the car this morning. I think she's gone looking for that boat. Well, good luck to her, I say. They're saying the gypsies have taken it, or maybe it was the *Maghrébins*. Don't see why she cares, do you? She never uses it—I mean, not since that redhead of hers went away.'

That redhead of hers. I wanted to say how wrong he was, but Joséphine's secret is not mine to give away. Instead, I said: 'Tell her I was here.'

He gave another mocking laugh. 'If you think I've got time to sit around and deliver your little messages—'

'Tell her I'll come back tomorrow,' I said.

361

'I'll be waiting,' said Paul-Marie.

CHAPTER TWELVE

☾

Friday, 27th August

When I got back to Armande's house, I found Alyssa waiting for me. Dressed in her black *abaya*, the headscarf covering her hair, she looked so unlike the girl I have come to know that I almost mistook her for someone else.

'I wanted to thank you before I left,' she said.

'You're going home, then?'

She nodded. 'Jiddo knows what I did. He says the *zina* was not mine. He also says Karim is not the man he pretends to be. My father is a good man, but perhaps too easily flattered, he says. And my mother . . . values appearances.' She gave a rueful little smile. 'My *jiddo* may be old, but he is a very good judge of character.'

'Will he tell your parents what happened?'

She shook her head.

'Will you?'

She shrugged. 'My *jiddo* says it would only do harm. There's no taking back what has happened. We can only pray that Allah will forgive, and try to continue with our lives.'

Is that even possible? Maybe it is, I told myself. Alyssa certainly thinks so; with the optimism of youth, she believes she can erase the past. But the past is an obdurate stranger that puts as many marks on us as we attempt to impose on it. Can Alyssa be content, living in that other world?

I tried not to think of what Inès had said. *A child sees a baby bird fall from the nest. She picks it up and takes it home. One of two things happens next. The baby bird dies almost at once; or it survives for a day or two, and the child takes it back to its family. But the scent of human is on it now, and the family rejects it. It dies of starvation, or a cat kills it, or the other birds peck it to death. With luck, the child will never know.*

But I am not a child, Inès. Alyssa is not a fledgling. Will her family take her back? I hope so. Maybe. Maybe not. If not, I think she is strong enough to survive alone, without their help. In the few days she has been with me, I have seen Alyssa change. No longer a frightened baby bird, she is starting to flex her wings. Can she really go back to the nest and pretend she doesn't want to fly?

We walked her to the al-Djerba house, where old Mahjoubi was waiting. He looked outwardly composed, but his colours were turbulent; grey shot through with blood-orange and black, betraying his anxiety.

'Will you be all right?' I said.

'*Inshallah*,' said old Mahjoubi.

Maya's face appeared at the door. 'I want to come, too. I want to show Rosette where my Jinni lives. Besides, he owes me another wish.'

Rosette looked at me and signed: *I want to go and see Foxy.*

'All right,' I said. 'But don't go too far.' I turned back to old Mahjoubi. 'Would you like me to come with you?'

'Thank you, no.' He shook his head. 'I think it

will be easier if I can speak to my son alone. It is time I did; it has been too long. Pride and anger have stood in my way. This would never have happened if I had not allowed my pride to stand in the way of my conscience. I will not let this happen again. I have been blind, but now I see. Allah give me strength to make others see, too.'

I nodded. 'All right. But if you need help—'

'I know where to come,' said Mahjoubi.

CHAPTER THIRTEEN

✝

Friday, 27th August

I awoke to the sound of tapping from the metal grille high up the wall. I ran over to the piled-up crates, now mostly submerged in floodwater.

'Vianne?'

It wasn't Vianne, of course. But it *was* Maya, and she had brought a friend. That might have given me hope, except that the friend was Rosette, who barely speaks, and when she does, makes little sense.

I tried not to let my frustration show. 'Maya. Did you tell Vianne I was here?'

She nodded. Beside her, Rosette was watching with eyes as round as collection plates. Through the grille, the two little girls looked like a pair of cartoon kittens spying on a very big mouse.

'Why haven't you brought her?'

She made a face. 'But you still owe me two

wishes.'

I suppressed the urge to scream at her. 'You know, Maya, I could grant your wishes a lot more easily if I wasn't locked up down here.'

The two little girls exchanged glances. Maya whispered something in Rosette's ear. Rosette whispered back, in a hiccupping voice interspersed with giggles. Then they turned to me again.

'My second wish is for you to bring back the cat.'

'*What* cat, for pity's sake?'

'You know, the cat that comes to our house. Hazi.'

'Maya, it's a *cat*,' I said. 'How should I know where it is?'

Maya looked solemnly through the grille. 'You made my *jiddo* better,' she said. 'But he's still sad, because of the cat. Now, would you please bring Hazi back? After that, we'll let you go.'

Père, I could have murdered her. It was like talking to Henriette Moisson. As it was, I gave a howl of impatience, and the two kitten faces pulled away as if a dog had lunged at them.

'Maya, Rosette, I'm sorry,' I said. 'It's just that I want to get out of here.'

She gave the grille a narrow-eyed look. 'Not until you give me my wish.'

There is nothing more futile than trying to argue with a five-year-old, especially not through a metal slot barely the size of a letter-box. I returned to my place on the cellar steps—three of which are now underwater—and tried not to give in to despair. It can be only a matter of time before someone hears about Maya's new game, and wants to see the Jinni for himself. Till then, I will try to be patient, and believe that there is some kind of sense to be found in this absurd situation. A week from now, I hope that I can look back on all of this and laugh at the misunderstanding. But at this moment, I see no light. And the water is still rising; not fast enough to present an immediate threat, but enough to be unnerving. I may not drown in here, *mon père*, but I may contract pneumonia. Is this what my God wants of me?

Here comes the call to prayer again. *Allahu Akhbar.* Underground, everything is curiously resonant. I have fallen inside a seashell, with the sound of the surf all around me. The voices of the everyday world float above me like jetsam. There is light, too, through the grille; brilliant, festive, fragmented light that dances and blinks like fireflies. The wind has dropped. The rain has, too. Maybe, at last, the Black Autan has run its course. I hope so.

Allahu Akhbar. Ash-hadu al-la. The sound of the seashell is potent: its voice as persistent as memory. It makes me think of the giant dune, the big white dune at Arcachon where we used to go when I was a child; the blinding run towards the sea; the endless climb back to the top with the sun on the sand like hammered bronze and the nape of my neck growing red as I climbed.

And now, for the first time, comes the thought that maybe I will die down here—alone, forgotten, unwanted. Who would miss me if I were gone? I have no family, no friends. My mother, the Church, prefers Père Henri. No one will look very far for me. And who would shed a tear for Reynaud, except perhaps Reynaud himself?

CHAPTER FOURTEEN

☾

Friday, 27th August

We had started to walk down the boulevard towards the little jetty. Maya and Rosette led the way, Rosette singing her wordless song. Maya joined in. Foxy and Bam seem to be made for each other. Half closing my eyes, I found I could see Bam as an orange light-scribble in their wake, though Maya's new companion remains at present invisible. Of course, I don't always see them. It has been months—perhaps even years—since I caught a glimpse of Pantoufle. As we reached the end of the road, all three of them vanished down one of the lanes that lead to the little boardwalk.

'Don't go too far,' I called after them. 'And stay away from the water!'

Anouk looked at me. 'Will Alyssa be OK?'

'I hope so,' I said. 'I can't interfere. The longer she stayed with us, the smaller her chances of going back home.'

'But she cut her hair, and everything. She likes football and Facebook and pop music. She even helped us repaint the shop. How can she go back to wearing a veil, and never going out alone?'

'It's her choice, Anouk,' I said.

'And what about Luc? You know he's crazy about her.'

'I know, Anouk.'

She looked mutinous. 'We came here for a

reason. You were supposed to fix things.'

She sounded so like Luc that I flinched. 'I can't always do that, Anouk,' I said.

'Then what's the point?' She was angry now, the tears starting in her eyes. 'What's the point of what we do, if in the end we can't save them?'

A baby bird, fallen from the nest.

'I never said I'd *save* anyone.'

'That's not true,' protested Anouk. 'We did it before. We can do it now. We made a difference to people's lives. Joséphine. Guillaume. Armande. Reynaud—'

And look at them now, Anouk, I thought. Eight years older, but what has changed? No one has been saved. A few expanding waistlines, perhaps; the fleeting warmth of memories. But go to the Café des Marauds, and Joséphine is still there. Paul-Marie, too, in his wheelchair. Guillaume, with his old dog. Armande, in the ground. And Francis Reynaud—all of them just names in the sand, blown away by the merciless wind.

Anouk looked accusing. 'You've given up. You don't believe we can change things.'

'That isn't what I said, Anouk.'

'Well, I don't care. I'll do it myself. We'll do it together, me and Rosette. We'll fix things for Alyssa and Luc. We'll find Reynaud. We'll fix up the *chocolaterie*. And then you'll *have* to believe—' She broke off, glaring, tears in her eyes.

'What's the matter, Anouk?' I said. 'Why is this suddenly so important?'

Anouk shook her head, stubborn as a toy soldier.

'Please, Anouk.'

She turned away. For a long time, she did not answer. I could feel her trying to hold it in, to

368

keep it under proper control. My little stranger has always been a surprisingly private individual; a hoarder of secrets and treasures and dreams, a puzzle box never quite to be solved. I waited.

'It's Jean-Loup,' she said. 'He isn't answering his mail. He promised he would, as soon as he was out of surgery. But the operation was three days ago, and he hasn't texted me, or posted anything on Facebook.' Now there were tears spilling down her face. 'No one's heard from him. No one at all. And he *promised*—'

I put my arms around her and pressed my face into her hair. 'It's going to be all right, Anouk. Everything's going to be all right.'

So *this* is why Anouk has been so brittle and restless these past few days: not because of Jeannot at all, but because of her friend Jean-Loup Rimbault—

'You don't *know* that. You can't be sure.'

You're right, Anouk. It's only words. The cheapest kind of magic words, like whistling past a graveyard. But sometimes words are all we have, and sometimes the ghosts are frightened away. Not every time, but sometimes—

And then, just then, something happened. Rosette, who had been playing in a side alley with Maya, gave a sudden hoot of surprise. I looked up and saw, coming under the bridge, an unexpected movement. Could that be a *houseboat*?

We ran to the bridge. It *was* a boat; no, not Inès Bencharki's boat, but a little dark-green riverboat; crooked chimney coughing smoke; pots of flowers on the deck. And from the bridge, we saw two more boats, one yellow, one black, already moored by the riverbank.

Rosette and Maya ran to see.

Anouk turned towards me, once more alight with expectation. 'You know what *this* means, don't you?' she said.

The river-rats were back in town.

The
RIVER-RATS

CHAPTER ONE

C

Friday, 27th August

The river-rats. An invasion of them, moored beside the old jetty; narrow wooden riverboats of the kind they never make any more; some brightly painted, some drab, like old potbellied caravans with their little tin chimneys and corrugated roofs. By noon, there were already a dozen of them round the back of Les Marauds. You could see them from Armande's house overlooking the river, and as evening fell we could see their lights beginning to shine across the Tannes and hear the sounds of activity as meals were cooked, greetings made, and the little floating community prepared to set up camp for the night.

Anouk is convinced it is a sign. Of what, she is uncertain; but to her, the return of the river-rats signifies a change in the wind.

Well, Anouk, you may be right. The wind has dropped. The sky is clear. On the Boulevard des Marauds, families are preparing to break fast on the seventeenth day of Ramadan. A river of stars overhead; the lights along the Boulevard; the constellation of riverboats scattered across the sleeping Tannes.

Tonight, we were alone at last. Alyssa has gone home, and the house is back to its normal size. But Rosette, who loves the riverboats, wanted to go and see them again; and Anouk wanted to check her messages, but of course there's no reception here.

I'll admit, I was happy to see them go. Too many people; too much to do; far too many anxieties. Half an hour alone, I thought, would give me back my perspective. I made a cup of hot chocolate and took it into the garden; the air is still cool after the long rain, and the scents of wet earth and lavender are just beginning to reawaken. Below me, the streets of Les Marauds. Above me, the stars.

I closed my eyes. Slowly, the sounds of the evening descend; the *chirr* of crickets; the church bells; the *tick-tick-tick* of the old house as it settles into the damp earth like a tired old lady into a chair. A ribbon of music—perhaps a flute— floats above Les Marauds. Eight years ago, when the river-rats came, I was preparing my first chocolate festival. Anouk was six. Roux was a stranger. Armande was still alive. Now, listening to that music, I can almost believe that nothing has changed. I can almost believe that *I* have not changed.

Everything returns, said Armande. *The river brings everything back in the end*. Dear Armande. If only it could. If only you were with me now. The things I could tell you—the secrets I know—

Everyone confides in *someone*. Much of the Catholic Church's appeal is surely the confessional and its promise of absolution. Reynaud held confession every day, without exception. Now that Père Henri is in charge, confession is a weekly event, timed to coincide with services. Some of the old people miss Reynaud. People like Henriette Moisson and Charles Lévy, who rarely speak to anyone otherwise. To them, he is more than just a priest; he is a friend, a confidant. Old Mahjoubi

373

was the same to the people of Les Marauds: and perhaps in my way I was too, in the days of the old *chocolaterie*. But to whom do *we* turn when we need to confess? Who is there to listen to me?

The chocolate had gone cold. I poured it into the bushes. The night, too, was chilly; I stood up, ready to go indoors. And then I saw something, on Armande's tree. We must have missed it last week, as we collected the last of the fruit: a single, perfect peach, just ripe; miraculously unblemished.

And so I picked it; its scent was faint, but came to life with the warmth of my hands. I broke it open and tried it. End-of-summer peaches are too often tasteless and watery, but this one was still good; still sweet; still slightly musky with the rain.

Armande was right; it's always a shame to let good fruit go to waste. I should plant the stone by Armande's grave, I told myself: she'd like that. There's plenty of room by the cemetery wall, and in summer the children will creep in and steal the peaches. She'd like that, too. I know she would. I put the stone in my pocket. Across Les Marauds, I could see riverboats still continuing to arrive, the coloured lanterns at their bows scrawling fire across the water. Why so many? Why today? And could Inès be among them?

It seems unlikely. And yet—

I know the travelling community. If anyone can find Inès, the river-rats will sniff her out. And as for Reynaud, wherever he is, surely the thought of the river-folk invading Lansquenet-sous-Tannes will be enough to bring him out from wherever he's hiding. He may not be the same Reynaud who tried to ruin my chocolate festival eight years ago, but his mistrust of outsiders remains. As soon as he hears the news, he'll come home. Everything comes home in the end.

I looked at my watch. It was past nine o'clock. Time for Rosette to go to bed. I knew where she and Anouk had gone; to the boardwalk, by the Tannes, perhaps to seek out old friends. I decided to go in search of them—it's only a ten-minute walk from the house—and headed off into Les Marauds, where the Ramadan lights along the boulevard were echoed by those on the river.

I walked past the al-Djerba house. The shutters were half open, and as I passed I saw them all having dinner—everyone laughing and talking— and the cat asleep on the window-ledge. That cat must have at least three homes. *Keep a cat indoors and all it wants is to go outside again. Keep it outside, and it cries to get in. People are not so different.* At least Maya got her wish. If only everything were as simple.

I passed the Mahjoubi house as well, but the shutters were closed. There was no sign of life. I hope Alyssa and her family have managed to find some common ground. And now, at the end of the boulevard, the shadow of the minaret falling across the alleyway that marks the entrance to Saïd's gym—and in the alley, a woman in black, carrying what looked like a cardboard box. I stopped in the shadows. The woman hadn't noticed me. She moved quickly and furtively, opened the door to the gym, went in—

Who could that be? I asked myself. Everyone was at dinner. And why would a Muslim woman enter an all-male gym anyway?

There was a little passageway at the other side of the gym. I waited there, hidden from sight, for

375

the woman to reappear. In less than five minutes she was back, but without the cardboard box. The woman was veiled from head to foot, but even so I recognized Zahra al-Djerba. I stepped out into the alleyway.

'Zahra?'

Her colours betrayed her. Behind the veil, I sensed her alarm. But her voice was calm enough as she said: 'Oh, it's you, Vianne. I was just dropping off some of old Mahjoubi's things.'

'To the gym?'

She gave a shrug. 'I didn't want to intrude. Besides—'

'You didn't want to see Karim.'

She started. 'Why do you say that?'

I smiled. 'Just something your grandmother said. And he *is* very handsome, isn't he?'

'Yes, handsome,' she said. 'And dangerous. Don't worry. He's hardly likely to turn *my* head.' I was surprised at her dry tone. After Alyssa's confession and my own first meeting with him, I had formed a certain idea of Karim. Women and men of all ages, from Omi to Alyssa, believe he's unfaithful to his new wife, but all of them seem to blame Inès rather than Karim himself—and yet Zahra seems almost amused at the thought that she, too, might fall for his charm. 'I'm sorry, I have to go,' she said. 'The others will wonder where I am.'

I watched her as she hurried back up the Boulevard des Marauds. I believed what she'd told me about Karim, but the rest still puzzled me. Why bring old Mahjoubi's things to the gym? And why does she mistrust Karim, when everyone else adores him?

376

I walked up to the door of the gym. As always, the neon sign was lit. Everything was quiet inside. I pushed at the door. It was open. Inside, the scent of chlorine over a watery, swampy smell; these old buildings flood easily, and the Tannes is at its highest. Other than that, I saw nothing unusual; nothing but the shapes of running machines and vaulting horses outlined in neon against the dark.

I called: 'Hello?' No answer.

I closed the door and went back on to the boulevard. Through the narrow passageway that leads down to the riverbank, I could see lights and hear voices and music. The river-gypsies were celebrating. I followed the boulevard towards the jetty; through the trees I could see their fires and shadows as they came and went. There's something about a campfire that has always drawn me. That's why I found myself moving, almost without being aware of it, towards the jetty and the lights, where someone was on the riverbank, roasting potatoes over a fire contained in a metal barrel. Two others were watching from the deck of a riverboat, and a third was practising monkey-jumps and shouting: *'Bam! Bam! Badda-bam!'*

I stepped out from between the trees.

'Maman!' cried Anouk. 'We found Joséphine! And look! Look who *else* we found!'

Joséphine had got up as soon as I arrived on the jetty. She was wearing jeans and a fisherman's sweater, and her hair was a pale corona in the lights from the water.

'I meant to come and find you,' she said. 'But—'

But I wasn't listening. All my attention was focused on the figure on the riverbank; the light from the campfire gilding his face, making his paprika hair into a circlet of wildfire—

'Hello, stranger,' the figure said.

Who else could it be? I thought.

It was Roux.

CHAPTER TWO

☾

Friday, 27th August

Joséphine began to explain. 'I went to look for the boat,' she said. 'I thought if I found it, then maybe Reynaud—' She shrugged. 'I didn't. I found Roux instead. And that woman was with him.'

Roux smiled. Roux has a very engaging smile, easy and at the same time curiously reluctant, which reaches all the way to his eyes. This time there was a question there. I climbed up on to the jetty and put my arms around him. He smelt of campfire smoke and of something unidentifiable, but familiar as the sound of the wind. Perhaps it was the smell of home. I found his lips with mine; we kissed. For a time, the question was answered.

I said: 'Don't you *ever* turn on your phone?'

He grinned. 'I lost the charger. And then, when I got your messages—'

'It doesn't matter any more. You're here now. But where's Inès?'

Now Roux told his tale. He'd come down by train two days ago, and had joined up with some friends in Agen. Everyone on the river knows Roux; he's done work on practically every boat from the

378

Garonne to the Haut-Tannes, and people trust him instinctively. They'd found the black boat downriver, moored illegally just out of Agen, with Inès and Du'a still on board. Roux had recognized it at once; he'd fixed the engine and brought it home.

'What about Inès?'

He shrugged. 'She said she'd been having problems here. She never meant to take the boat. But when it drifted downriver, she didn't know how to bring it back.'

'She told you all that?'

'Why wouldn't she?'

It's true, of course; people talk to Roux. There's something about him that invites trust. Children; animals; people in need; like the Pied Piper, he acquires followers wherever he goes. And yet, there is a remoteness in Roux that no one has ever overcome; a deep and quiet reluctance to talk about anything to do with the past; a refusal to explain himself, whatever the circumstances. Hence his refusal to discuss Joséphine, or even to mention Pilou's existence, though he must have known that his silence would make him look guilty.

But on the river, these things are allowed. No one asks too many questions. Friendships are made on the basis of a borrowed half-can of petrol. The river has only the present; the past is left behind on the shore. Names are most often nicknames; no one has any papers. Criminal records; past mistakes; broken families; none of that counts. Life is uncluttered and simple—

I looked at Joséphine again. I thought she seemed vaguely troubled, her colours tremulous and faint. Perhaps it's seeing Roux again, I thought,

379

with a flicker of unease. But that was absurd; more likely she's just anxious about finding Reynaud.

As for Roux himself—

A couple of days on the river have reawakened something in Roux. It's hard to say what, exactly; a kind of shine that was absent so long that I barely knew it was gone. A barge on a permanent mooring is not the same as a riverboat. There are rules to be followed; charges paid; and in Paris the riverside community is of a very different kind. Here, on the Tannes, he's free again. And the change is all the more striking in that he is unaware of it.

'Where are Inès and Du'a now?'

'I drove them back here in my car,' said Joséphine. 'Roux phoned me. I assume they went home.'

'You didn't see where?'

She shook her head. 'No. Is it important?'

Anouk was watching impatiently. 'Maman! Jean-Loup texted me!'

I hugged her. 'I'm glad. I'm sure he'll be fine.'

'And we have *potatoes*!'

'Potatoes?' I said.

Roux indicated the campfire. 'I found these potatoes growing wild all around the riverbank. Try one, Vianne. They're pretty good.'

I used a pointed stick to retrieve one of the roasted potatoes. Under the charred skin, it was good; floury, sweet and slightly pink. The others helped themselves too, and we ate them sitting on the deck, and between us, Joséphine and I told him about Reynaud, and Inès, and Alyssa, and everything that has happened here since the three of us arrived—

The story took a long time. When we had

380

finished, Joséphine went back to see to Pilou, leaving us alone again. Rosette and Anouk were already asleep, tucked up in the cabin.

The moon was starting to set, and the Tannes was blanketed with midges. Roux flung a handful of dried shavings on to the embers of his fire; the scent was sharp and immediate, lemon grass and lavender, sage and applewood and pine, like the campfires of my childhood.

I said: 'She told me about Pilou. And how she lied to Paul-Marie.'

'Oh.' His eyes were unreadable.

'I'm sorry.'

'For what?'

What could I say? I'm sorry for believing that you lied to me? For thinking that you could have led such a tortuous double life, while all the time pretending to be as open as the palm of your hand?

I shrugged. 'It doesn't matter now. I've missed you, Roux. We all have.'

He took my hand. 'So why not come home?' That question was in his eyes again. 'Vianne, you don't live here any more. You only came for a holiday. And yet, here you are, back in Lansquenet, doing all the same things that you did last time, getting involved—'

'You think I *shouldn't* get involved?'

He shrugged.

'But Armande brought me here. She wrote to me for a reason. She said there'd be someone who needed my help—'

He shrugged again. 'There always is.'

'What do you mean?'

He looked at me. His eyes were green as gages. 'Perhaps you're the one who needs Lansquenet, not

381

the other way around.'

He's wrong, of course. I don't need Lansquenet. But his words had opened up something in me, some secret cell of longing and grief. *Why do I do these things?* I thought. Why do I answer the call of the wind? Will there never be a time when I can be free of this restless need?

No, I'm not crying. I never cry.

We sat together on the deck. I found the place on his shoulder that fits my head so perfectly, and we sat in silence for a long time, listening to the crickets and frogs chirping among the rushes. Then, without speaking, we crept away into the shelter of the trees and made love there, in the moonlight, with the scent of green damp earth and the night settling around us. Strange, how accustomed we become to our familiar small routines; it struck me that we hadn't made love outdoors like this since we were last here.

Then we went back to the riverboat where Anouk and Rosette were still sleeping. Roux brought blankets on to the deck, and we lay there, watching the Milky Way turning like a Catherine wheel—

It took me a long time to get to sleep. Outside, the night had fallen still. Even the frogs were silent now, and the Tannes was a misty, luminous white. I got up and sat by the campfire, watching as the sky grew pale. Roux never finds it hard to sleep, just as he never remembers what time it is, or even what day of the week. If he were a Tarot card, he would be the Fool, whistling at the sky, shoelace undone, oblivious to all obstacles—the Fool who always tells the truth, sometimes without even knowing it.

And yet, he's wrong, isn't he? I never needed

382

Lansquenet. In a way I'm fond of it, but I never really belonged here. How could I? I'm a free spirit. I've travelled too far, seen too many things to fit into such a little space. Lansquenet-sous-Tannes. How absurd; that such a small, narrow-minded place should keep such a firm hold on my heart. What is it about Lansquenet? It's a village like any other here along the banks of the river Tannes. Quite an ordinary place; not as attractive as Pont-le-Saôul; not as historic as Nérac. Yes, of course, it has memories; but so does Paris; so does Nantes; so do a hundred different towns, a hundred different communities. I owe nothing to any of them. If they call, I do not hear. So why is this place different? Am I still a free spirit? Or am I just a tumbleweed, blowing wherever the wind takes me?

At dawn I went back to my place on the deck and tried to get to sleep again. I must have succeeded, because when I awoke the sun was up; and Roux was gone; the children were stirring sleepily inside the cabin; and the wind had changed again.

CHAPTER THREE

Saturday, 28th August

The woman in black came again last night. This time she brought a flask of mint tea, and slices of cold roast lamb wrapped in some kind of pancakes. I had promised myself that this time I wouldn't indulge in any undignified pleading, and so I took the food without a word; just looked up at her from the bottom of the steps, all but two of which are now submerged. As a result, I have to stand almost thigh-deep in water.

This seemed to make her uncomfortable. 'The water will stop rising soon,' she said. 'It hasn't rained at all today.'

I shrugged and didn't say anything.

'Are you all right? You don't look well.'

In fact, I feel like hell, *père*. I have been in the same wet clothes since the day I arrived here, and God knows what bacteria are floating in the water. I think I have a temperature; I'm shivering; my hand still hurts.

'I'm fine,' I said. 'I love it here.'

She eyed me over her face-veil. 'Vianne told me what you did. How you helped Alyssa when she jumped into the Tannes. And how you didn't tell anyone.'

Once more, I shrugged.

'So why did you try to burn Inès's school, and sabotage her houseboat?'

That final comment was enough to convince me that she wasn't Sonia. Her voice is different, anyway: drier and more nasal. I said: 'Talk to Sonia Bencharki. She knows I had nothing to do with it.'

'Sonia? Not Alyssa?' she said.

'Just ask her. Tell her why I'm here. She'll tell you what happened.'

She looked at me for a long time. 'Maybe I will do that.'

Of course, I have no certainty that Sonia would tell this woman the truth. But I don't have many options left. At least I've put some doubt in her mind.

384

I am not sure how this has happened to me. I always did my duty. It's these people, these *Maghrébins*. They're all as mad as each other. I've tried my best to help them, *père*, and where has it brought me in the end? I'm in the hands of a five-year-old girl, a lost cat and a woman in black. If I were not so tired, *père*, I might almost find it amusing. But I'm exhausted: what little sleep I managed to get on those two remaining dry steps was broken by dreams so vivid that they barely seemed to be dreams at all. Several times I was woken up by what seemed to be tapping at the grille; though when I went to investigate, on each occasion, no one was there. My mind must be playing tricks on me. My throat is dry. My head aches. I finished the flask of mint tea, but could not eat the food she had brought. All I want is to sleep now, possibly for ever. To sleep between clean linen sheets, my aching head on a pillow—

Dawn breaks. The call to prayer. *Allahu Akhbar. God is most great.* Those words are the first thing a newborn baby hears; the first words spoken in a new home. *Allahu Akhbar. God is most great.* And now, that half-hour's silence before the treadmills start again and the bells ring out from Saint-Jérôme's, where Père Henri will be saying Mass in front of my congregation—

But is it *my* congregation? The image of Père Henri Lemaître taking over Saint-Jérôme's— replacing the wooden pews with chairs; perhaps installing a PowerPoint screen—fills me with revulsion. But that does not entirely explain the violent sense of loss that I feel; the isolation; that longing for my ordered little place in the world. Even before all this, *mon père*, I was never one of them. Even though I was born here, I never felt I really belonged. I was set apart from the rest of them by something more than my calling. Standing here in the water, it seems so obvious to me now. Karim was right about one thing: no one will miss me very much. I never really touched their hearts; I only pricked their consciences.

Why is that, *père*? Vianne Rocher might say that it is because I do not make connections. I keep my distance. Is that so wrong? A priest cannot afford to be too friendly with his parishioners. Authority must be maintained. And yet, without my soutane, who am I? A hermit crab without his shell, helpless to every predator?

CHAPTER FOUR

☾

Saturday, 28th August, 9.40 a.m.

It was just after nine by the time he returned, with croissants and *pains au chocolat*. We ate them out on the deck, while Anouk made coffee in the galley and Rosette played with Bam on the riverbank.

'I would have been here sooner,' he said, 'but people kept stopping to talk to me.'

Père Henri is saying Mass today. The square will be full of people. Poitou does most of his business on Saturdays and Sundays; fancy cakes for lunch; fruit tarts; almond flans; the *pain Viennois* he only makes at weekends and on special occasions. The congregation usually calls first at the church, and

386

second at the bakery. The spirit must be fed, after all; not just with Scripture, but with pâtisserie.

'No news of Reynaud?' I said.

'No. Just that new priest, Père Henri. Went out of his way to talk to me. Said he respected my lifestyle choices and those of the travelling community, and wanted to know when we were leaving.'

I had to laugh. 'So—no change there?'

'At least Reynaud was honest.'

'And you think Père Henri isn't?'

He shrugged. 'I think he has too many teeth.'

Anouk ate her breakfast in three bites, then ran off to find Jeannot. Now that Jean-Loup has contacted her, her other friend takes priority again; her colours are fresh and green and clear, like innocent young love.

Rosette was nosing around the mouth of one of the alleys that led to the road. I asked her what she could see down there.

Maya, she signed. *Foxy.*

'Oh. So you can see him, too?'

No. He lives in a hole.

'A fox-hole?'

No. He wants to get out.

'Oh. I see.' Like Bam and Pantoufle, Foxy has already acquired a number of interesting characteristics. Bam has a mischievous streak that reflects Rosette's volatile nature. Pantoufle is a friendly companion. But Foxy seems to personify Maya's sense of rebellion—perhaps she's already conscious of the rules and restrictions surrounding her. That, and the fact that she chose a fox, the closest thing there is to a dog.

I checked the Boulevard des Marauds. Maya

387

was there, exuberant in her Disney sandals and *Aladdin* T-shirt. She waved to me before vanishing down the narrow passageway. But coming down the boulevard, some three hundred metres behind her, was a tight and purposeful little group, looking like chess pieces from afar—three black pawns and an old white king—heading towards the jetty.

The king was Mohammed Mahjoubi. I recognized his white beard; his bulk; his slow but dignified walk; the white *djellaba* he always wears. The pawns were women, all in *niqab*—at this distance, hard to know who they were. Was Inès among them? A field of tension lay over the group like a magnet on iron filings. All along the boulevard, doors opened, shutters clapped, people came out to watch them go.

Roux sensed it too and grinned at me. 'You think that's a welcome committee?' he said.

It wasn't a welcome committee. By the time they reached the jetty, more people had joined the little group. I recognized Alyssa, with Sonia and their mother, with Saïd Mahjoubi—another king— approaching from the other side. Then there was Omi, Fatima, Zahra in her usual *niqab* and Karim Bencharki, a step behind, dressed as always in T-shirt and jeans, looking controlled, but angry.

Omi greeted me with a croak of laughter. '*Hee*, what a circus!'

'What's happening?'

She had no time to answer. Approaching the jetty, Karim launched a staccato volley of Arabic, and made straight for the houseboat. Old Mahjoubi stood in his way. Karim tried to push the old man aside—

'What the hell's going on?' said Roux.

388

Saïd turned to Roux and said, 'These houseboats cannot stay here. This is all private property.'

'Really?' said Roux. 'Because the *curé* seemed to suggest that we could stay here indefinitely.'

'The *curé*?'

'Père Henri,' said Roux.

There followed another exchange in Arabic. 'I will talk to Père Henri,' said Saïd, addressing Roux. 'Perhaps he has not fully considered the effect this might have on our community.'

Old Mahjoubi shook his head. 'It is Ramadan,' he said. 'Everyone is welcome here, as long as there is mutual respect.' He turned to Roux. 'Stay as long as you wish. '

Saïd looked annoyed. 'I do not think—'

'Shall we refuse hospitality?' Old Mahjoubi's voice was soft, but still it carried authority. Saïd shot him a resentful look. Old Mahjoubi just smiled.

'Very well,' said Saïd at last. 'My father makes a valid point. We do not want arguments and conflict during our time of celebration. All we would ask is that you show respect, and keep your distance.'

Karim had jumped on to the deck of the boat and was looking into the galley.

'Excuse me. That's my boat,' said Roux.

Karim turned and stared. '*Your* boat?'

I stepped up to the jetty once more. 'Inès came home safely yesterday,' I said. 'Didn't she go to your house?'

Karim looked blank. 'No, she did not. You're saying she's here, in the village?'

Once more, Roux told his story. While the others were listening, I took the opportunity to ask Alyssa, 'How did it go yesterday?'

389

She shook her head. 'They're not talking to me. They think I've shamed the family.'

'They'll come round,' I said in a low voice. 'What about Karim?'

She shrugged. 'I'm *totally* over Karim.'

'Well, that's something,' I told her.

'He keeps wanting to see me in private. I said I didn't want to.'

'What about your sister?'

'*Meh.*' Alyssa shrugged. 'I think the baby's making her sick. She doesn't talk to me much any more, but I can tell she's tired.'

I glanced at Sonia, who was standing alone, looking at the river. There was something wistful about the way she stood; as I came closer I saw that her eyes were shining with tears.

'What's wrong?' I said.

She looked surprised. One effect of wearing *niqab* is to give the wearer the illusion of invisibility, and to discourage contact with strangers. Her eyes—kohl-lined and beautiful—nervously avoided my gaze.

'You're Vianne Rocher, aren't you?' she said. 'Alyssa told me about you.' There was a hint of censure in the flat little voice behind the veil.

I smiled. 'I'm happy to meet you,' I said. 'I hope you can both come and visit us.'

Once more, that startled look. Sonia Bencharki is not used to casual invitations from strangers. Under the veil, her colours were a sick and gaudy carousel. The girl had something on her mind. Sadness; fear; perhaps even guilt—

I caught Karim watching me from his position by the boat. I thought he looked uneasy at the sight of us together. Sonia noticed him watching, and

390

moved away a couple of steps. I followed her.

'Please. I can't talk to you.' The voice was almost inaudible.

'Why not?'

'I'm sorry. Just leave me alone.'

I let her go. There were too many people around for me to try to break through her reserve. Zahra said: 'She's shy, that's all. She's really a very sweet girl.'

Just like Alyssa, I told myself. Or at least, just like Alyssa had been before Karim Bencharki. Once more, I looked at Karim as he stood on the jetty, talking to Roux, and wondered how it was that one man had managed to gain so much influence over the little community. Yes, he is handsome. Yes, he has charm. And from what I have heard from Caro Clairmont, he has done a great deal to bring Les Marauds into the twenty-first century. His influence over Saïd has caused the mosque to grow more progressive; his work at the gym has given a focus to the young men of his neighbourhood. Strange, then, that his sister should adopt such a traditional image—unless, of course, the rumours are true, and the veil worn by Inès is simply a show of modesty that hides something very different.

But what I saw the other night—and here again, this morning—suggests that he, too, has a dark side. His treatment of Alyssa; his lack of respect for old Mahjoubi; and now, his arrogant dealing with Roux. We already know that he is capable of infidelity. Now, I'm beginning to wonder if he isn't capable of more. He has shown he can be aggressive. Is he also violent? Could Sonia be afraid of him? And what about Inès and Du'a? Are they deliberately avoiding him?

391

Zahra was watching me, a curious look in her dark eyes. It was the same look that had been in her eyes last night, around the back of the gym. Were they old Mahjoubi's things that Zahra had been carrying? Or did they perhaps belong to Inès?

I looked up at the minaret that stands at the top of the boulevard. Slender; bone-white; elegant; crowned with a silver crescent moon. And across the river, the little square tower of Saint-Jérôme's; plain; inflexible; unadorned. Two towers, facing each other across the Tannes like pieces on a chessboard—

'You know where she is, don't you?' I said.

Zahra nodded. 'I saw her last night. I told her about your friend Reynaud, and everything that has happened here. And then I spoke to Sonia.' She shot a glance at the girl, then spoke a few dozen words in Arabic.

'What did she say? Has she seen Reynaud?'

'No.' Zahra shook her head. 'But I know where he is. I'm sorry, Vianne. I have known almost from the beginning.'

I stared at her. 'But—why?'

She shrugged. 'I thought I was protecting Inès.'

'And now?'

She looked at me and smiled. 'And now, she wants to talk to you.'

CHAPTER FIVE

✝

Saturday, 28th August, 10.00 a.m.

Ten o'clock. the end of Mass. Even here, inside the whale, Père Henri continues to taunt me. Of course, I'd know my bells anywhere. Their voices are unmistakable. And in a minute there he'll be, sitting in my confessional, hearing their secrets, handing out *Avés*, once more taking my place—

A tap on the grille. It was Maya again. Maya and Rosette, in fact: two little pairs of feet, one decorated with Disney princesses, the other lemon-yellow. And a jaded-looking cat, firmly held by Maya and emitting a series of mournful yowls.

'So. You found the cat, then.'

She gave me a luminous, happy smile. 'Last night. I took him to Jiddo's house.'

'Wonderful.' In fact, *père*, I was feeling less than vibrant. My head was spinning, and my throat was so sore that I could barely make myself heard. 'What next, I wonder? A pony? A date with the Pope? A singing hat?'

'That's just silly. Hats don't sing.'

I tried to get a grip on myself. I must be light-headed with fever. The urge to laugh was almost overwhelming—and yet, *mon père*, I am not a man naturally given to laughter. I thought of Karim Bencharki's threats and managed to focus a little.

'Please. Maya. Did you tell Vianne?'

393

'Uh-huh. I told her all about you.'

'What did she say?'

'She said it was nice.'

I tried again. 'Listen, Maya. I'm not a Jinni. Karim Bencharki put me here.'

Maya put her head to one side. 'If you're not a Jinni,' she said, 'then how can you grant wishes?'

'*Maya!* Would you listen to me?'

'My *third* wish—'

There's no arguing with the implacable logic of childhood. For the first time in decades, I found myself close to tears. 'Please, Maya. I'm sick. I'm cold. I'm hurt. I'm afraid of dying here—' Suddenly, the narrow grille had become the screen of the confessional. But this time, *I* was the penitent and Maya the confessor. It was ridiculous, and yet I couldn't stop myself. Perhaps because I was feverish; perhaps because even a five-year-old girl was better than no confessor at all. 'I'm a priest, and I'm afraid to die. How absurd is that, eh? But I never believed in Paradise. No, not really. Not in my heart. Hell I *can* believe in. But heaven seems like the kind of thing you tell children when they're afraid of the dark. Faith is about obedience; adherence to rules; keeping order. Otherwise, we'd have anarchy. Everybody knows that. That's why the Church has its hierarchy; a stable pyramid of command; every member in his place and briefed on a need-to-know basis. The public accepts what we choose to reveal. God, in His turn, does the same. Order. Control. Obedience. Because if we let people know the truth—that even we have no *certainties*—then everything the Church has built over the past two thousand years would be nothing but a handful of paper and dust—'

394

I stopped to draw breath. In fact, *père*, I was starting to feel dizzy. Three days without proper human contact have left me feeling very strange. I stretched my fingers towards the grille—I thought if Maya saw me, she might believe my story. With an effort, I could just reach.

'Maya. I'm here. *Look* at me.'

Maya pressed her face to the grille. Rosette joined her; I saw her red curls shining in the sunlight. Both of them looked in at me; two earnest little faces, solemn and implacable. For a moment I imagined them as judges, ready to pass sentence.

'My *third* wish—'

I gave a howl. But my throat was so sore and my head so weak that all that emerged was a whimper. Maya went on oblivious:

'My third wish is for Du'a to come home. The riverboat came back, but Du'a and her *memti* weren't there. And so you must bring Du'a back, just like you did with Hazi. And after that, you'll be free. Just like Disney *Aladdin*.'

I gave up. It was hopeless. I'd given everything I had, and still it wasn't enough.

'I'm sorry,' I whispered. I'm still not sure why.

Maya's face withdrew from the grille. For a moment, Rosette lingered. I already knew that talking to her would be a waste of time, and yet there is a kind of intelligence in those curious, birdlike eyes.

'Tell your mother I'm here,' I said. 'Please. Tell *someone*. I'm begging you.'

Rosette made a soft clucking sound. Does that mean she understood? Then she put her hand on the grille. It felt like absolution. And right at that moment the pile of crates beneath my feet gave way at last, tipping me sideways into the dark and into the freezing water.

For a moment I was entirely submerged. For a second or two I panicked, struggling for the surface, then I hauled myself to my feet, pushed my dripping hair out of my eyes and slowly, painfully, made my way back towards the cellar steps.

CHAPTER SIX

☾

Saturday, 28th August, 10.15 a.m.

No one but Omi saw us leave. But as we turned on to the boulevard, leaving the scene on the jetty behind, I was certain I caught a curious look from under a loosely tied headscarf. Omi al-Djerba is too old for *niqab*; in fact, she tells me with glee, at her age, surely even *hijab* is an unnecessary precaution. Well, she may be old, but her eyes are still keen, and her curiosity is endless; so it didn't surprise me to see her, just a few minutes later, following at a distance, up the boulevard, past the al-Djerba house and towards the bridge into Lansquenet.

Zahra had persuaded Sonia to come with us. Sonia had seemed reluctant at first at the idea of seeing Inès, but Zahra spoke to her again in low and furious Arabic, a phrase in which I caught the name *Karim*, which seemed to persuade her.

Now she looked over her shoulder. 'Omi is following us,' she said.

'Don't let her catch up,' said Zahra.

The three of us quickened our step. Omi pretended innocence, looking at the view from the bridge. But by the time we had reached the Place Saint-Jérôme, she had abandoned all pretence, had picked up her skirts and was scurrying as fast as she could to catch up.

It was ten fifteen; Mass was over, but the square was still busy with people. A group of men were playing *pétanque* in the patch of red shale behind the church, and there must have been twenty customers in the queue outside Poitou's bakery. Some of them looked curiously at Zahra and Sonia in their black robes. In Les Marauds, *niqab* confers a kind of invisibility. Across the river, the opposite is true. A black robe catches the eye; a veil invites speculation. Joline Drou was coming out of Poitou's with a pastry box; the ribbon exactly the same shade of pink as her little church suit and pillbox hat. She gave us a look of compassion and passed by in a cloud of Chanel No. 5.

Zahra stopped outside the old *chocolaterie*. The *pétanque*-players were watching us now; a little group of middle-aged men, among them Louis Acheron.

'I bet she's a hot little number,' he said with a look of appraisal at Sonia. 'I wouldn't mind seeing what's under *that*.' He did not attempt to lower his voice; as far as Louis is concerned, all *niqabis* are blind and deaf.

'And *I* bet that man's penis is very small,' retorted Omi smartly, reminding me very much of Armande.

'Omi, go home,' Zahra said. 'This has nothing to do with you.'

Omi gave a cackle. 'Nothing to do with me, *heh*?

397

As if I didn't know you had my little Du'a hidden in there.'

'How did you know that?' said Zahra.

Omi grinned. 'The cat told me.'

Zahra shook her head irritably. We had already attracted too much attention to hold a discussion outside the shop. 'All right, you can come in,' she said. 'But don't go telling everyone.'

*   *   *

Zahra knocked. Du'a opened the door. For a moment I didn't recognize her. I'd only ever seen her in the same black robe as her mother; her hair covered up with a *hijab* tightly pinned around her face. But now she was wearing a pink *kameez* over blue jeans and sneakers, and her hair was in a long plait. I'd thought she was ten or eleven; now I could see her properly, I guessed her to be a little older, maybe thirteen or fourteen.

We followed her into the *chocolaterie*. With its walls newly painted, it looked almost as it had when Anouk and I first opened it. The stone floor was bare except for a small rug, some cushions and a low table; the house smelt of paint and incense.

Omi said: 'My little peach! So you took a trip downriver?'

Du'a nodded. 'We saw Rosette's dad. He helped us fix the engine.' She gave me a shy smile. 'He's awesome. Pilou talks about him all the time.'

'Is your mother here?' I said.

She was; in jeans and a red *kameez*; but unlike Du'a, she had not removed her veil. Even indoors, Inès Bencharki keeps her face hidden, her hair concealed beneath a black scarf. It looks slightly

398

indecent indoors, perverse, unmistakably hostile. The beautiful eyes were once more underlined with a strip of coloured fabric. Above it, her expression was blank, almost indifferent.

'I'm glad you're safe,' I told her. 'People were getting worried.'

She shrugged. 'I very much doubt it. I'm not the most popular person here.' She turned to Zahra, who, like Sonia, had removed her face-veil as soon as she passed the threshold. 'I told you to bring Vianne Rocher. Why have you brought a committee of fools?'

Omi laughed. 'As always, so welcoming. Why are you hiding away in here, when you know your brother is looking for you?'

'*Is* he now?' The voice was dry.

'Yes, and if you cared about anyone other than yourself—'

'Stop it, Omi,' Zahra said. 'You have no idea what's going on.' She turned to Inès. 'I spoke to the priest. You have to tell them your story.'

'You mean Reynaud?' I said. 'Is he here?'

But Sonia was looking at Inès with an expression of curious intensity. It was the first time I'd seen her without her veil, and I was struck by her resemblance to Alyssa. Both have the same small, delicate features; the large, expressive eyes; the golden stud in the nostril. But whereas Alyssa is vivid and bright, Sonia looks wan and colourless. There were dark circles around her eyes; her mouth was bracketed with sadness.

'Why did you go away?' she said. 'If you were going to come back like this, why did you go away at all?'

Inès shrugged. 'You don't understand.'

399

'Was I supposed to?' said Sonia. 'Karim and I were doing just fine before you came to spoil it all. And if you'd left us alone, then perhaps he and I would have had a chance—'

Inès gave a harsh burst of laughter. 'Is *that* what you think? That you had a chance?'

Slowly Sonia shook her head. 'I think you're an evil woman,' she said. 'You'll never let him get away. You put some kind of a spell over him, so he can't belong to anyone else. You pretend to be so modest, so pure, but everyone knows what you're really like. And if you think there's *anyone* left who still believes you're his sister—' She stopped, out of breath and trembling. Her face was paler than ever.

Inès indicated the floor cushions. 'Sit down,' she said in a dry voice. 'All this drama can't be good for the baby.'

In silence, Sonia obeyed. Her eyes were hot and fiercely dry. She looked so young at that moment— younger even than Alyssa—that I found it difficult to believe she was pregnant at all.

Then Inès turned to the rest of us. Her voice was hard and brittle. I checked her colours; beneath the veil, there was no sign of nerves or distress. In fact she seemed almost contemptuous; serene as only a woman can be who has given up hope of redemption.

'So, everyone thinks I have lied to them. That I am not who I said I was. That I am Karim's whore, and that Du'a is his daughter.'

Nobody answered.

Inès went on: 'Well, some of that is half right. But be assured, I am nobody's whore.'

'I knew it!' Omi said at once. 'You're his wife, aren't you?'

Inès shook her head. 'No. I am not.'

'I don't believe you,' Sonia said. 'Why else would he sneak out to visit you at night, when he thinks I'm sleeping? Why does he think of no one else? Why has he been like a crazy man ever since you went away?'

Inès gave a long sigh. 'I thought I could avoid all this. I thought that what lies between me and Karim could be buried at last and forgotten. I tried to warn you about him once, as I tried to warn your sister. But the war between Karim and myself has claimed too many casualties. I cannot be silent any more. I am sorry if this causes pain. That was never my intention.'

Sonia looked puzzled. 'I don't understand.'

'No, I don't suppose you do.' Inès sat down beside her. 'Make yourselves at home,' she said. 'This may take a little time.'

We seated ourselves on the cushions. Omi reached into a pocket and came out with a macaroon. 'If I have to listen to this, I need a little sustenance.'

Inès raised her eyebrows. 'Old Mahjoubi would say that you are riding the devil's donkey.'

'The devil's donkey or Shaitan's sheep. I'm old. Get on with the story!'

Above the veil, the smoky eyes narrowed in amusement. 'Very well. Let me tell you who I am. But first I will tell you who I am not. I am not Karim's sister. Nor am I his whore—or even his wife. *Alhumdullila*, I am his mother.'

CHAPTER SEVEN

☾

Saturday, 28th August, 10.25 a.m.

For a moment the room was silent. Then came a barrage of questions, exclamations, rebuttals. His *mother*? That was ridiculous. And even if it were true, then why would Inès want to hide it? Why attract suspicion, when she could have had acceptance, respect—

When finally the questions died down, Inès began her narrative. Her French is both heavily accented and unusually formal; the clipped and painfully accurate French of someone who has learnt the language from textbooks decades out of date. The beautiful eyes were expressionless; the voice as dry as dead leaves.

'I was sixteen years old when I had Karim,' she said. 'My family was poor. We lived on a farm in the country, my parents, three brothers, two sisters and I. When I was ten, my parents sent me to the city to work as a maid. I ended up in Agadir, working for a rich family. The family had three children; two little daughters and a son. At first I thought I was lucky. I went to school. I learnt to read. I studied maths and history and French. I learnt to cook and clean the house.' For the first time I thought her voice trembled. Then she went on. 'I was fifteen. The son, Mohammed, was eighteen. He came to my room one night as I slept. He said that if I told anyone, I would be dismissed. He raped me. I told

402

his mother. She threw me out. I told the police. They didn't care.'

Even at fifteen, I thought, Inès must have been a remarkably headstrong character. Treated as guilty by the police (the first thing they had asked her about the attack was whether she had been properly dressed), dismissed by her employers, she had tried to find work in another home. But no one would take her without a reference. She slept on the streets and begged for food. Twice she was arrested. On the second occasion, the police had conducted an intimate examination of her, and had discovered that she was pregnant.

'The police called my father,' Inès went on. 'He came to Agadir by bus—a six-hour journey. But when he heard my story, he turned his face away from me, and made the journey back alone. My family mourned me as if I were dead. My letters came back unopened. My mother sent me some money—not much, but it was all she had—and told me she never wanted to see me again. Six months later, Karim was born, in Agadir General Hospital.' Again, her voice seemed to tremble, but for a moment the flat tone took on a note of tenderness. 'He was so perfect. So beautiful. I thought if my parents could *see* him, then—'

'You thought they'd fall in love with him,' I said.

She nodded. 'It was a mistake. I knew as soon as I arrived. I had dishonoured the family. Ruined my sisters' chances. I'd spent all my money coming back home, but I had no home to come back to. I went to my elder brother's house—I was always his favourite. He'd been married for eighteen months to Hariba, a cousin of mine. They were not happy to see me at all, but still they took me in. And then, when my sister-in-law had gone out, *they* came.'

She was silent for such a long time that Omi broke in impatiently. '*Who* came?'

'A committee of fools. My uncle. My father. My brothers. They told me I was better off dead than living in dishonour. That I was a whore, that I had abandoned *hayaa*. That only blood could cleanse the shame of what I had done to the family. That if I had worn proper *hijab*, and behaved with respect and modesty, then this would never have happened. And then—'

And at that, Inès unpinned her scarf and drew aside her veil, and we saw—for the first time, *I* saw her: the Scorpion Queen, the Woman in Black, the ghost I have pursued for so long that I'd almost begun to doubt she was real—

Omi gave a startled squawk.

Sonia put a hand to her mouth.

Inès remained impassive. Zahra did, too—which made me think that this wasn't the first time she'd seen her unveiled—although her colours were shot with distress.

As for myself, it took me a moment to realize what I was seeing. I'd expected Inès to be beautiful. Everything suggested it—her posture, the grace of her bearing, the colour and shape of those green-gold eyes—so that for a second I even saw the woman Inès might have been. Perhaps not as young as I'd guessed her to be, but remarkable nevertheless; the lustrous hair; the elegant neck; the astonishing cheekbones; the arched brows; the beauty that even at sixty—or seventy, or eighty— will still be anchored there, bone-deep, like a diamond inside a knuckle of stone—

And then I *really* saw her. Like the optical

404

illusion that takes a moment to slip into place—two lovers into a demon face, a profile into a butterfly—never now to be unseen.

'They call it a *smiley*,' said Inès. 'You see them sometimes. In Tangier, in Marrakech—even in Paris or Marseille. They take a knife and they make a cut from *here* to *here*, from *there* to *there*'—she spanned the distance with index and thumb between her earlobes and the corners of her mouth. 'So that, for the rest of your life, you always remember to keep your *hayaa*. So everyone who looks at you will understand that you are a whore.'

CHAPTER EIGHT

☾

Saturday, 28th August, 10.45 a.m.

Her cousin had called for a doctor. It was he who put in the stitches—nine on each side, in shiny black thread, which, when it was removed, left a kind of permanent stain between every little pebble of flesh. The result is the face of a rag doll that has been ripped apart, then clumsily put back together again without quite matching the broken seams. It's gruesome and unutterably sad; one side of the face is lifeless, as if the woman has suffered a stroke; she tells us that this is because of the damage to the nerves. Without the veil, it is easy to see why her voice is so wooden and flat; she moves only the jaw as she speaks, like a ventriloquist's dummy. The scars are over thirty years old; stretched and laddered and polished by time. Once seen, it is difficult to see anything but those grinning scars; they catch in the throat like a fishbone, making you gasp and struggle for breath. To think of those scars on a sixteen-year-old; on a child the same age as Anouk—

'And so I went back to Agadir,' Inès went on in her toneless voice. 'I wore a veil, and slept on the street. There is no help in my country for dishonoured women. They have no rights, not even the right to give their child a surname. Religious charities do not acknowledge them. They are shunned by everyone. At last I found a day centre run by a Swiss foundation. The people there were good to me, although they were none of them Muslims. They helped me and looked after my child. They found me a job in a workshop, making clothes. I slept in the basement with Karim, and worked at a machine all day. I made dresses and saris and scarves, and stitched embroidered slippers. Karim grew. I worked hard. The couple who ran the shop were kind. The man was Amal Bencharki. I told him my husband divorced me. He didn't ask too many questions.'

When Karim was three, Amal Bencharki's wife died. They had had no children. Amal Bencharki was fifty-two. Most of his family lived in France. Amal offered to marry Inès and give her son a name.

'He didn't care about my face. In any case, no one would see it. I wore a *chadra* all the time— that's what they call the veil over there. Amal was lonely. He missed his wife. His family was far away. I think he just wanted company, and someone to cook and keep house for him. To be his maid. Well,

406

I could do that. I'd had plenty of practice.' Her lips twitched. It was almost a smile. Her mouth is very like her son's—or would have been, without those scars. But while Karim's is a slashed peach, hers is a grinning pumpkin, held in place by pulleys of flesh. Smiling makes it worse, of course.

Omi grinned in sympathy. 'You married him, then?'

She gave that ghastly smile again. 'I was going to marry him. But his family became suspicious. His brothers came round, asking questions. His father even came over from France. I didn't have any answers for them. Finally, I told them the truth.' She shrugged. 'That was the end of it.'

Amal Bencharki had given Inès money and papers to leave Agadir. The papers were in his dead wife's name, and Inès's photograph was in her passport. She had used them to give Karim a name, and to take them both as far as Tangier, hoping to lose herself in the big city.

'I became Inès Bencharki. The widow of a textile merchant from Agadir. I looked after my son and made clothes on a sewing machine in my room. I told Karim the same story, but as he grew older he started to ask questions. I told more lies. I sent him to school. I gave him everything I had. I wanted him to go to mosque, to have good friends, to have respect. He was a beautiful little boy. I know I spoilt him. That was my fault. But my Karim was all I had. They say *Jannah* is at the feet of the mother. For me, Karim was my *Jannah*. Allah was good because he was there. I wanted my son to have everything.'

She gave that dreadful rictus again. And yet, when she talks about Karim, I can see beauty in her face.

407

'I needed more money,' Inès went on. 'So when Karim was old enough to look after himself for a while, I went to Spain to pick strawberries. It was hard work. The hours were long. But the money was so much better there than anything I could earn at home, that I could not resist it. Karim was a clever student. I wanted him to go to university. But these things cost money; more money than I could earn in Tangier, making clothes. I spent three months in Spain that year, leaving my son alone. I suppose I did not exercise enough control over Karim. But he always seemed such a good boy, always so respectful. The next year I went to Spain again. Karim was barely seventeen. And this time, while I was away, he raped a girl at knifepoint.'

The girl was called Shada Idris; a twenty-two-year-old unmarried girl, whom Karim had met in a tea-house. A whore, by Karim's reckoning, in her jeans and spiked heels, her hair tied up in a fashionable style beneath her multicoloured *hijab*. She had agreed to meet Karim. He and his friends had been waiting.

At first he denied his involvement. He told Inès he'd only watched. But he'd kept a trophy—her bracelet—a single string of black jet beads. Inès had found it in his room and made him admit the whole affair.

He had told the police she was asking for it; besides, she wasn't a virgin. She lived with two other women near the big mosque in the city centre, and each took it in turns to mind the children while the others went to work. She already had an illegitimate child, a little girl whose name was Du'a—

'My little peach!' said Omi, glancing quickly

408

at Du'a.

Inès nodded. 'Don't worry, she knows. She has always known the truth. I brought up Karim in ignorance, and you saw what he grew into. But Du'a knows that *zina* is a slippery fish that will not be caught, but jumps from one hand to the other—' She smiled again. 'In any case, the child is not the criminal. I taught *that* lesson to my son, but the rest of it I left too late. I was ashamed, you see. I thought I could escape ever telling him.'

Shada had called the local police to report the attack against her. But as in the case of Inès, the police seemed more interested in investigating Shada herself. She was arrested for prostitution, and although the charge was dropped, it transpired that she had been living illegally in government accommodation. She and her child were turned out of their flat. Homeless now and desperate, Shada had gone to the housing association building, sat down in the middle of the square, poured a can of petrol over her head and set herself on fire.

Inès looked round at the four of us. 'What else could I do?' she said. 'My son must have a share in the blame. And so I told Karim the truth about his father—about myself; and I took the child Shada had left, and brought her up as my own. For a long time, Karim was angry. Angry at me for shaming him; still more angry at himself. He never looked at my Du'a, or spoke to her more than he had to. And yet she was a sweet little girl. I called her *my little stranger.*'

That phrase. *My little stranger.* At first I thought I'd misheard her. That she should use the very same phrase I'd always used for my Anouk—and yet it was oddly appropriate. Inès is no longer the

409

Woman in Black—she has a face, and in spite of those scars, I recognize it very well. We are alike, she and I. Both scorpions; both buffaloes.

Inès gave me a curious look. Her eyes were dark as wild honey. 'You see,' she said, reading my mind. 'We are not so different, after all. Some of us choose our family. Some of us are chosen. And sometimes the choice we have to make is between two halves of a broken heart. This has been my choice, Vianne. It has not been easy. Listen to me, and ask yourself if you would have acted differently.'

CHAPTER NINE

☾

Saturday, 28th August, 11.00 a.m.

'Karim was a beautiful boy,' she said. 'soon, he became a beautiful man. Women liked him; so did men. He knew how to charm them. He wanted to study in Paris, he said: I gave him the money to travel. But a year into his college course, he wrote to say that he had dropped out; he wanted to marry a French woman he'd met while he was studying. The woman was older than he was—she worked at one of the embassies—*and* she had money. She was besotted. She gave Karim everything he wanted. I admit, I suspected from the start that this was why he was marrying her. It seemed her family did, too. One day I received a phone call from the woman's mother. She had made inquiries. She knew that

410

her daughter was not the only woman Karim was seeing. There were others—*several* others—and worse, there had been certain rumours—'

Inès gave her harsh little laugh. 'I recognized the story. A girl at a party had been raped; but she had been drunk, her account was unclear. Another student had been raped in a park, near a nightclub. Both were classmates of Karim's. Both times, his name was mentioned. Neither incident was reported to the police. And yet, I knew. In my heart, I knew.'

Inès had come to Paris and forced Karim to a confrontation. He'd denied the two assaults, but there was something in his eyes that told her he was responsible. Looking through his belongings, once more she found his trophies. A necklace; an earring; a headscarf that still smelt of perfume. They were just whores, he said sullenly. The capital was full of them. They had no shame or modesty; why shouldn't he take advantage?

'And yet I loved him,' said Inès. 'He was my gold and incense. I knew that I had been at fault. I had indulged him far too much; I thought that I could change him. By then he was twenty-three years old; Du'a was eight, and going to school. I thought that if I could get Karim to go to mosque more regularly, to study the Qur'an, to respect women and himself, then this behaviour would disappear. I made him come back to Tangier with me. I made him break off the engagement. I started to think that he had changed—but all of you have seen my son. He shows a golden face to the world. People want to love him. Time passed; I found him a job working for an importer of textiles. Karim was well spoken, intelligent; always polite and respectful. He

411

often travelled on business; he always brought back gifts for me. Sometimes I was uneasy—once, when a girl in our apartment block was raped outside, by the rubbish bins; once more when a young girl came to the flat, asking for Karim. But my son always had an answer; an excuse; an alibi. I wondered if my suspicions were simply *waswaas*, unfounded fears. And then came Saïd Mahjoubi—first a customer, then a friend. They met on a trip to Mecca, and soon became close. At first I was glad. Saïd was a good man, honest and devout. I hoped he would be a good influence.'

Instead it was the other way round. Karim was the one with the influence. Little by little, the younger man had worked his charm on the elder. Saïd was already susceptible; resentful of his father; jaded by current events in France; nostalgic for a country and a time that had never been his own. Karim fed him a pretty version of everyday life in Tangier; spoke of family and respect and of his return to Islam. Saïd was impressed, and within a year was talking about a possible marriage between Karim and his eldest daughter.

At first, Inès was uneasy. But Karim had changed; he was sober; polite; he really seemed to be serious. Besides, she *wanted* to believe; she wanted him to be married. Sonia was a good Muslim girl from a decent family; and from the pictures she'd seen of her, she was also beautiful. Inès allowed her doubts to fade. The ceremony was arranged.

One problem remained—her secret; the scandal of Karim's parentage. He'd introduced himself to Saïd as the son of Amal Bencharki, and had allowed Saïd to believe that Inès was his

412

widowed sister.

'If Saïd had seen my face,' said Inès, 'he would have guessed the truth. And so I let him believe the lie. I became Karim's sister.'

The wedding had duly taken place. Inès had come over with Du'a for the ceremony. She had not intended to stay for good, but something had alerted her. Perhaps the easy atmosphere of the community of Les Marauds; the girls unveiled, in Western dress, some not even wearing *hijab*. She blamed old Mahjoubi's leadership; the old man was no scholar, and his interpretation of the Qur'an was wholly unconventional. He allowed too much freedom to his flock; he was too lenient with *zina*. His rivalry with Francis Reynaud verged on the inappropriate; he was openly hostile to the *niqab*, read all kinds of unsuitable French books and was even rumoured to drink alcohol. She decided to stay, at least for a while.

Karim was surprised and unhappy. But there was nothing he could say without giving away his secret. Over the months Inès had tried to combat the shortcomings of old Mahjoubi's regime. She set up a school for Muslim girls; promoted *niqab* and traditional dress; and by her association with Karim, who had already won hearts and minds on both sides of the river, quickly became a prominent member of the female community of Les Marauds. She was an oddity to them—both virtuous and curiously liberated—living independently, but going to mosque every day and setting a good example. People started to copy her, then to compete with each other. Modest attire began to be seen as a statement, rather than a constraint. Gradually, the young women of Les Marauds began to look to Inès

Bencharki as a role model and a guide.

Meanwhile, Saïd Mahjoubi was doing his best to do the same with the men of the village. The gym had always been a regular meeting-place for them; with Karim in charge, it now became a magnet for bored and disaffected young men. Karim has a shine; I've seen it myself. Attractive to women; outgoing with men; deferential to his elders, but quietly unconventional enough to make an impression on the young. While Saïd preached a gospel of tradition, respect and a return to Islam, in the gym Karim used Islam to promote his own opinions; opinions formed on the streets of Tangier, where women who do not wear *hijab* are considered fair game to predators. To some of the men of Les Marauds, this kind of talk had subversive appeal. Young men who had once been shy acquired a certain swagger. Friendships between Les Marauds and Lansquenet gradually waned. Brothers became increasingly protective of sisters who did not wear *hijab*, and as the more traditional style of dress gained in popularity, the community became increasingly polarized. Saïd grew more outspoken in his disapproval of his father's leadership, while old Mahjoubi fanned the flames of unrest by speaking out against the *niqab* and preaching integration.

Within six months, the character of Les Marauds had subtly changed; and nobody really understood how or why it had happened. Was it Karim's influence? Was it Inès? No one knew. But beneath the surface of the quiet little community, something was gaining momentum; something that would soon become a war.

CHAPTER TEN

☾

Saturday, 28th August, 11.10 a.m.

'A war,' said Inès. 'Imagine that! A secret war between mother and son. Neither of us spoke of it. That would have been to admit that there was mistrust between us. But Karim hadn't really changed; he'd simply become more careful. He had a new wife who adored him; even so it wasn't enough. He praised the *niqab* in public, but his fantasies were of Western whores, and I knew it was just a matter of time before *zina* found him again.'

Once more, Inès looked at Sonia. She had listened to all this without comment, but now she was shaking her head.

'No. I don't believe it. You are wrong. My Karim would never—'

Inès put a hand on Sonia's arm. 'I know all this must be hard to believe. I know how cruel it must sound. I too found it hard to believe, once. I tried to blind myself to the truth. But it started with porn on the internet. I found it on his computer. After that, it was internet sex. I caught him at it one time, with a girl from the village. Her name was Marie-Ange Lucas, and her profile said she was sixteen. In fact, she was fifteen, but Karim didn't care. She was a whore, he told me. Why else would she accept to meet a boy she didn't know for sex? My intervention came just in time. Karim broke off contact with Marie-Ange. I thought he'd learnt his lesson, but he'd simply found more attractive meat. Your sister, Alyssa, whom he seduced, then drove to try and kill herself—'

By this time, Sonia was ashen. 'I don't believe you,' she whispered.

Inès shrugged. 'I'm sorry,' she said. 'I should have spoken out before. But I thought I could control him. I thought that if I stayed nearby, then I could always intervene. I tried with Alyssa. Then with Vianne, whose arrival in Les Marauds—and with a pretty daughter—had already attracted attention. But by then things had started to happen. Someone set the school on fire. Rumours were spread about me. The priest who tried to help me was warned away by friends of Karim's. I moved back into Karim's house, but old Mahjoubi did everything to make me feel uncomfortable. And then I realized that Karim was beginning to notice my little Du'a.'

'No,' said Sonia, pulling away.

Inès stood up. 'The other day, Du'a lost one of her slippers. A red embroidered slipper that we had brought with us from Tangier. She and I looked for it everywhere, but it was nowhere to be found. And so I waited until Karim was out, and found *this* in his wardrobe—'

She stepped into the kitchen and came out with a metal box. Opening it, she tipped out the contents on to the little table. I saw bracelets, earrings, beads, scarves—and one embroidered slipper, scarlet, and stitched with small glass beads—

Inès ran her elegant fingers over the collection of objects. 'The bracelet he took from Shada Idris. One of Alyssa's earrings. A ring that belonged to his fiancée. And this—' She touched the red

416

slipper. 'My son was getting ahead of himself, taking trophies in advance.'

But something else had caught my eye among the pile of trophies. A little woven bracelet—yellow, with a blue shell charm—the kind of thing a child might make, perhaps as a gift for her sister—

'It belongs to your daughter, does it not?' said Inès, seeing my expression.

I picked up the bracelet. I knew it well. Anouk had been wearing it when we arrived—and, now that I came to think about it, I hadn't seen it for several days—

'Maybe she dropped it,' said Inès. 'Maybe she left it lying around. But Karim had already noticed her. It would have been just a matter of time.'

After finding the box of trophies, Inès had moved with Du'a into the houseboat. A temporary solution, at best; but all she could think to do at the time. While appearing to be the most dutiful son, through rumour, malice and subterfuge Karim had somehow managed to turn the whole of Les Marauds against Inès, except for Zahra, who knew the truth, and who had always tried to protect her.

'My son rarely acts on his own behalf,' explained Inès with that painful smile. 'He lets other people act for him. They think they are making their own choices, but in fact they are simply doing his will. That writing on the wall of my house. The fire. Even the houseboat—' She looked back at Sonia, whose face had become ghastly with realization. 'He *meant* for you to do those things,' she said. 'He set you in motion. He knew I couldn't expose him without exposing myself as well, and he thought he could play the innocent and blame it all on you—'

Sonia shook her head. 'Please. I didn't mean to

417

hurt anyone. I only wanted you to go.'

'Of course you did. I know,' said Inès. 'But even if I had gone, Karim would never have felt entirely safe. I know too much about him. He wanted rid of me for good, but first he needed a scapegoat. At first I thought it might be you. But even though you loved him, he knew that you were no murderer. So he came up with a better plan. And Monsieur le Curé played right into his hands.'

Reynaud. I'd almost forgotten him. 'Where is he?' I said. 'Is he all right?'

Zahra looked awkward. 'I'm sorry, Vianne. I was taken in at first. Like everyone else, I was certain that Reynaud had started the fire. And then, when Karim caught him that day actually holding a petrol can—'

'Where is he, Zahra?' I said.

'He's in the cellar under the gym. I'm sorry. I should have told you. But Karim was so upset, and I thought—'

'Of course he was.' That was Inès. The hard, dry voice was flatter than ever. 'Monsieur le Curé's intervention arrived at exactly the wrong time. My son, having tried all other plans, was planning to deal with me at last. He thought that, if I disappeared, Reynaud would be held responsible. And if Reynaud were never found—' She shrugged. 'The Tannes is a dangerous river, especially after the rain. It might take weeks to find a body, after which time the cause of death might not be possible to determine.'

There was a silence as all of us struggled to understand what she was saying. Karim, a murderer? Surely not. And yet, it all made perfect sense.

'My son had run out of time,' she said. 'He was afraid that for Du'a's sake I would speak out against him. The houseboat made us vulnerable. Perhaps he would have made it look as if we died in an arson attack. Perhaps he would have sunk the boat, and tipped our bodies into the Tannes. But when he came to fulfil his plan, Monsieur le Curé was there.'

Now Sonia spoke up. 'I know. He saw me. I—confessed to him.'

'You did?' Inès looked amused. 'Well, whatever you said, it kept him there just long enough to spoil Karim's plan. Karim must have seen him watching the boat. He would have been a witness. And so my son attacked him, thinking perhaps to use him as a convenient scapegoat later—but I had heard and seen everything, and while Karim dealt with Reynaud I untied the houseboat and steered it away downstream.' She sighed. 'At the time I did not know whether Reynaud was alive or dead. I'd seen him fall. That was enough. But when Zahra told me what she knew—'

Now Omi interrupted, her cracked old voice hoarse with amusement: 'You mean Monsieur le Curé has been in that cellar all this time? *Hee*, I bet he's mad as fire—'

I looked at Zahra. 'The gym?' I said. 'That's why you were there last night.'

She nodded. 'I brought food,' she said.

'But why keep him there at all?' Sonia was still puzzled. 'If what Inès says is true—'

'He needed him alive,' said Inès. 'If he intended to blame Reynaud for whatever happened to me, it would not do for the police to find out that the suspected murderer had died days *before*

419

the victim—'

'He was waiting for you to come back,' Sonia said.

Inès nodded. 'I think he was.'

'But now,' said Sonia slowly, 'Karim knows that you are here.'

There was a long pause, during which the realization settled like dust. Then Inès got to her feet and quickly retied her face-veil. Sonia did the same, and within seconds we were all on our feet, even Omi, who was already reaching for another macaroon.

This must be Reynaud's fourth day in the cellar under the gym. I know those cellars; dark and damp, often flooding in the rains. And to think he'd been there all the time. Loyalties run deep in Les Marauds. Karim's friends would not have betrayed him. But the gym belongs to Saïd, after all. Did *he* know? Did his father know?

I dreamt of you, old Mahjoubi had said from his sickbed on Wednesday. *When I tried to perform istikhaara. I dreamt of you, and then of her. Take care. Stay away from the water.*

I'd thought at the time he was talking to me. Half delirious, he'd seemed barely to understand who I was. Had he been speaking of Reynaud? Like the Woman in Black and myself, old Mahjoubi and Francis Reynaud are reflections of each other. Did old Mahjoubi guess the truth? Could his dream have been something more?

CHAPTER ELEVEN

☾

Saturday, 28th August, 11.25 a.m.

We came out into the place Saint-Jérôme. the sun was already scorching hot. The last of the rain is gone from the streets, and the cobblestones are bronzed with dust. A flock of pigeons that had been feeding outside the door took flight in a sudden clap of wings. The square was almost deserted now; Poitou's bakery was closing; the *pétanque* players had packed up their things, heading for home and iced *floc* underneath the persimmon trees. Only one figure remained beneath the arch of Saint-Jérôme's; the squat, sad figure of Paul-Marie Muscat sitting in his wheelchair, half in, half out of the shadows like the Knight of Cups on the Tarot card.

'Congratulations, you've done it again,' he called across the square to me. 'Tell me, did you get any special training for what you do, or are you just a natural?'

I said: 'I don't have time to talk. This is an emergency.'

He laughed. 'You don't surprise me. It's always urgent business with you. People to see, places to go, marriages to ruin. Eight years you've been away, and I'm not saying it was perfect, but you've not been back three weeks and everything's a shambles.'

I must have looked surprised, because he laughed again. 'Haven't you heard? She's leaving me. For good this time. She's running away with the river-rats. Just like the Pied Piper.' He belched, and I realized he was very drunk. 'Tell me, do they pay you, Vianne? Is it good money? Or do you work for love?'

'I have no idea what you're talking about,' I said. 'But give me half an hour, and I'll come back and you can explain everything. Drink some coffee. Wait for me.'

That laugh again, like a broken drain. 'You slay me, Vianne. You really do. Wasn't it you who told her she ought to tell the truth? To tell me that that brat of hers isn't the fucking redhead's, but *mine*? And now she's come clean with the whole thing, now she's robbed me of eight fucking *years*, the bitch announces she's leaving me, like somehow that gives her permission?'

I looked at him. 'She told you?'

'Oh, she did *nothing* but tell me. As if telling me was going to fix everything. And I have *you* to thank for that, don't I, Vianne? What next, eh? What's so urgent in Les Marauds? Some guy beats his wife? Call Vianne! Cat stuck up a tree? Call Vianne!'

Inès, Du'a and the others were already on their way to the bridge. 'I'm sorry,' I said. 'I have to go.'

'And leave me to miss the excitement?' Furiously, Paul-Marie began to push his wheelchair across the square. The going was rough, but not impossible; his big arms pumped like pistons. 'Oh, no. I'm coming, too. I want to see what the deal is.' He started to follow me down the street, shouting at the top of his voice: 'Come on, everybody! Come and see Vianne walk on water!'

He moved surprisingly quickly as he lumbered over the cobblestones. Behind him, doors were opened, shutters unlocked. Our little group—unusual enough to command attention even in ordinary circumstances—soon attracted followers. Poitou came out of his bakery; Charles Lévy stopped weeding his garden; customers at the *terrasse* of the Café des Marauds craned their necks to see what was happening, abandoned their drinks and came running.

I saw Guillaume, carrying Patch; Joséphine, looking concerned; Caro Clairmont, still wearing an oven glove on one hand. By the time we had reached the boulevard, we had acquired a dozen followers, and more were arriving from Les Marauds; Fatima al-Djerba and her husband Mehdi; her daughter Yasmina; her son-in-law Ismail. There were less friendly faces, too: the Acheron boys and their retinue; Jean Lucas and Marie-Ange; a handful of men from inside the mosque, looking tense and suspicious. Louis Acheron was pushing Paul-Marie's wheelchair, while Paul called out deliriously: 'Just like the Pied Piper!'

Joséphine came to find me. 'What's going on?'

I told her. But in the noise of the people now gathering outside the gym, it was hard to know if she'd understood. 'You're telling me Reynaud's in there?'

I nodded. 'We have to talk to Saïd. We have to explain what's going on before this turns into a riot—'

The growing crowd was gathering at the mouth of the alleyway. The gym was open, and a number of patrons—all of them young men, in T-shirts and shorts—were standing by the entrance. Karim was not among them. It was almost unbearably hot;

423

the midday sun was like a spike hammered into the top of my head. The crowd, too, had a heat of its own; a smell like metal and juniper. Beneath the awning of the gym, there was a triangle of shade so stark that I could barely see the faces of the young men. They were in shadow; I was in sun; we faced each other like gunslingers across the length of the alleyway.

I started to walk towards the group. Joséphine was behind me. But Zahra and the others held back. Even now, for a woman to enter the gym was almost unthinkable; even Inès seemed to hesitate as I made my way towards the door.

One of the patrons blocked my way. I didn't know his name, but I recognized him as one of the men who had been with Karim on the day we first met.

I said: 'I need to speak with Saïd.'

The man shook his head. 'Saïd is not here.'

Behind me, my unwelcome retinue had grown increasingly noisy. Concerned villagers like Narcisse and Guillaume had been joined by a larger group, clearly looking for trouble. I counted three of the Acheron boys; one had pushed over some plant pots from a nearby window-ledge. Another was trying to topple one of the large dustbins in the alley behind the café. Caro Clairmont called for order, thereby creating yet more noise; Marie-Ange Lucas was openly filming the scene on her mobile phone.

There were some river people, too; I recognized their clothes; their hair; the way they kept to the back of the crowd. Roux was among them, his red hair unmistakable in the sun. There was no sign of Anouk or Rosette. Du'a, too, had vanished. I hoped that Omi and Fatima had taken her to safety.

Paul-Marie Muscat yelled: 'The river-rats! Trust *them* to be part of this!'

This provoked a double surge in the crowd as some people turned to see, only to push into others who were trying to move forward. Beside me, Zahra protested as someone snatched at her *hijab*. There was a crash from the alleyway: the dustbins had finally succumbed.

I looked at the man who was blocking my way. 'Please, let me in.'

He shook his head. 'This is private property.'

'Is Karim Bencharki here?'

Once more he shook his head.

'Do you know where he is?'

A shrug. 'Maybe the mosque. Who knows? Now get out of here before we call the police.'

Meanwhile, Paul-Marie was enjoying himself. His raucous voice cut through the crowd, shouting: 'Didn't I tell you? Didn't I say? This was bound to happen some day! Let them in, and the next thing you know there's anarchy. *Vive la France!*'

The chorus went up. A rival chorus, in Arabic, arose from the opposite corner. Someone threw a stone.

'Vive la France!'

'Allahu Akhbar!'

The most frightening thing of all is perhaps how fast these things develop; the morphic resonance of hate, dragging us into its vortex. Later, I heard the stories; the baffled, slightly shamefaced accounts of punches thrown and insults hurled; of broken windows, toppled bins; theft and damage to property. Like seagulls over a carcass, pecking out shreds of the truth, the rumour-mongers did their work: Reynaud had been murdered by *Maghrébins*. Reynaud had gone mad, and killed someone. Reynaud had killed a *Maghrébin*, although only in self-defence. The *Maghrébins* had kidnapped a French girl and were holding her inside the gym. The river-folk were in league with *Maghrébin* traffickers. Reynaud had tried to bomb the mosque and was being held till the police arrived. Rumours grew wilder on both sides. Slogans flew like banners.

'*Allahu Akhbar!*'

'*Vive la France!*'

There is no police force in Lansquenet. We have never needed one. Trouble arises so rarely, and when it does it is usually up to the village priest to try to resolve the conflict. But even if he had been there, I doubt Père Henri would have intervened. Francis Reynaud might have known what to do. Reynaud, who, in defiance of the law or of political correctness, knocks heads, grabs collars and distributes insults as well as *Avés*. But Reynaud was gone, and Père Henri was preaching a sermon in Pont-le-Saôul.

Another stone flew; this time it struck one of the men in front of me. He staggered back, one hand to his head. Blood ran through his fingers.

'Fucking *Maghrébins*! Go home!'

'French pigs! Sons of whores!'

I tried to push through into the gym, but too many people stood in my way. The man who had been hit with the stone was looking shaken, blood running down the side of his face, but more of his friends had joined him. Another stone flew; a window smashed, high up on the wall of the gym.

Someone was pushing through the crowd.

I recognized Roux's voice at my side. 'What's happening?'

'Where are the children?' I said.

'I left them back at the boat. They're fine. What's all this about Reynaud?'

Behind us, on the boulevard, a sound had begun to carry above the rising cacophony. It was a high, thin, ululating sound; eerie and penetrating. I'd heard it before, in Tangier; at funerals and demonstrations. But to hear that sound in Lansquenet—

'He's underneath the gym,' I said. 'We have to get him out of there.'

'We do?' said Roux. 'Since when was he your special responsibility?'

'Please,' I said, raising my voice over the rising sound of the crowd. 'Help me. I can't do this alone. I'll tell you everything later—'

And then, from inside, came a figure I knew. Bearded, in white; unsmiling; Saïd Mahjoubi faced us with a look of stony contempt.

'This is an outrage. What do you want?'

Inès, standing at my side, tried to explain in Arabic. I caught Karim's name, but nothing else. She took another step forward.

He pushed her away. 'Get out of here, whore.'

Inès dealt him a ringing slap.

At my side, I saw Roux start to react, and put my hand on his arm.

Saïd stared blankly at Inès, astonishment veering to anger. The marks of Inès's fingers were clearly visible on his face. He took a threatening step. Roux moved in to intercept him. For a moment, their eyes met. Then Saïd lowered his gaze.

'This woman is poison,' he said to Roux. 'You

427

people know nothing about her. I know what she is. Why she hides her face. Not out of piety, but shame—'

And at that, he darted forward and pulled at the strings of Inès's veil and tore it away, revealing the ruined features I had seen only a few minutes ago, in the *chocolaterie*—

For a few seconds, nothing happened. A crowd has a certain energy, a momentum, like that of a flock of circling birds, which takes time to change direction. Inès stood motionless, facing Saïd, making no effort to hide her face, or to retrieve the fallen veil. Saïd and his companions were subjected to the full impact of the *smiley*.

'Shame?' said Inès. 'Is *that* what you see? My son has made a fool of you. Yes, my *son*. A fool, and worse. He has pulled a veil over your eyes. He has made you forsake your daughter. Why do you think she ran away? Why did she try to kill herself? Why did she seek help from strangers—yes, even a *kuffar* priest—instead of from her own family?'

Saïd frowned. 'I don't understand.'

'I think you do. You spoke of shame. The shame is for a man to believe that when he lusts after a woman, *she* is the one responsible. Only a fool believes that Allah can be swayed by such miserable excuses. Your father may be a stubborn old man, but he is worth ten thousand of you.'

And then Inès turned round and addressed the people in the alleyway. Those closest to her fell back a step; the rest took a few seconds longer; ripples running through the crowd until at last there was silence.

'Look at me, all of you,' said Inès. 'Look very closely at my face. This is the face of cruelty, of

428

bigotry and injustice. This is the face of hypocrisy, of guilt and of intolerance. These things are not a matter of religion, race or colour. A crime committed in Allah's name does not cease to be a crime. Do you think you are better than God? Do you think you can fool him with your talk of justice?'

The voice of the Woman in Black was strong, her eyes as hard as mica. She made no attempt to cover herself, but stood to face them squarely, with pride. One by one, they dropped their gaze. Even Paul-Marie Muscat was speechless, his red face turning white. Marie-Ange Lucas, who had been filming the scene on her mobile phone, dropped her hands to her sides. Even Roux stood motionless, staring at Inès with a look of slow-dawning comprehension in his eyes.

Once more Inès turned to Saïd. 'Now take me to my son,' she said.

CHAPTER TWELVE

Saturday, 28th August, 11.40 a.m.

No treadmills today. That's peculiar: usually here, inside the whale, the sound is a constant heartbeat. And yet, it is not silent. There seems to be a crowd outside—a market? I don't think so. Every crowd has a certain pulse, a recognizable tempo. A congregation sounds different from a marketplace, a sporting event, a playground, a classroom—

429

I cannot make out individual voices, but it seems to me that the crowd is large—perhaps even as many as a hundred people, up there, in the real world.

In spite of my increasing fatigue, I cannot help feeling curious. The cadence of the voices suggests that some are French, some Moroccan. What would bring so many people out on to the boulevard?

Once more, I go back to the air-vent, where I can hear them more clearly. There is nothing to see from here, though: just the brick of the opposite wall and a few dandelions growing between the stones. I crane my neck to see more. Nothing. A demonstration? Some of the voices sound angry; others merely excited. But there's a resonance in the air, like a string tightened to breaking point. Something is about to snap.

Once more I try to see through the grille. If I stand on the pyramid of crates, I can just see, in the blurry corner of the screen, a vague impression of movement, of shadows flirting with the ground.

'Maya?' My voice is almost gone. It sounds like a broken clock movement, clicking at the back of my throat. Calling for help is futile. Even at its most powerful, my voice could never cut through the noise. And yet—

That impression of movement again, this time closer, and accompanied by a pair of feet. I know they are not Maya's. Under the hem of the long black robe, a pair of pale-blue sneakers.

'Hey!' I rasp in my ruined voice. 'Down here!'

A moment's pause. Then a face appears at the grille. It takes me a few seconds to recognize Inès Bencharki's daughter. In those black headscarves, it's sometimes hard to tell who's who, and besides,

430

the child has never spoken to me. I'm not even certain of her name.

The dark eyes widened, then came a smile, almost startling in that solemn little face.

'So *you*'re Maya's Jinni!'

That's wonderful. I'm so glad my situation amuses you. I'll have you know that so far I have granted all three of her wishes—

Another flurry of movement. A second pair of sneakers, or what might have been sneakers at some time or other. Now they are as grubby and disreputable as the face appearing at the grille. Jean-Philippe Bonnet, I presume, otherwise known to some as Pilou.

'What the hell is going on?'

'I think it's a riot. It's awesome.'

Awesome. What a word. All I need now is the damn dog.

'We came here to get Vlad out of the way. He doesn't like crowds.'

My wish has come true. A snuffling nose now appears at the grille, tipped with a wet black truffle. Vlad barks.

'It's OK,' says Pilou. 'They've come to get you out of here.'

'What? *All* of them?'

'Kind of. I think some people just came for the ride.'

That's even better. Witnesses. When I walk out of here, dripping wet, with a three-day beard and a face like death, naturally the first thing I will want to see is half of Lansquenet, gawping at me. To say nothing of the police, or the fire brigade, or whoever else may have joined the circus. And Père Henri—will *he* be there too? Oh my God. Just take

431

me now.

'Are you all right?'

'I'm *awesome*.'

'Hang on. It won't be long now.'

Suddenly, there comes a man's voice close by, over the rumbling of the crowd. He is speaking Arabic, but I know Karim Bencharki's voice. There comes a violent scuffling; the dog barks; the boy's face withdraws; the long black robe blurs with dust. The pale-blue sneakers skid backwards in a sudden arc, then vanish from sight.

'Hey!' That's the boy's voice. 'Hey! What are you doing? *Hey!*'

And then the girl begins to scream. The dog is still barking furiously, and for a moment the scuffed sneakers seem to indicate that some kind of tussle is going on. Then, there is a heavy thud; the boy falls against the wall. His head hits the ground just centimetres from the grille; I see blond hair; the curve of a cheek; a single, crawling line of blood.

Then a silence, deafening, even against the noise of the crowd.

And the door to the cellar swings open.

☾

Saturday, 28th August, 11.40 a.m.

The scent of chlorine was like a slap after the dusty heat outside, and the light was so dim in comparison that it took me a few seconds to adjust before I could see clearly. A big, bare room, once painted white, but now mostly grey and patched with damp, with a row of machines to one side—treadmills and cross-trainers—and on the other, a rack of free weights. Right at the back of the room, two doors, one leading to the changing rooms, the shower room and the storage cellars; the other leading out on to the walkway that links all the riverside houses.

Roux led the way. Inès followed us. Joséphine was close behind, with Zahra trying to stop the crowd from entering the gym. Outside, I could hear Omi protesting: '*Hee*, will someone let me through? This is better than Bollywood!'

I turned to Saïd. 'Where's Karim?'

'He went out by the back door. The priest is in the cellar.'

I looked at Roux.

'Get Reynaud,' he said. 'I'll go out and find Karim.'

C

Saturday, 28th August, 11.45 a.m.

The cellar was flooded and smelt of rot, wet plaster and the river. There was barely any light. Standing on a pile of crates on the far side of the room, Reynaud looked like a shipwrecked sailor on the smallest of islands; his face a distant blur of dismay, his hands outstretched as if in entreaty.

When he realized who we were he jumped down into the water—it was almost up to his shoulders—and started to move towards us. He moved as if exhausted; one hand raised to shield his eyes. He

433

looked like a man in the throes of a nightmare so vivid that he no longer even dares to believe that he may ever awaken.

'Quickly,' he rasped in a broken voice, as soon as he reached the cellar steps. All but the top two were submerged; he managed to climb halfway up, then stumbled and fell in the water. Joséphine took one of his arms. I took the other, and together we managed to haul him on to his feet and up the steps.

'Quickly,' he repeated.

'It's all right,' I said. 'You'll be all right.'

In fact he looked anything but all right. His face was pale beneath the three-day growth of beard. His eyes were screwed shut against the light, and his breathing was harsh and asthmatic. A fit of coughing seized him, and for a moment all he could do was double up, trying to breathe.

'You don't understand,' he told me. 'Joséphine's son. The Bencharki girl—' Once more he succumbed to an attack of coughing, gesturing wildly with his hands.

'What is it? What's wrong?'

He tried again. This time his voice was stronger. 'Karim took the girl. In the alleyway. Pilou tried to stop him. I think he's hurt.' He waved an arm at the far wall, and I understood where he was pointing; to the narrow passageway that links the boulevard to the riverside. I knew it well; it was the place where Maya claimed her Jinni lived—

Inès was already out of the door that leads on to the walkway. Joséphine had dropped Reynaud's arm, but stopped when he fell to his knees again.

'Francis—'

He waved an impatient hand. 'Don't waste time.

434

Just get the boy!'

And then, we both heard the screaming.

✝

Saturday, 28th August, 11.45 a.m.

My eyes are unused to this dazzling light. The single bulb from the corridor has become the midday sun. I shield my gaze against it, but even so, it feels like looking into the eye of God. And against the brightness, three figures stand, enclosed in a triple corona of light—

I recognize Vianne and Joséphine. But who is the third? Could that be Inès? But the nimbus that surrounds her makes her hard to recognize, and the long robe looks like folded wings. Have I seen an angel? Much as I would like to believe in the possibility of a divine intervention, there is no time at present. I manage to tell them what happened—at least, enough to alert them to the danger Karim presents. The three of them run to intervene—I hope they are in time, *père*—leaving me at the top of the steps, half in and half out of the water.

The last of my strength is spent, *père*. A part of me just wants to die. But this is Lansquenet—like God, it will not let me go so soon.

Outside, I hear cries of alarm coming from the river. What is happening out there? I try to haul myself to my feet, using the side of the door for support. But my legs do not work any more; my head spins; my eyes hurt. And then I hear the sound of footsteps in the corridor; voices exclaiming in Arabic; the sound of the whale as it surfaces—

The light is still too bright for my eyes. All I can see are robes and feet; sandals, slippers, moccasins. These are the feet of my enemies. They will trample me into the dust.

A hand clasps my outstretched right arm.

'*Alhumdullila,*' says a voice.

Second only to Père Henri on the list of people I'd rather not see, it is Mohammed Mahjoubi. He lifts me from out of the jaws of the whale, and though the light still hurts my eyes, now I can see him quite clearly: white beard; white robe; face like a Gospel of wrinkles—

'Thank you, I can manage,' I say.

And then I go out like a candle.

☾

Saturday, 28th August, 11.50 a.m.

We came out on the boardwalk, on the far side of the passageway that links the river with the boulevard. It's an irregular kind of walkway; in places, only a metre in width, but broadening as it reaches the gym, becoming a kind of terrace. These terraces are a feature of the disused tanneries; poised over the river like acrobats on their wooden stilts. Nowadays, few people use them, and all of them have been condemned.

Roux was by the balustrade. Karim was barely ten feet away. He was holding Du'a with one arm and a can of petrol with the other. Both of them

436

were drenched in it; Du'a had lost her headscarf, and her hair and face were wet. The smell of petrol was everywhere; the air unsteady with its fumes.

Roux gave me a warning look. 'Don't move. He has a lighter.'

It was a Bic, a cheap plastic Bic of the kind you can buy in every newsagent's in France. Easy to use; reliable; disposable as a human life. Now he dropped the petrol can and held the Bic in Du'a's face.

'Don't come any closer,' he said. 'I am not afraid to die.'

Inès spoke to him urgently in her rapid Arabic.

Karim just smiled and shook his head. Even now, his colours gleamed without the slightest trace of fear. He turned to those of us watching from the jetty and the road, and I sensed the force of his charm again; the potency of his beauty. *Even now, he expects to win. In a battle of wills between himself and Inès, he doesn't believe he can possibly lose—*

Still holding Du'a with one hand, he beckoned Inès with the other. The sun shone starkly on her face—pale after thirty years of *niqab*—her green eyes crazed with reflections.

Looking at them together now, I could see the resemblance; like something glimpsed underwater, reversed and fractured by the light. He has her mouth, with its tender curve; her arrogant cheekbones; her bearing. But there's a weakness in Karim that is absent in his mother; something yielding, like spoilt fruit. It's there in his colours; under the skin, a barely perceptible softness.

'See what she is? The lying whore,' he said, addressing the growing crowd. 'This is *her* fault— just look at her face. Look at what she has done to

437

me.'

Inès said, in French: 'Let Du'a go.'

He gave a crack of laughter. 'They're all in it together, you know,' he said. 'Whores stick together. They always tell the same lies.' He yanked sharply at Du'a's hair, forcing her head back painfully. 'Look at her! Look at those eyes and tell me she doesn't know what she's doing!'

Further down the walkway, I saw Paul-Marie in his chair, with Louis Acheron by his side. Alone of all the onlookers, they seemed to be enjoying the show. Roux was still standing ten feet away, too far to risk intervening. A second was all the time it would take for Karim to use the lighter. And yet Roux was considering it. I could see it in his posture; the tension at the back of his neck; the subtle shift to the balls of his feet—

Then, from the little alleyway, I heard a sudden cry of alarm.

'There's someone here! A body!' It was Omi al-Djerba. '*Hee*, it's my Du'a's little friend—' Clearly, from where she was standing, she hadn't yet seen the tragedy beginning to play out by the Tannes. But Joséphine had caught her alarm. For a second she turned on Karim. 'What did you do with my son?'

He shrugged. 'He got in my way.'

'I'll kill you,' she said. 'I'll kill you if you touched him—'

Around us, the crowd was silent. No one but Inès dared speak. In the sun, the reek of petrol was almost overpowering. The air seemed to shimmer with tension. From the jetty, I saw Paul-Marie, his face no longer flushed, but the colour of old ash. Could it be that Paul-Marie was actually *afraid* for his son?

Joséphine had already gone to see to Pilou in the alleyway. I couldn't see what was happening; like Roux, I was fixed in place. Only Inès and Karim moved now, watching each other like wary cats.

'Let Du'a go,' said Inès. Her voice was low, but commanding. 'I'll do what you want. I'll leave Lansquenet. I'll go back to Tangier. I'll never come back—'

'As if *that* would do any good now!' said Karim, his voice rising like an adolescent's. 'You've always been there to mess up my life. Reminding me I was born in shame. That wasn't my fault!'

'Karim,' she said. 'You know I never blamed you for that.'

He laughed again. 'You didn't have to! I saw it every day, in your face.' Once more he addressed the onlookers: 'See her face? It means she's a whore. They're *all* of them whores underneath. Even under the *niqab*, they're watching you. They're testing you. They're always on heat. They're Shaitan's army, soft as silk, until they get their hands round your neck—'

Once more, he laughed. The Bic lighter—it was a red one, just like a strawberry lollipop—shone merrily in the sun. A click—

Du'a screamed. But the flame hadn't caught.

Karim shot us that rainbow smile. 'Oops. Try again.'

I moved half a step forward. From the door at the back of the gym, Saïd Mahjoubi was watching.

'Why Du'a?' I said to Karim. 'Why choose her? She's an innocent.'

'How would *you* know?' Karim said. 'All I need do is look at you and I know what kind of woman

439

you are. Where I come from, men know how to deal with women like you and your daughter. But here, in France, they talk about lifestyle choices, and free will—'

Now Alyssa was at my side. 'Just let her go,' she told him. 'No one wants to see you hurt. And Du'a has done nothing wrong.'

The honey-kissed eyes lingered on her. 'My sweet little sister,' he said, and smiled. 'Remember what I told you? Paradise opens its gates during the month of Ramadan. If only you'd had the courage to do what I am going to do, then maybe this wouldn't have happened. We could have been together. But instead you listened to Shaitan's whisperers, and now—'

'You think Allah is fooled, Karim?'

The voice that came from behind us was only slightly familiar. A strong, commanding, masculine voice, filled with wrath and energy. At first I thought it must be Saïd, but Saïd was still standing at the door. He looked like a man dragged out of a dream. His face was glossy with disbelief.

I turned and saw, to my surprise, old Mahjoubi standing there. But this was not the old man I'd seen at the al-Djerbas' house. This was Mahjoubi transfigured; Mahjoubi revitalized and reborn. He approached the boardwalk, and the crowd stood aside to let him pass.

'There's a story some of you may know,' he said in his new, compelling voice. 'A scholar and his disciple were on a journey together. They came to a swollen river. They saw a young woman standing there. She could not cross the river alone, and so the scholar picked her up and carried her to the other side.

440

'Many miles later along their road, the disciple said to the scholar: "Why did you help that woman, master? She was alone, unchaperoned. She was young and beautiful. Surely, this was very wrong. She might have tried to seduce you. And yet, you took her in your arms. Why?"

'The scholar smiled and said to him, "I carried her across the river. But *you* have been carrying her ever since."'

There was silence as old Mahjoubi finished his tale. All faces turned towards him. I saw Paul Muscat, still ashen; Caro Clairmont; Louis Acheron; Saïd Mahjoubi, looking like a man who has suffered a paralysing stroke.

Then Karim spoke again. His voice was lower than before, and for the first time his colours showed a sign of uncertainty.

'Get away from me, old man.'

Mahjoubi took a step forward.

'I said, get away. This is a war. A holy *jihad.*'

Mahjoubi took another step. 'A war against women and children?'

'A war against *immorality*!' Now Karim's voice was strident. 'A war against the poison that threatens to infect us all! Look at you, you old fool. You don't even see what's under your nose. You don't understand what has to be done! *Allahu Akhbar*—'

And with those words, he shoved the Bic into Du'a's face. There was a *click*, and then a *whoosh*, and then all of these things seemed to happen at once:

A kind of sigh came from the crowd as Karim's right arm blossomed with flame. So did Du'a's *abaya*; she screamed; and for a split second I saw

441

Karim's expression through the heat haze; his ecstatic look changing to one of realization as the flames leapt on to his face, turning from blue to yellow, and then someone came hurtling towards him—a figure in black, with ferocious intent. It was Inès; her arms flung wide; her black *abaya* parted like wings to embrace the flaming figures.

She took Karim by surprise; he fell sideways against the balustrade, still holding Du'a with one hand. The wood was brittle, old pitch pine bleached blond by two centuries of sun and rain, and the force of the impact was enough to send the three of them over the edge, trailing rags of fire and smoke, into the slipstream of the Tannes.

Almost at the same time, another figure came hurtling through the broken balustrade. He moved as smoothly as a bird diving into the river. I barely had time to recognize his red hair and to call his name—

'Roux!'

We ran to the balustrade. For a moment we saw nothing but the shreds of Du'a's *abaya* floating downstream from the jetty. Then something surfaced; a flash of red; a blur of something paler; and then we saw Roux, swimming towards the bank, with Du'a clinging to his neck—

Later, we found that the discarded robe had taken most of the damage; beneath it her *kameez* was intact, and even her hair was barely scorched. But, though Roux went back to look, Inès and her son were gone.

CHAPTER THIRTEEN

Wednesday, 1st September

It took Our Saviour three days to rise. It took me a little longer. I can't help feeling sorry for that; I hear it was quite a business. They carried me home—or someone did: if I am to believe the accounts that are circulating around Lansquenet, there must have been a hundred or more in the group that rescued me.

Imagine the tableau: Caro Clairmont in the role of the Magdalene; Père Henri as Saint Peter. Yes, *he* was there—she texted *him* rather than calling the police—and as soon as his sermon in Pont-le-Saôul was finished, he came running to save the day; by which time the crisis was over and his flock barely noticed he was there.

He wanted to give me the Last Rites. Caro would have let him, too, if Joséphine hadn't intervened. From what I hear from Jean-Philippe—who, I am glad to say, was undamaged but for a headache and a nasty cut on the scalp—the intervention was both Rabelaisian and (according to Caro) unnecessarily aggressive. She ejected Père Henri Lemaître forcibly from the sickroom, at which point he was subjected to further abuse from Henriette Moisson, who, recognizing the *perverti* who tried to impersonate Monsieur le Curé, chased him out of the house with a broom, screaming like a Fury. Vlad was outside, explains Pilou. He doesn't usually bite, but the combination of Henriette's cries, the flying broom, the unfamiliar priest, well—

I think the word is *awesome*.

The bodies of Inès and Karim Bencharki were found by police divers on Monday. Still locked in that final, fervent embrace; her charred black robe enshrouding them both. Joséphine told me her story. I wish I'd known it sooner, *père*. I wish I could have known her face.

As for myself, I spent three days half in, half out of consciousness. Delirium, pneumonia, dehydration, exhaustion—all briskly dealt with by Cussonet, the village doctor, and Joséphine, who has barely left my side since the moment I arrived.

During that time, she tells me, there has been a stream of visitors. Some of them I remember: Guillaume Duplessis; Charles Lévy; Luc Clairmont and Alyssa Mahjoubi. Many from Les Marauds, bringing gifts, mostly of food. And, of course, Vianne Rocher: Vianne with a flask of hot chocolate; Vianne with a handful of *mendiants*; Vianne with a jar of peach jam and a smile like a summer sunrise.

'How are you, Monsieur le Curé?'

I smiled. (I'm getting better at that.) 'I'll mend. Though I may need chocolate.'

She gave me an appreciative look. 'I'll do my best.'

'How's Du'a?'

She shrugged. 'It's going to take some time. The al-Djerbas are looking after her.'

'Good. They're good people. What about you?'

'I thought we might stay another week. At least until you're back on your feet.'

That took me by surprise. 'Why?'

444

That smile again. 'Oh, I don't know. Perhaps I'm getting used to you.' She reached into her pocket and pulled something out. I was expecting a chocolate. Instead, I saw in the palm of her hand a single, dry peach stone.

'The last of Armande's crop,' she said. 'I was going to plant it by her grave. And then I thought of your garden. You don't have a peach tree, do you?'

'No.'

'Then plant it,' she said. 'Next to the wall, where it's sunny. It might take a few years to bear fruit, but with time and patience . . . In China, the peach is a symbol of eternal life, did you know that?'

I shook my head.

I took the peach stone, not wanting to say that I might not be here to see it grow. My house belongs to the Church, after all, and my position is precarious. Today, the Bishop called me. Joséphine picked up the phone. He wants to drop by tomorrow; there are things to discuss, he says. I imagine Père Henri Lemaître has already told his version of the story. I do not expect an endorsement. Although my name has been cleared, I doubt whether this will change anything much. I have brought the Church into disrepute; defied the Bishop's orders; caused friction with Les Marauds. I have no defence; I am guilty as charged. And yet—

While I was inside the whale, I had plenty of time to think. To remember what is important. To understand where I want to be. And I have realized that Lansquenet is more than just a parish to me. I cannot leave, even though the Bishop will probably ask me to. If that means giving up the Church, so be it, *père*. I'll start again. Perhaps try my hand at

445

carpentry, or gardening, or teaching. It's hard to imagine, but then, *père*, I've never had very much imagination. Still, it's easier for me to picture that than accepting another parish.

At Saint-Jérôme's, Joséphine tells me I am sorely missed. Since the incident with Vlad, Père Henri has not returned. The bells have been mute since last Saturday, and no one has come to say Mass since then. Perhaps he's waiting for me to leave. Perhaps the Bishop has told him to stay away until I am gone.

Dusk, and the moon is rising. I can see it from my bed. I sleep with the shutters open; I have never liked the dark. Since my time inside the whale, I find I like it even less. When I awake from uneasy dreams, I want to see the stars.

Next door, in the parlour, I can hear Joséphine moving about. Nothing I can say to her will persuade her to go home for long. She goes back for an hour at a time to see Pilou and to check the café, but Paul is looking after the place, and doing a reasonable job, for a change. Perhaps this ought to surprise me. But since what happened in Les Marauds, I find that very little does. People are not always what they seem, and even a wretch like Paul-Marie may one day live to surprise us.

I can see Vianne's peach stone on my bedside table. How very like her to give it to me. Vianne, who never stays in one place long enough for any kind of seed to grow. Eternal life. Well, I never. The moon is in its last quarter, and across the Tannes I can just hear the sound of the evening call to prayer. Here, in the real world, it no longer sounds as threatening. I left those fears inside the whale, along with a lot of other things. I doubt if this makes me a better man. But something inside me *has* changed; something I am just beginning to explore, as a man might explore, with the tip of his tongue, the tender place inside his mouth from which an aching tooth has been pulled.

I am not sure how it happened. But what began with Vianne Rocher has ended with Inès Bencharki. And now, for the first time in seven days, I know that I will sleep tonight, and that when I awake there will be stars.

CHAPTER FOURTEEN

Thursday, 2nd September

This morning, I rose, in defiance of Cussonet's orders and Joséphine's disapproval. I was shocked to discover how weak I was, and how long it took for me to get ready. But a visit from the Bishop is rare, and I had no intention of facing him from a horizontal position.

I showered and dressed with particular care, and after some hesitation, chose to put on the old soutane that I have not worn in years. *It may be my last chance to do so*, I thought, and was vaguely surprised at the pain I felt. Joséphine had gone to check on Pilou, and so I went into the kitchen to find something for breakfast.

Joséphine had told me that a number of people had brought gifts of food. This was no exaggeration—in fact, every surface was burdened with dishes, tins and boxes. There were casseroles and quiches and tarts; biscuits, fruit and pastries; bottles of wine; jars of jam; roasts and tagines and curries and soups and an enormous stack of those Moroccan pancakes. Opening the fridge, I found cheeses, ham, cold meats, pâtés—

Bewildered by sheer volume and variety, I made coffee and a piece of toast, and for the first time in over a week, went out into my garden.

Someone has weeded my flowerbeds. Whoever it was has also pruned an unruly climbing rose, as well as planting a dozen pots of red geraniums and staking out some hollyhocks that had been in danger of collapsing.

I sat on my bench and watched the street. It was early; just past eight o'clock, and the morning sun was gentle. Birds were singing; the sky was clear, and yet I felt a sense of dread. In all my years as priest of Lansquenet, the Bishop has visited only four times, and never for social reasons. I guessed that, after Père Henri's failure to deliver the message, he meant to deliver it himself.

I know, I know. It's ridiculous. But I am a priest, *père*—more than that, I am the priest of Lansquenet. To leave Lansquenet is unthinkable; to give up the priesthood, equally so. Either way it would mean giving up half of my heart. It's impossible.

I heard the clock strike the quarter. The Bishop was due at nine o'clock. His verdict was inevitable; so was my sentence. I would have paced, but my sickness had left me too weak. Instead I sat and waited with increasing misery for the sound of his car down the boulevard—

Instead, I saw Omi al-Djerba walking slowly

448

down the road. Maya was with her, running ahead with the curious waddling gait of small children. It's unusual to see people from Les Marauds on this side of the bridge, but since the events of last week, I'm told, it has been a more regular sight.

Maya got there first and looked at me sternly over the wall. 'So. You're up at *last*,' she said. There was a world of condemnation in those five syllables.

'Well, I've been quite ill,' I said.

'Jinn don't get ill,' said Maya.

It seems my release from the cellar has done nothing to shake Maya's belief in my uncanny powers. Even the revelation that I am a priest has left her mostly unmoved. She fixed her solemn eyes on mine.

'Du'a's *memti* died,' she said.

'Yes, Maya. I'm sorry.'

Maya shrugged. 'It wasn't your fault. You can't fix everything at once.'

This matter-of-fact response was enough to make me laugh aloud. It was a strange, unhappy sound, but it was laughter nevertheless. In any case it surprised Omi al-Djerba, who peered over the wall at me with a look of reluctant approbation.

'Well,' she declared, 'you look awful.'

'Happy to oblige,' I said, putting down my coffee cup.

She made a face that I took for a grin. She is so old that her wrinkles have evolved a topography of their own, each with its own set of expressions. But her eyes, which are baby-blue with age, still have a surprisingly youthful shine. Vianne says she reminds her of Armande, and now, for the first time, I can see why. She has the kind of irreverence that only the very old, or the very young, can

449

achieve.

'I heard you were leaving,' she said.

'You heard wrong.'

Caro Clairmont, I suppose. You can usually trace gossip back to her door—especially when it's bad news. My instinctive response surprised me a little; though Omi nodded approvingly.

'Good,' she said. 'They need you here.'

'That's not what I've been told,' I said.

Omi made a derisive sound. 'Some people don't know *what* they need until they're about to lose it. You should know that, Monsieur le Curé. *Hee!* You men! You think you're so wise. But it takes a woman to show you what's right under your nose.' She laughed, exposing gums as pink as Maya's rubber boots. 'Have a macaroon,' she said, pulling one out of her pocket. 'It will make you feel better.'

'Thanks. I'm not a child,' I said.

She made that noise again. '*Meh.* You're young enough to be my great-grandson.' She shrugged and ate the sweet herself.

'Isn't it still Ramadan?' I said.

'I'm too old for Ramadan. And my Maya is too young.' She winked and handed Maya a sweet. 'You priests. You're all the same. You think fasting helps you to think about God, when anyone who can cook would tell you that fasting just makes you think about *food*.' She grinned at me. All her wrinkles grinned, too. 'You think God cares what you put in your mouth?' She popped another macaroon. 'Ah. That will be your bishop.'

That was the sound of a car approaching; the double-bump over the camel-backed bridge; the sound of its straining engine as it rattles up the cobbled street. Most of the streets of Lansquenet

450

are not really built for cars. Most of us drive (I myself do not), but we know how to handle our vehicles, coaxing them over the bumps in the road, slowing down for the ancient bridge, speeding up only at the far end of the boulevard. The Bishop is not familiar with the peculiarities of our streets, and the exhaust of his silver Audi was blowing alarmingly by the time he stopped in front of my house.

The Bishop is in his fifties; square-shouldered, square-jawed, more like an ex-rugbyman than a cleric. He must have the same dentist as Père Henri, because he has almost the same teeth. This morning they were ferocious in their whiteness and good cheer.

'Ah, Francis!'

'Good morning, *monseigneur*.' (He likes to be called Tony.)

'Such formality! You're looking well. And this is—' He looked curiously at Omi, who stared back at him, unabashed.

I gave her a warning glare. '*Monseigneur*, this is Madame al-Djerba. She was just about to leave.'

'Was I?' said Omi.

'Yes,' I said.

'It's just that I've never seen a bishop before. I thought you'd be in purple.'

'Well, thank you, *madame*,' I said. 'And now, the Bishop and I need to talk.'

'Oh, don't mind us,' said Omi. 'We'll wait.' And she sat down on the garden bench with the look of someone prepared to wait indefinitely, if required.

'Excuse me, what are you waiting for?' said the Bishop.

'Oh, nothing much. But everybody wants to see

451

Monsieur le Curé back on his feet. A lot of people have missed him.'

'Really?' The Bishop gave me a look. His surprise was far from flattering.

'Oh, yes,' said Omi firmly. 'That new priest was no substitute. That kind of priest may work in the big city, but not in a village like Lansquenet. *Khee!* It takes more than a few committees to get to the heart of a village. Père Henri has a lot to learn.' And then, just as she spoke, there came the sound of bells from Saint-Jérôme's. *My* bells, ringing for Mass, although it wasn't Père Henri's day.

The Bishop frowned. 'Isn't that—?'

'Yes.'

The bells were too loud to be ignored. We went as far as the end of the street and looked into the empty square. There was no sign of anyone, and yet the church door was open. The bells rang on. I went to the door. The Bishop, after a moment's hesitation, followed me inside.

The church was filled with people. As a rule, my congregation numbers forty or fifty at best, at Christmas or Easter. The rest of the time, I'm lucky to see a couple of dozen; sometimes fewer. But today, the pews were all full; there were even people standing at the back. Three hundred people, maybe more—half the population of Lansquenet— waiting for me inside Saint-Jérôme's.

'What *is* going on?' said the Bishop.

'*Monseigneur*, I have no idea.'

'Monsieur le Curé! Glad you're well.'

That was Paul-Marie Muscat, at the back in his wheelchair. Pilou was sitting beside him, with Vlad, a piece of string firmly attached to his collar. I saw Joséphine next to them, smiling as if her heart might break. Then, Georges Poitou and his wife. The Acheron family—*all* of them, even the eldest son, Jean-Louis, who never usually goes to church. Then Joline Drou and her son, Jeannot; Guillaume Duplessis; Georges and Caro Clairmont—Caro, with an air of concern that made me want to wring her neck. Narcisse, who takes Communion twice a year, if he remembers to, but rarely attends otherwise; Henriette Moisson; Charles Lévy; even the Englishman, Jay Mackintosh—

And then there were people who, for good reason, had *never* been part of my congregation. Zahra al-Djerba. Sonia Bencharki. Alyssa Mahjoubi. Their father, Saïd. And old Mohammed Mahjoubi, too—all of them carrying flowers and fruit. And, of course, there was Vianne Rocher. And Anouk, and Rosette, and the river-rats; ragged people, tattooed people, crowding my church to the vaulting—

And on every surface, every ledge, there were candles. Hundreds, *thousands* of votives, every single one a prayer; on the altar; by the font; beneath the statues of Saint Francis and the Virgin. We don't have as many on Christmas Eve; but today, on a Thursday morning in September, Saint-Jérôme's was like a cathedral.

'Glad to see you well, *mon père.*'

'Did you get my flowers?'

'I hope you enjoyed the wine, *mon père.*'

'Will you be taking confession?'

I turned to the Bishop. 'I had no *idea*—'

But *monseigneur* was smiling. There may have been a little frost in that toothpaste-commercial smile, but the Bishop is politician enough to know when to change allegiance.

'How wonderful to see so many here,' he said, addressing the villagers. 'Yes, of course—don't crowd Père Francis—I'm sure he'll agree to say a few words.'

Well, *père*, I have never said Mass to such a large crowd of people. Of course, I had nothing prepared—but to my surprise, the words came to me more easily than ever before. I don't remember quite what I said, but I talked about community, and what it really means to belong; and of the kindness of strangers; and of being in the darkness, watching the light from the windows of other people's homes; and of being inside the whale, and of being a stranger in a foreign land—and when I had finished, the Bishop was gone.

As Vianne would have said, the wind had changed.

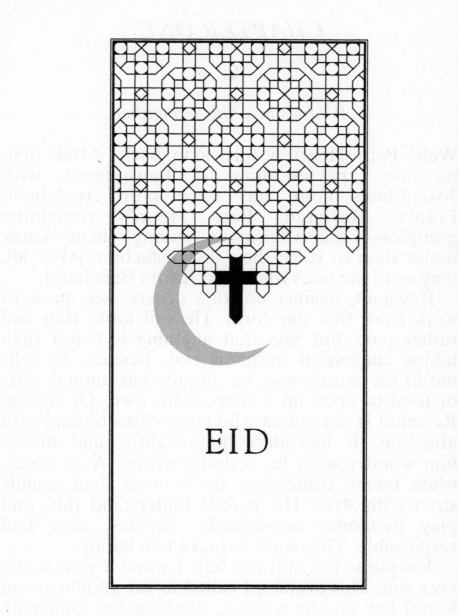

EID

CHAPTER ONE

☾

Wednesday, 8th September

Well, Père Henri never came back. After that, no one expected him to. Lansquenet, with Joséphine's help, has once more reclaimed Francis Reynaud. Père Henri's remaining groupies—Caro Clairmont among them—know better than to voice their dissatisfaction. After all, they were the ones who fêted Karim Bencharki.

Reynaud, against doctor's orders, was back to work from that day forth. He still looks thin and rather pale, but says that anything is better than taking confession from his bed. Besides, he tells me in his caustic way, he already has enough gifts of food to open up a shop of his own. Of course, Reynaud is not a man who knows how to deal with affection. It bewilders him slightly, and makes him wonder what he is doing wrong. As a result, when taking confession, he is more than usually strict with *Avés*. His people understand this, and play penitence accordingly. Besides, they feel responsible. They want to make him happy.

Joséphine has still not left. I wonder now if she ever will. This evening I called to say goodbye, and found her on the *terrasse*, drinking hot chocolate and watching Pilou sitting on the side of the bridge. Pilou had his fishing-pole, and Paul-Marie was beside him, with Vlad lying next to him on the road. I could only see Paul from the back as he sat there in his wheelchair, but there was something about his posture that made me want to look again—

'I know it's stupid,' said Joséphine. 'People don't change. Not really. But over the past few days he's been—' She shrugged. 'You know. Just different.'

I smiled. 'I know. I've seen it too. And no, people don't often *change*—but sometimes they grow, if you give them the chance. Look at Reynaud.'

She nodded.

Of course, you'd have to know him very well to sense the change in Monsieur le Curé. But something has altered, something that few other people would notice. I do, because it's in his colours. And Joséphine, because—

'Did you see? They finished the old *chocolaterie*.'

I shook my head. 'I'll have to look.'

I'm aware that over the past two weeks Luc Clairmont and his father have been working hard to restore the place. Roux volunteered to help them, which is why we've barely seen him, but on my way to the café today I omitted to check on their progress.

'What's going to happen to the place now?'

She shrugged. 'Your guess is as good as mine.'

I know what she's thinking. It's been a week since Reynaud left his sickroom. School terms are beginning again. It's time to get back to Paris. And yet—

'You can't leave today,' said Omi, when I tried to tell her this morning. 'Tonight is the end of Ramadan. Tonight, there'll be *harira* soup and barley soup and sixteen kinds of *briouats*, and roast lamb and spiced couscous and *chebakia* and stuffed dates. Plus I'll be making coconut *sellou* to my mother's recipe, and you will never forgive yourself

457

if you miss the chance to taste it.'

We are all invited, of course. People from both sides of the Tannes; even the river-gypsies. There's not enough room in the al-Djerba or the Mahjoubi houses to accommodate everyone, but the nights are still mild, and the jetty is the ideal place for a celebration. Already, trestles and benches have been set up on the riverbank, while the boats closest to the jetty are decked with lanterns and fairy lights. All the women will be dressed in their best and brightest clothes—no black today—and scented with patchouli oil and amber and cedar and sandal and rose. There will be games for the children, the minaret will be illuminated and I have made a batch of chocolates, with pistachios, cardamom and gold leaf, tied up in twists of coloured paper, to be given out to everyone.

Not everyone will come, of course. The Acherons remain opposed, and some of the young men from the gym are also refusing to take part. Even so, Lansquenet has never seen such a gathering. *Maghrébins*; river-rats; villagers and visitors, all here to celebrate the end of a time of sacrifice—

'No wine, of course,' said Joséphine. '*And* no dancing. How does that work?'

I laughed. 'I'm sure you'll manage.'

She looked at me. 'You make it sound as if you won't be there tonight.'

'Of course I'll be there.'

Of course I will. But there's something in the air, Joséphine; something that smells of car exhausts and fog on the Seine and plane trees and rain on the September streets. I know what it is. You know it, too. You've felt the pull of the changing wind. Outside in the square, there's an autumn scent. The

458

shadows are starting to lengthen. Anouk is talking to Jeannot—earnestly, her hand in his—while Rosette and Pantoufle and Bam chase each other like clusters of leaves around the cobbled corners. The light is rosy and somehow sad—the nostalgic light of summers past—and I sense that something is over, but what? The whitewashed church tower is rosewater-pink. The Tannes is a sheet of hammered gold. I can see all of Lansquenet, from Saint-Jérôme's to Les Marauds. And the people—I can see them too, their colours rising like strings of smoke against the fading summer sky.

So many people. So many stories. All of them interwoven with mine, into this cat's-cradle of light.

In his garden, Francis Reynaud waters his peach stone and thinks of Armande. On the deck of the black houseboat, Roux lies on his back and waits for the stars. On the bridge, Paul-Marie watches his son catch a perch, and smiles warmly—an unfamiliar sensation, which he has to check with his fingertips, as a man may check his moustache for crumbs after eating a sandwich. In the mosque, old Mahjoubi gets ready for prayers. The spire of the minaret floats in the sun. In an alley in Les Marauds, François and Karine Acheron sit with Maya around a box with a couple of puppies inside. Du'a sits on the riverbank, watching the Tannes. She no longer wears an *abaya*, but jeans, a *kameez* and her red slippers. Alyssa Mahjoubi sits with her; her short hair is uncovered, her eyes full of tears.

You see, everywhere I look, there are things that connect me to Lansquenet. Stories; people; memories; insubstantial as heat haze, and yet they have a resonance, as if those strings of light could play a tune that might finally lead me home. So

459

the *chocolaterie* is finished at last. I feel a strange reluctance to look. Better, perhaps, to remember it as I first saw it three weeks ago; a ruin, scorched and abandoned. But then, I've never been very good at leaving things behind. I tried, but I have always left fragments of myself there too, like seeds awaiting their chance to grow.

I leave Joséphine and Roux to get ready for the evening's celebrations and walk out into the Place Saint-Jérôme, where the last frame of summer is fading to grey. And yes, the chocolate shop is there, just as it was the day I left; flowerpots on the window-ledge; shutters painted geranium-red; all whitewashed and gleaming and new again, waiting for someone—

Someone like you—

The sound of the *muezzin* floats across from Les Marauds. At the same time, the church clock strikes the half-hour. Jeannot Drou has gone home, and Anouk is on the street corner, the shadow of Pantoufle at her feet like a signpost marking our road.

Above my head comes a small, creaking sound. It's the wooden sign above the shop door; fixed to the wall by a bracket. Its voice is small, but persistent; the voice of a tiny bird that chirps: *Try me. Test me. Taste me.*

I look up. The sign is blank, ready to be painted. I can almost see it now, in red and yellow lettering; as if the events of the past eight years have been neatly and prettily folded away, leaving no rough edges, no blanks, just the gloss of recovered time.

And it smells of the Americas; the court of Montezuma; spiced, in golden goblets and mixed with wine and pomegranate juice. And it smells of cream and cardamom; of sacrificial bonfires; of temples and of palaces; of vanilla and tonka and mocha and rose. The scent is overwhelming; it rushes through me like the wind; it sweeps me off my feet like love—

Will you stay, Vianne? Will you stay?

Anouk and Rosette are watching me. Both of them have friends here. Both of them are a part of this place, as we are a part of Paris; bound by a hundred invisible threads, which must be broken when we leave—

I reach out my hand to touch the door. It, too, has been painted geranium-red. It's my favourite colour; Roux, who painted it, must have known. And now can I see the faintest glow, etched in gold around the frame like the tiniest, sweetest of glamours? From the corner of my eye I can see Bam, watching me. Since we arrived in Lansquenet, Bam has been very visible. Now, today, so is Pantoufle; his solemn eyes blink at me from the shadows.

I try the door. It is open. Doors are always open here. It opens a crack: inside, in the dark, is that a flash of kingfisher-blue, a scrawl of exuberant orange? My children are learning, I tell myself, with a strange little tug of pride. They know how to summon the wind. But is it enough? Is it ever enough?

Across the river, in Les Marauds, Roux is getting ready. I know the signs; that distant look of other places in his eyes. Roux would never live in a house. Even a houseboat is limiting. And Lansquenet is *small*, Roux. Small people. Small minds. In the end, you came with me because you knew she'd never leave—

Quietly, I close the door. Above my head, the invisible bird gives its tiny, persistent call: *Try me. Try me.*

I hold out my hands to my children. Anouk takes one: Rosette, the other. The call of the *muezzin* falls silent now over Les Marauds. The sun has set. We don't look back. We have a party to go to.

ACKNOWLEDGEMENTS

Once again, heartfelt thanks to the unsung heroes of this book: to my agent, Peter Robinson; my PA, Anne; everyone at Transworld, especially Marianne Velmans; Kate Samano; Deborah Adams; Claire Ward for the jacket design and Louise Page, who organizes publicity with such efficiency and good cheer. Thank you to Mark, who maintains my website; to the Shed, for Zen moments of inspiration; to Vlad, the Boys, the Melancholy Baritone (in fact, to most of the West End) and to all my friends on Twitter, for biscuits, encouragement and elegant conversation. Thanks too to the proofreaders, copy-editors, sales reps, booksellers, festival organizers and all those who work behind the scenes to keep my books in print. Most of all, thanks to all of you; to the readers, without whom Vianne Rocher would never have found her voice.

And lastly—because we all need something to cling to—to Kevin and Anouchka, who stop the wind from blowing me away.

Joanne Harris achieved international fame with her novel *Chocolat* in 1999. It was shortlisted for the Whitbread (Costa) Prize, and made into an Oscar-nominated film starring Juliette Binoche and Johnny Depp, and in *The Lollipop Shoes* she returned to the story of Vianne Rocher in Paris. She is the author of many other bestselling novels, the most recent of which is *Blueeyedboy*. Her hobbies are listed in *Who's Who* as 'mooching, lounging, strutting, strumming, priest-baiting and quiet subversion'. She plays bass guitar, is currently studying Old Norse, and lives with her husband and daughter in Yorkshire, about fifteen miles from where she was born.

Meet up with her at www.joanne-harris.co.uk or follow @joannechocolat on Twitter.